THE
INSIDER

Mari Hannah

ORION

First published in Great Britain in 2018 by Orion Books,
an imprint of The Orion Publishing Group Ltd
Carmelite House, 50 Victoria Embankment,
London EC4Y 0DZ

An Hachette UK company

1 3 5 7 9 10 8 6 4 2

Copyright © Mari Hannah 2018

A CIP catalogue record for this book is
available from the British Library.

ISBN 978 1 4091 7407 3

Typeset by Input Data Services Ltd, Somerset

Printed and bound in Great Britain by Clays Ltd, Elcograf S.p.A.

www.orionbooks.co.uk

For Daisy and Finn

THE INSIDER

1

It was the news they had all been dreading, confirmation of a fourth victim. For DS Frankie Oliver, the journey to the crime scene brought back memories of her father driving her around Northumberland when she was a rookie cop, pointing out the places where he'd been called to investigate serious incidents throughout his own police career, giving her the benefit of his advice along the way. He'd been doing this since she was a kid, only with less detail, leaving out the unspeakable horrors the locations represented. Back then, they were words. Just words. Narratives that, if she were being honest, excited her in ways they should not. And then there was the night he stopped talking: an experience etched on their collective memory forever more – a night too close to home.

Flashlight beams bobbed up and down, illuminating sheets of horizontal rain. The detectives stumbled along the Tyne Valley track, heading east on the Northern Rail line linking Carlisle to Newcastle. No light pollution here. Under a dark, forbidding sky, it was difficult terrain, rutted and sodden so close to the water's edge. The swollen river thundered by, a course of water liable to flash flooding. Red alerts for the area were a regular occurrence. At midday, Northumberland's monitoring stations had warned of a serious threat to those living nearby. If the Tyne rose quickly, Frankie knew they would be in trouble. Many a walker had slipped into the water here by accident.

Few had survived.

Lightning forked, exposing the beauty of the surrounding landscape. A high-voltage electric charge, followed by the rumble of thunder in the distance, an omen of more rain to come. The lead investigator, Detective Chief Inspector David Stone, was a blurred smudge a hundred metres in front of her, head bowed, shoulders hunched against the relentless downpour.

Mud sucked at Frankie's feet as she fought to keep up, two steps forward, one back, as she tried to get a purchase on the slippery surface. Her right foot stuck fast, the momentum of her stride propelling her forward, minus a wellington boot. She fell, head first, hands and knees skidding as she tried to stay upright. Dragging herself up, she swore under her breath as brown sludge stuck to her clothing, weighing her down.

Unaware of her plight, David was making headway, sweeping his torch left and right in a wide arc close to Eels Wood. He had one agenda and Frankie wasn't it. With a feeling of dread eating its way into her gut, she peered into the undergrowth blocking her passage. Where was a stick when you needed one? As she parted the brambles, there was an ear-splitting crack, a terrifying sound. Before she had time to react, a tree fell, crashing to earth with an excruciating thump, unearthed by a raging torrent of water filtering off higher ground, its roots unable to sustain the weight of a century of growth, landing metres in front of her.

Frankie blew out a breath.

Only once before had she come closer to violent death. Hoping her luck would hold, she vaulted the tree and ploughed on. From an investigative standpoint, the situation was grim. Had there been any footprints adjacent to the line, they were long gone. As crime scenes go, they would be fighting a losing battle to preserve evidence, assuming they ever found the body spotted by an eyewitness, a passenger on an eastbound train. Where the fuck was it?

Frankie expected to see the dragon ahead, a wide-eye LED searchlight used by emergency services, an intense beam of white light guiding her. As far as the eye could see there was no light visible, other than the beam of David's flashlight. Worrying. Exasperating. Frankie couldn't be arsed with this. Pulling her radio from her pocket, she pressed the transmit button hoping her link to Control wouldn't be affected by the appalling weather. It would be a heavy night in the control room, for sure.

'Oliver to Control. We're in position. Can you repeat the coordinates? We're seeing bugger all out here.'

Silence.

'Damn it! DS Oliver to Control. Are you receiving? Over . . .'

A pause before her radio crackled to life: 'Control: go ahead.'

Wiping rain from her nose with the back of her hand, Frankie repeated her request, yanking at the drawstring on the hood of her raincoat to stop water getting in. A useless exercise. She was well and truly drenched. 'Have a word with first responders, will you? If they're guarding a crime scene, they should know where the bloody hell they are. We need help here.'

'Copy that. I'll get back to you.'

Ending the transmission with one eye on Stone, the other on the rising river level, Frankie stopped walking. There was no point continuing without an update. By now it was glaringly obvious they were in the wrong place, a thought that seemingly hadn't occurred to Stone. He was still on the move, the space between them extending with every second that passed.

'Guv, hold on!'

She was wasting her breath, her voice lost on the wind. David was head down, keen to reach the scene and do what was required. Back at base, he'd been distracted. Before Frankie had time to ask him why, the call came in and they were racing to the car, burning rubber as he sped out of Northern Command HQ, barking orders into his radio to get things underway. It was unlike him to lose his cool. What in hell's name was eating him?

What happened next shook Frankie to her core . . .

An icy shiver ran down her spine, every hair on her head standing to attention, a physiological reaction to imminent danger. With the roar of the wind, she couldn't hear but she could feel. She looked behind her. Nothing. There it was again. A definite vibration through her unbooted foot. She swung round. Eyes front. Up ahead Stone was oblivious, his worst nightmare on its way. She screamed at him to get off the track. He kept going. A man on a mission with no clue of what was going down. Kicking off her remaining boot, Frankie sprinted barefoot, precariously close to the water's edge, dislodged gravel cutting her feet as she ran – or tried to – a sudden release of hormones providing a vital burst of energy.

'Guv, stop!'

He was too far in front to hear her cries.

As the south side of the river burst its bank, she clung to a tree for safety, self-preservation her priority now. Unable to go on or go back, she had to do *something*. If she didn't get out of there soon, she'd be swept away in the raging torrent and washed downstream.

If David didn't move . . . She didn't want to think about that.

The vibration through the soles of her feet increased. Frankie panicked. Realising she'd never get to him in time, she used her torch – three short bursts; three longer ones; three short – a last-ditch attempt to save her boss from certain death. International Morse code was the distress call every police officer was sensitive to and, finally, she had his attention.

As if in slow motion, he turned to face her, lifting his hand to shade his eyes as she shone the torch directly at him. In the distance, over his shoulder, Frankie spotted a pinprick of light.

4

Oh fuck!

It disappeared as her guv'nor blinded her with his own flashlight, peering through the darkness, with his back to imminent danger. Seeing the depth of water all around her, he'd be more worried about her predicament than his own. Frantically, she waved him off the track, a sob leaving her throat as he walked towards her. He thought she was calling for help.

'No!' she screamed.

A horn blasted behind him. Simultaneously, the light illuminating Frankie's face disappeared and the freight train was upon her. It whooshed by, feet away, rattling down the track. Frantic, she shone her torch along the railway line. No movement. She dry-heaved. Thirty seconds later, David rose to his feet. He'd thrown himself clear with seconds to spare. Frankie sunk to her knees, almost waist deep in water. *Jesus! That was a close call.*

2

The late news was full of it. They knew nothing. The way he liked it. Last week, the third victim had been identified: Margaret something-or-other – his grandma's name, not that that was of any consequence. Margaret had served a purpose, though the fact that she too was a grandmother pricked at his conscience slightly. Not enough to stop the hatred boiling in his gut or to make him reconsider. She'd done nothing to him personally. It was what she represented that made him choose her. He liked to think of her as – what was the term? A means to an end.

For days, he'd dominated the headlines, everyone talking about the killer who'd evaded Northumbria's elite murder squad. *Inept* was the word reporters used. They took every opportunity to knock the police and, when an informant tipped them off that the Senior Investigating Officer had abandoned not only the case but his profession too, the press had a field day, claiming that the stress of an accelerating triple-murder investigation had got to him. A carefully planned retirement was the excuse given. It was bollocks, of course.

What did they know?

And now there were four.

He had to admit he was thriving on the notoriety. Yes, there had been a moment when his courage had deserted him, but it soon passed, as most things did when they got going. First-night nerves. Nothing more. In the end, he got over it. The anger was enough to propel him forward. Stephanie had a lot to answer for. All he'd done was what she'd drummed into him, time and time again: *Concentrate on what's important.*

He had . . . He was.

Steph – she wouldn't let him call her that – was like a

broken record. She'd always been opinionated, a woman who liked the sound of her own voice, the type to impart what she considered to be advice that only she was qualified to give; the type to spout forth at every opportunity, classifying people, rating and pigeonholing them as she saw fit. It wore him down, and he was done with her arsey attitude. She'd live to regret her actions . . .

But not for long.

Scanning news channels, he was enjoying the drama his actions had caused. His career hadn't been all it was cracked up to be. He'd been forced to make so many sacrifices, both in his professional and personal life, and this infuriated him. For a while, he'd been treading water, but then he'd realised he had other options. It was a moment of clarity, like he'd thrown a magic switch, illuminating the darkness. He knew then that with a little creativity he might help the bitch to see more clearly. Bizarrely, she was also the conduit through which he would regain his self-respect.

He wouldn't dwell on the one that got away.

Number four was fresh in his memory. As he boarded the train, his victim had been reading a document spread out in front of her, a thin strip of red ribbon trailing from her bag. He'd seen enough of those to know what it was: the binding for a legal brief, an advisory document.

Perfect.

She didn't look up as he sat down. Too busy on the phone, that edge to her voice that he couldn't abide. He didn't need to see her face to know that she was the one. Placing his ticket on the seat beside him, he'd dropped his head into his chest, crossed his arms and shut his eyes, feigning sleep, his baseball cap pulled low to avoid a face-to-face with the conductor as he passed through the carriage.

Fifteen minutes and three stops later, the train slowed, approaching Stocksfield station. Perfect. No sign of the conductor. The woman opposite hung up the phone, folded her briefing document, tying the red ribbon around it in readiness to leave. As she slipped it into her bag, he let his mobile drop to the floor, accidentally on purpose. It skidded across the aisle. A bloke would have glanced down and stepped over it but, true to form, his plan worked. Most women were accommodating, even with strangers. Number four was one of those, a gracious lady, taught to do the right thing, never to turn a blind eye to a person in need; the kind to say I'm sorry even when it wasn't her fault, but she also had that look of irritation, like he'd bothered her unnecessarily. That look alone would determine her demise.

He'd faked a yawn, searching his pockets, then the aisle, his back to the only other passenger in the carriage. As the woman bent to pick up the device, her coat fell open: a show of cleavage, soft skin, firm breasts, a hint of lacy underwear beneath a black dress. Their fingers kissed as she passed him the mobile, a frisson of excitement coursing through him as the train stopped at the platform. He'd never get over the thrill of that first touch, a combination of anticipation and fear.

At first, her hazel eyes avoided his.

'Sorry,' he said.

That polite apology was all it took to put her face straight. He wasn't attracted to her sexually. The point of the exercise was far more complicated than that. He was royally pissed off. Someone had to pay – and she'd do nicely. It was a question of respect. Women like her made it easy for him. The daft cow even spoke to him as the carriage door opened, exchanging a word with the nice man on such a horrible night.

For her, it was about to get so much worse.

Indiscriminate killing wasn't his thing. What he wanted was validation. And to get that, he'd been told he had to prove himself. Initially, he'd thought the police weren't playing ball. They hadn't a clue. Even if they had, what did he care? He'd been careful to build in insurance in case things went tits up. As the ligature tightened around the woman's neck, he thought of the one who'd made his life a misery, an image so clear-cut, he could've sworn he caught the overpowering whiff of her perfume. Classy. It sent his pulse racing. If four wasn't enough, he'd go on with his quest, perfecting his craft until she started listening . . . really listening. He was saving Steph till last.

3

They raced towards the correct location with new intelligence, Frankie stripping off in the back seat as David drove. The witness had sent them up a blind and perilous alley near the Tyne Valley village of Wylam. By process of elimination, uniformed officers had taken the initiative and found the crime scene, but communications were down when they attempted to update the control room. They were standing by, west of Stocksfield, fifteen minutes away.

Grateful for his new four-by-four, David's eyes were firmly on the slick road, his advanced driving skills fully deployed. Even with the wipers on full pelt, he was struggling to see through the windscreen as he reissued orders to stop the trains. His earlier instruction hadn't been acted upon.

The controller was astounded. 'Your request went out as soon as we received it, guv. I logged the call myself at eleven ten. That route should have been off-line forty minutes ago.'

'Well, it's still active. The damn thing nearly mowed me down.'

'Sorry, boss. It's no excuse but, according to my screen, Network Rail are dealing with a landslide yon side of Gilsland. They're clearing the line—'

'Without stopping the trains?' An icy shiver ran down David's spine. Having come close to death a few minutes ago, he gripped the steering wheel a little tighter, his stomach taking a dive. The train had been travelling at speed when it passed Eels Wood. It wouldn't stop until it reached Carlisle. By his calculation, it would plough into the railway crew in minutes. 'That's less than thirty miles away,' he said. 'Get on to their control centre. They need to contact the driver now!'

'I'm on it.'

The radio fell silent.

In 2004, Cumbria had experienced a horrific accident near Tebay that had claimed the lives of four maintenance workers on the West Coast Main Line. The county didn't need another disaster. David drove on autopilot, feeling a sense of disconnect, appalled by the images in his head, vaguely aware that he was not alone. He tried not to dwell on the unimaginable. He'd done all he could to avoid catastrophe. Was it enough?

Silence in the car.

He glanced at Frankie. She was as shaken as he was by the potential loss of lives. Rarely was she lost for words. Control would act immediately. The question was: would they do so in time? David imagined the controller blasting his counterpart at Network Rail, relaying his message forcefully, an urgent attempt to avoid fatalities. If successful, that was one problem solved . . . but there were other things on the SIO's mind.

Trying to get his head around a major investigation already underway had proven difficult – and then some. Earlier in the day, he'd met with the head of CID, Detective Chief Superintendent Philip Bright, a man respected and feared by every Northumbria detective. It was a baptism of fire for any newly promoted SIO. David was under intense pressure to find the man striking fear into the community. Women across the county had been warned to stay alert.

To add insult to injury, the team he'd been put in charge of knew more about his triple – probable quadruple – murder investigation than he did. Detectives were wary of a new boss taking over in the middle of a protracted enquiry, especially one newly arrived from the Metropolitan Police. Understandable. Continuity was key. His methods wouldn't necessarily be the same as the outgoing SIO's. With his own way of working, David could turn the case on its head and the team would have to suck it up. It was not a good place to be – for anyone.

His predecessor, DCI Gordon Sharpe, was popular. His surname matched his skills, his eyes, his tongue. A cool operator with an impressive detection rate, he commanded the loyalty of the rank and file, though Bright was far from impressed that he'd put his ticket in without time for a proper handover, at the height of a major investigation, leaving others to take on the responsibility.

David had a mind to solicit the same level of respect from his new squad, but first he had to prove himself. No SIO could work in a vacuum. Without Frankie, a DS with a raft of local knowledge, he'd be finished before he started. And then there was the other problem; the one that had been eating him up for weeks.

Coward.

Revealing his innermost secret to his second in command would hurt, though it had to be done. His was a cut so deep and so raw he'd struggled to come to terms with it, unable to confide in the police psychologist or lay it on former Met colleagues. Only his brother knew the whole truth, part of the reason he'd quit the Met, taken a demotion and transferred to Northumbria. Now Luke was gone it was time to come clean to Frankie.

Another glance in her direction.

Moving from general CID to the Murder Investigation Team had been a big deal for both of them. It had come on the back of a successful investigation, an outcome for which he'd received a commendation, even though she'd done most of the work and deserved it more. He'd leaned on her heavily during the case, his past catching up with him. It was time to put it to bed. He *had* to tell her.

Do it!

Get it over with.

With every moment's delay, the situation weighed more

heavily on his mind. It wasn't that he didn't trust her. He did. It was more a question of self-preservation. Keeping his secret hidden was a vital part of his armour, an invisible security blanket that gave him the strength to cope with his job and the mundane business of everyday life, albeit on a reduced basis. From the moment shots were fired, he'd existed in a void. Part of him died that day. He wouldn't downplay it. That wouldn't be right. Frankie had to know the truth.

All of it.

It was vital to share it with her before embarking on a pro-tracted enquiry that would make or break them both. The offender was clever. Forensically aware. The deaths of three women had eluded his predecessor. Now there were four. When Sharpe passed the baton without solving the case – an astonishing failure – it prompted a heated argument with the head of CID. Bright's words arrived in David's head: *What copper with an ounce of self-respect would give up on their last case and walk. You have one chance, Stone. Don't blow it!*

David glanced in his rear-view mirror. Frankie was in the back seat pulling a thick jumper over her head. Her hair was dripping, face covered in mud. Despite fresh clothes, she was shivering uncontrollably. She hadn't said a word since they left the riverside. He changed down, took a bend in the road, accelerating out of it, houses flashing by on either side, dim candlelight emanating from within.

A power cut was the least of his worries.

'I have something to tell you,' he said.

'Me too. I need a bath.' Frankie laughed, one foot on the back seat, her right leg cocked at the knee, tying shoelaces, her waterlogged boots discarded in the front footwell. 'I hope you weren't peeking, guv. Not that I give a shit. In fact, I'd like a quid for every copper who's seen me in my undies. Mind you, don't repeat that. It might be misconstrued.' She looked up, a wry smile developing. 'You're wet through. Can't we stop and get you dry?'

'I'm fine . . .'

David was anything but, though he intended to finish what he'd started. He wouldn't allow her to derail him now. And still he choked on his words, teetering on the brink of a disclosure she'd earned the right to hear. Putting a hand on his left shoulder, she climbed into the front, cursing as her sweater snagged on the centre console. Freeing it, she settled into her seat, pulling her safety belt across her body, clipping it in place.

'We're already late, guv. We really should stop. Five minutes won't make a difference. It could be hours before we get back to base.'

'I can't—'

A sideways glance. 'No spare clothes in the boot? Shame on you. My flat is smaller than this car.'

'That's not what I meant, Frank. No one can move without my say so.'

'Let 'em wait.' She ran a hand through her wet hair. 'You're no good to them if you catch pneumonia. The victim isn't going anywhere, is she?'

'Frankie, button it. What I have to say is important.'

'Can it wait till we get back to HQ?'

'No.' David flinched as another crack of thunder shook the car. The flash of lightning that followed was fortuitous, exposing a thick branch in the centre of the road. He changed direction to avoid it, throwing her around in her seat.

'Watch out!' she yelled.

David braked hard as an animal darted across the road in front of them, missing them by a whisker, literally and metaphorically. In his wing mirror, he watched the terrified creature cower at the side of the road. The village of Stocksfield was otherwise abandoned. A ghost town. Not a soul about. The odd candle in a window, indistinct figures peering out at freakish weather for the time of year, devastating gardens and fencing, scattering litter bins. One of them was missing a dog.

14

'That's us.' Frankie was pointing to a light in the distance: the dragon.

David turned the wheel. His moment was gone.

4

An outer cordon prevented access to Stocksfield railway station. An officer in a high-vis jacket held up a hand as they approached. David let his engine idle as Frankie wound down her window, a strobe of blue illuminating their faces. As she spoke to him, the SIO's eyes scanned the scene, settling on a black-and-yellow height barrier directly in front of him, beyond which an inner cordon flapped in the wind. He panned left. A CSI transit van was blocking entry to a short strip of tarmac. Beyond it, a metal gate led to the discovery site, concrete bollards separating the area from the car park. It turned out that Frankie knew the officer. Unsurprising. She was a third-generation cop and knew a lot of people on the force: uniform, detective and civilians.

'What's the story, Ray?'

'If you could drive under the barrier and park up behind our vehicles. Designated access to the body is tricky. We're asking everyone to walk north of the restricted area, turn right at the concrete bollards and keep to the south side of the footpath. The gate is chained and padlocked. You'll have to climb it, Sarge. We think the victim may have been dragged through the gap to the north of the gate so we're keeping everyone away from there.'

'Good job.' Frankie thanked him.

The officer nodded, allowing them through.

David drove on, swung the wheel hard left, then reversed into a spot as instructed. Frankie was out of the car before it had properly come to a stop. The SIO got out too, his penetrating eyes scanning the car park, clocking three vehicles. Over the gate was an area of uneven waste ground, around seventy or eighty metres in length. He focused on a huddle of bodies about halfway along the empty plot of land, backlit by the dragon. It was chucking it down, the rain bouncing off saturated ground. Once over the gate, they used flashlights, scanning the area on the way in: rusting rail tracks poking through tall weeds; a rotting wooden spool that had once held heavy-duty wire, a section of which was still attached; concrete sleepers and assorted debris contained in an oil barrel. A second gate, also padlocked, barred entry on to the track beyond; the vanishing point where the line disappeared to the left under a graffiti-covered bridge.

In silhouette, a second officer in uniform was walking their way, a big bugger, thickset like a bouncer, a heavy utility belt protruding beneath a fluorescent jacket two sizes small for him. Water cascaded over the brim of his service cap as he tipped his head to one side. Relatively new to Northumbria, David didn't expect or receive recognition from him.

Anticipating a challenge to their presence, Frankie took a step forward. 'I'm DS Oliver. This is DCI David Stone, the SIO.'

'Sarge . . . guv.' The giant was a man of few words.

The victim lay face up across four abandoned railway sleepers, lips parted slightly, arms by her side, hands palms down. There was a wedding band on the third finger of her left hand. Nails, manicured to match her lipstick, shone bright red as rain washed over them. A river of mascara ran from bloodshot eyes, blackening ash-blonde hair on either side of her face. Her clothing and jewellery were intact, her handbag placed neatly by her side.

Frankie raised her voice to make herself heard above the gale-force wind rushing through the trees. 'It wasn't theft then,' she said. 'Nor sexual assault, by the looks of it. I suppose that's a blessing for her family, but not much of one.'

David agreed. There were no injuries visible beyond a ligature mark on the victim's neck. Motive was anyone's guess. He'd find it eventually, but he'd lay odds on it making little sense, to him or anyone else in their right mind. A desire to kill could never be justified. He studied the expression on Frankie's face, a mixture of sadness and rage, an emotion so strong he felt the urge to comfort her. The only female present, it occurred to him that she might view the scene in a different light to the rest of them. The victim was around her size. An easy target. Vulnerable. From an early age, it would have been drilled into them both: *be careful; watch your back; stay safe*.

David was about to speak when Frankie turned away. She'd seen enough. Convinced that Operation Trident had found its next victim, she made a beeline for Foley, the Crime Scene Manager, greeting him like they were old mates, no hint of stress visible as it had been a moment ago. She deserved a BAFTA for effort alone.

More introductions.

Nods were exchanged between the two men.

Frankie eyeballed Foley. 'Any ID on the victim?'

'Joanna Cosgrove. Thirty-seven – today as it happens, according to her driving licence.'

David waited for Frankie to speak but she seemed preoccupied. For a split second, it occurred to him that she might know the victim and didn't want to say as it would rule her out of the investigation.

He turned to Foley. 'Is she local?'

'Two miles that way.' Foley was pointing east. 'There are photos in her wallet, guv. One of Joanna with an IC1 male and a couple of teenage kids, one of each. The lad is the spitting double of her.'

David rubbed at his forehead, sickened by the portrait the CSI had drawn. Murder was like a pebble dropped in still water, each ripple representing a family member affected by tragedy. There were multiple victims to every suspicious death. He'd break more than one heart tonight.

'My lads did a vehicle check in the car park,' Foley said. 'The one on the western edge is hers.'

'Northumberland plate,' Frankie said, finally finding her voice. 'Grey BMW, 16 Reg?'

'That's the one.' The CSI was taken aback.

David wasn't.

Frankie was a diligent investigator with a sharp eye. If they were in a pub, she could memorise, in impressive detail, the customers she'd passed on the way in, even if she was standing with her back to them. They had often played the game to see who was the most accurate. She'd always come out on top. She'd been playing that game since she was five years old with her father and grandfather. There had been a Frank Oliver in the Northumbria force since 1966. In their day, observation was a must. If your sergeant asked you what you'd seen, and you didn't know, you'd get marked down.

Frankie had a question for Foley. 'Did you find her car keys?'

'In her coat pocket. Which would suggest she wasn't close enough to use her fob when she was jumped.'

'Is that right?' Frankie's tone matched her sardonic expression. She didn't actually say, 'Do your job and leave the detecting to us,' but she may as well have. 'Joanna does what I do . . . What most women do . . . We never open a car door from a distance. It's unwise.' Her cutting remarks floated away on the wind, but Foley had got the message. He wouldn't make the same mistake twice.

David caught Frankie's eye. 'Get in touch with Control. We need the car transported. We can't examine it here.' As she made the call, he turned to face Foley, pointing toward three ghostly figures through a curtain of rain, none of them recognisable. 'Which one is the pathologist?'

'Collingwood has been and gone, guv. She had to shoot off,

another call-out. A male,' Foley added, to put the SIO's mind at rest. 'She recorded time of death at 23.40.'

'The victim was strangled from behind?'

A nod. 'Same MO as the other three.'

A CSI camera flashed as Frankie hung up the phone.

Foley's eyes strayed towards the deposition site. 'My lads processed the scene as best they could, though if you find DNA on the body, I'll eat my hat. It's been tanking down since we arrived. The victim has been washed clean.'

David didn't need telling that evidence recovery had been problematic. The situation was dire, his crime scene little more than a swamp. He couldn't think of a worse set of circumstances. 'Did it not occur to you to erect a tent?'

'We tried, guv.'

David opened his hands. 'Then where is it?'

'Up there.'

The Crime Scene Manager swung round, aiming his torch across the railway line and upwards. David and Frankie followed the beam of light. A torn sheet of white canvas flapped in the wind from a hawthorn tree, thirty feet above their heads, as if poking fun at them. No one laughed. Humour wasn't welcome here. It had been a tough operation for everyone. More than once tonight, the weather had beaten them. Like every officer on duty, the three were cold, wet and miserable, ready for their beds. Fat chance tonight, David thought. There was a death message to deliver and it couldn't wait till morning.

'I'm sorry, guv. We did our best.'

The SIO waved away Foley's apology. There were times that the elements won the tug-of-war when it came to preserving evidence. In those circumstances, CSI teams did what they could, and that was all any Senior Investigating Officer could reasonably expect of them.

'How long will you be?' David asked.

Foley consulted with a colleague.

The forensic photographer looked up. 'Almost done, guv.'

He'd been doing his thing a few feet away, a valiant attempt to produce a visual record of the general layout of the crime scene before turning his attention to the murder victim. Taking detailed images of anyone in the dark was a challenge at the best of times – more so tonight, given that both subject and photographer were exposed to wind and rain. Frankie and David watched him change lenses, then set about taking close-ups of Joanna Cosgrove from a variety of angles, adjusting lighting to get the most accurate shots, aware that his grim photoshoot would be scrutinised by investigators later and, when the time came, produced as evidence in a court of law. He was packing up now.

Foley's team were done.

David gave permission for the body to be removed. He was keen to get Joanna out of the rain and into the morgue for a more thorough examination. He looked on as the grim task of lifting her began. Those handling his victim did so with as much care as they would a live casualty, placing her in a body bag and securing her on a stretcher for transportation to the morgue – a deeply traumatising scene he'd witnessed many times throughout his police career, though it never got any easier.

With feet squelching and slipping in the mud, the wretched procession covered the short distance to the gate. Two officers climbed over it, receiving the stretcher on the other side. As Joanna was locked in the back of a van, David vowed to find the callous bastard responsible for her death. Failure wasn't an option he could contemplate.

He glanced sideways.

Frankie's head was bowed. Crestfallen was the word on the tip of his tongue as he studied her, wondering what was going through her mind. Undoubtedly, she'd seen her fair share of dead bodies: road traffic fatalities, suicides and accidents, murders, too, in the initial stages, but she was now his 2ic

21

with all the responsibilities that a second-in-command post entailed. This was her first crack on a Murder Investigation Team – Stone's first in Northumbria. For both, the case had just got personal.

5

The major incident room was a hive of activity when David Stone emerged from briefing the head of CID. A cacophony of voices fielding telephone calls, gearing up for an even more difficult case than anyone could have imagined at the start, DS Abbott and DC Mitchell among them, seconded from general CID at the SIO's request due to the scale of the enquiry he was about to undertake.

The murder wall made grim reading: CATHERINE BENNETT (28), ALISON BRODY (34) and MARGARET ROBSON (59). Mitch was adding the name of the latest victim – JOANNA COSGROVE (37) – formal identification having taken place during the night.

Frankie's voice came from over David's shoulder. 'Morning, guv.'

He turned. 'Morning, Frank. Briefing at nine?'

'I'll pass the word on.'

'I want the whole team in attendance. No excuses.'

'Understood. Have you seen the morning papers?'

He nodded, fury lighting up his eyes. 'Join me for an update when you're done.'

Frankie raised an eyebrow. 'Such as it is . . .' She flicked her eyes left, towards the team they had inherited, dropping her voice to little more than a whisper. 'Allegedly, this lot have been working flat out for weeks and got nowhere. What makes you think we'll accomplish more?'

'I have you,' he said. 'You're worth four of them.'

She grinned. 'Can I have that in writing?'

'In triplicate.'

David walked away. He was aware that she didn't rate all the detectives in the room, but they were stuck with them for

23

now and there wasn't a damned thing they could do about it. An assessment of individual capabilities would have to wait, though in time he'd decide who to keep, who to send on their way. He intended to consult Frankie on every appointment, tap into her knowledge of MIT personnel.

He yawned – for lack of air, not exhaustion. Though that would come later.

It was gone three when he got to bed – and he was up at six – but this morning he was running on adrenaline. In the early hours, he'd left Alan Cosgrove heartbroken, unable to process the appalling circumstances of his wife's death. David glanced at his watch. It wasn't yet eight. He imagined the couple's teenage children in their beds, blissfully unaware that they would never celebrate their mother's birthday or see her alive again. Their father still had that awful task to face.

Every parent's worst nightmare.

Last night, David had assured him that his team would be working round the clock to find the person or persons responsible. In return, Cosgrove gave him an accusatory stare: *If you'd done your jobs, my wife would still be alive.* The man had every right to be angry. The newspapers were fuelling the frenzy, sensationalising the fact that a madman was bumping off women indiscriminately across Northumberland. These deplorable murders had to stop but the hacks weren't helping. If truth be known, they were making matters worse, terrifying women, warning them to stay indoors.

Lacking any theories of his own, David sat down at his desk. It would be a while before the post-mortem results were in, an agonising wait, but there was much to do: liaising with the office manager, tracking Joanna's last movements, hunting for witnesses who may have seen her on the train, if indeed that was how she'd travelled to Stocksfield. She could have taken a taxi or a bus but, given the weather warning for people to stay off the roads, that was unlikely. The SIO flicked through the reports in his in-tray, many addressed to Sharpe.

He'd linked the incidents under Operational Order 81/17.

David read on . . .

Operation Trident was so-called due to a cluster of incidents within a three-week period. While Sharpe wasn't stupid enough to think that the offender would stop at three, it occurred to David that false optimism may have factored in his choice of operational name. David understood where he was coming from but, after a short break, Joanna had been murdered. He hoped that she'd be the last victim even though, in his heart, he knew different. Serial offenders rarely stop of their own free will.

Before his involvement, crime pattern analysis experts had worked hard to inform the Murder Investigation Team's approach to the case overall, comparing crime and geographical data across all enquiries to give them a head start, though in truth their predictive capability had been lacking thus far, with two exceptions: all victims had been strangled; all, including Joanna, were middle-class, professional women with high-end jobs, a young celebrity among them.

The report he'd been reading hit his desk.

A big sigh . . .

He picked up another document, equally depressing. The cost of the enquiry was spiralling out of control, a consideration for him and the head of CID. Fortunately, Detective Chief Superintendent Bright had promised him every resource in his efforts to stop the rot. The call log was mounting as people woke to the devastating news that another woman had lost her life, each telephone message generating a possible action, a further strain on an overstretched budget. Thousands had come in since the investigation began. Detectives were working flat out to clear the backlog, each one aware that the body count might rise further.

6

A tap on his door made David look up. Frankie poked her head in. He beckoned her closer. She looked as unhappy as he felt as she pulled up a chair and sat down. He'd asked her to monitor calls, liaise with Northern Rail and British Transport Police in the hope that CCTV might kick-start the enquiry into Joanna's death. The detective sergeant's miserable expression would suggest she'd lucked out. Seconds later, David's reading of her proved right.

'Rolling stock on that route is ancient,' she groaned. 'There is no CCTV.'

'And at the station?'

'Power was out, remember? Our guy couldn't have picked a better night to make his play. Apart from us, and the rest of the emergency services, there were few people about. Anyone crazy enough to venture out was wrapped up against the storm: caps, hats, hoods. Our guy would be no different. He could've been wearing a fucking balaclava and no one would have raised an eyebrow . . . What the . . . ?' Frankie's eyes grew wide. She swore under her breath. 'Has Bright seen that?'

'Unfortunately . . . He's going ballistic.'

'Hardly surprising.'

She'd spotted the front page of the newspaper on his desk, with its damaging headline: *Another Victim: The Sleeper Strikes Again*. There could only be one reason for attaching the pseudonym. Overnight, someone with knowledge of the scene – CSI or copper – had leaked a vital piece of intelligence to a journalist who shouldn't be party to the information – and the local rag had run with it.

Frankie looked worried, for them both. 'The question is, what are we going to do about it?'

'What do you think we should do?'

'You don't want to know what I think, guv. It isn't polite.'

David was in no mood for humour.

He crossed his arms, letting out a big sigh. It went without saying that the staging of Joanna Cosgrove's body on railway sleepers was not something he wanted in the public domain. Information like that should be strictly under his control. The fact that a leak to the press may have come from within his team didn't bode well so early in the investigation. He was livid.

'Keep your eyes and ears open,' he said. 'We need to shut the leak down before any more damage is done.'

'Bright will expect nothing less.'

'Tell me about it.'

'We'll find the loudmouth, guv. And when we do . . .'

She let the sentence hang, studying him closely. David looked on edge, even more so than he had the night before – understandable, given the newsprint screaming out from his desk – but his expression went deeper than concern or even irritation that someone was compromising the investigation and, in so doing, undermining his authority. It brought to mind his wish to offload on the way to the crime scene. Frankie couldn't recall exactly how he'd put it – only that it was important – and that events had overtaken them and it never got said.

'We should take five,' she said. 'Coffee? Last night, you said you had something important to discuss.'

David shook his head.

'No coffee, or no chat?'

'No coffee. If I have any more, I'll get the shakes. And this' – he tapped the newspaper – 'is not what I wanted to talk about.'

Now Frankie was even more concerned. 'Is it Ben? Because if it is, now's not the time. You know it'll lead to a row. We rarely agree on how to handle him.'

'We?' Ben was the nephew David had taken in when his brother died, ending *his* life as a single man with no ties. Already the lad was cramping his style. Gone was his privacy. His peace. God forbid that he might want to take a woman home – other than Frank, and she didn't count. 'On second thoughts, I'm happy to share him.' He grinned. 'Would you consider joint custody?'

'Turn of phrase, guv. I'm not ready to play happy families.'

'Me either . . . I don't know why I let you talk me into it—'

'Don't tell me he's being difficult. He promised me he wouldn't give you any grief.'

'He hasn't . . . much.' David got up and opened the window a touch, registering nothing as he stared through the grubby glass. Right now, Ben was the least of his concerns. He tuned Frankie out, his mind far from Northumberland. He took a deep breath. *For fuck's sake, tell her!* If he didn't do it now, he never would. There had never been a better time. He sat down again, wiping his face with his hand.

'Well if it isn't Ben, what is it?' Frankie never missed a trick. 'You didn't lose your crocodile shoes, did you?'

Ordinarily, David would have laughed at her reference to Jimmy Nail. Since he'd arrived back in the north-east, she'd ribbed him relentlessly about his homesickness and tendency to see the area through a haze of old memories, and yes, his crocodile shoes too.

'It's time I explained why I left the Met and came north.'

'What?' She stared at him in disbelief. 'You *really* want to have that conversation now? Here?'

'I do . . . I have to.' A big swallow, a dry mouth.

The smile slid off Frankie's face. 'David? I'm sorry, I didn't mean to upset you—'

'Her name was Jane . . . DS Jane Vincent.' There, he'd said it. That wasn't so hard now, was it? But he could see Frankie making up the rest, imagination in overdrive. He had to put her straight. The secret he'd been hiding was no love affair.

28

No critical illness . . . It was murder, plain and simple. 'She died in my arms, Frank . . . Four shots at close range.'

'What?' Not much knocked Frankie sideways, but this had. 'When was this? Were you armed response?'

'No.' Having spent years in a Met firearms team, he could see where she was coming from, but she was wrong. 'We were colleagues in a Major Incident Team, much like this one.'

'Then how? I don't understand . . .'

'We were off duty at the time. Jane had just come out of an abusive relationship. The night it happened, she rang and asked for help, pleading with me to get over to her flat. Her ex had threatened her on the phone. She wouldn't call it in and begged me not to. She was ambitious and didn't want to make it official. Her supervision was a twat. You know the type. Jane thought he'd accuse her of bad judgement and mark her down for it. I went over with a bottle of wine. As we sat talking, the boyfriend let himself in and shot her right in front of me.'

'Jesus, David! I remember this.'

Of course she did, along with every detective in every force across the land. 'Before we get into this four-hander, I want you to understand why I froze during our last investigation. It was unforgivable. I owe you an explanation.'

'You owe me nothing.'

'We can't move on without one, Frank.'

'It doesn't matter—'

'It does to me. So, shut the fuck up and let me do this.'

Their eyes met briefly, a moment of heartbreak and sorrow. He didn't want to tell her – and she didn't want to listen – and yet he felt compelled to explain why he'd floundered during an abduction case, reacting badly to a witness turned suspect, a female doppelgänger who reminded him of Jane. Frankie had taken up the slack and he'd pushed her away, unable to bring himself to discuss it. Despite her efforts to get to the bottom of his bizarre behaviour, he'd not taken her into his confidence. And he couldn't let that happen again. She was racking her brains now, rifling through her internal filing system, trying to recall the exact details of the execution of his ex-colleague.

'They caught him, didn't they?'

'Eventually . . .' David glanced out the open window, thoughts of that night crowding in on him. He was back in Jane's flat, reliving the worst moments of his life, a montage of memories scrolling like movie credits behind his eyes. It took a while to compose himself. 'I didn't see his face, just a hand pointing the firearm. I already had his details and photographic evidence of what he'd done to her. He pulled the trigger as he opened the door.' David was beginning to unravel.

'Take your time,' she said.

He didn't want her sympathy. He couldn't handle that. He just wanted to get it said and put it behind him. 'She begged me not to let her die.' His voice broke as he spoke. 'I tried stemming the blood but there was too much of it. I knew she wouldn't make it.'

Frankie sat forward in her chair. 'But you told her what she wanted to hear, right?'

He nodded. 'She trusted me to tell her the truth. I lied . . . and kept on lying until . . .' And still he couldn't say it. 'I did everything I could but she was beyond saving. I knew that the minute he fired off the first round. She took one in the chest. She was gone before the medics arrived.'

Frankie fell silent. She was good like that, knew when to keep her mouth shut and when to let rip. Had it not been for her, there would've been no second chance for him: following his transfer; during their last investigation in general CID; nor last night when he was almost wiped out by that train. He suddenly felt vulnerable. Exposed. Like he had on the afternoon he'd walked back into the West End Central nick in the heart of London's Mayfair after Jane's funeral, the eyes of his Met crew staring at him as he entered the incident room.

'My team were amazing,' he said. 'No one blamed me—'

Frankie bristled. 'Why would they?'

'I don't know, but the fact they didn't somehow made it more difficult to live with.' The flashback hit him like a brick. There was no physical similarity between the two women, but David saw Jane sitting in Frankie's chair, a pair of ice-blue eyes staring back at him, her face twisted in agony. The palpitations came thick and fast. He told himself to get a grip. 'I should've known better,' he said. 'I should have leaned on her to get her boyfriend charged. I did fuck-all to prevent it happening. I have her blood on my hands, Frank.'

'David, you don't really believe that any more than I do. You didn't report the abuse at her request. You're no mind reader. How could you possibly have known what he'd do?'

'All the same, I should've seen it coming.'

'Should you? Jane didn't or she'd have acted. Her ex sounds like a fucking lunatic.'

'He is—'

'There you go then. None of this is your fault. None of it!'

Frankie's sympathy had turned to anger. She was glaring at him. Judging him. Reading him. David didn't care. He wasn't yet ready to tell her everything: that at one point he was heading for the nearest tall building; that he'd become so depressed life hadn't seemed worth living; that it had taken every ounce of energy to get up in the morning. It would sound defeatist if he said it aloud. Frankie wouldn't understand. How could she? She was strong. Nothing could make her feel that way.

Her eyes were pleading with him. 'David, don't torture yourself. I've heard enough. I can't possibly imagine what you went through, but do yourself a favour – shift the blame to where it belongs or this will kill you.'

'It *is* killing me. Why do you think we're having this conversation?'

She glanced at the door to the incident room, then back at him. 'You certainly pick your moments.'

'I know, but I want a fresh start. I can't operate without all my cards on the table.'

She blew out a breath.

He understood her frustration.

She looked small in the oversized chair – and fidgety. Only to be expected. Cut one member of the police family and the rest bled. Although she wasn't big physically, Frankie had a heart the size of a house. She was on his side. He sensed it. She'd known that something catastrophic had gone down when he was a DCI in the Metropolitan Police but not the fine detail.

Not for the want of trying, he imagined.

She'd have trawled the internet trying to find out what had triggered his sudden departure from the capital but the chances of her finding anything were slim. With forty-five thousand officers across a hundred and eighty police stations, it would have been like looking for a needle in a haystack. For all intents and purposes, Jane's death was a domestic incident between ex-lovers. A murder, yes. But not the random killing of a police officer by some crazed villain or terrorist. As an eye-witness to the killing, Stone had been forced to hang around until the trial was over, but it had taken many months to get Jane's killer to court. Even if Frankie had tried to investigate, the timeline wouldn't match. She might have had a stab at what it was but, short of ringing the incident room and asking outright, she had no way of knowing the truth of it, and she'd never betray a colleague in that way. Such an enquiry from an outside force would've raised suspicions, exposing David's weaknesses, ending their professional partnership. Besides, Frankie had more integrity than that. And because David did too, he struggled on . . .

He had to get it said.

'I was a basket case for months. I couldn't talk about

it. I couldn't visualise Jane in any way but dying the way she had. Every memory of her deserted me. It was as if she never existed beyond that room. I know it sounds crazy—'

'Didn't you see the Met psychologist?'

'It didn't help.' David ran a hand through his hair. 'I know it sounds pathetic, but I was stuck, unable to move forward. Luke was the only one I could talk to. When he died, so did my counsel outside of the job. He was the one who kept me afloat, Frank. I'd never have got through it without him. I should've told you about this long before now.'

'Look, David, I can listen but it sounds like you need help I'm not qualified to give. I'm not passing the buck here, but this is not my business and we have too much on to dwell on the past.'

'Even if I'm unfit to hold office?'

'Don't be daft—'

'I wasn't, not in London anyway—'

'Oh please! If you still think that, you may as well hand over your warrant card and piss off.' Frankie paused but she was nowhere near finished. 'Look, what happened to you was bloody awful – I'm not denying that – but you've got to put it behind you. And, for the record, I'm not carrying you for the rest of your career.'

'Fair comment.' Her words stung a little, though David knew what she was trying to achieve and for whose benefit. Now his secret was out there, he expected to return to normal and pull his weight. 'Frank, I'm well aware that if it hadn't been for you I'd have drowned during our last case. I let you down badly and I'm sorry. If anyone deserved a promotion out of it, it was you.'

'You're wrong, David. This is your time, not mine. And you'd better make a good impression or you'll be out on your ear. Extenuating circumstances won't cut it with Bright. He won't stand for failure and, frankly, neither will I. When we leave this room, you need to act like you own the place.' She climbed off her high horse.

He smiled for the first time since she'd entered the room. He felt better for having told her. A knock at the door prevented him from letting her know how much.

She jumped up and yanked it open.

Mitch was loitering outside. 'We're ready for you, Sarge.'

Frankie glanced over her shoulder, a challenge in her eyes: *You coming or not?*

7

His revelation had come as no surprise. Frankie had always known that he was broken by something in his past. During their last case in general CID, an enquiry spanning both ends of the country, they had gone back to David's old stomping ground and, frustrated by his odd behaviour, she'd had a quiet word with one of his ex-colleagues, trying to find out what in hell's name was wrong with him. The Met officer clammed up, telling her not to push him, forcing her to back off. She wouldn't break a confidence. Frankie let it go then and she'd do the same now, though she had a theory that the mindless slaughter of four defenceless women across Northumberland had sparked the need for David to bear his soul. It had upset her to see him struggle to get the words out and, if she were being honest, it angered her to listen to his negativity. He had a job to do and she intended to see that he did it.

Loathing Jane's killer almost as much as he did, Frankie pushed open the door and led the way into the incident room. She turned to face him, the formality of rank reasserting itself in case she was overheard. She was well versed in protocol.

'Good luck, guv.'

'I appreciate your support.' The smile was forced.

She dropped her voice to a whisper. 'You can do this, David. I'm here if you need me.'

'Thanks, Frankie.'

Their eyes locked.

In that pivotal moment, she felt sure that, having finally plucked up the courage to explain his past, he'd begin to look forward, not back. His promotion to the rank he'd held within the Met had secured his future. Privately, Bright had told her that David had accepted the position as Sharpe's replacement with one condition, repeating his words verbatim: *With respect, sir, I'd like to pick my own second in command. No DS Oliver and you can swing for it. That's non-negotiable.*

She'd laughed like a drain.

No Northumbria detective who valued his or her job, apart from DCI Kate Daniels, had ever had the temerity to talk to him that way. Fortunately for David, the head of CID rated Frankie too. Early on in her service, he'd marked her as one to watch. He'd worked with her old man for many years and, though Stone didn't know it, had encouraged her to give up her uniform in favour of plain clothes. Bright hadn't hesitated in rubber-stamping her appointment as David's 2ic.

In the crowded room, murder detectives were seated, note-pads at the ready, everyone waiting for the briefing to begin. David assumed his position at the front. Frankie seemed to be holding her breath as he scanned the room waiting for conversations to end. He had a matter to raise that would rattle someone in the room. There was a hush as detectives paid attention; young and old, black and white, male and female eyes now bearing down on him, everyone keen to hear his take on the case. That would change. The SIO took a step forward, feeling under intense pressure, like he was standing on the gallows waiting for the trapdoor to open.

'I've been in conference with Detective Chief Superintendent Bright this morning, so I know that you've been working round the clock on this enquiry. Whatever you were doing, drop it. We have no credible suspects and we're doing this my way from now on. I want fresh eyes on this investigation. We'll be concentrating on the latest murder victim and l intend to review the evidence going forward.'

This didn't go down well.

A detective at the front snorted, pissed off at having to change direction. Stone understood that. It had happened to him many times. He'd learned over the years to drop one ball and pick up another as priorities changed. He'd agreed a strategy with Bright and was sticking with it, even if it made him unpopular in the short-term. He could have fired off the unpalatable truth, that Bright was growing increasingly frustrated by the lack of progress. Over and above their social status, the team had found no link between the victims; they were killed on different days of the week in a geographical area that had no obvious connection: a beach, a graveyard, a riverside location, a railway siding; they were not in the same age group, nor were they similar in appearance; and, most importantly, CSI's hadn't found a shred of forensic evidence at any of the scenes, nor did they have a clue on motive.

Worrying.

David kept his thoughts to himself. He needed this merry band onside, though he'd kick ass if he had to. 'My door is open to those of you with a beef . . . But know this: if you don't like the way I work, you can walk. I'll find replace-ments. This is a major investigation. Detectives are queueing up for a crack at it.' His eyes travelled around the room. 'And, while we're on the subject, when I find out who in this room blabbed to the press about railway sleepers – and believe me, I will – they'll be out on their ear. Any questions?'

None were forthcoming.

In the comfort of his office, he'd thought long and hard on whether to raise the matter, but decided that not to do so at the outset would have been viewed as a weakness by those assembled. Having put it out there, he'd demonstrated that he wouldn't turn a blind eye to any buggering about, driving home the idea that he was no patsy when it came to leadership.

He felt himself relax.

'OK, let's start with the victim. Joanna Cosgrove, maiden name Wallis, was pronounced dead at the scene last night by pathologist Beth Collingwood. A post-mortem will take place today. The IP was fully clothed and found close to a railway line on the south side of the Tyne in the village of Stocksfield. CSIs processed the scene, but you all know what it was like last night, so I'm not hopeful that it'll take us very far. A PolSA team is there now.' Police Search Advisers were consultants used in every UK force to plan and manage search activity.

'Uniforms are covering house-to-house,' Stone added. 'No joy yet, but we can hope. I want every commuter on that train route identified and interviewed. I want someone to liaise with British Transport Police. It's important to nail down Joanna's movements by close of play. Any questions?'

'The MO is the same as the other three?' Mitchell asked.

David nodded. 'Strangled from behind. Personal effects left with the body. Joanna's handbag had been deliberately placed next to her. It was not lying on its side, as you might expect following an attack of this nature. It seems our offender likes to tidy up after himself.'

'No robbery then?' Mitch wasn't asking.

David shook his head. 'The contents of her bag were untouched as far as we can tell. Inside was a legal brief relating to a fraud prosecution. Joanna was a solicitor specialising in criminal cases so it's not beyond the bounds of possibility that she might have known her assailant. Her purse contained seventy-five quid in notes and loose change, as well as personal items: lipstick, comb, expensive Mont Blanc pen and house keys, two sets. Car keys were found in her pocket.' He scoured the room, taking in every face. 'Let me make one thing clear: the words "serial killer" are no longer in your vocabulary. Remember that when you're dealing with the public, or indeed the press when they're demanding a statement. We're in the national spotlight. I expect you all to toe the line or face the consequences.'

He paused, allowing his words to sink in and note-takers to catch up. An image popped into his head of Frankie in a beautiful hallway, dripping water all over a polished wooden floor while he delivered the death message.

Heartbreaking for all concerned.

'DS Oliver and I informed the IP's husband of her death in the early hours and formal identification has been made. Alan Cosgrove was at home for most of the evening with the couple's two teenage children. When his wife failed to return home, he went to the railway station to look for her but there was no one around. Her vehicle, a grey BMW, was in the station car park. It's been uplifted and is being examined as we speak. Mr Cosgrove returned home to wait and went to bed when Joanna didn't show.'

Looks were exchanged, muttering at the back.

David ignored it. 'Mr Cosgrove was too traumatised to be questioned last night. I'll return to this at the evening briefing after I've paid him a second visit.'

Abbott raised a finger. 'Are crime scene photographs available for viewing yet, guv?'

'They are. The video isn't great in view of the atrocious weather conditions last night.' David found the office manager in the sea of faces, a man with slightly receding hair, a weathered face and metal-framed specs, a dead-ringer for Tommy Lee Jones. 'Charlie, I'm raising an action for the convenience store opposite the station, Orchard House Veterinary Centre and Broomley First School. Concentrate your efforts on Stocksfield and any strangers hanging about. There are bus stops on either side of the road outside the station. Lean on the house-to-house team. Make sure they're asking the right questions, particularly of people who use the bus.

39

They might have seen something. Lastly, for those of you who doubt my strategy, there's a reason I'm concentrating on Joanna. There's a distinguishing factor between her and the other three victims I'm hoping might lead somewhere. The scene was staged.'

8

Those who'd been to the scene knew this already. To the rest, news of this nature was like an incendiary device exploding in their midst, recharging a team who, it had to be said, had been flagging when Frankie arrived at work first thing. If she was any judge, this was exactly why the SIO had left the revelation till last, though she was sure the detectives had seen the newspaper headline. David was taking the lead, as he was destined to do. He'd been there before and knew what was expected of him. From her point of view, they made a good pairing. She had a lot to thank him for, not least of which was giving her a leg-up in an organisation that didn't understand the meaning of the word meritocracy. Working in the Murder Investigation Team had its downside – it was gruelling work, long hours, emotionally taxing – but investigating the ultimate crime was every detective's dream. In her case, payback after years of hard graft. She had plenty of insight to offer but, as his bagman, she also stood to learn a lot.

A voice drew her back into the room.

'Guv?' Mitchell's hand was in the air. 'If there was staging in this latest incident, can we link it to the other three?'

'Not conclusively. We'll know more following the PM, but I'm praying that we're not looking for more than one offender.' David paused. 'The change in the way the body was dealt with post-mortem interests me. The offender could just be dicking us around – because he can. But if he's getting cocky, he might make a mistake. I want you on your toes and ready for him.'

Detectives were responding, nods and shared looks, whispers floating around the room. David was holding his own and yet was fully aware of his team's reluctance to accept a new SIO. Their scepticism was justifiable, given their loyalty to their old boss and his methodology. It was natural to favour Sharpe over an incomer, familiarity being more comfortable than working with an unknown quantity. The team's relationship with Sharpe was built on close contact and, mostly, positive results, although it had Frankie wondering what had triggered the sudden departure of a man of his calibre and what her new colleagues *really* thought of being abandoned mid-case. Bright had castigated him for it, privately and publicly, though Frankie wondered if Sharpe was ill – or one of his family was – a fact that he'd kept quiet. There could be any number of reasons why he'd jumped ship.

Frankie had no doubt that David would prove himself a worthy replacement in time. He was well thought of in the Met, a fully paid-up member of his team, well liked by everybody, including his former Met guv'nor. Presently, he had detectives eating out of his hand.

A Technical Support civilian was on his feet with information to impart. 'Guv, I came in early to examine Joanna's phone. Were you aware that she'd called home at nine-o-nine last night and left no message?'

David glanced at Frankie.

She shook her head. 'Her husband didn't mention it to me.'

'Me either.' The techie sat down but the SIO wasn't finished with him yet. 'Did Joanna make any other calls?'

'No, but she did receive one. The number is registered to Alan Cosgrove. It was a missed call—'

'Married-couple syndrome,' an old detective joked. 'My wife never answers either.'

'That's because you're a misogynistic dinosaur,' Frankie said.

Everyone laughed.

'Any idea where she was when she tried to call home?' David was eyeing the techie.

'Not yet, sir. I've been on to her service provider. They're getting back to me.'

'When they do, let me know.'

'Sir.'

'Anything else?' There were no takers. With the benefit of some new information, David had every reason to feel positive. He wrapped up the meeting and threw a glance in Frankie's direction. 'We better go.'

'Cosgrove?'

He nodded, keen to get over there now the dreadful news had sunk in and offer his personal support to the bereaved husband. Although David's altruism was genuine, holding the hands of a murder victim's family was the job of the FLO he'd appointed that morning. His and Frankie's priority was pinning down Joanna's last movements. Gaining insight into her life meant that they would eventually understand her death. To allow her passing to go undetected would be a travesty, handing victory to her killer – and they weren't having that.

9

The sun came out as they left Northern Command HQ and drove up the coast road, jammed with traffic, temporary roadworks for essential maintenance slowing their progress. Skirting the city, the route took them west, then south, passing through a sentry of trees on either side of a dual carriageway, a wonderful cloudscape in the distance. Thirty minutes later, Frankie looked left as they passed over a bridge, glimpsing the receding River Tyne, before Stone followed the sign to the sleepy village of Stocksfield where Joanna Cosgrove had lived.

On its western edge, they passed through a set of traffic lights. Up ahead, council workers were clearing away debris left in the wake of the storm. Otherwise, the village was peaceful, the railway station back in business, a thorough search carried out at dawn, though the crime scene – invisible from the main road – would remain taped off until the SIO gave the order for its release.

Streets with pretty names flashed by. Outside Broomley First School, warning zig-zags dissuaded parents from parking outside. They passed sports fields, took a sharp bend in the road and then drove up a steep incline. During last night's identical journey, this was the point at which David understood why Joanna had taken her car to the station and not walked. Stocksfield was a sprawling commuter village, its population of two and a half thousand spread across a wide area.

He glanced at Frankie. 'Is this it?'

'Next one, guv.'

'It looks different in daylight.'

He passed one turning, indicating when he saw a signpost for Hedley-on-the-Hill. The Cosgrove house was set back from the road about halfway up, around two miles from the crime scene. It stood on a large plot with a stunning view over surrounding countryside, a new build made to look old.

Running on empty, Frankie knocked on the door, her eyes gritty, like someone had thrown half of Bamburgh beach in there. There was no answer. *Odd.* At David's request, she'd called ahead to ensure that it was a convenient time to call. Children were involved. Neither detective wanted to arrive as Cosgrove broke the news of their mother's death. His silver Mercedes was on the driveway.

Frankie glanced at her boss, a raised eyebrow: *We're expected.*

'Let's try round the back.' David indicated a side gate and led the way.

They found Joanna's husband alone in his garden, sitting in the shade of a stunning clematis-covered gazebo that had survived the summer storm. He drew hard on a cigarette, dark glasses covering his eyes, a young brown Labrador spark out at his feet. His bereft mother-in-law had just left, he told them, taking his traumatised children home to stay with her and their grandfather for a few days.

'I didn't want to go,' he said. 'I know Barbara means well but I couldn't bear to leave the house right now. I feel close to Joanna here.' He glanced from one detective to the other, barely in control of his emotions. 'This was her favourite seat.'

Frankie had dealt with victims all her working life. Questioning family members whose pain was this raw and this visible never got easier. The fallout from criminal activity, whether violent assault, robbery or murder, blighted the lives of those affected and those left behind. Last night, the words 'we're sorry for your loss' sounded hollow, even when spoken with genuine regret by her boss. Cosgrove had given David hard eyes in return. This morning, Frankie had hoped he'd be less hostile. It didn't take her long to realise that he hadn't moved an inch. Neither had he forgiven David's predecessor for failing in his duty to protect. In Cosgrove's eyes, as incumbent, the new SIO was equally responsible for his wife's death.

Conscious of an awkward atmosphere developing between the two men, Frankie took the lead. 'We're trying to piece together Joanna's movements last night, sir. Would you like to go inside the house or talk here?' If this was the couple's special place in the garden, she wouldn't contaminate it.

Appreciating the gesture, the man hauled himself to his feet. He dwarfed David by several inches and made giant strides into the house via an open patio door. The dog and the detectives followed him in. In a vast breakfasting kitchen, he pointed at a state-of-the-art coffee machine and told them to help themselves. They both declined but Frankie made one for him, strong and black, and took it to the table where he was now sitting. He was unshaven and looked like he hadn't slept a wink.

Without thanking her, he took the cup. 'What do you want to know?'

Frankie glanced at David. His nod was almost imperceptible, her cue to proceed, information-gathering more important to him than exercising rank. Frankie was grateful for his confidence in her ability. She excelled in talking to victims and had the know-how and patience to elicit the right answers.

'When did you last see Joanna?' she asked.

'At eight a.m. when she left for work.'

'And what time were you expecting her back?'

'She never said.' Cosgrove took off his sunglasses revealing red-rimmed watery eyes. He had the look of American actor Jeff Goldblum: angular features, square jaw, redundant laughter lines, an oddly attractive man with grey flecks in dark hair. Frankie guessed that he was a few years Joanna's senior. 'She had a last-minute strategy meeting scheduled for the late afternoon with her associate, Joseph Cohen. They were planning an early dinner afterwards.'

'Any idea where?'

'No, sorry.' Cosgrove shook his head, a guilty expression. 'To be honest, I never asked. Joseph is a friend and senior partner in the law firm Joanna works for. They often dine out together and he normally takes care of reservations. They may have eaten at his private members' club. They do that sometimes. It depends how they're feeling, if they want any fun with their fillet. Joanna likes the food but not the atmosphere. It's a little too stuffy for her liking.'

'Northern Counties?' Frankie asked.

'No, the other one. Martin's on Grey Street. You'll have to talk to Joseph. I'm sorry to be so vague.' Frankie made a note of the club and Cohen's name as he continued to talk. 'Joanna went out in two minds whether to stay in town or travel home.'

'Which hotel might she have used?'

'None. She has a bolthole close to the law courts,' Cosgrove explained. 'She and Joseph were listed to appear there this morning in a long-running fraud case . . . Joanna often stays in town if she has a late night or the weather's bad—'

'And yet she was found in the village.' It was a statement, not a question.

Cosgrove dropped his head in his hands and didn't comment. Frankie gave him a moment. She couldn't make up her mind if he was weeping or avoiding her questions, irritated by a police presence when all he wanted was to be left alone to grieve. Or maybe he had a guilty conscience for having laid the blame on police the night before. In the absence of a suspect, the man had to point the finger at someone.

'Sir?' Frankie moved on. 'How had Joanna been recently? In herself, I mean.'

The bereft husband raised his head, eyes filled with tears. 'What do you mean?'

'She hadn't received any strange calls or mentioned anything that was bothering her?'

'Are you suggesting she was stalked?'

'We don't know yet. Had she been acting differently?'

He shook his head. 'No . . . nothing like that.'

'And you, sir? What were your movements yesterday?'

'I'm on standby.'

'For what, if you don't mind me asking?'

'I'm a commercial airline pilot. Long haul.'

Cosgrove got up, helping himself to something stronger than coffee. As he sat down again, Frankie's mind was racing: *three victims, one after the other, then a gap.* She tried not to look at David but he sure as hell was looking at her. She could feel his gaze boring a hole in the side of her head.

'And the week before last?' she asked.

'I had a three-day layover in Cancun.'

Nice. 'And the week before that?'

'I was in the sim . . . flight simulator. Fucking pain in the arse.' Another flash of offence, his eyes flitting between the two detectives. 'What is this? I'm a suspect now? You people really are the pits.'

You people.

'That's not what I'm suggesting, sir.' Frankie didn't flinch. She had to think on her feet. 'Joanna's killer is targeting women on their own. She may have been followed when you weren't here, that's why we need your movements and hers.'

'I understand,' Cosgrove apologised. 'But if that had been the case, she'd have said. If I was in the air, she'd have called her father. He'd have been straight round. And he'd have made damned sure I knew if there had been anyone giving her grief.'

'She may not have been aware of a tail.'

A tear escaped Cosgrove's right eye. He brushed it away with his index finger and Frankie pressed on: 'I realise how upsetting this is for you, but we need your assistance and we need it now.' Cosgrove nodded, a gesture for her to proceed.

'Do you have a rigid rota for days off? It would help if I knew how they're worked out.'

He shook his head. 'Duty hours and flying hours are convoluted, worked out on the number of time-zones you cross. If you're on a bullet – there and back, no stopover – calculations take this into account. If not, then a different formula applies. As I said, it's complicated. Look, if you want my rota I'll print one off. I have nothing to hide.'

'That would help a lot,' Frankie said. 'And if you could possibly let us know who else might have access to that rota, we'd like that too.'

'Yes, of course.'

'What did you do yesterday while Joanna was at work?'

Cosgrove hesitated, his brow creasing in concentration, his gaze travelling across the room to the mantelpiece, a collection of family photographs. 'I ran the kids into Hexham where they go to school, came back here and did some gardening, made a few calls, pottered about. I had a pint and a sandwich in The Feathers around one, then spent the afternoon reading. Joanna had left a meal in the Aga for me and the kids. I went out to collect them at around four. I can't have been gone more than half an hour.'

'You were home after that?'

'For the most part, yes.'

'For the most part?'

'I was planning a belated birthday surprise.'

Cosgrove drifted off someplace else. Another glance at the mantelpiece. More tears. A slug of his drink. Frankie could see the man was broken. She didn't have the heart to push him on it. They would talk many times during the course of the enquiry and she'd return to specifics later.

Despite her initial reaction to his working patterns – frequent trips away followed by days off at home with nothing to do – no one was seriously suggesting that the grieving man was involved in his wife's murder. And yet, as David had told

MIT detectives, there was a fundamental difference between her death and that of the other three women. She'd been laid out carefully and Stone had yet to confirm categorically that her death was linked to the others.

Frankie changed tack. 'Can I return to Joanna for a second, sir? Am I right to assume that she had no set hours, no routine for travelling to and from work?' It was necessary to ask. Such behaviour made victims vulnerable to attack. If that had been the case, Joanna could easily have been followed.

Cosgrove gave a nod. 'Joanna's movements depended on her workload. She came and went at different times of the day and night. If she was writing up legal arguments, sometimes she worked from home.'

Frankie's eyes settled on a desk in the corner. 'Is the laptop hers? None was found at the scene.'

'No, it's in her office.' He pointed to a hallway leading off the living room. 'Second door on the right.'

As Frankie asked another question, David got up to fetch it. No doubt he'd have a quick poke around while he was in there. She'd bet money on it. 'Were you aware that Joanna called you last night?'

'Yes, but not at the time she called. I'd taken Bradley for a walk.' Half asleep, but hearing his name, the dog wagged its tail once, receiving a pat from its master. 'Stupidly, I'd left my mobile in the house.'

'Joanna left no message?' Frankie already knew the answer.

'No, but my daughter said my phone had been ringing. The kids don't answer when I'm on standby. Not that I mind, but they know that sometimes I don't want to be found. Living in the sticks has its advantages. Poor signal is one of them. When I realised I'd missed Joanna, I figured she was staying out.'

Frankie seized on the contradiction. 'And yet you went out to meet her?' That's what he'd said last night.

A nod. 'The weather started to get worse. I was restless

. . . worried in case she'd decided to come home after all. We both love this house but it's a nightmare on the steep bank in bad weather and she hates driving in a thunderstorm. Having missed her call, I wanted to be sure.'

Time for an observation. 'The station is quite a way from here.'

Cosgrove shrugged. 'A couple of miles.'

Frankie glanced at the Lab at his feet. 'Wasn't Bradley frightened by the conditions?'

'I left him in the house and took the car. I was going to drive Joanna home and drop her back at the station this morning. Anyway, it was a fruitless exercise. She didn't get off the train.'

'Did you call her?'

'Yes, but she didn't pick up.'

'Mobile or landline?'

'Mobile. She doesn't have a landline in her flat.'

That tallied with what David had been told during the briefing. For a few moments, he'd been standing in the doorway, listening as the interview progressed. 'Did you get out of the car at the station?' He sat back down, placing Joanna's laptop on his knee.

'No, I was a bit late. I had to stop once or twice to shift debris off the road. There was litter everywhere.'

David's turn to nod. 'Her car was there when you arrived?'

'Yes.'

'Did you see the train?'

'It was pulling away as I pulled in. There was no one on the platform, none that I could see from my vehicle anyway. The only person I saw was an elderly lady in the car park. Poor sod could hardly stand up in that gale. She was having trouble holding on to her car door. I was about to get out and help when she managed to climb in and pull it to. I don't think she liked the look of me.'

'What made you think that?' Frankie cut in.

51

'She took off like a Gulfstream jet.'

'Can you remember the make or colour of her car?'

'Small. Light-coloured . . .' Cosgrove sighed, tired of all the questions. 'I didn't take that much notice.'

'So you can't help us with the registration number?'

Cosgrove shook his head.

'Not even a partial?'

'No, I'm sorry.'

'OK. Do you remember any other cars in the car park, apart from Joanna's?'

Cosgrove shut his eyes, the better to imagine the scene, then opened them again. 'Three or four, could've been five.'

'And where exactly did you park?' David asked.

'Why is that important?'

'It helps build a picture of who was in the area and where they were in relation to one another. It's important to identify anyone we might need to talk to as quickly as possible. The first twenty-four hours in any investigation is crucial.'

'You should've thought about that for victim number one, not waited until now. Isn't that what we pay our taxes for?' Another dig at police. Seeing the wounded expression on the faces of those trying to catch his wife's killer, Cosgrove took it back, apologising for having a go at them. 'As I said, I saw the train pull out of the station. I stopped at the barrier and reversed on to the area on the south side of the car park.'

'Outside the bollards, facing east?'

'Yes. I waited a few moments, which was when I saw the lady I mentioned. I followed her out of the car park when Joanna didn't show.'

Stone shifted in his seat. 'What time was this, sir?'

'Quarter to ten.'

'One last question: could your wife have taken another train, one that might have got her in before the quarter to ten?'

'I doubt it. And she wouldn't take the last one. Too many drunks.'

This was not what Stone was driving at. Frankie had already checked the timetable and knew full well that Joanna wasn't on the last train due in at 23.02. She was seen – if not dead, then close to it – by the eyewitness who raised the alarm at 22.40. If she rang home at 21.09 and didn't get off the 'quarter to ten' as her husband put it, then how did she get back to Stocksfield?

10

Stone and Oliver let themselves out. Closing the front door quietly behind them, they set off down the garden path through borders of overgrown lavender, releasing its scent as their legs brushed against it. As he reached the gate, David paused, looking back over his shoulder. Inside and out, the house was beautifully appointed, the interior full of family memorabilia and yet, it struck him that it was not a homely place to be. Last night, after breaking the awful news, they had moved through into a living room strewn with unopened gifts, cut flowers in vases, balloons and birthday cards on every surface. One in particular had caught his eye. It was signed: With love, Joseph xx.

David had noticed it as the bereaved man chose a photograph from the mantelpiece, a good likeness of his wife detectives might share with the press. As SIO, David was planning an appeal for the public to come forward. A major part of the investigation into Joanna's death would concentrate on the last weeks of her life. When he noticed the inscription, he remembered thinking that Joseph might have been Joanna's son. Now he knew different. Question was: did it mean anything? A birthday greeting from a colleague was perfectly innocent and yet David felt on edge. There was something missing in that house – and it wasn't just Joanna.

Unable to rid himself of the feeling, he opened the car doors and climbed in. Maybe he was wrong. Maybe what he'd picked up on was the void that sudden death creates. Emptiness outstripped love in the homes of victims left behind and those of bereaved relatives. Joy turned to misery. People stopped talking to one another. Rooms felt icy cold. You could feel distress leaking from the walls.

'What?' Frankie had picked up on his concern.

He didn't look at her. 'What did you think of him?'

She spoke through a yawn. 'What do you mean?'

'I'd like your first impressions, that's all.'

'He's crushed, David. And angry . . . He has every right to be.'

'With me?'

'With everybody: you, me, Sharpe, the police generally. He thinks we're inept and maybe he has a point. What did you expect? His life fell apart. He wants a scapegoat and you happen to fit the bill. I wouldn't take it personally.'

'I'm not.'

'Aren't you? Then what are you getting at?'

Another glance at the house. 'To be honest, I'm not sure. Forget I said anything. I'm probably wrong—'

'About what?' She waited. 'Well, *something* triggered the question.'

Now he looked at her. 'When you were interviewing him, I got the distinct impression that we weren't the only ones he had a problem with. He was angry with Joanna too. And when you asked him where he was yesterday, he sidestepped the question with what he wanted us to hear, though his emphasis was on the word *belated*. He seemed resentful. You saw the gifts, the balloons, cards. The family had gone to a lot of trouble. Don't you think it's odd that she would meet with Cohen on her birthday rather than spend the evening with them?'

'Not really. She's a pro with a heavy case on her hands by the sounds of it. I've worked plenty of birthdays and I'm guessing you have too. It's not a hanging offence. I'm surprised it even crossed your mind.'

'Yeah, maybe I'm overthinking things.' He turned the engine over. 'Chase Joseph Cohen when we get back to base.'

Frankie held up her notebook. 'Already on the To Do list.'

David reversed the car, a difficult manoeuvre on to a main

road. Unable to see, he pulled forward, negotiating a three-point turn to give him greater visibility.

'Where next?' Frankie was looking left, checking the traffic from her side. 'The crime scene?'

'No. Have you eaten today?'

Frankie shook her head. 'No time.'

'Well, if the pub Cosgrove mentioned isn't far away, we might pick up some gossip from the locals and, if we're really lucky, grab a burger while we're at it.'

'Burger?' Frankie grimaced. 'Wash your mouth out! My body is a temple.'

'Mine's not. I'm clamming and there'll be nowt left in the canteen when we get back.'

'Sounds like a plan.' She was pointing uphill. David swapped indicators, left for right, and pulled out on to the main road. 'You don't know the pub?'

Stone shook his head. 'Don't think so.'

'You've been away too long, guv.'

11

The Feathers was a two-hundred-year-old drovers' inn, up the road in the village of Hedley-on-the-Hill, a gastropub Frankie knew well, the hub of a small community, though people came from miles around to eat there. The village itself was peaceful, a friendly place to live, Frankie mentioned as David pulled the SUV into a small car park. She could tell from his agreeable expression that this was his kind of pub, his kind of area, though that came as no surprise to her, living in the countryside as he did.

They got out of the car.

Frankie was halfway to the pub's entrance, talking to herself, when she realised Stone wasn't listening or even following. He'd walked a little way down the road for a look around before turning back and retracing his steps with a question for her.

'Did you look at the incident log this morning?'

'That's like asking did I breathe.' Frankie placed a hand on her heart. 'I'm crushed that you'd even ask. This village doesn't get a mention, if that's what you're after. There's very little crime here. I'd be surprised if it has ever cropped up on a crime stats search.'

'And lower down the valley?'

'In Stocksfield?'

A nod.

Frankie shook her head. 'No incidents of serious violence in the recent past.'

'Has there ever been?'

'A siege that ended badly. A forty-odd-year-old was shot by a police marksman – a sad state of affairs for everyone involved – but that was over a decade ago in 2005.' Frankie flicked her eyes towards the pub's front door. 'If you're still hungry, we better get inside.'

Customers spoke in hushed whispers, a subdued atmosphere in what was normally a thriving, happy pub. Stone got his burger, albeit a posh one, Frankie opting for salmon straight from the North Sea, neither saying a word as they wolfed it down. The food hit the spot. David declined coffee when Frankie ordered one. He gestured towards the bar. On both sides of the counter, there were mournful expressions. Bad news had spread quickly. It was time to go to work.

Taking their drinks with them, they made their way across the room. Frankie took care of the introductions, explaining that she and Stone were investigating Joanna Cosgrove's murder. No need for covert questioning. These were decent folks.

A man spoke up: square-jawed, piercing eyes, a fresh pint of dark ale in his hand. 'Alan was in here yesterday. I told him he'd not be wanting to fly in that bloody awful wind. He said he'd flown in worse.' He looked at the others in the company. 'I wasn't sure whether he was pulling my leg. Maybe he was.'

'Wouldn't surprise me,' another man said. He glanced at the detectives. 'He's ex-Army Air Corp. Gulf War veteran. Top bloke.'

'How did he seem to you?' David asked.

'Friendly. Same as always.'

'He's a regular?' Frankie asked.

'We all are.' The man turned his head away, his attention drifting to a seat in the corner. 'He sat over there, didn't he, Helen?'

The landlady looked up from pulling a pint. 'He read the paper as usual and finished his crossword before he left. He pops in once or twice a week when he's at home. The family eat here a lot. I'm devastated by what's happened. Joanna was such a lovely woman, a real laugh.'

'He must be heartbroken,' the man who'd begun the conversation added. 'They've been married for twenty years. Not that you'd know it. They were still very much in love. I can't believe that, hours after he left us, she was gone. It doesn't bear thinking about.' He glanced at the SIO. 'I don't know whether to visit or stay away from him, to be honest with you. What do you think, DCI Stone?'

Frankie jumped in before David could answer. 'I'd leave it a few days.'

'Aye, that's what my wife said, pet.'

He meant no offence. 'Pet' was a term of endearment in this part of the world, not a poke at Frankie's authority. If that had been the case, she'd have put him straight.

'Your wife knew Joanna Cosgrove?' she asked.

'Aye, the news has knocked her for six.'

'It felled us all,' the redheaded woman standing next to him said. 'They were a lovely couple. We often saw them around. Alan's not from round here, but you'd never know it. He gets involved in all the local activities, including Helen's annual barrel race. Last week, he gave a talk to the Northumbria Gliding Club in Leadgate. They loved it. Funny and informative was the way my husband described it—'

'And Joanna?' Frankie asked.

'Blissfully happy, as far as I could tell.'

'Absolutely,' someone else said.

Half an hour later, feeling the benefit of having fuelled up, on nosh as well as information on the Cosgroves, Stone and Oliver made their way back to the car. As they reached it, Frankie turned to face her boss. 'So, they were liked and respected by everyone. Talented, funny, pillars of the community. No enemies as far as that lot are concerned. And he still had the hots for her. No wonder he's so angry, David.'

No wonder you are . . .

No wonder I am.

'We've got to stop this violent bastard before another family has to suffer.'

They locked eyes over the bonnet of his SUV, aware of how urgent their task was. A fugitive was out there somewhere, wrecking lives, causing havoc. The investigation was like a ticking bomb strapped to their chests, the clock running down. It was only a matter of time before the killer struck again.

David patted his breast pocket, then both trouser pockets, searching for car keys, a look of panic crossing his face. He was about to go back inside when the redhead they had spoken to appeared at the door, dangling keys in front of her face.

'You left them on the bar,' she said. 'I do it all the time.'

'Thanks.' David looked suitably embarrassed.

'You will get him soon, won't you, DCI Stone?' She was clearly worried, preoccupied with the murders, troubled by the fact that he was unable to offer a timescale, never mind the certainty she craved. 'I have a daughter,' she said softly. 'She has a right to feel safe.' She walked away then, leaving the detectives in a worse state emotionally than when they arrived.

In silence, they climbed into the car.

'You can see her point.' Frankie strapped herself in. 'Talking of kids, how's Ben doing?'

David waggled his hand from side to side: so-so.

It wasn't an answer as such.

Frankie let the matter drop. Her attempt at diverting his attention away from the investigation hadn't worked. The SIO was deeply troubled, in no mood for small talk, distracted by a grim reality. The redhead was right. The region's female population – old and young – were fearful of a killer exercising power over them. Wherever they went, whether he was there or not, they felt a monster lurking in the shadows.

They deserved better.

As they drove downhill heading for the crime scene, Frankie wondered if she'd done the right thing, encouraging David to assume responsibility for his nephew. As a single man, working long hours, taking on someone else's kid was never going to be easy for him. The fact that he'd done it reluctantly sat heavily with her. She hadn't been in possession of all the facts when she'd pushed him into it. He had a cottage to renovate, his brother's death to cope with – and yet she'd piled on the pressure, unaware that he was also grieving for an ex-colleague, his worst nightmare, a horrific experience that had dogged his life for months. On top of that, a promotion to the MIT was a big deal for him, bringing with it extra responsibility. Frankie hoped that acting as surrogate father to Ben wouldn't be the final grain of sand that would tip her guv'nor over the edge.

She sighed, concentrating on the road ahead.

There was activity in the distance. Officers in uniform were knocking on doors, part of the house-to-house team. Two more were questioning a man in the doorway to a shop. At the entrance to the station car park, a couple of women with grim expressions chatted conspiratorially on the pavement. An elderly male was doing his bit to keep the village clean, picking up litter caused by the summer storm, placing it in a wheelbarrow, while another pinned a leaflet to the community noticeboard. A village scene like any other.

Frankie's phone rang as David pulled into Stocksfield station: DC Mitchell.

She took the call. 'Mitch, tell me you have good news.'

'There's something you need to be aware of—'

'I'm aware of too much already and it's all depressing,' Frankie said.

David was about to leave the car.

She grabbed his arm. 'Hang on, Mitch. I'll put you on speaker. The boss is with me. Has Beth Collingwood confirmed what time she wants us yet?'

Mitchell's voice filled the car. 'No, sorry.'

'Chase it up,' David said. 'We need to be there when she does the PM.'

'Will do, guv.'

In her wing mirror, Frankie noticed a man standing outside Orchard House Veterinary Centre. He was chatting to a copper she knew, part of the house-to-house team. The more information they could gather here the better. 'You had something to tell us, Mitch?'

'There's been an interesting call to the incident room.'

'Are we talking a witness, a confession, what? You seem in two minds—'

'Nothing gets past you does it, Sarge?'

'Get on with it, man. We're busy.'

The young detective apologised even though he knew Frankie wasn't seriously ticking him off. He'd seen her in full flight and this didn't come close. 'The first, an elderly woman, called as you were leaving. She saw a man loitering as she walked off the train last night. And get this: he was standing near the metal gate to the right of the car park.'

Frankie's eyes met Stone's as she spoke. 'In the scrubland or outside of it?'

'In, she thinks.'

'What time was this?'

'Around nine forty-five.'

'Quarter to ten,' came out like a mumble.

'Same difference . . . Did I miss something?'

Frankie ignored Mitchell's confusion. 'That could be our guy . . . or Alan Cosgrove . . . although he claims he remained in his vehicle, assuming he's telling the truth. If it was the killer, your witness is bloody lucky to be alive.'

'Yeah. The caller said the man stood still when he saw her. She got in her car and drove away. I asked if she saw anyone else – I was hoping she might have seen the victim, but she said not.'

'Cosgrove said Joanna wasn't on that train,' Frankie said.

'The fact that he didn't see her, doesn't mean she didn't get off,' David reminded her. 'He said he was late, remember? Mitch, was she able to describe this man?'

'No, guv. He was wearing a dark raincoat with the hood up.'

'She's still worth a look. What's her name?'

'Annie Parks. She lives at Bywell on the north side of the Tyne.'

'Text me her details. We'll get over there as soon as we're done here.'

Frankie was beside herself. This was the only reported sighting of a possible suspect in this recent spate of deaths. Across the four murders, many men had owned up to being in the vicinity at the time the killings took place. All had been ruled out. This new mystery man needed identifying fast. Annie Parks could well be a key witness.

'We're at the crime scene now,' Frankie said. 'We'll drop by and see her, then swing into town to Joanna's place of work. There's a colleague of hers we need to see urgently. Unless we're held up, we should be back in a couple of hours.'

12

Stone's face was set like granite as they entered the restricted area. Oliver watched him closely. The gratuitous killing of four innocent women had got to him; devastating their families, causing them unimaginable pain. His sensitivity to the bereaved was one of the things that drew Frankie to him. They were similar in that regard. Perhaps, in her case, over-sensitive for reasons he wasn't aware of, but that conversation was for another day. There was no point revisiting the scene in daylight to have a proper look around if she wasn't 100 per cent focused.

Her father's voice arrived in her head: 'SOCOs pick up shit and bag it, Frank. They're not paid to observe. That's where you come in. Think laterally and you won't go far wrong. If there's graffiti on a wall, find out who put it there. You never know where it might lead. Everything you see is a signpost. Potentially, it could solve a case.'

With his advice lingering, Frankie took some photographs on her mobile phone for her own use. As she examined the railway sleepers, an image of Joanna lying across them in the pouring rain flashed before her eyes.

She turned to face David. 'Why stage this one and not the others?'

'I don't know,' he said. 'Maybe he's getting more confident.'

'I hope you're wrong. Actually, I think there's more to it than that.'

'You have a theory?'

An incoming text alert stopped her from verbalising it. Stone checked the screen, Frankie eyeing it over his shoulder: *Dick Abbott*. He turned away, read the message and pocketed the phone. A big sigh.

'Any news?' Frankie could hope.

'Not the kind we want. The PolSA team found nothing of value.'

'Figures. The killer is too clever to make basic mistakes like that. Whatever he used to kill Joanna is probably in the drink on the way to Tynemouth.' Frankie's attention shifted to the giant wooden spool they had examined by torchlight last night, a trail of rusty wire still attached. 'Foley's team collected a sample of this but it's too thick to have been used as a ligature. You'd need bolt cutters to get through it. There was some thinner stuff over there he could've used. The CSIs took that too, but it would've cut into her neck causing a deep wound. None was visible, not to me anyway.'

'I agree,' David said. 'I studied close-ups of all four victims this morning. To the untrained eye, Joanna's injuries look the same as the others. Blue plastic rope, probably washing line, is what we're after. Collingwood found microscopic fragments embedded in the wounds of the first two victims, Catherine Bennett and Alison Brody. Even though it was missing from the third, Margaret Robson had the same twisted pattern of bruising. The offender will have come equipped.'

Think laterally and you won't go far wrong.

'Unless all four deaths aren't the work of one man.'

'That's your theory?' David raised a sceptical eyebrow.

'Just floating the possibility. You said yourself this one is different. How do we know some moron hasn't read all the hype in the newspapers and decided to join in? I know we kept certain details from the press, but if you wanted rid of someone, is there any better way than to jump on the bandwagon, passing it off as someone else's handiwork? Joanna was placed with such care, David. She was lifted on to these sleepers, almost a mark of respect. Who would do that? More to the point, why would they? Unless they knew her . . .'

'Point taken. Collinwood will rule Joanna in or out conclusively when she does the PM.'

Frankie checked her watch. 'What's keeping her? I'd have thought she'd have been on the blower before now. She's normally shit hot.'

'She's got two on today.'

'Yeah, well ours is more important.'

'They're all important, Frank.' David was equally exasperated. 'The incident she ran off to last night was a fatal stabbing. The difference is, they've got someone locked up for it. We haven't. Collingwood has priorities too. Sometimes, they'll coincide with ours. Often as not, they won't. Get used to it.'

'She's probably pissed off that we arrived late,' Frankie huffed.

'As I recall, you were busy trying not to drown—'

'I was saving you from ending up as mincemeat, mate! If you want to blame anyone, talk to Control. They were the ones issuing the wrong coordinates.'

'The comms were down—'

'Yeah, well those four words nearly ended up on your gravestone. I hate misinformation.'

'Spilt milk, Frank. Suck it up and move on.'

'You said that out loud, guv.'

Frankie turned away, scouring the scene, mind back on the job.

A stone wall ran the length of the site where it abutted the main road. Part of the wall had crumbled away, leaving a gaping hole of dislodged stonework. The oil barrel she'd seen last night was gone, along with its contents. Forensic scientists would pore over every fag end, old can or bottle top, any scrap of trash that might have been discarded by the man terrorising the neighbourhood and the wider Northumbrian community. David had asked them to fast-track results. Ordinarily, it would take days or even weeks, but the body count they were dealing with had elevated the case. They were top priority. If there was anything in that barrel that might aid their investigation, it would be found.

There was evidence of a fire close to the deposition site. In view of the prevailing weather at the time of Joanna's death, Frankie didn't believe it had any relevance. Could've been there weeks: a rough sleeper keeping warm; kids hanging out; a caravanning tourist finding a quiet spot for a BBQ close to a handy car park; a villager burning rubbish. She may never find out. But in her head, her father's wise words kept bubbling to the surface, reminding her not to discount anything: *Potentially, it could solve a case.*

13

When Frankie turned around, David was nowhere to be seen. She'd been so deep in thought, she'd not heard him take off. He was a hundred metres away, on the other side of the metal gate, heading for the car park. Minutes later, she joined him. He was studying the bay where Joanna had parked her vehicle. It was now empty, a patch of diesel on the tarmac where it had once stood – an old stain, not new.

'She obviously cared about her car,' he said.

'How d'you work that out?'

'This bay is wider than the rest.'

'Maybe it was the only space available.'

'I doubt it. Didn't you notice how she parked to one side? If you ask me, she was looking after her investment. Her BMW is an expensive piece of kit.'

'Yeah, well her caution may have contributed to her death,' Frankie said. 'It's furthest away from the station exit, not seen from the road or the railway line, yards from where she was killed.'

As a train pulled in, Frankie turned her back on him.

Across the car park, there was a ramp leading to the station platform. She imagined Joanna walking down it in the dark, coat pulled close, keen to get home, unaware that the date of her birth would also be the date of her death. Frankie didn't voice that thought, but it lingered as she strode towards the platform. At the ramp, there was a tourist information board with a map of the area. Underneath, a list of helpful data: accommodation, local attractions, a selection of pubs and eateries, bus timetables and taxi facilities, emergency service numbers and cycle paths. Tourism played a big part in the economy of the area, supporting local businesses, creating jobs. Visitors from all over the world flocked to Northumberland National Parks, including the World Heritage site of Hadrian's Wall, nine miles away. Tyne Valley villages were popular – this one perhaps less so today.

Frankie continued up the ramp, block-paved in red, freshly painted blue railings on either side. At the top, a red footbridge crossed the railway line, straddling the track: Platform 1, across the bridge for eastbound travellers; Platform 2 westbound on the south side of the line. As stations go, this one was pretty. In the distance, in either direction, a bend in the track hid the route from view.

David arrived at her shoulder.

Frankie followed as he walked west, deep in thought. He stopped walking at the end of the platform, glancing off to his left, his attention drawn to the railway sleepers where the victim had been found.

'This was the point our eyewitness noticed Joanna's body. I read his statement this morning. The train was pulling in and, therefore, not going very fast. He wasn't sure if she'd collapsed while walking or tripped and fallen. The position of her body suggested otherwise, which is why he raised the alarm, alerting the conductor who rang Control. Just as well he did; she might've lain here for days, weeks.' David met Frankie's gaze. 'I don't know about you, but I rarely look out of the window when I'm travelling. Like everyone else, I'm checking my phone, eating, reading, people watching.'

They walked back down the platform in silence.

Frankie stepped aside to allow a young woman to pass by, the voice of the redhead arriving in her head: *She has a right to feel safe*. A fleeting glance between detective and rail passenger, a knowing look, a moment of solidarity in the face of adversity. There was an expression of defiance in the girl's eyes, an unspoken message that she'd not be intimidated, let alone go into hiding. It didn't stop an urge to warn her to be careful, not that Frankie expected another offence in this location, but you couldn't rule it out with a dangerous offender on the loose. The impulse passed and she carried on taking her photographs.

Further along, she came to a sudden stop.

'Yeah right.' She swore under her breath.

David pulled up sharp, intrigued by her sudden outburst.

Frankie pointed at a blue sign with white lettering that seemed to poke fun at them: IMAGES ARE BEING MONITORED FOR CRIME PREVENTION, PUBLIC AND STAFF SAFETY. A telephone number was listed, offering further information. 'Shame the power was out,' she said, her cynicism subsiding. 'CCTV might not cover the car park but, had these cameras been active, they would've confirmed whether Joanna was on that train and she might still be alive.' It was David's turn to curse their bad luck. He was downhearted and angry that Mother Nature had backed the other side. Frankie tried to stay positive. 'Maybe the witness Annie Parks can help us with that.'

14

Bywell was a beautiful village, unchanged for centuries, a favourite of local historians. At school, David had learned that it was the family seat of Lord Allendale, son of the third Viscount Allendale, a legacy of conservation the current dignitary was proud to maintain on his 2,000-acre estate. The village had two churches. St Andrews, known as 'the White Church', an Anglo-Saxon place of worship, and St Peter's, 'the Black Church', formerly the home of Benedictine monks.

Annie Parks' home was the quintessential English country cottage, a property tucked away near the river bank, surrounded by trees. She was a while coming to the door. Mid-to-late seventies, she was in good shape, deeply tanned like she'd recently been somewhere exotic. She had high cheekbones and silver hair, cut short.

'Mrs Parks?'

'Ms.' She leaned on her walking stick, a wicked grin. 'I never understood the need for men, to be honest.'

'Me either,' Frankie said, 'but I'm afraid we're stuck with them.' She grinned at the SIO and then refocused on the homeowner. 'I'm DS Frankie Oliver and this is my boss, DCI David Stone – one of the good guys, I promise you. We're here in response to your call. May we come in? Assuming it's a convenient time to talk.'

The living room was small, cosy, full of antique furniture. David waited for their host to sit before accepting an invitation to do likewise, perching himself on the edge of a high-backed leather chair. Annie Parks settled in hers, liver-spotted hands held loosely in her lap, brown eyes fixed on her visitors. Her beauty hadn't faded any. Some women got better with age. Annie was one of them. She reminded the SIO of his nan – independent, outspoken, salt of the earth – a woman who'd endured unimaginable trauma in her lifetime: losing her husband, daughter and son-in-law, then bringing David and Luke up as her own. It was that or local authority care. Without her unconditional love and support, he couldn't hazard a guess as to where he might have ended up – wrong side of the law, most probably.

There was a fine line . . .

He aimed to put their host at ease. 'We have one or two questions, Ms Parks, nothing to worry about.'

'Please, call me Annie. My late father insisted on Annabelle, but it sounds so . . . unlike me.'

David preferred Annie and told her so. 'How did you hear about the incident?'

Her smile melted away. 'Word of mouth. Village gossip mainly. What an awful business. I gather your police vehicles kept a few people from their beds in the early hours. Have you identified the victim?'

'Yes, we have.' David wasn't about to share Joanna's identity and Annie had the good sense not to ask. 'The detective you spoke to this morning said that you'd seen a suspicious man close to the station car park when you got off the train last night.'

'That's right.'

'Well, before we talk about that, I'd like to ask a few questions about your journey home from Newcastle. I assume that's where you got on the train?' He took in her nod. 'It's vital that we trace the victim's movements before and after she arrived in Stocksfield. We're keen to identify anyone who might have seen her.'

'I understand.'

Locating Joanna's photograph from his briefcase, David handed it over. 'Did you see this lady last night?'

Annie put on her specs, a flash of recognition crossing her face that raised the hopes of the detectives. She was not overly upset, as she might have been had she known Joanna personally. 'I've seen her before,' she said, 'but not last night. She travels alone mostly, though occasionally with a young woman I took to be her daughter. They're very alike. We've nodded the occasional hello but nothing more. Poor woman . . .'

'So, you'd have recognised her if you'd seen her?'

'Definitely. Maybe she was in the other carriage. There were two.'

'Perhaps.' David was gutted at the notion that Joanna's life might have turned on the off-chance of choosing the wrong carriage on her way home to celebrate her birthday with her husband and their kids. 'Were there any passengers in your carriage you could describe to me in detail?'

'Three women and one man, or maybe two, but I can't for the life of me remember what they looked like or what they were wearing. I'm sorry, Detective Chief Inspector. I had my head in a book the whole way. None of them got off at Stocksfield, I'm fairly certain of that.' Annie took off her specs, returning Joanna's photograph. 'That route is never busy at night, except the last train. I tend not to take that one.' She echoed Joanna's fear of rowdyism and drunkenness her husband had alluded to earlier. 'Without a sheriff riding shotgun, disorderly behaviour at night is not uncommon. The last train is not the safest place to be for a woman on her own. I'm . . .' She stopped short of finishing her sentence, a sad expression on her face. 'I'm sorry. That sounds ridiculous in view of what happened yesterday.'

'Not at all,' Frankie said. 'Everyone has to be vigilant. Statistically speaking, men are more at risk than women, Annie. Remember that. We don't want you worrying unnecessarily. What happened last night is rare.'

'Really?' She was referring to the recent spate of deaths. Frankie had no answer to give and Annie wasn't finished. 'Times have changed – and not for the better,' she said. 'Have you seen the crime figures? Up ten per cent in rural areas. Public protection is no longer a priority, it seems. There are fewer police officers on the streets than I can remember in my lifetime. A sad state of affairs. We lost our village bobby years ago but there was always a police station locally. You'd be hard-pressed to find one now. As far as I can see, it will only get worse.' It wasn't an accusation, rather a statement of fact neither detective attempted to disagree with.

Nevertheless, David's tone was conciliatory. 'You're right, Annie. Our visibility isn't what it once was and for that I can only apologise. That said, I now need your help and that of the local community if we're to find the person responsible for last night's attack. To facilitate that we must identify and interview everyone who travelled on that train, where they were sitting, whether alone or together, including individuals you didn't like the look of, anyone who said something odd or acted suspiciously. So, if anything untoward happened during that journey, we'd appreciate the heads up.'

'There was no trouble on the train.' Annie swallowed hard, fear creeping into what had been a confident gaze when they first arrived. The penny had finally dropped. 'Oh, my goodness . . . are you saying that the person who killed that unfortunate woman was on the train with us?'

'It's a possibility,' Frankie said. 'No more at this stage. We're still making enquiries. Let's stick with the victim for now. The fact that you didn't see her doesn't mean that no one else did.'

Annie nodded, let out a big sigh.

Slipping Joanna's photograph back in his briefcase, Stone withdrew a carriage plan he'd had the foresight to put in before he left the office in case he happened upon a witness during the day. He showed it to Annie. 'Can you indicate exactly where you were, front or rear carriage, direction of travel?' He handed her a pen. 'Feel free to draw on it.'

The glasses were back on.

Annie took her time, writing ME in shaky handwriting

where she'd sat, her preferred seat affording easier access than some, she said. She was placing the letters M and F in seats surrounding her, adding a number beside each one – representing male, female and approximate age. When she was done, she looked up, anticipating the next question. 'None of the people I saw were regulars.'

Stone and Oliver were impressed.

Annie fixed her eyes on the SIO. 'You may have noticed that I use a stick, Detective. Though it pains me to admit it, I need assistance getting on and off the train. No one left my carriage before the conductor came to help me, I'm certain of that. The lights were out, so I didn't see anyone on the platform. If your victim got off the rear carriage, she'd have disappeared . . . I mean, reached her car before I did . . . or not, as it turned out. By the time got to my vehicle, I was the only one about, except the man I saw.'

Excusing herself, Frankie got up and left the room.

David watched her go. She'd be calling base, making sure that someone interviewed the driver and conductor immediately. In view of the information they had collected so far, the SIO was as sure as he could be that Annie was the woman Joanna's husband had seen struggling with her car door in a gale-force wind. He had no intention of telling her that another witness was in the car park at the same time. The reason for that was threefold: he wouldn't give credibility to Cosgrove's story; he wanted to collect Annie's account independently; but most important of all, he didn't want to scare her.

He handed her an A4 sheet. 'Can you indicate on this diagram where exactly your vehicle was and what you saw when you entered the car park?'

'My car was here.' She indicated a disabled space at the north-eastern corner of the car park, close to the ramp leading from the platform. 'The man I saw was standing in the shadows here.' She drew an X beyond the metal gate at the western end.

'Behind the metal gate, not in front?'

'Behind.' There was no hesitation.

'The power was out last night. Wasn't it difficult for you to see?'

'When you live in the sticks, you carry a torch, young man.' She looked out through the open window. 'I need a torch, even here. It's as black as coal when I get home some nights. I'm far-sighted. I'd never get my keys in the lock without one.'

'Was the man you saw carrying anything?'

'Not that I noticed.' She took a breather, her attention on the diagram. 'Was that where . . .' She didn't finish her sentence and David didn't fill in the blanks. From the look of her, Annie had already made the jump. He felt sorry for her. Trips to Newcastle would never be the same after this. Worst-case scenario, they may even end. Without careful handling, she would carry the fear with her until the day she died. David hoped not. Her evidence had been considered and precise, enabling him to build a clearer picture of what had gone down last night, corroborating what he knew already.

He pressed on. 'We're nearly done, Annie. You've been a great help and I'm enormously grateful. One last question: did you see anyone else in the car park?'

'No, but there was a car in the cut with its lights on. I assumed it was that man's. To be honest, I was nervous of him. I got in my car and drove away.'

It had to be Cosgrove.

Didn't it?

15

Joseph Cohen's office was palatial. Situated on the top floor of a four-storey Grade 1 listed building in Grainger Town, it was almost directly opposite the city's Theatre Royal in the historic heart of Newcastle. Having spent all morning in court, Cohen was debriefing a client when Stone and Oliver arrived unannounced, asking to see him. They had been waiting twenty minutes by the time they were finally shown in.

Cohen stood up as they entered: tall, thin, impeccably dressed. The man looked pale and drawn. Not only had he lost a much-loved colleague to a violent and unexpected death, he'd lost an important fraud case too. Frankie had discovered the result on the way over there, after a call to a friendly court official.

Offering his condolences, David shook hands with the lawyer and introduced himself. 'Thank you for seeing us, sir. I can see this is a very bad time. This is DS Frances Oliver. I'm DCI Stone. I'm sure you know why we're here. We're sorry to intrude but we need some information about your meeting with Joanna Cosgrove yesterday.'

Cohen nodded. 'I've been expecting you. Please, take a seat. Can I get you anything to drink?'

'No, thanks, sir. Time is crucial, as I'm sure you can appreciate.'

'I understand.' Cohen looked away, then back at the DCI. 'I'm still trying to get my head around it. Joanna was a brilliant associate and a valued friend. She'll be a great loss to this firm and to me personally.' He made a steeple with his hands. 'You're linking her death with the other three?'

'That will be determined when post-mortem results are in.'

'But you're not ruling it out?' Cohen held up a hand. 'Sorry

'. . . I've been a criminal lawyer long enough to know how these things work. I shouldn't have asked. Before you start, how are Alan and the children bearing up?'

'You've not spoken?' Frankie hid her surprise well.

'Briefly,' the lawyer explained. 'But I was called into court. It doesn't pay to keep the judiciary waiting, as I'm sure you know.'

Frankie did know. There had been many a time during her career that she'd been reprimanded by a trial judge for lateness. It mattered not that she'd been delayed for good reason – once for having jumped from her car to render CPR to a woman who'd collapsed in the street as she was driving by. Excuses were reserved for those in the dock, not the officers who'd put them there. Courtrooms were as much about drama as justice.

'I had Haynes this morning,' Cohen said. 'I didn't want to put his back up.'

A shiver ran down Frankie's spine.

Haynes' nickname was the Smiling Assassin.

'We've not seen the children yet,' Frankie said. 'They're with their grandparents, though personally I think they'd be better off with their father. Mr Cosgrove is as well as can be expected, given the circumstances, if a little angry with the police for not apprehending someone sooner—'

'That's Alan.' A shrug from Cohen. 'We're good friends, but he can be . . . heavy going at times. I wouldn't take it to heart, either of you. In legal terms, he has an unrealistic view of what is possible within the constraints of your job. He's pro-police, believe it or not, but he has no concept of what's involved, let alone what it's like to operate under PACE.' The Police and Criminal Evidence Act made Stone and Oliver's jobs more difficult, Cohen's a damned sight easier. 'Every time an offender is bailed, Alan crows about it. Why he ever married a defence lawyer is beyond me. Joanna and I used to laugh about it. I'm afraid he's of the lock-'em-up-and-throw-away-the-key brigade. I wouldn't put it past him to support capital punishment . . . especially now. Sorry, I'm rambling. You have questions to ask.'

'We'll be brief,' David said. 'Alan told us that you and Joanna had a meeting late yesterday afternoon and that you were going out to dinner afterwards.'

'That's correct.'

Cohen seemed to drift off, the memory of his final meeting with Joanna clearly upsetting him. He glanced out of his office window, his jaw bunching as he fought to control his emotions. Frankie chanced a glance at David. Those engaged in the business of criminal justice weren't immune to grief. It was a different scenario altogether when you knew the victim personally. No one knew that more than he did. Though he wanted Cohen talking, the SIO gave him a moment of reflection.

'We're sorry for your loss, sir.'

Cohen turned to face him. 'Just catch the bastard that took her from us. I'm afraid to say it, but I'm with Alan on this one. A rope is what's required.'

Frankie could see that he meant every word. 'Mr Cosgrove told us that you and Joanna might have eaten at your club. Did you?'

'No, though I'd made a reservation. Joanna was in a good mood. She fancied Blackfriars. She loves . . . loved anything medieval. The building has a wonderful atmosphere and the food is excellent. We ate at seven and I suggested going for a drink afterwards—'

'Did you?'

'No, she was keen to get away.' Cohan almost choked on his words. 'I wish I'd been more persuasive.'

'How did she seem to you?' David asked.

'Perfectly fine. She was convinced we'd win in court this morning – we might have, had she been there. The case against our client was strong, but she'd found an irregularity that helped our cause. I heard the news of her death minutes before I was called by the usher. As you can imagine, I wasn't firing on all cylinders. I would have asked for an adjournment only my client, unaware of what had befallen Joanna, was keen to press ahead. I bet he feels differently now. The case didn't go quite as we'd planned.'

'Was Joanna intending to stay in town last night?'

'Why do you ask?'

'Her husband mentioned that she might,' Stone said.

'That makes sense.' Cohen allowed himself a half-smile. 'But no, she was heading home, desperate to surprise the kids who I gather were a bit glum when she said she might not be back. It was her birthday.'

When the car turned right instead of left, the opposite direction to the one Frankie was expecting, she glanced at David. 'I thought we were heading back to Middle Earth?'

'You thought wrong.' Despite his black mood, he grinned at her reference to Northern Command HQ, located at the eastern end of Hadrian's Roman Wall on Middle Engine Lane. If there was a pseudonym available, detectives always found it. At his promotion do, Stone had been dubbed the Northern Rock. Frankie, he wasn't too sure about, but there would be a nickname for sure. 'Collingwood left a message,' he explained. 'Our attendance is required at the morgue.'

Home Office pathologist Beth Collingwood was as Frankie had described her: shit-hot, a top-notch professional who would not be rushed into making a quick decision. To look at her, you'd never know how taxing her job was or that she'd accumulated both medical and law degrees, let alone published an impressive list of professional papers on her specialism. She was a diminutive figure, no more than five one, dressed in raspberry-coloured scrubs that looked like pyjamas, booties, cap and face mask. Wisps of purple hair poked out from under the elastic of her cap, the colour matching her spectacles exactly. She couldn't look less like a Clinical Professor of Forensic Pathology if she'd tried.

Introductions dispensed with, she went about her business, as relaxed as any doctor tending the sick, bringing her considerable expertise to bear on a suspicious fatality. She was charged to report on her findings to the Senior Investigating Officer and would make herself available to testify in a court of law where/if evidence was refuted by defence advocates, or if called upon to do so by the trial judge – assuming they ever found Joanna's killer.

Assisting two Northumbria SIOs had taken up Collingwood's entire day. She'd done much of the nasty stuff before Stone and Oliver arrived, performing tests on blood and bodily fluids, examining organs, taking nail clippings and other samples for laboratory analysis. She had to be certain that no disease or medical condition might have accelerated Joanna's death or caused her to collapse, that she had in fact died at the hands of another.

For David, attending a post-mortem where weeks before the same procedure had been performed on his brother's body was emotionally draining. He'd lost both parents as a kid, but losing Luke was still raw, taking on his nephew a responsibility that was proving difficult, given his current workload. Somehow, he managed to separate the personal from the professional and concentrate. He was relying on Collingwood to give insight into Joanna Cosgrove's death, an understanding he couldn't possibly second-guess. Despite outward appearances at the crime scene, nothing was a foregone conclusion.

During the post-mortem procedure, more photographs had been taken of Joanna's injuries, her clothing removed, bagged and labelled for forensic testing. Scientists would take fibre lifts and samples, hoping for evidence that might track the offender down, now or in the future. Collaboration between departments was essential when it came to the ultimate crime.

In all, the post-mortem process took around an hour and a half to complete, the surgeon recording her findings verbally into a microphone, answering each query as it was raised by the SIO, providing a running commentary of what she was doing and seeing – some of which neither detective present recognised as human.

Collingwood was new to David. He watched with sharp eyes and couldn't help but be impressed with her meticulous attention to detail. Frankie rated her and that was good enough for Stone. When she was done, she peered over her specs at her assistant, a geeky-looking male of equally small stature who'd been attentive throughout, handing her medical instruments and turning Joanna's body when instructed. He'd not spoken a word during the examination.

A nod was all he needed to start reconstructing and cleaning the body ready for storage. It would be some time before the victim would be released to an undertaker. Joanna's husband and children would have a long wait to lay her to rest. Collingwood scrubbed up and turned to face her expectant audience. The cap was off, the purple hair sticking out at odd angles.

She didn't hang around. 'Cause of death is strangulation but, sadly, we all knew that. These seemingly random killings are a puzzle. As I told you before, there was no sexual assault—'

'Ruling it out as a motive doesn't mean there was no such element,' Frankie said sharply. 'Exercising the ultimate power over women can give a perpetrator an immoral high on its own. That's what they get off on. And they don't give a shit about who they hurt along the way.'

'Thanks for the lesson in criminology,' Collingwood said. 'But that's not my field, as well you know. I'm neither psychologist nor psychiatrist but, if it makes you feel any better, I couldn't agree more. However, there are differences in this case—'

'Differences?' David was all ears.

'Yes, unlike the other three victims, there are minute traces of something under Joanna's fingernails.'

'Skin?' Frankie's tone was flat and unfriendly, bordering on hostile.

David couldn't fathom why and had no time to indulge her. He focused on the pathologist. 'You were saying, Doctor?'

'Not skin, unfortunately. It's some kind of waxy substance, but it might still help you.'

'Yeah, right,' Frankie said. 'Our guy is proving difficult to pin down, Beth. He was careful, well covered, and it was pissing down. He took the ligature home most probably. Assuming you identify the substance, he's clever enough to have disposed of where it came from. Unlike fictional crime, some of the cruel bastards in the real world get away with it. Too many . . .'

Collingwood gave an embarrassed smile, her focus on the SIO. 'My job is a thankless task most days, DCI Stone, but I'll thank your DS to be more grateful.' She was trying to lighten Frankie's mood but, for the first time since he'd entered the morgue, David could see tension in Collingwood's body-language. The pathologist was uncomfortable, Frankie rigid beside her.

Collingwood combed a hand through her hair, her focus switching between the two detectives, eventually settling on Oliver. 'I appreciate how difficult murder is to deal with, and to pick up where your predecessors left off, but believe me when I say that this is progress. Frank, your man got sloppy.' There it was again, that same discomfort between the two women. 'We only need to get lucky once.'

'Luck has nothing to do with these cases.' Frankie took a step away, pain etched on her face. 'How many more before we find him?'

Collingwood caught her upper arm and gave it a squeeze. The two women were now talking in code. David had no bloody idea what was going on, but he guessed that they had a history neither intended to share with him. Frankie wasn't upset. She was more galled than he'd ever seen her. Like all colleagues, they'd had their moments since they began working together but this was something else. These two highly qualified professional females knew something he didn't.

Worrying.

'I'm sorry.' Frankie was avoiding eye-contact.

'For what?' David said.

'Nothing. My outburst, I'm tired that's all.'

'That's bollocks. You're unstoppable. You never tire of chasing villains.' He could see that she wasn't in the mood for banter. In the absence of a way into the conversation, he supported her excuse, telling the pathologist that it had been a very long day.

Mistake.

Frankie looked through him, a scornful expression: *What do you know?*

The surgeon shot her a warning look as if to say: Don't do this, now's neither the time nor the place. 'Frank, you know that I rarely stick my neck out but, taking all the victims together, notwithstanding the ligature wounds, I have something else to say that might be of interest.'

The detectives waited.

'Given that Joanna's body was so obviously staged, I checked over my notes to see if anything struck me as odd before I began today's exam. I found a parallel that makes little sense to me and one that hadn't occurred until now. None of the first three victims had injuries consistent with having fallen to the ground.'

Stone and Oliver exchanged a look.

'That's interesting,' David said. 'Frankie said earlier that Joanna was lifted onto these sleepers. Almost a mark of respect.'

'That's it exactly.' Collingwood took a moment of reflection, consulting her notes, a way of buying herself more time. She looked up, a haunted expression on her face. 'Notwithstanding the fact that they all died, it seems to me that, to a greater or lesser extent, all four victims got the kid-glove treatment post-strangulation. Joanna more so, you might argue. It's as if they were laid down with care after death, as you or I might handle a child who'd fallen asleep.' She seemed to gag on that last sentence.

16

Here we go. One minute he was driving east, the next Incontinence Man was making a day of it, asking him to pull over. An unscheduled stop on the way back to Newcastle was not on his agenda. The delay was an irritation he could well do without. Ignoring the request to break the journey, he floored the accelerator, his speed climbing: fifty . . . sixty . . . seventy miles an hour, the arsehole giving him earache the whole way. The Military Road ran close to Hadrian's Wall – linking the villages of Greenhead and Heddon-on-the-Wall – so-called due to its construction by eighteenth-century forces to fend off a Jacobite rebellion from the north. The road was long and straight, much like a Roman road, with no stopping places along the narrow carriageway.

'Fuck it! You'll have to pull in, man. I'm busting for a piss.'

'Will this do?' He slowed, pointing at a brown tourist information sign: THE SILL.

'Yeah, do it! I'll have a slash and we can grab a coffee, maybe some grub. I could eat a scabby horse. I've heard the rooftop view is spectacular.'

'If you like that kind of thing.'

'You've got no soul, mate.'

True.

Hiding his displeasure, he indicated his intention to turn in, complying with his passenger's demand to use the men's room, keeping his composure, acting normal so as not to draw attention to his preoccupation. Incontinence Man had no idea that he had stuff on his mind, priorities much greater than his.

They unzipped their flies and didn't speak as they urinated

in the shiny new facilities. No graffiti yet. It would come. As they moved to the wash basins, his mind wandered. He needed to up his game. Make the bastards understand that he was serious. For all his efforts, the MIT weren't listening. Arguing with Steph had got him nowhere, although it pleased him that he now had a name – in the press at least: *The Sleeper*. He liked that.

It was time to get creative.

As they made their way out of the gents, he tuned his companion out, uninterested in his boring conversation, giving an occasional nod to indicate that he was listening. Handing over a tenner at the door to the café stopped him carping about his empty gut.

He wasn't the only one who was hungry.

There were candidates here – women of means, women who never gave him a second glance as he headed for a seat, a purple couch in the corner. He sat down with his back to the view, watching customers sip their wine and dig into their food. Many females were deep in conversation, oblivious to their surroundings and anyone not in their company, their default position. Everyone else, including him, was shit on their shoes.

He loathed them all.

All too soon, coffee and sandwiches arrived: honey roast ham and Northumberland cheese. While he hadn't planned on stopping, he ate what he'd been given – fuel for later – while enduring more monotonous chat that didn't fire his jets. He was running out of patience when the man giving him earache pushed his chair away from the table and stood up.

'I wanna grab some photos from the roof. Coming?'

Finally . . .

He thought he'd never go.

'Not my style. Besides, it's heaving up there.' He opened his newspaper, content to read about himself, enjoying the thrill of being noticed. 'You go ahead. Let me know when you're done.'

He'd clocked people taking in the vista from the rooftop as they walked up the hill from the car park, other sightseers getting off the AD122 bus. Public transport was essential here and pay machines required your car registration number, a difficulty for anyone with murder in mind, except that *he* wasn't in his private vehicle, so it caused no headache for him – now or in the future. Besides, he had legit company, an alibi should he ever need it. His new job required no second skin.

'Gimme ten. I'll meet you at the car.'

He watched the sad bastard wander off through a patio door. Like everyone else outside, Incontinence Man wanted in on Northumberland's newest tourist attraction, UNESCO World Heritage Site, the UK'S National Discovery Centre.

Well, they got that right.

A smirk.

Inside, the accents echoing around the cavernous room were not all local. People had come from far and wide to gape at nothing that interested him: some shonky Roman ruins up the road at Housesteads Roman Fort – a pile of old stones as far as he was concerned. Big sky, sheep, and not a lot else. For him, the draw was within the building, not without. If he'd been on his own, which one would he choose today?

He turned the page.

There was no rush to make another selection. The murder squad were looking for him on a train that had no CCTV. How cool was that? The old lady had been in touch. Like he cared. She was old. Behind the cloak of darkness, she wouldn't be able to give a description of him if her life depended on it. If the incoming SIO was taking his lead from her, he could carry on with impunity.

He glanced over the top of his newspaper. A woman in a blue cashmere cardigan caught his eye briefly before turning away. He was wavering . . . Nope: far too nice, he decided.

Like the last one. Amiable wasn't the type he was after. If anything, the opposite was true. Then a female voice drew his attention, ridding him of the need for self-justification. This was not a voice, more a fog horn, sounding off from table 23. His eyes seized upon her as she called out to a passing staff member, demanding something she could easily have fetched for herself. The young woman she was barking at stopped dead in her tracks, then scurried off to do her bidding.

His anger rose quickly.

Another glance at the gobby cow: fully made up, dyed ash-blonde hair, an asymmetric bob – the business for someone in their mid-fifties trying to look thirty-five. Her tongue-lashing was unnecessary, her hard expression ordering others to pay attention. She might require another teaspoon; what she needed was a charm transplant. He blew out his cheeks, the eruption from the woman at table 23 reminding him of Steph: obnoxious, up herself, all powerful, making others look and feel small. Tailor-made.

Shame he wasn't alone.

17

Although the traditional evening briefing was a chance to recap, murder detectives wanted answers to questions they had been discussing while Stone and Oliver were out, the main one being: could the Northern Rock and his sidekick live up to their high expectations? Many in the room were sceptical and jaded – never a good sign – but the majority sat patiently as David called for order. 'Before I begin, can I remind everyone that Joanna Cosgrove has extended family, some of whom are abroad. Her details are not to be released until they've been informed. Is that clear?'

Heads were nodding.

'OK, let's deal with scene issues first. Soil and plant samples have been collected from in and around the crime scene. We may get something from that if we recover footwear and clothing further down the line. However, despite an extensive second search, PolSA failed to recover anything that might have been used as a ligature. House-to-house are struggling. They've checked with the school, the vet's practice, bus passengers, and come up with nothing of value to us. There's been no mention of strangers lurking in Stocksfield over the past few weeks, and no one's mentioned anyone local acting out of character. There's no construction going on either, so no builders hanging about. On the face of it, whoever killed Joanna slipped in and out unnoticed – but don't be too depressed, the news is not all bad. We *are* moving forward. We will find the offender we're hunting if we keep at it.'

Detectives looked at one another, a roll of the eyes almost, like they'd been there before – and no doubt they had – but they had never come close to finding the person responsible for the deaths of Catherine Bennett, Alison Brody or Margaret

Robson. With Joanna Cosgrove now dead, David had to find a way to win over his new team. It wouldn't be easy, he could see that, but he had to try. He was keen to move on and share something more positive.

'For the first time since these murders began we have a key witness in Annie Parks, the old lady who rang the incident room this morning. Frankie and I went to see her this afternoon. She's been very helpful to us. The man she saw acting suspiciously within the boundary of the crime scene undoubtedly frightened her, though it was too dark to see him clearly.'

Abbott raised his hand. 'Are we to assume that Annie was the woman Cosgrove saw in the station car park?'

'Yes.' Stone liked Dick. He might've been general CID for most of his service, not a detective many in the MIT knew that well, but he'd done his homework. 'Her car is a Toyota Yaris, hybrid automatic. Glacier Pearl. Cosgrove described it as small, light-coloured. Annie is also unsteady on her feet, which fits with what Cosgrove told us. What he didn't and still doesn't know is that she needed help getting off the train. Annie was less able-bodied than Joanna. The way I see it, the victim was quick to leave the train and was grabbed before it pulled away, prior to her husband's late arrival—'

'Allegedly,' someone said, a disbelieving tone.

The implication was clear to everyone. Smarmy looks passed around the room like a Mexican wave. 'The idea that Cosgrove was the man Annie saw occurred to us too,' David said, 'but it could equally have been someone else waiting for a loved one, or the man whose collar you so desperately want to feel. No one wants that more than I do, but we need to find the bastard first.'

More smirks.

David ignored them. 'The most likely scenario is that Joanna gets off the train and is dragged through the gap by the metal gate. Strangled. Our man is making his way out of the waste ground by the time Annie gets to her car. He's hovering, I think, because by this time Cosgrove has arrived and parked up. He sees the train pulling out, waits a second for Joanna, and sees Annie struggling with her car door. She gets in and, scared to death, takes off like a bat out of hell, but it wasn't Cosgrove she didn't like the look of. I'm betting it was our man.'

'Surely Cosgrove saw him too,' a DC at the front said.

'Not necessarily,' Frankie jumped in. She stood up and moved to the murder wall, where she'd pinned a sketch of the scene before the meeting began. 'Cosgrove claims he arrived as the train was leaving.' Using her forefinger, she drew his route on the map as she spoke. 'He moves towards the height barrier here but doesn't pass through. He reverses and parks here with the rear of his vehicle in front of the metal gate, about halfway along the "cut" as Annie put it. If our guy is exiting the scrubland, he's in Cosgrove's blind spot. Which explains why he didn't grab Annie when he might have done. Whoever this guy is, he wants no witnesses. In my opinion, he's made a big mistake. Consequently, Annie may need protection. The SIO has sanctioned a panic alarm.'

'In Bywell?' It was almost a snort. 'By the time anyone gets there, she'll have a rope around her neck—'

Frankie stared at the grunt with contempt. She could be caustic to fellow officers on occasions and didn't much care for the softly-softly approach if they weren't showing a positive attitude.

David studied her, expecting an explosion. She was uptight, below par and oddly exposed. Floundering was the word that sprung to mind. It occurred to him that telling her about Jane might not have helped before a big case, but that couldn't be the reason she was in a state. No, he decided, her mood had plummeted last night at the crime scene, but she'd recovered quickly, and this morning he'd seen no sign of anything untoward. Then, as the day went on, her anger had returned, especially when they were with Collingwood at the morgue. Right now, it was focused on the smartarse in the front.

'Thank you for pointing that out, DC . . . ?' It was a put-down. Frankie knew his name.

'Bridges, Sarge.'

She eyeballed him. 'Well, Bridges, Annie now has access to our direct line. Her nephew is staying with her and she isn't going anywhere until the offender is caught. Does that satisfy you?'

The SIO let it ride. Frankie had a point. Bridges was one detective who'd be out on his ear if she got her way. She didn't rate him. If David were being honest, any murder detective he'd ever known was better than the shower he'd inherited from Sharpe. This team needed re-educating. Somehow, he had to find a way of motivating them into finding the sick fuck terrorising the region's female population. Thankfully, he had Frankie and Abbott with forty years of policing between them. Even Mitchell, a copper with very little CID experience and none whatsoever in major crime, had the attitude he was after, the enthusiasm of the highly trained detectives he'd worked with in the Met. Frankie, Abbott and Mitchell were professionals whose loyalty he could rely on. Tried and tested. The rest? He didn't have time to indulge their lack of faith in him. He had no choice but to lead by example. If he showed an ounce of disillusionment, he was sunk.

He eyeballed Bridges. 'Happy now?'

'Guv.'

Stone gestured for Frankie to carry on. She hesitated. Whatever was bothering her, it wasn't Bridges. She could handle guys like him standing on her head. If David was to hazard a guess, it was something else. Something more personal.

A memory stirred . . .

We couldn't have lost another.

That simple message accompanied a gift David had received

93

from Frankie's grandfather on his promotion to the rank of DCI. The old man was giving thanks for getting her to hospital in time to save her life during their last investigation. Now David came to think of it, there had always been a sadness in her he hadn't been able to reach. Maybe the hint that she'd lost someone close was her grandfather's way of telling him to tread carefully. David had wanted to ask her about it but had never found the right time. In the end, he held back: it might've opened a wound too painful. She looked like she'd rather die than be in this room.

He recognised the signs.

With the eyes of every MIT detective bearing down on her, she took her time, showing her backbone, unwilling to let Bridges derail her. 'Cosgrove claims he sat in the car the whole time and didn't see anyone apart from Annie. She doesn't recall seeing anyone in his vehicle. Unsurprising. Her eye was firmly on the guy at the gate. Assuming – wrongly as it turned out – that the car we now know to be Cosgrove's belonged to the loiterer, Annie legged it as fast as she possibly could. That said, there are a few discrepancies between the two, or should I say three witnesses, if you count the lawyer Joanna had dinner with on the night she died. Does anyone here know Joseph Cohen personally?'

Abbott's hand shot up. 'He plays with a straight bat,' he said, anticipating her next question.

'That's good to know.' Frankie was back in control. 'I'd like to talk about Alan Cosgrove now. After missing a call from Joanna, he'd assumed she was staying over in Newcastle but, just to be sure, he went out to meet her off the nine forty-three train. But, and this is important, according to Cohen, Cosgrove knew that his wife was intending to travel and surprise their kids on her birthday. I don't want to read too much into this. Maybe she was a woman easily swayed, although Cohen claims this is not the case. He said, quote: "If she'd made up her mind, she rarely changed it," unquote.'

The team were now listening, making notes.

'Joanna also called Cohen from the train, just a few last-minute thoughts about their court case. He described her as untroubled. The two were friends as well as colleagues. If anyone was bothering her on the train, I'd have thought he'd have known about it.' Frankie paused. 'I can tell you with certainty that both Joanna and Annie were seen on CCTV at Newcastle Central station, though Annie didn't notice her. Hardly surprising. As I said, she requires help on and off the train. I'm not sure how that works. Maybe she was held back by staff until everyone else boarded – or was put on first. According to Annie, there were three women and one or two males in her carriage. She couldn't describe them, but none left the train at Stocksfield. Even if that's the case, these passengers need identifying. I've requested details of anyone who bought a one-off ticket, but many others will have been season-ticket holders, like Joanna, or paid for the journey during transit. The conductor would've had close contact with anyone who did this.'

'Where are we with that line of enquiry?' David asked.

Frankie glanced at Abbott.

'No joy,' he said. 'I've tried driver and conductor several times.'

'As soon as we're done here, give them another call. We *need* that intel.'

Pushing away concerns that his 2ic might be struggling, David turned to face the team. 'Now, I have a theory I'd like to share with you. As we said before, last night's attack is different from the others in that it was staged. The offender went to the bother of laying Joanna out on railway sleepers. This afternoon, the pathologist conducting the post-mortem confirmed that none of the victims had injuries associated with having fallen to the ground after strangulation, so we're looking for one killer. It may have been an opportunist attack during a power cut. Maybe not. I'm taking Annie back to the crime scene tonight to see if we can get more detail from her on the suspect. Any questions?'

A hand went up. 'Did Cosgrove report Joanna missing at any point?'

'No, but remember she has a place in town. She often stays over.'

'Did he call her?'

'Yes, but her phone went to voicemail.'

'And then?'

'He went home to bed when she didn't make an appearance at the station car park.'

'Or maybe she did.' Dick threw it out there again and was right to do so. 'We only have his word for the fact that he was late.'

His suggestion hung in the air a moment.

'All options are open at this point,' David said.

Another hand went up. 'Have we confirmed that Joanna was due in court this morning?'

'Yes, I checked,' Frankie said. 'Our two witnesses appear to corroborate what the other is saying, but again there are a few anomalies we need to get our heads around. One: Cohen is adamant that Joanna wasn't intending to stay in town. Two: Cosgrove didn't tell us that Annie was carrying a torch. We need to speak to him again.'

'Is Cosgrove a suspect?' Mitch said.

'That notion occurred to us when we interviewed Annie,' Stone said, glancing at Frankie. 'I'd be inclined to think not, though he doesn't deny he was in and around the area of his wife's death. He could even have been sitting in his car while Joanna was being murdered yards away, though that stays within this room. If he was guilty – and remember we think the same man murdered all four women – he'd hardly draw attention to himself. So, let's not hang him out to dry until we delve further into it. I'm more interested in the man Annie saw.'

'With respect, that's bullshit,' Dunne said. 'The man Annie saw could well have been Cosgrove. If my opinion counts, I figure he gave himself a reason to be there in case he was seen . . . and he was, by Annie Parks. If you ask me, he's the clear suspect in this case, irrespective of how many passengers got off the Stocksfield train.'

This kind of interaction was exactly what David was after. Everyone chipping in, throwing ideas around. But then Dunne went too far.

'I don't buy any of this,' he crowed. 'Cosgrove was clearly expecting Joanna, and yet when she didn't show up, he went out to meet her and then thought nothing of it? C'mon! Sharpe would've—'

'Would've what?' Frankie lost it then. 'You think you could do better? Be our guest.' Frankie and Dunne were the same rank. He resented the fact that she'd been chosen as the SIO's bagman, giving her the edge over him. A complaint to Bright had fallen on deaf ears. She glanced at David, fire in her eyes. 'Guv, shove up. We have an expert in our midst.'

Dunne glared at her.

'Too shy?' Her smile was more of a smirk. 'Thought so.'

Expecting a verbal punch-up, David cut her off. 'Cosgrove seemed genuinely devastated by his wife's death. He was in the house in his pyjamas when Frankie and I arrived to break the news.'

'Yeah, freshly showered,' Dunne snorted.

Dunne had friends in the room. He was taking the piss out of David and Frankie didn't like it. 'Whoever killed Joanna has already killed three times,' she said. 'Are you seriously suggesting that Cosgrove would take his wife out and offer himself up as a contender for prime suspect? He's an intelligent man. Why would he?' It was a serious point but also a dig.

'I don't know.' Dunne was showboating now. 'You said

yourself, our guy is clever. As I recall, you also said he's forensically aware, someone in the know perhaps. Well, Cosgrove would know a lot about police procedure and forensics if he's married to a defence lawyer, wouldn't he?'

18

With a heavy heart, Frankie pushed her key in the front door of the semi-detached house she'd been born in and grew up in. As she let herself in and hung her coat on a peg in the hallway, she heard the TV from deep within the den her father called his man pad, the only room in the house where he could escape the many females in his life: Frankie, her mum, her grandma, her sister, Rae, and Rae's civil partner, Andrea. They were in and out of his home at regular intervals, like bees to a hive.

'Back already?' The shout out was not intended for Frankie.

When she poked her head into the den, her father was in his favourite chair, watching a news channel, beer can in one hand, *TV Times* spread out on his knee. He seemed pleased, if a little surprised to see her standing on the threshold so late in the day. The last twenty-four hours had been a bloody nightmare. After a long shift – she couldn't recall a worse one – Frankie had never been more pleased to see him, even more so to discover that he was alone.

'Hi, Dad.' She kissed him on the forehead. 'Where's Mum?'

'On the pull with Fay.'

Frankie grinned. 'Girls' night out?'

'A twenty-year reunion from work, no less. Not my cup of tea. Fay is Mum's plus one tonight.' Fay was Frankie's aunt.

'Oh hell, I forgot. Mum went then? She was in two minds when we last spoke.'

'She took a bit of persuading, but you know your mum. She'd hate to miss owt. Mind you, it took her forever to get dressed. "Everyone will look better than me," she said. I kid you not, she's had every piece of kit out of her wardrobe and tried it on twice. This place was a catwalk at teatime. I told her she was drop-dead gorgeous in every outfit, for all the good it did.'

Though Frankie's mother was carrying a few pounds more than she ought, her father loved her to bits. Since they got together, he'd never so much as looked at another woman. They had been childhood sweethearts from the age of sixteen, far too young to commit to monogamy in Frankie's opinion. Still, they enjoyed the kind of relationship she wanted . . . one day.

'Did Mum know you were coming?' her father asked. 'She didn't mention it.'

'No. Just thought I'd drop by.'

Frank Snr looked at his watch, then at her, a retort unsaid: *At this hour?*

'Actually, I'd like to stay over. Is that OK? I've got an early start tomorrow.'

'Of course!' He gave her an odd look. 'Since when do you need to ask?'

He'd spent the best part of his thirty-year police career as a detective, having followed his father into the job and worked his way up. Retired or not, they both kept up to date with every major incident that made its way into the public domain. Like most ex-cops, they couldn't help themselves. They were so proud when Frankie finally made it to Northumbria's elite murder squad. From the look of him, her father had guessed that things were not going to plan.

Frankie threw herself into her nan's chair, a family heirloom passed down through the generations which she'd insisted on handing over early, 'on the off-chance anything happens to me'. The woman was an unmitigated hypochondriac with one foot in the grave, to hear her tell it. Already in her late eighties, she was universally loved within the family, a matriarch expected to outlive everyone.

'You look stressed.' Frankie's father handed her a beer.

A hiss escaped as she yanked the ring-pull. The drink was welcome. Frankie hated to think what she must look like through her father's eyes. Studying her, he made no mention of her dishevelled appearance. A heavy silence did nothing to assuage his concerns that something was up.

And up it definitely was.

Instinctively, he knew she was in trouble. 'You've got to step up another gear now, Frank.' A bit of friendly advice, nothing more. 'It's your responsibility not only to lead a team and deal with detectives under your command, but also fit in with Stone's way of working. It's a tall order in anyone's book, but it's what you've always wanted. Make the most of it.'

Frankie *was* trying.

She looked around a room that hadn't changed a whole lot since she was a kid; a lick of paint, new curtains now and then, the same worn furniture, photographs of his daughters proudly on display, the way her father liked it. The smell and feel of his den was a constant reminder of when she was growing up. Good and bad memories were here, hours spent sitting with her dad. Despite a self-imposed ban on the female form, he'd let her sneak into his sanctuary whenever things were tough.

'What's wrong?' Picking up the remote, he killed the TV.

'Nothing,' she lied.

'Yeah right.' He raised an eyebrow, letting her know that he wasn't born yesterday. 'You want to climb up on my knee and spit it out? Unfortunately, I'm out of lollies.' When she didn't answer, his expression turned serious. 'Not even a smile for your old man? Must be serious.'

'It is.'

'Let me guess. Sharpe's team are giving you a hard time?'

'That as well . . . and we have a snitch among us.'

'Yeah, I saw the papers.'

'Of course you did.' Her money was on Dunne.

Frankie pinched the bridge of her nose, playing for time. Guys like Dunne had no place in an elite murder squad. There were bad apples in every department, in every industry and

101

every walk of life; nevertheless, she had to concede that he had a valid point to make about Cosgrove and he'd managed to push it home with equanimity. What was presently making her blood boil was the fact that her father had been talking to Bright, checking up on her, but she couldn't handle another row. As spent as she was, like a homing pigeon she'd headed to his den on autopilot to ask for advice.

He waited patiently, not wanting to push her.

This was painful. Frankie didn't want to upset him, but she had to talk to someone and there was no one in the world she'd rather consult, not even Andrea, a Traffic cop she'd met at training school, a fellow officer she was closer to than her own sister, Rae. 'I choked when I saw the victim last night,' was all she managed before her voice broke.

'We all do at first,' her father said. 'You'll get used to it. It takes time.'

How could he be so matter-of-fact? 'Will I, really? You make it sound so easy.' Tears pricked the back of Frankie's eyes. She stalled. 'It affected me in ways I didn't expect. When we arrived at the crime scene, I could barely look at her—'

'What exactly *did* you expect?'

'Her name is Joanna, Dad.'

Silence.

The temperature in the den plummeted, the colour draining from her father's face, his expression turning sour. He didn't try to cover his distress and, when he spoke, his tone was harder than before. 'Whatever her name, she deserves your attention, Frank. This is not about you any more. It's about the victims and those they left behind. They're the ones that matter now. They need closure—'

'We need closure!'

Seeing how upset she was, her dad got up and kneeled on the floor beside her chair, taking her free hand in his. 'Sweetheart, don't you think I know that?' His thumb stroked the top of her hand, soothing her, calming her, or trying to.

He'd always been able to read her. She didn't need to tell him that dark memories were running through her head, over and over, like a neverending nightmare, or that cold sweat was soaking her navy shirt. 'What you're feeling will pass,' he said gently.

'Will it? Really?' There was a hard edge to her voice.

'It will, I promise you.'

Frankie looked away, her eyes drawn to the wood panelling on the opposite wall, a photograph of his firstborn hanging there. If only her father would take his own advice. He was acting like he'd put the past behind him . . . Only she knew different. He was as stuck in a rut as she was.

She turned to face him. 'All that anger I worked on is back and it's suffocating me.'

'You'll never get over it, Frank. None of us will. How do you think I feel? Investigating murder is difficult for anyone. But if you want to fulfil your true potential, you must move on and use what you're feeling to help others.' He paused before delivering the sucker-punch: 'It's that or fold . . .' He let the sentence trail off. Frankie's glare didn't stop him from ramming his point home. The truth stung but he didn't hold back. 'Bright won't like it if you do. He's the head of CID, for Christ's sake. He put his faith in you. Do you have any idea how rare that is? You'll never get another opportunity if you tell him you're shipping out.'

He was being cruel to be kind.

Maybe she needed to hear it. Her old man had always supported her and wasn't being serious. He knew as well as she did that it would be professional suicide to fall at the first sign of trouble. She couldn't do it. In her family, joining the police was like taking a room at the Hotel California. The job stayed with you, even after you checked out. Frankie was a detective through and through. Although she felt trapped in a situation she had no control over, she couldn't dump this case on David – whether they were at odds with one another or not.

She didn't mention that or react to her father's provocation. 'What if I can't do it? What if we never find the vicious shit who killed those women?'

'You can and you will. It's what you were born to do. I really believe that, Frank. What's more, you're good at it.' He tried for a smile that didn't quite come off. 'You know that, right? You can't afford to fall apart because of a name, love. Those victims are relying on you.'

Frankie was wilting under his intense stare. He pulled her to him, put his arms around her, holding her like he used to when she was a child, offering words of comfort, trying his best to give her something positive to hold on to. She pulled away. She could take anything but sympathy.

She felt herself welling up.

'Please don't . . .' Her father wiped his face with his hand. 'We've done enough crying, Frank. You'll have me going if you start and what will your mum say then, eh?' He was halfway there himself, so close and yet unable to reach her emotionally. Hauling himself up, he went back to his chair. He looked deep into her eyes. 'You can't fool me, Frank. There's more to this, I can sense it. What are you not telling me?'

She took a swig of beer.

'C'mon, let me help.'

'It's not only me . . . it's David.'

He wasn't expecting that. 'What about him?'

She could tell her father anything knowing that it would go no further, but she felt guilty breaking a confidence bestowed on her less than twelve hours ago. David was struggling with a difficult team. After the briefing, he'd bollocked her for losing her rag with Dunne when all she was doing was trying to support him, telling her that if she had something unsavoury to say in future, she should do so in private, professionally – but there was so much more to it than that.

Frankie felt like a kid who'd been sent home with a note for her dad: *must try harder*. In the end, she decided to put her faith in him, the last thing she'd intended when she arrived. What other choice did she have? They drank more beer and he listened patiently as she gave a blow-by-blow account of David's experience in London, sharing his exposé about his murdered colleague – the horrific circumstances in which she'd died – and how he'd carried the burden for months and felt the need to offload so he could start afresh as SIO. The whole lot came spilling out.

Now her father understood.

As she snitched on her boss, she watched her old man closely. He was crushed, the disclosure upsetting him more than even she'd anticipated. He glanced at his daughters smiling out from the shelf above his desk, Joanna in the centre. There were so many parallels between David's experience and his own. Frankie felt bad now – worse than she had in the years when she'd dared to broach a taboo subject in his house. She wanted to hit pause and rewind, take it all back, but what was said could never be unsaid. In hindsight, she should have chosen Andrea as confessor this time around.

Suddenly, Frankie was eleven years old, the sound of weeping ringing in her ears. Back then, she hadn't known the meaning of grief, only that what she was feeling made her want to bolt from the house and hide. Truth be known, what she really wanted was to curl up and die. This word grief was etched on her parents' and grandparents' faces, along with words Frankie did understand: shock and disbelief.

She stood.

She had to get out of that room.

'I remember that case,' her father said softly.

Frankie was at the door, rigid, with her back to him. It was unforgivable, telling him. It had summoned emotions that were raw years after an event that had placed an indelible stain on their lives, a seismic shift in the dynamics of her whole family. It was impossible to blot out something so deeply personal.

'Frankie, come and sit down.'

She stood still, on the edge of tears. She wanted to run, and keep on running, but she turned slowly and made her way back to him, the photographs on the shelf drawing his eye and hers. 'I'm sorry, Dad. I shouldn't have said anything.'

'Don't be daft. Who else would you tell?' He'd always had her back and, though he was stating the obvious, trying his utmost to raise her up, what he did next made her bawl all over again. He thought of others before himself.

'Sounds like David needs our help.'

She nodded. 'He's lost perspective, Dad. He's not hunting the fuckwit who killed those women. He's hunting the man who killed the woman he loved.'

'Is that so bad? You feel that way too. I know you do.'

'We're not talking about me.'

'Aren't we . . . just a little?'

She ignored that one. 'With everything else that's going on, I don't know if David can put it behind him, so soon after it happened, or even if I can.'

'You can.'

She wiped her eyes. 'Not if today is anything to go by. I'm a basket case. We both are.'

She jumped at the sound coming from the hallway, then realised that it was the clock chiming the hour, not her mother returning. She'd take one look at Frankie and that would be that. Frankie relaxed, told herself to get a grip. She was a grown-up with new responsibilities and David to look after. He was worried about her too. She could feel it, even if she didn't want to admit it.

'He deserved none of this,' she said.

'So help him . . . And while you're at it, help yourself. You've done it before. You can do it now.'

'I . . . he can't know we've spoken—'

'You know me better than that, Frank. You think you're the only two detectives with baggage?'

106

'No.'

'Well then.'

This was like déjà vu. Him giving her advice on how to cope; her not really listening. Frankie didn't want to talk any more. She wanted him to shut the fuck up and go to bed, but she couldn't leave him now. The damage was done. He stood up and put strong arms around her. She fell into his embrace, allowing her body to relax, her head dropping to his chest, accepting the warmth on offer. She felt like a small child.

His voice was a broken whisper: 'I've been there too, remember.'

'I know, Dad—'

'There's a lot you don't know.'

Frankie pulled away.

'When I was on the floor emotionally, I never believed I'd be able to carry on. Your mum was a brick. Joanna's death nearly killed her too, but she had you and Rae to look after. She couldn't afford to fold. She dragged me like a drunk from the gutter and stuck with me till I got my shit together. It took a long time, but I got there in the end. You will too and so will David. We may be coppers but we're also human. I told you before, it's OK to stumble . . . so long as you don't fall.'

She quoted him: 'What doesn't kill you makes you stronger.'

'Exactly.' He'd told her that years ago and it had stuck. 'I'm not saying it'll be easy, but David needs your support. You owe him. We both do – and I'm not talking about your sideways move to the Murder Investigation Team. As far as I'm concerned, that had nothing to do with him. You earned it. But he saved your life and that's a huge debt to repay. If you support him, I'll support you. Deal?' He took in her nod. 'And not a word to your mum.'

19

Annie wasn't a bit nervous about returning to the crime scene so late at night. She was dressed up, fully made up, resembling an old movie star. If the matter wasn't so serious, she might even have been excited by her role tonight. David half expected her to tell him that, despite Joanna Cosgrove's death, the show must go on. Her nephew came along, as did four volunteers from HQ, a Traffic detail and a photographer to video the scene, the SIO explaining what would happen when they got there.

Reversing his vehicle into the disabled bay, where Annie's had been parked the night before, David got out and walked round the car. Opening the passenger door, he helped her out, asking her to stand in the same position where she'd first set eyes on the unidentified man. He'd arranged for the lights in the car park to be switched off at a given time, recreating similar conditions to the ones she'd faced as she came down the ramp from the train. He could do nothing about street lighting or the weather. It was balmy and still, if a little eerie in the moonlight.

He turned to face his eyewitness. 'Annie, I'd like you to watch the Traffic car and hold up your hand when it reaches the position of the car you saw last night. Can you do that for me? The driver will stop on your signal.'

The old lady nodded, one hand on her walking stick, the other on the roof of his pool car.

The SIO used his radio to communicate with Andrea McGovern, a woman he'd got to know since he paired up with Frankie in general CID, before their move to the Murder Investigation Team. 'Stone to Alpha 1: Back into the cut slowly, please.'

The Traffic car began to reverse, pulling up when Annie raised her arm.

'Is that about right, Annie? If not, we can move it back or forward. Take your time, we need to get this spot on.' David had to be sure.

'It's perfect as it is.' There was an irritated edge to Annie's voice. 'My legs might be gammy but there's nothing wrong with my spatial awareness or my brain. I'd appreciate it if you wouldn't patronise me, Detective. That's exactly where the car was parked, or I wouldn't have said so.'

Aware that the operation was being recorded, her nephew stifled a grin.

David remembered Annie's comment earlier in the day and wanted to tell her that he wasn't the kind of man she had no use for. It made him think of Frankie and her joke that he was one of the good guys. He wondered if she still thought that and where she was right now. When he'd sent her packing from the incident room, declining her offer to accompany him, she'd stormed out of the station car park in a mood. It wouldn't last. She'd be fine after a good night's sleep.

He hoped.

His apologies to Annie were accepted gracefully and so he moved on. 'Were there any lights showing on the vehicle, Annie?'

'Dipped headlights, not main beam.'

He didn't question it, merely raised his radio to communicate with Andrea. 'Leave your lights dipped, Alpha 1, and remain in situ.' He turned back to his star witness, his only witness to the stranger lurking in the shadows. 'You're certain that the man you saw was standing behind the metal gate and not in front?'

He followed Annie's gaze across the car park.

She closed her eyes and thought for a moment. 'Yes, behind the gate. Definitely. That's what I saw.'

A gust of wind came out of nowhere, rustling trees,

whispering through the long grass edging the wasteland, the tail end of last night's appalling weather. For a moment, David was behind the metal gate staring at Joanna Cosgrove's body, every detail in sharp focus. Beside him, Annie shivered, as if someone had walked over her grave too.

'Are you cold?' He thought he'd better check.

'No.' She pulled her coat around her.

'OK standing?'

'Yes, it's moving I'm not good at. Don't fuss.'

David raised an eyebrow to her nephew. He was around forty-five, square-jawed, thick-necked with deep-set eyes. He looked like he could handle himself on and off a rugby pitch, his chosen sport, as they had discussed on the way to the scene. Though he hadn't mentioned it, the SIO had him down as a prop forward.

The man grinned.

'My aunt doesn't need a guardian,' he said. 'If she was the target of this creep, she's capable of seeing him off with the bullets that come out of her eyes. As you've already witnessed tonight, she's cocked and fully loaded. She scares the hell out of me, I can tell you.'

David shook his head, warning Annie's nephew not to spook her.

'Don't worry, DCI Stone. No need to walk on eggshells, eh, Annie?'

'Absolutely not.' A mischievous wink from the old lady. 'It'll take more than one man to intimidate me. Many have tried. Few have succeeded.'

Her comment raised a smile from both men.

Much as he was enjoying the banter, David was forced to press on. 'You've already indicated where you saw the man standing last night. Can you please confirm, for our recording, that you've not seen the officers in the accompanying police vehicle?'

'Correct. Is it relevant?'

'It's important that you didn't see them up close, Annie. This is not an identity parade but we're treating it as if it were. The height and build of the man you saw is very important to us.' She appeared satisfied with his explanation and David carried on. 'One by one, I'm going to ask the officers to make their way from the police vehicle and stand in the location given. I'd like to establish how tall the man was, so please try and visualise what you saw. If you could indicate how much of the gate obscured his body, all the better. How much of his chest could you see, how big or broad he was?' He took in her nod. 'And anything else you can think of that you didn't tell us earlier; for example, if he wore glasses—'

'No glasses.' There was no hesitation.

David used his radio again. 'Officer 1, please leave your vehicle and proceed to the north side of the gate.'

When the officer was in place, Annie said without prompting: 'He was a little further to the right.'

Stone gave the order. As the officer made the adjustment, another thought occurred to David. He turned to face Annie. 'I'd like you to wait until all four officers have completed this task and then choose which one you think best fits the physical description of the man you saw. If you'd like to repeat this process at any time, that's not a problem.' When Annie had seen enough of Officer 1, Stone repeated his instructions to Officers 2, 3 and 4. In every case, the build was different. They were all wearing dark jackets with their hoods up.

At the end of the process, Annie said: 'I'd like to see Officers 1 and 2 again, please.'

Stone gave the order.

'The man I saw was like Officer 2 in height and build.'

Annie was done and for that David was very grateful. She'd chosen an officer of medium build, around five six. If she was as good a witness as he thought she might be, her information had ruled out Cosgrove, who was at least six five and much leaner.

20

The operation at Stocksfield station had gone well. Annie was a reliable witness. She'd provided vital information into four deaths. David took her and her nephew home to Bywell, made sure they were OK and then drove east. Despite the hour, he'd asked Andrea to go for a drink. She was due to finish her shift and God knows he needed one after his minor spat with Frankie. Fortunately, Andrea had come double-crewed, her co-driver offering to drop her off and take her car back to base so she could rendezvous with David at the Boathouse, a bar she knew well.

Stone drove through the village of Crawcrook, turning left for Wylam, making it in time for last orders. As he got out of the car, a warning signal from a freight train passing through the station opposite the pub sent a shiver right through him. It had been a challenging twenty-four hours.

He went inside to await Andrea's arrival.

The pub was busy, several customers standing at the bar. David bought two drinks, then made his way across the stone-flagged floor to a table at the end where an inglenook fireplace held a hefty wood-burning stove, a stack of dry logs piled up beside it. On the wall opposite, the landlord had proudly displayed the awards he'd won: West Northumberland Pub of the Year being one of many.

Another freight train rattled by.

Another shiver.

As he sat nursing his half-pint, dwelling on the day's events, he felt relatively pleased with progress. The first few days of a murder investigation were always manic, but Annie had given a good account of herself. Despite her bluster, there was no bad in her.

Andrea appeared in the doorway, combing back short, spiky blonde hair. She'd replaced her jacket with a casual one but, try as she might to disguise it, she still looked like a copper, her uniform trousers and heavy-duty shoes a dead giveaway, not to mention her tendency to nail every punter on the way in.

David stifled a grin.

She'd never be able to work undercover.

'Is this for me?' She was pointing at the spare half on the table.

'No, I'm meeting a civvi.' Stone grinned at her confusion, pointing at the Doc Martens on her feet. 'Is that your idea of incognito?'

'I've got news for you, mate. You may be in plain clothes but you smell as much like a copper as I do.'

He pushed the drink towards her. 'Thought I'd better get one in before closing time. Not that this lot look like they're going anywhere. If it's flat, I'll get you another.'

'It's cold and it's wet. That'll do me. I can only stop for one.' She pulled out a stool, threw a long leg over it and picked up her drink. 'You look knackered.'

Stone yawned. 'I am.'

'How did the op go?'

'Good. Thanks for your help. The witness will do well for us in court.'

'She reminded me of Miss Marple.'

'Stocksfield isn't that different from St Mary Mead.'

The smile slid off Andrea's face as she put her beer back on the table. 'How's Frankie doing?'

David wondered if the question was loaded. Did she know that he'd ticked Frankie off at base? The two were as close as any women he'd ever met. Apart from being sisters-in-law, they had known each other for years. David had gone out with them several times, together with Frankie's sister Rea. The four of them got on. If anyone would know what was upsetting Frankie, Andrea would. After all, that's why they were here. The nightcap had been his idea, a chance to pick her brains.

'I don't know is the honest answer,' he said finally.

The Traffic officer was instantly on her guard. A car pulled on to the steep incline outside the pub's Georgian sash window, blinding her with its headlights. Squinting, she changed position until they were switched off. She watched David over the top of her glass, then put it back on the beer mat. 'You haven't broken any rules in the Frank Oliver Handbook of Dos and Don'ts – Rule 9, for example?'

David laughed as Frankie's voice arrived in his head, quoting her daft rulebook: *Rule 9: Keep me sweet.*

Andrea wasn't laughing. 'You've been arguing again, I can tell. Call it women's intuition—'

'You make it sound like we're at each other's throats all the time.'

'Aren't you?'

'I thought she might have been in touch, that's all.'

'To say what?' Andrea was fishing.

'Nothing,' he lied. 'You speak most days.'

'We do, but not today funnily enough.' She studied him. 'I called her from the car on the way over here but she's not picking up.'

'I called her too, with the same result.'

'Is there something going on between you two?'

'Not that I'm aware of.'

Andrea wasn't buying his bullshit. 'Then how come she's not here?'

'She's exhausted.'

'Yeah, right.'

'She is! We were up half the night. One of us needs to stay awake tomorrow.' David was tempted to ask what might have triggered Frankie's uncharacteristic dark mood, but he knew better than to read too much into it without all the facts to hand. He must get to the bottom of her inability to concentrate, her adverse reaction to the victim, and why she'd allowed Dunne to rattle her in the incident room. As her supervision, David couldn't afford not to, but he'd rather get the details from the horse's mouth. Maybe she was just having an off day, but even as the thought occurred to him, he dismissed it. She was bigger than that. He let it go and so did Andrea. Well, he thought she had, until she pulled out her phone.

'Mind if I make a call?'

'Suit yourself.'

She punched in a number, lifting the device to her ear.

The volume was on high. David could hear the ringing tone across the table. It was unlike Andrea to make a call if she was in company. She thought it rude, an opinion she voiced loudly if she saw anyone checking Twitter or emails when off duty or out on the hoy. She'd once told him that she didn't have time in her life to waste on social media.

The phone was still ringing.

David willed Frankie not to answer, assuming it was her that Andrea was trying to reach. He relaxed as she returned the phone to her jacket pocket, eyes fixed on him. 'That's odd,' she said. 'I happen to know that Frank Senior is on his own tonight and he's not picking up either. What do you make of that?' It was a leading question.

David was on the back foot. 'Maybe they're doing the same as we are.'

'No, Frank will be waiting in for Julie. She's out on the town with her sister. Besides, you know as well as I do that my father-in-law never fails to answer my calls. Unlike you, he thinks I'm cool.'

'It's late. He probably turned in.'

Andrea gave Stone a pointed look.

He wouldn't tell her that his 2ic had recoiled from Joanna's body at the crime scene. Frankie had worked her arse off to get into a Major Incident Team and he wanted to keep her

115

there. It would be disloyal to discuss her inability to fulfil that crucial part of her job, even with family – especially with family. Bad-mouthing her to someone she so obviously cared for would be the ultimate let-down. He couldn't do it.

He wouldn't.

Stone wondered if Frankie was with her father now, if there was a reason they were ignoring the phone. Andrea obviously thought so. They drank, no longer in a mood for conversation, unlike regulars at the bar who were having a high old time celebrating someone's birthday. Smoke drifted in through the open door. Stone could do with a cigarette, though he hadn't smoked in years. He felt awkward as the conversation dried up. Andrea must've felt the same. She'd never been one for small talk, but it was a gap she found impossible not to fill.

'How's Ben?'

'Shit!' Stone palmed his brow, then told another porky. 'I've not seen him much. He was out when I was in and vice versa—'

'That's bollocks, David. You forgot about him, didn't you? You actually forgot!' Andrea shook her head, a raised eyebrow, a filthy look. 'For God's sake don't tell Frankie. If she finds out, she'll go all Mother Teresa on you. You're supposed to be looking after him. You promised.'

'Yeah well, he'll get over it. I've been a copper long enough for him to know the score. He's stroppy, probably pleased that I'm otherwise engaged. He hasn't commented on my absent-parent routine, not to me anyhow. As for Frankie, you'd have to ask her. She's closer to him than I am.'

'That's because she puts herself out to spend time with him.'

David threw his hands up. 'It's not *my* fault. It's hard to hold a conversation with someone whose eyes never leave an iPad screen and who is incapable of anything more than a grunt over his Crunchy Nut Cornflakes . . .' He grinned. 'He's even worse if it's Coco Pops.' David looked at his watch, saw an out and took it. 'But if it makes you feel any better, I'll head off and check on him now.'

Andrea wasn't amused.

Ben was slumped on a threadbare sofa watching a movie when Stone finally got home to Pauperhaugh. His nephew didn't even register his arrival. The living room of the tiny cottage was a dump, crisp packets and empty, squashed beer cans littering the floor – but it wasn't all bad news. There was no tell-tale smell of cannabis and he no longer resembled a sack of garbage. He'd cleaned himself up and looked much healthier than when he'd moved in. Maybe he was beginning to see sense after all.

David watched him for a moment.

Ben was like his dad, around six two and well-built with a mop of blond hair. The lad had lost his way when his mother died. He was fourteen when it happened. He'd got in with the wrong crowd and fallen foul of his father, David's brother, Luke. His death – a fatal RTA – was more recent. True to form, the first thing Ben had done afterwards was make the wrong decision and drop out of university. He was going back in September. Finishing his degree in Journalism was part of the deal David had struck with him.

While he'd shunned the idea of taking Ben on initially, David had bent under pressure from Frankie, with Andrea and Rae backing her point of view. As the lad's sole living relative, David had little choice but to give it a go and, in exchange for his support, Ben had promised to adhere to a few house rules: drop the attitude; no smoking in the house; no weed in or out; clean the shower; hang up your clothes; take the bin out occasionally. Though the lad wasn't there yet, there had been a definite improvement – for them both. Ben was less hostile, David less authoritarian, man and boy having to compromise. For David, the adjustment from single man to father figure would take a little getting used to.

'Good movie?' he asked.

Ben made a sound that might have come from one of the pigs at the farm at the bottom of the garden. David could describe the sound but would never be able to spell it. There was no comparable word in the Oxford English Dictionary. Despite the late hour, and with Andrea's words ringing in his ears, he'd made up his mind to spend a little time with his nephew before retiring, an effort to make up for his absentee-ism, but it didn't go according to plan.

'Has the plumber been?' He'd been waiting for one for weeks.

'Yeah.'

'Good. When's he coming back?'

'Dunno.' Ben turned up the volume.

'Is that my cue to leave?'

'Wot?' The lad never turned his head.

David tried again. 'I brought a couple of beers. Want one?'

'Yeah, but I'm watching this.'

David sighed, put the cans on the table. Reminding his nephew to clear up his mess, he sloped off, a grin not a scowl on his face. He was too tired to mention who was paying the bills.

With the TV running next door, David couldn't sleep, so he took a seat at the desk he'd built out of some wood he'd found in a reclamation yard in Boldon. The proprietor had told him that it had come from an old brewery that had gone into liquidation. He'd smiled at the pun, intended or not, but the salesman was clueless.

David ran his hand over the desk.

The wood was solid, rich in colour, the grain beautiful as well as tactile, exactly what he was after. He'd inherited the single-storey cottage from his late grandmother and planned to strip and renovate it in his spare time. In exchange for bed and board, Ben had offered to help, but there had been no sign of that since the lad moved in, though his great-grandmother would have approved of the arrangement. Family had always been a priority for her.

The room David was sitting in used to be hers. So strong was her presence, he almost turned to glance at the saggy bed behind him where she'd drawn her last breath. Instead, ignoring the racket and laughter from the living room – it was nice to know that Ben hadn't lost his sense of humour – David woke up his laptop, logged on and made a list of things he wanted to take to the team in the morning.

21

At her father's invitation, Frankie had agreed to stay over for a day or two. He wanted her close and she understood why. He was as concerned about her as she was about David – as she was about him. Talking about Joanna had upset them both. Frankie had gone to bed long before her mother got home and almost choked on her toast trying to keep up appearances at breakfast. Luckily, her mum was too busy giving a hilarious account of her reunion to notice that her daughter wasn't her usual self, that she'd not said a word since she'd walked into the kitchen and surprised her, nor that she'd wasted her time cooking a fry-up that neither Frank Oliver seemed interested in eating. Frankie tuned her mother out as her mobile bleeped an incoming text:

Cosgrove may be a big hit with cabin crew but he's no walking cliché. He's clean, a family man, as everyone in The Feathers said he was. Annie was a star!

Frankie put away her phone, keen to know more and chuffed that Annie had come through for David. Her father eyed her across the table, curious to know what was going on. He could tell the text was of interest, but her mother was still chuntering . . .

'I bet you two planned the whole thing to get me out of the house,' she said.

'We did.' Frank Snr winked at his daughter over his coffee cup. 'It's the only way we could get a word in edgeways, eh, Frank?' He arched an eyebrow towards his wife, a wry smile on his face. 'You look a bit green, love. Feeling OK?'

She punched his arm and got up to fetch more coffee.

When her back was turned, Frankie's father flicked his eyes to the door, sending an unspoken message: *Whatever it is, go! Get it over with. Make your peace with David and focus – I'm here if you need me.* So, taking a deep breath, Frankie kissed her mum and dad goodbye, climbed into her car and headed to Northern Command HQ.

Frankie had been in conference with Stone this past hour. With Cosgrove out of the picture, David wanted to concentrate on the man Annie Parks had seen loitering near the metal gate at the crime scene. Her description fell short of a photofit, but height and build would come into play should any interesting suspects emerge.

It was a start, nothing more.

Frankie stood in the doorway, steeling herself to enter the incident room. Whether she approved of them or not, everyone in the MIT was doing his or her bit. The whole team looked fatigued – even though it wasn't yet mid-morning – but Frankie and David didn't hold the monopoly on wanting to nail the man currently terrorising the north-east; every officer on duty, across the force and beyond, plainclothes or uniform, was hell-bent on apprehending the offender they were hunting.

Images of all four victims dominated the murder wall. There was no suggestion that any one of them had been stalked in the days leading up to their deaths, no complaints at home or at work, no concerns expressed to family members. On the one hand, the killer appeared to be choosing his victims randomly; on the other, selecting women by type, a conundrum Frankie puzzled over as she took a breather. She wondered what he was up to now: singling out another innocent female, taking a break until the heat died down? After her temporary setback last night, she was on a mission to stop him.

She'd noticed how focused David was this morning too, as if a weight had been lifted since he'd shared the trauma that had haunted him for months. Having sought advice from her old man, and feeling better for having unburdened herself, she understood her guv'nor's need to offload. She was convinced that fate had brought him north. Some things were meant to be – their professional partnership was one of them.

Despite their collective baggage, obtaining justice for victims would drive them both. These women – grandmothers, mothers, daughters, sisters, nieces, aunts and cousins – had been taken long before their time. Stone and Oliver could never bring them back, but they could give it their best shot to apprehend the person responsible for their deaths.

It's what you were born to do.

Her father's words subsided, the buzz of a busy incident room taking over. Across the room, Frankie noticed the statement reader working his way through statements passed back from the outside enquiry teams. Indexers were working hard to keep HOLMES fed. Without the Home Office Large Major Enquiry System, they'd be screwed, a sentiment her grandfather didn't share. When he and her father had joined the force, a card system was used for keeping track. Frankie couldn't imagine how officers of their generations had coped with investigations of this scale and considered herself lucky that all major enquiries were now computerised.

There had been a flood of phone calls from concerned members of the public since David had sanctioned an appeal for witnesses to come forward. Experienced civilian calltakers as well as rookie detectives were manning the phones due to the high volume of calls coming in. They had taken hundreds since the enquiry began, many that hadn't yet been updated on HOLMES. Keen to clear the backlog, David had asked Frankie to assist the receiver. The SIO trusted her – and so he should; they could afford to miss nothing and she excelled in weeding out the important stuff.

Sitting down at her desk, she slipped her warrant card into

a slot on her computer to access HOLMES, painfully aware that the team around her were struggling. They needed a boost, something more than Annie's information to latch on to. Dunne had stopped her on the way in, sheepishly asking her opinion on whether a criminal profiler would help their cause. Sharpe had used one, but David wasn't keen. Frankie stood somewhere in the middle. She was wary of Dunne, wondering what he was up to. Looking to drive a wedge between the incomers was her best guess. If he thought she had leverage with the SIO, he might be trying to use her. Equally, if it turned out that they were dealing with a serial offender like Sutcliffe – who'd gone on killing until his subsequent arrest – then a profiler may well be the way to go.

'I'll have a think,' she'd said.

Dunne appeared to accept that, even apologised for being a twat yesterday. Distrusting his motives, she didn't reciprocate. As far as she was concerned, he now had to prove himself. Maybe yesterday's spat *was* over and done with. Maybe not. Grown-ups fell out occasionally and then got on with the task in hand. He'd never make her fantasy Major Incident Team, but he didn't need to know that.

Frankie sat back and rubbed her eyes. She'd been reading for about an hour, and though she'd discounted nothing during that time, neither had she found anything that jumped out at her waving its arms. Most appeals drew a small percentage of time-wasters. Even callers with genuine information to impart were often classed as low priority. The police asked for it – 'If you have anything to tell us, no matter how unimportant you may think it is, please call the incident room' – and they invariably got it. What she'd been reading was a bunch of shit.

Or was it?

She sat forward, scanning her computer screen, homing in on the message below the one she'd just read. The next one in the queue was unusual, in that it hadn't come in on the phone as most of them had; it had arrived as an email from a woman named Rebecca Hill – a referral to Northumbria Police via British Transport Police. An officer passing the buck, Frankie guessed. The tone of it read more like a complaint than an observation.

On the face of it, the message was of low significance, a communication that had nothing to do with Stocksfield, or the scene of Joanna Cosgrove's death. But, having read the content, it might have something to do with the man the team were hunting. Frankie googled Rebecca Hill. There were several social and professional profiles of women of that name, including a list of the Top 10 on LinkedIn, some successful, but none local. On the second page, however, she found her target in a *Guardian* article praising the Global Leadership Award Rebecca Hill had won from the Society of Women Engineers in 2010.

Drumming her fingers on her desk, Frankie wondered. This might, just might, lead to something. Picking up her internal phone, her finger hovered over David's extension number. She'd left him preparing an update for Bright and didn't really want to disturb him. On the other hand, she was excited by her find. She reread the email and went for it. Stone picked up almost immediately.

'Guv, it's me. I know you're busy, but have you got a minute?'

'Sure.'

'We've received an interesting email concerning an incident in Durham, initially reported to British Transport Police. The caller claims it's her second attempt to draw attention to a suspicious character she'd seen on a train. BTP did nothing with it initially, but when Joanna's death hit the press, the caller wouldn't let it lie. She rang them again and was referred to us. It's a gut feeling, nothing more, but I think we should follow it up.'

'We will,' he said, 'but not yet – I want you with me this morning.'

'I did some digging, guv.'

'I'd expect nothing less—'

'Hear me out, please. Hill is a chemical engineer living locally. Same profile as our victims: top-notch professional, I mean. She's a high-flyer, graduate of Newcastle University, a big noise who works for a major pharmaceutical company based in North Tyneside. She's highly qualified with letters after her name. I'm well impressed.'

'Me too, but how does it take us anywhere?'

'It took me less than two minutes to find her on the net. Our man may also be trawling cyberspace to find his targets. I appreciate that it's a long shot—'

'It is.' Stone cut her off. 'Durham is miles away.'

'Ten, fifteen minutes by train.'

'They're not short enough odds to justify our time right now, Frank. I don't see it as a high-priority action.'

'OK, you're the boss.'

Dunne was watching as she put down the phone. He'd heard her side of the conversation and could see how bitterly disappointed she was. A sideways glance at two of his old team mates was more of a smirk. Frankie felt like wiping it off his face but was conscious of Stone's warning that she should keep it civil. Dunne caught her eye. A malicious remark to a colleague incensed her. Unable to take any more of his bullshit, she was on the move . . .

22

'Don't ask,' Abbott said as the SIO marched into the incident room wanting to know what was going on. Daft question, all things considered. Across the room, a slanging match was developing, Frankie and Dunne at its centre, other detectives gathering round, all work on hold. Abbott scratched his head. 'This is not like her – and what it has to do with Joanna is anyone's guess.'

David frowned. 'Joanna?'

'Beats me.' Abbott shrugged. 'Whatever it was, it made her kick off. Dunne's a wanker. He's been twisting the knife, trying his hardest to get her going all morning—'

'Looks like he succeeded.'

'I'd give them a few minutes,' Abbott said. 'It'll blow itself out.'

'The hell it will.'

Dunne was still mouthing off and he wasn't holding back. He was ridiculing Frankie, something to do with her detection rate that David didn't quite catch and understood even less. He moved closer, careful to remain within their blind spot, but close enough to earwig their row as they continued trading verbal blows, an attempt to intervene on hold until he found out what was going on.

'Ask him . . . if you dare!' Dunne's tone was spiteful. 'Daddy's gone now, in case you hadn't noticed, along with your protection. It's common knowledge that you arrived via the back door. The old boys' network isn't what it once was, Oliver. Or maybe it was something equally underhand that got you in.' He glanced briefly at his audience. 'We're all wondering who you're screwing – the Northern Rock or Bright?'

'Fuck you!'

David caught her wrist as she drew her arm back, ready to throw a punch, exactly what Dunne was after. When Frankie realised who it was who'd grabbed hold of her, she stopped struggling and David let go of her.

'DS Oliver, get your coat and meet me at my car.'

She didn't budge.

'Move it!' The SIO rounded on Dunne. 'If anyone is getting screwed around here, it's you. You'd better have a bloody good excuse for this when I get back or you're out.' He looked at the mob surrounding him. 'And that goes for anyone else who'd like to go with him. Now, piss off back to work the lot of you or get the hell out of my incident room. This is a murder enquiry, not a bare-knuckle fight.'

David watched them trundle back to their desks. If this problem escalated, it would take everyone's eye off the ball and he wasn't having that. On his way out of the room, he used two fingers to point at his eyes, then at Abbott's, flicking his head towards Dunne as he sloped off, muttering under his breath. He was trouble.

Abbott nodded his understanding.

Once through the double doors, David practically frog-marched Frankie along the corridor and out of the building, ignoring her complaints. Realising she was on a hiding to nothing – and that no explanation she offered justified brawling, no matter the provocation – she fell silent as she strode across the car park. She'd disobeyed a direct order not to mix it with Dunne and David was far from happy.

He could see she was upset.

Tough: if she behaved like a four-year-old, he'd treat her like one.

The Wall's End pub was within walking distance but too close to home for the SIO's liking. He blipped open the doors of his SUV, conscious of eyes at the windows on the floor above. Dunne and his pals would be up there, waiting for him to give Frankie a dressing down.

They didn't get their way.

Ignoring the temptation to look up, David climbed into the car and started the engine, head-checking the car park as he reversed out of his spot. He didn't say where they were going – he didn't know – and Frankie cared even less. She stared straight ahead as he pulled away. No doubt the prying eyes above had occurred to her too. He wanted her gone before the rumour mill started up. There were no secrets at Middle Earth.

He was heading for Plessey Woods, then changed his mind in favour of somewhere closer. The short journey passed in a blur, an atmosphere of bad feeling in the car, during which neither detective spoke. After five minutes or so, David took the sign for Tynemouth, then North Shields, turning at a signpost for the Fish Quay and Riverside. He could see cranes in the distance as he continued down the hill. Stone glanced to his left. Looking at Frankie was like seeing his reflection in a mirror. Whatever she'd lost her rag about, he had to find a way to help her over it.

Stopping the car on Quay Road, he yanked on the handbrake, swivelling in his seat to face her. 'Out!' he said. 'You're going to walk it off and tell me why you and Dunne were scrapping.'

'Hardly scrapping, guv.'

'Don't split hairs.'

They got out of the car.

The storms were over, the summer returning. It was a blistering day, not that Frankie seemed to notice. She was feeling another kind of heat; one David didn't understand. What had been said by Dunne at Middle Earth was killing her. 'You should know better than to let him wind you up. You're bigger than that. Dunne is unpleasant but he's not stupid. He knows how feisty you are and so does every detective in the force—'

'Yeah, yeah. I've heard it all before.'

'And you'll hear it again and again until you start listening.' He cared about her but she frustrated him. He had to get through to her somehow. 'You have a reputation you feel you have to live up to, is that it?'

She gave him hard eyes. 'No!'

He started down the road, the smell of the sea and the screeching of gulls unable to lift his mood, as it normally would. Frankie fell in step and when he spoke, his tone was softer. 'You really do not want to take him on, Frank. It'll end in tears. If you want my honest opinion, you should never have joined a force where your old man or his old man have made enemies.'

'You think I should run off to the Met like a sad fuck?' Frankie bit back.

'Your father begged you to join Durham Constabulary. Why didn't you?'

'I wanted to join my home force, that's why.'

He didn't rise to the bait. 'We can't always have what we want, Frank. Dunne had himself down as my bagman and you, or should I say we, put his nose out of joint. You didn't expect him to welcome us with open arms or congratulate you on your appointment, did you?'

She slipped her sunglasses on and didn't answer.

'And, for the record, this sad fuck didn't run away. I chose to go south.'

'Yeah, just like you chose to come home again.'

Her second dig stung, but again David ignored it. She knew she'd hurt him. He could see that. Arguing with her wasn't going to get him anywhere. 'What did he say to you about Joanna?'

'What?' Taken aback by the question, Frankie lied to cover it up, her face colouring ever so slightly. 'Nothing.'

'As I told you once before, you'd be hopeless at poker. What did he say?'

'It was nowt, guv. Honestly . . .' She climbed down. 'Look,

can we forget this? I'm sorry for my outburst. It won't happen again.'

They turned right and on past a blue metal gate with the words FISH QUAY AND MARKET welded into the design. David pointed at the Old Low Light Café up ahead. They went in and he ordered lemonade with a dollop of ice cream to cool her down – even though she looked like she was dying for gin. They took their drinks through the back door where tables and chairs sat empty. Despite the glorious view where the River Tyne met the North Sea, they had the place to themselves. No chance of being overheard.

David put his drink on the table. 'Frank, talk to me. What did he say?'

'He made me angry, that's all. What do you care, anyhow? The guy's a tosser!'

'One you have to work with for the time being.' He was almost pleading. 'For God's sake, what is wrong with you? What if Bright had walked in while the two of you were locking horns?'

'If he'd heard what he said, he'd have decked the foul-mouthed bastard and sacked him on the spot.'

'Is that what you want, another man's career on your conscience?'

'Dunne has no career. I think he tipped off the press. Be honest, so do you – and you need to do something about it.'

'You have proof?' David got no answer. 'Thought not. Well, when you do, let me know. Anyone could be responsible, even the offender himself. Did that thought ever cross your mind? It didn't, did it? You're too distracted to get your arse in gear and do your job.' He looked away, trying to reel himself in before he said something he might regret.

A flock of gulls had perched on old staiths covered in algae and seaweed, the smell of which floated towards them on the breeze. Like David, the birds waited expectantly; in their case, for small fishing boats to come ashore with their tea; in his, for Frankie to get over her strop and calm down. David didn't need to be a betting man to work out that he was the one with the longer odds.

When he turned to face her, she was still smouldering. 'C'mon, Frank. If Dunne is guilty of passing information to the press, I'll be the first to hang him out to dry. But making life difficult for him won't buy you any friends. It'll do the exact opposite. You've seen his cronies. They're tight. If you make this a power struggle, you'll lose everything. Whatever he said to you, it's not worth it.'

She was seething, hands curled into hard balls, knuckles almost white.

Though David couldn't see her eyes clearly beneath her sun specs, he could tell from her rigid body language that he wasn't getting through. 'You think I don't know about uncontrollable anger?'

She snapped. 'You didn't hear what he said.'

'I just asked you what he said. You chose not to give a proper answer.'

Frankie looked out to sea.

Stone watched her closely. He wanted to support her and yet she was making it bloody difficult. She had been fine on the way to the crime scene, but since then she'd rapidly gone downhill and he couldn't figure out why. She'd lost her temper with Collingwood at the morgue and hadn't been able to control herself when Dunne had a go at her. She was a loose cannon and he couldn't afford that. He had to rein her in. Maybe he'd reach her if he showed some honesty.

'If you won't talk, will you at least listen?' He was almost pleading.

A shrug was her answer.

'For God's sake! We haven't got time for this, Frank.'

'Whatever.'

He hesitated. 'I didn't tell you the whole truth about what happened in the wake of Jane's death—'

131

'You don't need to. I'm not dumb. I can imagine.'

'I don't think you can.'

'Then tell me.' It came out like a bark.

She wasn't really interested but David was running out of ideas. 'Everywhere I went, I saw her. I had to keep reminding myself that she was gone.'

'You were grieving. Shit happens.'

'Yeah, well, grief affects us all.' He was edging closer, but Frankie wasn't playing.

'If you're going to tell me that you two were—'

'No, that's not it. When we first met, she was with someone . . . the wrong one as it turned out, but I wasn't to know that at the time.' Stone held her gaze, taking a deep breath before continuing. 'I had strong feelings for her, I won't deny it, but I missed my chance. That didn't stop the arsehole who killed her alleging that we were having an affair, or that the deceit had driven him temporarily insane. It sparked an internal investigation. My guv'nor knew it was bollocks but she had to go through the motions with Professional Standards.' He paused, staring at the glasses on the table. 'You throw mud, some of it sticks, Frank.'

'He couldn't possibly prove that.'

'Yeah, well there's no smoke without fire. The crime scene photos included two glasses and a bottle of wine, lots of daft photos on our phones, off duty and pissing about, enough evidence that we were close. His barrister made his play and Jane's parents had to sit through that while Laughing Boy got his kicks. It wasn't my name I was worried about him trashing, it was hers . . . And now it's yours.'

Frankie seemed to have calmed down considerably. 'Why are you telling me this?'

'Because you need to hear it.' He dragged a hand through his hair. 'I despised him for what he'd done. In killing her, he'd killed a bit of me too, leaving a hole where my self-restraint used to be. Sound familiar? I couldn't take part in the investigation and, with time to kill, all I could think of was getting revenge. Which is why I worry that you'll let Dunne provoke you into doing something you'll live to regret.'

'What do you mean?'

'I think you know.'

She snorted. 'You didn't really think I was going to deck him, did you?'

'That's what it looked like, to me and a couple of dozen witnesses. If you want to have it out with a bully, there are better places to do it than in a crowded incident room. Look, I know how destructive anger is. Believe it or not, after what happened in London, I had the same urge to kill as Jane's ex. Worse than that, I had the capacity to do it . . . in cold blood. If I'd had a firearm, I'd have emptied the barrel across that courtroom and never blinked an eye.'

'No, you wouldn't.' She shifted uncomfortably in her seat.

'Yes, I would.'

'You're talking bollocks.'

'I'm not bluffing, Frank. As crazy as it sounds, I was a murder detective with a plan to off someone. It ate me up for weeks. Drove me nuts. I couldn't shake it off, neither did I want to. The thought was there, day and night. If I couldn't get to him before he went inside, I'd bide my time until I could. That was plan A. I began to fantasise about him swaggering from the prison, me squeezing the trigger, pumping him full of holes, showing him as much mercy as he showed Jane.'

Now she was listening – intently. What's more, she knew he was serious. David had crossed the line by telling her of his experience, but he had an ulterior motive. Abbott suspected that Dunne knew what was bothering Frankie and was playing on it, baiting her, knowing that if he gave her enough provocation, a sudden loss of control had the potential to ruin her life, as David's anger had almost ruined his.

'That must've been scary,' she said.

'It was.'

He caught her eye.

Even though a thin blue line threaded her body in place of veins – and what he'd said flew in the face of everything she believed in – she wasn't judging him. In that moment, the dynamic between them changed. For the first time since they'd met, he knew that, to a greater or lesser extent, she'd been there too.

Maybe she still was.

'I don't expect you to understand any more than my Met colleagues did,' David said. 'Few of them saw the full effect Jane's death had on me. I left London to talk it over with Luke. Once I was on that train there was no going back. When I crossed the Tyne, I had already decided to cut and run. Maybe I am that sad fuck after all—'

'You're not . . . I went too far. Though I never understood how you could take a hit in rank to transfer. Given the same circumstances, I don't think I could.'

David looked deep into her eyes. 'I saw it as a penance—'

'That's rubbish! You have nothing to beat yourself about.'

'Do you?' He was trying to draw her out.

'I can't talk about it, David.' She held his gaze. 'I'm sorry.'

'But there is something?'

She nodded, a big sigh. 'I'm not shutting you out . . . I just can't.'

'OK, so we'll handle it.' Finally, he was getting somewhere. 'Frank, when you almost lost your life, I took it badly. Ask Andrea. I'd coped with it once, I'd never have survived a second time, at least not in the job I was meant to do – the job we are both meant to do. I'd have walked, for sure. I have you to thank for the fact that I didn't. I owe you and I want to help if I can.'

'Hey! Don't go all maudlin on me. I'm a third-generation cop, remember? That means I'm not allowed to die before I give birth to a successor.' She was beginning to relax.

'You want kids?'

'One day, maybe . . .' She caught his surprise before he could hide it. 'Don't look so shocked. I'll have you know that my maternal instincts are a hundred per cent intact. No need to panic just yet, mind. For the record, I'm not remotely interested in settling down, so you're stuck with me. Unless Kit Harington has been dumped, then I might have to reconsider.' She put her hands together, looked up at the sky, then dropped her head, smiling eyes meeting his across the table. 'If he calls, I'll be sure to let you know.'

'It's good to know you'll be around a while.' Stone wasn't buying her humour – it was all a front – but he'd reached out to her and she'd responded . . . finally. 'Frank, we're a team.' He smiled then. 'I won't pry if you don't want to talk about what's bothering you, but know this: you only need to ask.'

She looked down and nodded.

It was a defining moment.

23

They finished their lemonade and walked away from the Old Low Light. As they exited the café's backyard, Frankie caught sight of a man in one of the sheds to her right. He wore a long blue apron and was gutting fish. She loved the fish quay. It was a real place, a working place, full of interesting characters who made their living off the sea. It was alive and thriving, the reason she'd chosen to live at the coast.

They walked past the Dockmaster's House – an intriguing building standing within the confines of a seventeenth-century ancient monument, Clifford's Fort, a defensive gun battery guarding the mouth of the River Tyne – and on past benches, brightly painted and made from old pallets, where visitors sat eating fish and chips, with keen-eyed gulls screeching overhead. A few minutes later, they arrived back at the SUV in a better mood than when they had left it. As Frankie reached for the door handle, David paused before unlocking the car.

'Are we good?' he said.

'We're good. I'll up my game, David. I promise.'

The interior of the vehicle was like a sauna when they climbed in.

Leaving the door wide open, Frankie turned to face him. 'You said you wanted me with you when we spoke on the phone earlier. Did you have something specific in mind?'

'Yeah, we need to change direction.'

'I thought you'd agreed a strategy with Bright to keep the focus on Joanna.'

'I did, but while the team are doing that, you and I need to start at the very beginning. I have it on good authority that Sharpe wasn't firing on all cylinders when he ditched the investigation. His wife fucked off with a guy half her age

136

who has form. They were dishing the dirt to a divorce lawyer, claiming irretrievable breakdown on the grounds of psychological abuse. Word is, they had their eye on a substantial portion of his salary. Sharpe put his ticket in and buggered off before they could lay their grubby hands on his commutation. He was crushed, Frank. Came home one day and she was gone. Just like that. No warning. No note. She dumped him by text.'

'I knew there must be a reason.'

'Rumour has it that he took off to the South of France in case they make a land grab there too – I gather he has a villa by the sea.'

'Lucky him.'

'My thoughts exactly. Anyway, I'm concerned he may have missed something.' Stone started the car and pulled out into traffic.

They passed Mariner's Lane, heading north to the first crime scene on the fringes of Blyth where Catherine's Bennett's body had been found. David turned along the coastal route to Tynemouth and Cullercoats, Frankie people-watching as he drove. Along the seafront, kids played chase in a park, restaurants were busy. As the road wound itself around the headland, she caught sight of St Mary's Lighthouse in the distance, arriving in Blyth a few minutes later, a town that had been through major redevelopment in recent years. Traditional industries of coal mining and shipbuilding had long since vanished, though other commercial enterprises had taken over: renewable energy, marine science and technology, the Port of Blyth handling up to two million tonnes of cargo every year.

David and Frankie parked up and got out. They were heading for the beach or, more accurately, to some relics on the dunes.

'Catherine was found right here.'

David was indicating a spot halfway between a semi-circular

gun emplacement – filled in to form an amenity shelter – and a derelict battery observation post. There were no visible signs that anything untoward had happened on the rough ground between the two structures, or that the police had been crawling all over the promenade weeks ago, let alone that a young woman had lost her life there.

Frankie shook her head. 'When did Sharpe give the go-ahead to release the scene?'

'As soon as crime scene investigators moved out. He had no choice, Frank. Hard to contain it without a sentry on duty 24/7.'

'S'pose.' Her attention was drawn to an information sign attached to a rusting post sticking out of the ground:

A unique First World War Observation Post that housed the Battery Commander and his signallers who passed his orders on to the whole Battery. Under the revolving armoured turret on the top floor was the Battery's rangefinder, used for setting the direction and angle of the guns to increase accuracy.

Frankie glanced at the concrete blockhouse further along, a hexagonal pillbox with a window cut out at the top of the sea-facing wall. 'Can you imagine what it was like in there with artillery bombarding the coast in wartime? Bloody terrifying. So many lost their lives—'

'Yeah, all very sad, but that's not why we're here.'

Frankie turned to look at him. 'Why are we here then, guv?'

'Like I said, I think Sharpe may have missed something.'

David bent down and picked up a small pebble that caught his eye, rolling it between finger and thumb. Thinking time. Absent-mindedly, he slipped it into his pocket. His action reminded Frankie of seaside trips she'd made as a young 'un, feet clad in brightly coloured wellington boots, armed with fishing net, bucket and spade. Paddling in rock pools, collecting stones and shells along this coastline with her dad and her sisters was a favourite pastime of hers, Rae's and especially Joanna's. Good times. A memory to hold on to when things got tough. David hadn't noticed the excursion into her past, but his expression grew more serious, prompting her to ask if she'd missed something.

'Not sure,' he said. 'You saw the crime scene stills. Catherine was slightly built, easily overcome. She was lying here on the grass. Car keys in her pocket. No purse. She was successful, the youngest victim at just twenty-eight, but think about that for a second. So far, we've been working on the assumption that our punter has been choosing his victims randomly, but he didn't pick Catherine out on the day she died. He couldn't have. She'd taken a walk on the beach and was dressed appropriately, not a hint of slap, no outward sign of wealth to ring her as a target. She was unrecognisable from her celebrity photos. The killer must've known her . . . or knew of her.'

'I take your point, but she didn't live here, David. She was visiting her parents up the road.'

'True, but she was a talk-show host and after-dinner speaker. He could easily have seen her picture in the press, watched her on TV, heard her on the radio. She was a regular contributor: bright, intelligent, often controversial, specialising in women's issues. Her feminist ideology made her very popular. The opposite is equally true.'

'Marmite.'

'Exactly. Opinionated women in the public eye have their critics. Ambitious feminists are constantly under attack. They put up with all sorts of shit, physically and virtually. It might be worth pursuing.'

'Guv, Sharpe had a good look at the issues she supported and found nothing. Couldn't she just have been unlucky, wrong time, wrong place?'

'All options, Frank. My predecessor may have done a job on her email and social media accounts, but how thorough was he? As I said, his head was all over the place. He was under immense pressure, dealing with a multiple-murder investigation with no time to sort out his domestic life – and the team we inherited hardly inspires confidence, does it? Even Bright admits we got the thin end of the wedge. We need to be absolutely certain that there were no disgruntled males bothering or stalking Catherine. We owe her that much.'

Frankie was nodding, saddened by the loss of someone so young. 'When we took the case, I listened to her on BBC Radio 4's *Late Night Woman's Hour*. She was hilarious.'

'Homework?'

'That's what I'm paid for. You want me to take another look at her antecedent history and social media account?'

'I'll put Dunne on it. He's got nothing better to do than shout his mouth off.'

Frankie went on to voice her uncertainty that Dunne should be involved at all.

David cut off her objections. 'He knows I'm watching him, Frank. He won't dare put a foot wrong while his position within the MIT is under scrutiny. Trust me. He's exactly who we need right now.'

Frankie couldn't disagree more.

24

Frankie's phone rang as they left the beach. She stopped walking to answer it, her focus on the colourfully painted beach huts on Blyth promenade. There were twenty in all, ten per row, each with a little outside space, room for a deckchair or two, fenced off individually to keep dogs and toddlers safe. Beyond them, wind turbines rolled majestically in the distance under a deep blue sky punctuated with fluffy white clouds. This was holiday heaven for those free to enjoy the sunshine.

Abbott came on the line: 'It's me, can you speak?'

'Yeah, what's up?'

'The receiver came across an email she thinks needs immediate action. It was passed to us by British Transport Police—'

She cut him off. 'Would this be Rebecca Hill?'

'You a mind reader now?'

She laughed. 'No, I raised it with the guv'nor this morning—'

'There's no action on the system.' Dick sounded confused.

'There won't be. I did nothing with it. It doesn't fall in line with his policy.'

'Then maybe his policy is wrong. Hill fits the profile, Frank. Can't you give the boss a nudge, see if he'll reconsider?' Abbott wasn't dissing David – he'd never do that – just offering an alternative point of view Frankie happened to agree with.

'OK, I have her details on my phone. I'll have a word with him.'

'Will you get back to me? I'm happy to take care of the interview—'

'No, leave it with me. We're out and about. Depending on the guv'nor's take on it, we might swing by there on the way back to Middle Earth.'

She hung up.

Stone was curious. 'Who was that?'

'Dick. Remember the chemical engineer we talked about this morning? She's caused a bit of excitement in the incident room.'

'Is this a set-up, Frank?'

'No, I swear!'

Rebecca Hill lived on Moorfield in High West Jesmond. It was a terrace property with kerb appeal, circa 1910, much sought after with south-facing views of the Little Moor, an urban green space registered as common land, a site of conservation interest, much loved by those lucky enough to live there. It was a handsome double-fronted Victorian villa, very close to the city, yet with a definite semi-rural feel.

When Hill opened the door, Frankie took care of the introductions.

On the way in, the smell of bacon wafted along the hallway from the kitchen where a female who couldn't sing was belting out Whitney Houston's 'I Wanna Dance With Somebody'.

Guessing that the girl was probably wearing earphones, unaware of strangers entering the house, Frankie smiled. 'It's hard not to sing along to that one.'

'Kids!' Rolling her eyes, the chemical engineer excused herself and disappeared.

Stone was sporting a wide grin.

'What?' Frankie whispered. 'There's nowt like a bit of Whitney when you fancy it, though you probably prefer Alan Price.' She started humming 'The Jarrow Song'.

Stone laughed, pointing at her. 'Grow up. She might hear you.'

'You think?'

Hill was giving someone what for in the next room.

'Fine,' Frankie said. 'I forgot the next line anyway.' She

142

made a crazy face, her best ear listening at the kitchen door. There were hushed angry voices behind it.

'Sorry.' Hill was back. 'I thought she'd taken her breakfast up to bed.'

She showed the detectives into a smart living room, beautifully done out. With an eye for style, the homeowner had managed to retain period features and yet had created an airy, contemporary interior: light colour scheme, blinds at the windows, minimal furniture. It was a world away from the reds, golds, greens and heavy drapes of the Victorian era.

With her mind now firmly on the job, Frankie studied the woman as she took a seat. Physically and mentally smart, Hill was keen to assist the investigation. Stone had asked Frankie to lead the interview. She'd found the witness after all and he wanted her to take the credit.

'Thank you for ringing in,' she began.

'I hope I'm not wasting your time. I know how busy you must be.'

'I understand you reported an incident to British Transport Police some weeks ago. I gather you were travelling.'

'That's right, though they didn't follow it up.' Hill was clearly irritated. 'When I saw reports of what had happened to that poor woman they found close to the railway line, I got in touch with them again and was directed to your control room. I was happy with that. British Transport Police didn't want to know.'

'What prompted the initial call?'

'A horrible experience. I was on my way back from a business meeting on the eight o'clock from King's Cross, an uneventful journey until the train stopped at Durham. A man boarded there. He was young, late twenties–early thirties. I've come across some odd characters in my time, but this creep freaked me out.' She looked uncomfortable talking about it. 'I'd had a bit of a run-in with the train guard over my ticket and she'd come back to tell me that I had to pay extra because

I'd boarded the wrong train. Like it matters! Anyway, this man boarded at the far end of the carriage and walked towards me, taking a good look at every female passenger as he passed through, before his eyes fell on me. He took a seat facing me.'

'Did he speak to anyone? To you?' A bit of wishful thinking on David's part.

'No. It sounds stupid now I'm telling you, but he had such an intense stare that it made my skin crawl.'

'But, technically, he'd done nothing against the law?'

'Not that I could mention to the guard, especially after we'd had words over the ticket. She'd have told me to take a hike. But the more I thought about this young man's fucked-up behaviour, the more worried I became, especially after the recent murders.' She looked at Frankie, as if she needed a woman's perspective to add weight to her argument. 'It's hard to explain. Believe me, I don't frighten easily, but this man's interest was sinister. I couldn't wait to get off.'

Frankie was angry. No wonder women and girls rarely came forward to report intimidation if all they got was the brush-off. When she was a teenager it had happened to her once or twice on public transport and the guard, and on one occasion the bus driver, looked at her as if she were stupid, a silly bitch who should dress more appropriately if she didn't want to attract the attention of men. The memory made her seethe so much that her fingernails bit into the palms of her hands. What if her sister had asked for help and been turned away? Frankie's heart was hammering in her chest now. It felt like it might burst through her rib cage. Her mouth had gone dry.

It's what you were born to do.

Frankie took a long, deep breath, her father's words giving her strength to leave the footpath she'd visited behind his back every year since she was eleven years old. That was one secret she could never share with him. Pushing that thought away, she climbed back into Hill's living room where it was safe and warm, ready to resume the interview, but David had noticed her hesitation and was already filling the void.

'Did the man stay on the train?' he asked.

'No,' Hill said. 'The service terminated in Newcastle.'

'Did he attempt to follow you?' He wanted chapter and verse.

Hill looked out of the sash windows over the lush green moor. It seemed to give her comfort. There was no doubt in Frankie's mind that she was reliving, in technicolour, her experience that night, worrying for her safety, and the safety of the young woman they had heard singing a moment ago. The voice of the redhead they had encountered at The Feathers arrived in Frankie's head: *I have a daughter . . . She has a right to feel safe.*

And the killer wasn't choosy when it came to age.

No female was safe.

'Ms Hill?' David was still waiting for an answer.

'I didn't wait around to look,' Hill said. 'I usually take the Metro but that night my partner came to the station to collect me. I'd been away a few days.'

'Did he see the man?'

'She . . . and no, we left immediately. I was pretty shaken up.'

Stone looked embarrassed. 'Excuse the assumption.'

The woman shrugged. 'I'm used to it.'

'Still . . .' David looked like he wanted to dig a hole and climb into it.

Frankie came to his aid: 'I don't suppose you still have your tickets?'

Hill shook her head. 'I have the email, if that's any good to you.'

'That's perfect.'

The engineer pulled her laptop towards her and printed off the email. Frankie took it from her. The booking summary detailed an Advance Single (first-class) ticket costing £285.50, bought on her company credit card over a month ago, the journey scheduled to take place shortly after the death of the third victim, scientist Margaret Robson: mother, grandmother and a leading light in her field of expertise.

Frankie passed the email to David.

He scanned the document and looked up at the witness. 'Your reservation suggests that you were due to arrive into Newcastle at 22.54, that you were in coach M, seat fifty-five, a forward-facing single seat.'

'I always book that seat if it's available. I prefer to sit on my own, so I can work. Lucky for me the seat was unoccupied, even though I was on the wrong train.'

Frankie pointed at the laptop on Hill's knee. 'May I?'

Hill passed it over. 'Can I get you some tea?'

'We're fine, thanks.' Frankie opened the Virgin East Coast app, Stone looking over her shoulder, so close she could feel his breath on her neck. To find what she was after, she keyed in a journey she had no intention of taking and waited for the seating plan to load. She got up and took it to Hill. 'So, you were in seat fifty-five. Can you indicate where the man was sitting?'

'This one.' Hill pointed it out. No hesitation.

'Seat thirty-six?' Frankie had to be sure.

Hill was nodding. 'It gave him a good view of me, as you can see.'

'And vice versa. Describe him for me.'

'He was white. Brown hair. Piercing blue eyes.'

'He really rattled you, didn't he?'

'You could say that.'

'You're doing great, Rebecca. Do you remember what other seats were occupied?'

'Not many. My end of the carriage was almost empty beyond York. Both forty-seven and forty-nine were taken when we left London, but the occupants got out at York, I think . . .' She hesitated. 'Actually, I couldn't swear to that. It could've been Darlington.'

Frankie made a note. 'What about the four-seater table opposite you and the one in front of that: seats forty-three to forty-six, fifty-one to fifty-four?'

'Also vacated at York. As I said, the carriage was quiet at my end. I was petrified when he moved closer because there were other seats available. It was very intimidating.'

'I can imagine.' Frankie sat back down, taking the computer with her. 'Could you estimate how tall he was?'

'About my height.'

'And you are?'

'Five six.'

'How do you know this if you were both sitting?' Frankie asked. 'It's difficult to estimate when people aren't standing. You said yourself he was a few rows in front of you. I'd imagine it's hard to guess height, let alone see eye colour from that distance.'

'I need the computer plan to explain.' Hill got up and moved towards them. With her focus elsewhere, David gave Frankie a nod.

He stepped aside to allow Hill in.

'When I got up to leave, he did too,' she said. 'Fortunately for me, the man in *this* seat stood up.' She indicated which one on the screen: seat thirty-nine. 'He was much taller and struggling with an overly large suitcase. Anyway, he was blocking the creep from getting to me. I glanced over my shoulder to see if he was still behind me or making his way to the other door. I had no wish to meet him on the platform. That's when I saw his eyes. They were fixed on me and level. He was smallish for a bloke. I remember thinking that, if he tried something on, at least my knee would reach his balls.'

Frankie smiled and, for the first time since their arrival, so did Hill.

'Do you remember anything else about him?' David said.

'I remember everything about him. He was wearing a dark raincoat. No logo on it as I recall.'

'No hat?'

'A black beanie and heavy framed glasses.'

Frankie bristled. 'How did you see his hair colour if he was wearing a beanie?'

'He had thin dark sideburns, neatly trimmed.'

Or he wanted her to think that.

Frankie didn't dwell on it, though it could have been a disguise. She fired off another question. 'Do you think you might recognise him if you saw him again?'

'Without a doubt. I can't get those eyes out of my head.'

Stone and Oliver exchanged a hopeful glance.

'You've been very helpful,' David said. 'I'll send someone round to take a formal statement and it may be necessary for us to visit again.'

'No problem. I hope you catch him soon.'

Frankie wondered if the woman walking her out had been a target of the man the press had dubbed The Sleeper. She'd never voice that theory, but Hill was a definite profile match with the other victims. More importantly, the general physical size of the creep she'd encountered on the train was identical to the description Annie Parks had given for the man hanging around at the fourth crime scene. As the bolt on the door slid home, it occurred to Frankie that the engineer may have come closer to the killer than she knew.

25

He'd thought about sinking a pint at the Commissioner's Quay Inn, but he didn't fancy that. He needed to stay focused. A clear head. An even clearer direction. He crossed the road, heading to a seat shaped like an upturned boat where he wouldn't be seen. Pulling his beanie down over his ears, he stared out at the North Sea, lifted his binoculars as a salvage vessel chugged into Blyth, a marine services boat following in its wake. A larger ship was berthed in the foreground, the ID on its side confirmation that it was far from Dordrecht in the western Netherlands. He knew about boats.

After a stunning day, the sky was layered like a rainbow, strips of blue, pink and purple reflected in the water beneath, the black silhouette of a single wind turbine directly in his eyeline. The motion of its giant blades and the sound of waves slapping against the harbour wall aided concentration. His mind wandered for a moment or two, then it was off and running.

It was time to turn the tide.

He did his best thinking by water. The sea air and the expanse of sky made him feel like anything was possible. And it was. In no time at all, a plan began to take shape. It was beyond brilliant, so obvious it made him wonder why he hadn't thought of it before.

Closer to home . ...

That was the way to go.

How ironic would it be if he managed to capture the attention of the police by taking out one of theirs? There were so many female officers to choose from, several who'd fit the bill, women who possessed the same attributes as Steph. Formidable was the adjective others used to describe them. He could think of something better. Something less complimentary. Top brass loathed them. The wimps that worked for them trembled in their presence.

Well, *he* was no coward.

In his head, they were mere obstructions standing in his way, cannon fodder with the potential to improve his circumstances over time. Yes, if he took this route, maybe the press, the public and the MIT would realise that he was serious. And, with any luck, Steph, dear darling Steph, might take note too.

Mind you, it would be tricky taking out an officer equipped with techniques in self-defence. No room for error. If he were to achieve it, more planning would be required. What a coup de grâce it would be if he could pull it off. He would choose a woman of stature, someone popular, an officer everyone would miss, one who'd make the most impact. He could almost hear the Chief giving condolences to the family, vowing to throw every resource at the case.

Yup, this plan of his definitely required more thought.

Walking concentrated the mind. He got up, the ball bearings rattling from the spray can in his pocket, a quick glance over his shoulder. It was risky returning to the beach – the first crime scene – but he had a job to do, so he wandered off in that direction, joining others out for an evening stroll. When he got home, he'd log on and do some research. He'd make a list of probable candidates. He almost chuckled as his plan clicked into place. The police took every opportunity to bang their drum. If they could push a female in front of the camera, all the better – even a dead one.

26

Stone and Oliver approached Middle Earth more buoyant than they'd left it, Dunne and his nonsense overtaken by matters far more serious. It had been a good couple of hours. Frankie felt almost high. It had been a long time since David had seen her this animated. She was out of the car before it came to a stop, keen to get inside and share the positive news with their MIT crew, such as it was. Swiping her card to gain entry to the back of the building, she held open the door.

'We've made real progress today.' She let the door go. 'I was in a foul mood when we went to Blyth—'

'Really?' David joked. 'I never noticed.'

She punched his arm, setting off at a brisk pace for the incident room, her enthusiasm transferring to her feet. 'What I was going to say, before I was so rudely interrupted, was that I was expecting very little. But your observations were spot on, guv.' The formality of rank was like a light coming on automatically each time she stepped over the station threshold. 'We came away with so much more, and now we've seen Rebecca Hill, I think we're finally on to something.'

'I hope you're right.' He could hardly keep up.

'Mind you, I'm scratching my head about the timing of the offences, aren't you? I mean, why do three in close succession, then take a break? Do creeps like him take a holiday like the rest of us?' Without stopping for an answer, Frankie vaulted the stairs, two at a time, glancing at him as she reached the top. 'Am I overthinking this?' He opened his mouth to speak, then shut it again as she carried on. 'Maybe he just didn't see anyone he fancied knocking off for a while. Sorry, that was a bad choice of words. What I'm saying is, once these arseholes get a taste for it, they usually can't help themselves. I don't mean they can't stop, in the psychological sense, I mean they don't want to. It's a control thing. They feed off the power. They like the way it makes them feel.'

'I agree.' David pushed through a double door into the corridor. 'That's why most of them go on killing until they get caught.'

'Not that I'm complaining that he slowed down,' Frankie said. 'I'd hate for there to be an escalation, but you see what I'm driving at. These offenders are rare, but not rare enough. I'd like to wipe these men off the face of the earth.'

Frankie stopped talking as a probationer in uniform politely stood aside to let them pass. David acknowledged his greeting with a nod and carried on walking, the squeak of new boots receding behind him. It lifted his spirits to see the young officer so keen to impress. It felt like yesterday when he joined up, throwing on a blue suit that made him feel self-conscious but also ten feet tall.

'That was amusing?' Frankie had misread his walk down Memory Lane.

'Not in the slightest. Sorry, I was somewhere else.'

'Did you even hear what I just said?'

'I did, and I apologise for going off-piste. For what it's worth, I couldn't agree more. One offender like ours is one too many. That's where we come in, although you can't apply logic where there is none. We'll catch him if we keep at it. We made progress today in Blyth and got lucky finding Hill, though we can't be sure that the man she saw and the one we're hunting are one and the same. In the meantime, we'll be re-examining the other crime scenes, but first we need to regroup.' David stopped outside the incident room. 'I asked Abbott to put the team on standby for a mini briefing. Sharpe's lot will be waiting, daggers drawn.'

Frankie grimaced. 'Office politics are such a pain.'

'Want me to fetch your Kevlar vest?'

Stifling a grin, she pushed the door open.

When asked for an update, Abbott told them he had news and was given the nod to share it. He got to his feet to see and be seen. 'We now have confirmation that three men boarded the train with Annie and Joanna in Newcastle. The good news is, they're all season ticket holders and have already been spoken to. The bad news: it didn't take us anywhere. Unfortunately, they all travelled in Annie's carriage. They remember her because she's unsteady on her pins, but none recalled seeing Joanna, either getting on or off the train. I was gutted, to be honest. Anyway, not to be outdone, I checked CCTV at the Metro Centre, which was in working order.'

'They were spared the power cut?' David asked.

'Yes, and I found evidence that two males boarded the train there, one of whom was smallish and loosely fits the description of the bloke we're interested in.' He glanced at the SIO. 'There's a copy in the evidence locker, guv. There's no clear image, I'm afraid. He's a pro and kept his head down to avoid security cameras.'

'Of course he did . . .' Frankie said. 'It's classic behaviour. I have a mate on air support. Only the other day he was telling me how obvious it is to spot who he's looking for when he's in the air. Ninety-nine per cent of people – the innocent ones – look up when the eye in the sky passes overhead. Those with something to hide, don't. It's the same with CCTV.'

David agreed. 'I want all Metro Centre cameras, inside and out, trawled to see if we can spot this guy—'

'That'll be a waste of time and resources,' one of Dunne's cronies said, leaning back in his chair. 'Pound to a penny, he'd gone there to dump his car and never went inside.'

'Thanks for volunteering,' Frankie said.

The detective groaned.

Abbott was still on his feet, steamed up about something, unusual for a detective of his experience. He had the face of a rookie on a first assignment. 'The conductor remembers the

IP and two men in the rear carriage. It was quite a night. Joanna was desperate to get home and said as much when he checked her ticket. Ditto, one of the males. The other was asleep, a ticket on the seat beside him. The conductor checked it and let him be. A ruse, I suspect, if this was our man. And here's the interesting bit . . . Just before the train pulled into Stocksfield, remembering that Annie needed help getting off, the conductor left the driver's cab to assist her and when he did his rounds again to check for new passengers, neither the sleeping man or Joanna was there.'

'What about the remaining passenger?'

'He stayed on board until the train terminated its journey in Carlisle.' Abbott was really rocking now. 'I also spoke to the train driver, guv. There's never more than one or two folks boarding the westbound train from Stocksfield at that time of night – but, on that night there were none. And if that's not enough to convince you that the guy who got off is our offender, I may have something that will.'

'Oh?' David said.

From the expressions on the faces of the officers facing him, Abbott could tell that the SIO wasn't the only one intrigued. 'The conductor is sure that the ticket on the seat beside the sleeping passenger was for a journey to Hexham, which means he got off earlier than anticipated. Who pays for a journey they don't take?'

There was silence in the incident room.

'He remembers that?' Mitch was unconvinced.

'I was sceptical too and questioned him at length,' Abbott said. 'But he gave a satisfactory explanation. Passengers often fall asleep and overshoot their stop. He was intending to give this guy a nudge before Hexham in case he ended up in Carlisle. It happens a lot, especially on the evening trains. All part of the service, apparently.'

'Good man,' Frankie said. 'Any description?'

'Dark clothing, hat and glasses. That's the best he could do.'

Stone and Oliver were both on the same track, Hill's interview still fresh in their minds.

'It's enough to convince me,' Frankie said. 'No mention of size or height?'

'Nothing that's any use to us.' Abbott grimaced. 'Medium build, he said. Beyond that, he hasn't a clue. He never saw the guy get on or off, just found him slumped in his seat when he passed through checking tickets. He thought he might have had one too many before boarding.' Dick turned his gaze on the SIO. 'The Sleeper is an apt name as it turns out, guv.'

Frankie glanced at David. 'He's everything we said he was: an opportunist, a watcher, a thinker. Maybe he knew the power was out further west. There is an app for most things these days. He parks at the Metro Centre, buys a ticket for Hexham and falls on his feet when he sees Joanna. We'll struggle to ID him, I reckon, but maybe we can ID the guy who remained on the train. When Dick was talking, it made me think. The description Annie and the conductor gave could fit thousands of men. On its own, it's not enough. I know we got a lot from Rebecca Hill, but this Carlisle passenger may have got an even closer look at him, spotted something we're unaware of. Potentially, he's a vital witness.'

'I'm on it,' Abbott said. 'We have a clear image of him. And he's a season ticket holder, so it shouldn't be too difficult.'

'Who's Rebecca Hill when she's at home?' Dunne asked. 'Never heard of her.'

'Then take your head out of your arse,' Abbott said. 'We discussed her this morning!'

Giving Dunne a black look, David stood up as Abbott sat down. 'Frankie and I have not been idle.' He updated the team on the interview they had just come from, recounting Hill's distressing experience on the Durham train, adding brown hair, possibly sideburns and blue eyes to the description of the man they so desperately wanted to speak to.

'She got a good look at him,' Frankie added. 'If this was our

155

man, and we both think it might be, then it's worth getting an e-fit prepared.' Electronic facial identification was a revolutionary computerised technique, used in ninety per cent of UK forces.

'Action that,' David said. 'And make sure they know we need it urgently.' He scanned the room. 'While Frankie and I were in Blyth, it occurred to us that this is where our offender may live.' He explained his reasoning, pointing out that it was unlikely that the killer would have recognised the first victim, Catherine Bennett, if she was casually dressed and free of cosmetics. 'Whoever killed her may have picked her out from her TV show or in the press, but we now have eyewitness statements that suggest she's around the same age as the man we're looking for. Mitch, I want you to go over her antecedent history with a fine toothcomb. She may have gone to school with him or known him in the past. She was brought up in the area.'

'Everyone knows she was born in Blyth,' Dunne said. 'She's probably the only good thing to come out of the town. We completed all the usual lines of enquiry at the beginning of this investigation.'

'Then check the unusual ones,' Frankie said. 'We have more information now.'

'For fuck's sake, she's a household name with a Wiki page!'

'Yeah?' Frankie came straight back at him. 'And we all know how accurate that is. It's a great tool but, in case it passed you by, it has openly editable content, unreliable for our purposes. Only a fool would count on it.' It was a clear dig.

David backed her up.

'Where was her car found?' Frankie asked.

'In the beach car park. There was nothing flash about it that might draw the attention of the arsehole who killed her.' Dunne was grandstanding again. 'Anyway, I thought we were concentrating on Joanna.'

There was a row brewing.

David put a stop to it. 'We're concentrating. Period. That's all you need to know. Priorities are fluid, so get used to it. We now have a partial description of our target with the promise of more if we can find the Carlisle witness. Annie's sighting of this bloke was from some distance away, in the dark. She's also elderly. Her evidence is unlikely to swing a jury or cut it with a judge. The conductor on her train had little to add to what we had already, but with careful handling, we may be able to jog his memory. However, Hill's description is less sketchy and they all agree on age. It may be a long shot, delving into Catherine Bennett's past, but with what we now know, or think we know, it will shorten the odds. You have your instructions. Now get on with it.'

With that, the SIO ended the briefing.

27

Since he'd taken over the investigation from Sharpe, David had felt the heavy burden of needing to crack the case. He might be dealing with a clever offender but, for the first time since he'd been handed the flagging investigation, he felt upbeat and on track, and so did Frankie. With Hill's help, he hoped to get a decent composite image of the offender, but that would take time. If he could find the Carlisle traveller too, that would be an unexpected bonus. Saving lives was the only thing that mattered.

Frankie had been silent in the car, reading up on the second victim, familiarising herself with the actions Sharpe had issued and what progress had been made into finding the killer of Alison Brody. Pathologist Beth Collingwood had been the one who'd linked her death to Catherine Bennett, having found the same microscopic fragments in both victims' neck wounds.

Closing the file, Frankie turned to face David. 'Initially, I'd wondered if he was substituting the victims for someone else, someone he'd fallen out with perhaps or is jealous of: mother, wife, girlfriend. The problem is, the victims are not physically alike, neither are they the same age group. It's definitely their status that is getting up his nose. Ambitious high-flyers, all of them. That's what he can't cope with, but why?'

'Who knows what goes through the heads of these morons,' David said. 'And if it is a status thing, who's to say that said mother, wife or girlfriend isn't a high-flyer?' As Frankie mulled this over, he turned left off Dipe Lane into Boldon Cemetery, parking his SUV in front of the gatehouse. A blue tractor stood idle on the driveway, presumably the modern method of grave-digging, its glaring colour incongruous in such peaceful surroundings. He didn't voice the fact that it angered him so much, but somehow it did. Grabbing a bottle of water from the door pocket, he climbed out of the four-by-four and took a drink, his eyes scanning grounds bathed in sunshine.

Frankie wandered across to a noticeboard she'd seen on her way in, then turned to face him. 'Well, this explains why he chose to kill Alison much earlier in the evening than the others.' She pointed at the opening times. 'She was murdered on a weekday. They close at eight p.m.' Glancing over her left shoulder, she said: 'C'mon, it's this way.'

They walked away from the main gate.

A path led from the entrance, a right-hand dogleg at the top. A long, paved avenue fringed by trees on either side ran the full length of the burial ground. There was no one around. Alison had been found by the relative of someone who had long since passed away. The eastern edge of the graveyard backed onto the village's golf course. This was the older part of the cemetery, darker and less populated than the other side, significantly so. Some of the gravestones were crooked and unreadable, many of the plots obliterated by overgrown ivy. Others stood straight and proud, one with a gothic top catching her eye, its epitaph making her heart ache. There was no bible passage, quote or poetry verse, merely a heartfelt inscription from a loved one. It made her think of Alan Cosgrove and his children and the families of the other victims waiting to bury their dead.

A quick Google search explained why the ground to the left of the path was practically empty. It was marked as general, whereas other sections – Frankie had to accept, the busy ones – were consecrated. Jesus reigned here.

Where two paths crossed, she stopped walking.

'This is it,' she said.

'Where exactly?' David looked around. 'One plot looks much like any other.'

Prompted by him, she accessed crime scene photographs she'd sent to her iPhone before they left the office, preparation for what was to come. She searched the ground, took a few steps forward, a few more, comparing the images with what she could see. 'This is the one.' There was no flat or upright headstone here, just a weathered granite kerb marking out the dimensions of a large plot.

She turned the phone to face him.

David gave a nod.

What Frankie saw next sent a shiver right through her, a stone cross with a simple engraving, etched in an ornate font: *At Rest.* 'He's toying with us,' Frankie said under her breath.

David looked at her. He hadn't noticed the cross, let alone the inscription.

She pointed to it. 'This must be his idea of a joke. Maybe Dunne didn't tip off the press about The Sleeper – maybe the offender did it himself.'

David scrutinised the plot. On first inspection, it appeared to offer few clues beyond the fact that Alison had been found there, presumably accosted as she walked through the cemetery or sat on a nearby bench. Much like Joanna, who'd been dragged a short distance through a metal gate from the northern edge of a station car park, out of sight and away from the railway line. His eyes seized on something tucked into one corner of the kerbed parcel of land that made his heart race. He took a photograph before picking it up; a stone, small enough to fit comfortably in his hand, a tiny natural hole at its centre. He glanced at Frankie, the hairs on the back of his neck rising.

'What?' she said.

He held it up between finger and thumb. 'This doesn't belong here.'

She was perplexed. 'It's a stone—'

'A holey stone,' he corrected her.

'I know what it is, so what?'

'But do you know what it represents?'

'Do I need to?'

'Perhaps you do. My association with these stones is death, Frank. My nan called them Odin stones. She gave me one years ago to ward off childhood nightmares, thinking it might help me over the grief of losing my parents—'

'And did it?' Frankie had an ulterior motive for asking.

'No. It's nothing but an old wives' tale—'

'There you go then. Throw it away. We haven't got time for a lesson in folklore.'

She was about to make a move when he spoke again. 'You and I might not believe in it, but what if our offender does?' Her expression went from puzzlement to intrigue as he reached into his pocket, pulling out another stone about the same size as the first. He never said a word as he compared the two. He looked up, locking eyes with her. 'I picked this up in Blyth at the scene of Catherine Bennett's murder.'

Frankie laughed. 'You're winding me up, right?'

'No, I'm deadly serious.'

'Have you lost your mind? They're all over the beach, man!'

'Hold that thought,' he said. 'It's not just my nan who believes in such nonsense. Historically, these stones were considered powerful, worn on the person for protection, hung at doorways to ward off evil spirits, placed near a bed so the sleeper remained free of nightmares.'

Frankie shuddered.

Just hearing the word 'sleeper' made her skin crawl.

And still her boss wasn't done. 'You'd expect to find a stone like this on a beach – they're all over the north-east coast – but not in an inland village. Remember what Beth Collingwood said about the victims having been lowered to the ground following their deaths, like some care had been taken—'

'You're saying this is a calling card?'

'I'm saying it's a possibility.'

Frankie wasn't yet on board. 'We're dealing with a fruitcake who has no stop button, David. He's not fallen into the trap of leaving anything of himself at the crime scenes—'

'Bar these, if I'm right.'

'Why would he?'

'That's for you and me to find out.'

Frankie was shaking her head. 'Will you take a friendly piece of advice from someone who cares about you? This is a theory too far. If you feed it back to the team, you'll be laughed out of the office.'

He shrugged. 'I've got broad shoulders.'

'Great! You're going to need them.'

'You're right to be sceptical, but people place all manner of memorabilia close to the graves of loved ones,' he argued. 'Flowers, seashells, baby booties. You name it, you'll find it. All I'm saying is, what might seem odd to you and me could make perfect sense to the man we're hunting.'

'Except his victims aren't loved ones.'

'I didn't say I had all the answers, Frank.'

She took a few paces away and then back. 'Even if what you say is true, that's not a lot of use, unless we can work out what they mean.'

'Then help me do that. At least hold off rubbishing the idea until we can examine the other two scenes.'

'Excuse my lack of confidence, but you're not selling it to me. Strangling women and then protecting them after the event makes no sense.'

'To us,' he reminded her. 'Frankie, we can't afford to ignore this. It could be a personal stamp, a ritual unique to him, an integral part of his behaviour.'

Her father's voice arrived in her head.

Everything you see is a signpost.

162

28

David bagged his dodgy evidence on the off-chance that the Odin stones were somehow symbolic, serving the emotional or psychological needs of the man they were desperate to apprehend. With his words ringing in her ears, Frankie followed him to the car and they left the cemetery heading for Middle Earth. Having found a stone at the first and second crime scenes, she was content to reserve judgement, but had a mind to take a drive to the third and fourth deposition sites to satisfy herself that none had been left there. Neither location was near the coast and, as David had been at pains to point out, it would be weird to find such an item inland. Finding two could be a coincidence, three or four was a different ballgame entirely.

With this uppermost in their minds, they drove out of the cemetery and back to the incident room, David telling her to keep quiet about their find. It might turn out to be unimportant but, if the opposite was true, they needed to be careful. 'Until we find out whether or not we have an informer on our team, trust no one.'

'That's my default position,' Frankie said. 'You should know that by now.'

'Does that extend to me?'

She grinned. 'No exceptions.'

Frankie hated loose ends. She was keen to rule David's half-arsed theory in or out. Sadly, it would be dark soon, so she took off her jacket and sat down at her desk. Left with no alternative but to wait till morning, she logged on to her computer and did a bit of research, finding pages and pages of material on the stones David had found. Across the world, the meaning of these fascinating objects differed, as did the name. She came across an example of this in Dorset, where they were known as Hag stones, used as protective charms against malevolent witchcraft by the county's fishermen.

'Yeah right,' she mumbled.

Uninterested in myth and legend, she clicked off Google to check on HOLMES, locating the stills and videos for the third and fourth incidents to see if she could spot any similar stones. She was concentrating hard and hadn't noticed the hum of the conversation dying around her, or the fact that the team were packing up for the day. It wasn't until Abbott dimmed the lights and approached her desk an hour later that she looked up.

Apart from him, the incident room was empty.

Frankie loved having the office to herself and often stayed late to clear paperwork, though her involvement in this multiple-murder investigation had scuppered that tradition. Overtime was on everyone's wish list, but the incident budget had already overrun considerably. A few motivated detectives were operating on a timescale of goodwill to keep the momentum up.

Dick was one of them.

Moving her work out of the way, he perched on the edge of her desk, handing her a brew. Thanking him, she put the mug down and sat back in her seat, hands behind her head. They had worked together for most of her career. He'd been her supervisor when they were in uniform, transferring to the CID a year or two before she passed her sergeants' exam. She'd followed him in three years later. Working on a Major Incident Team was an ambition they shared. She was hoping that his temporary secondment would be made permanent. He was worth ten guys like Dunne.

'Are you OK?' he said. 'You look exhausted.'

'It's been a tough day.'

'Yeah, I was there, remember?' He gave a wry smile. 'Looked

like you were holding your own until the guv'nor intervened.'

'I didn't mean Dunne, you idiot. He's the least of my worries. I meant the fucking ghost we're trying to find. How could he move in and out of four areas without being seen?'

'He has been seen—'

'Yeah, by an old lady who couldn't give us a description worth a jot.'

'The e-fit might help—'

'With what? I know I was the one who suggested it – and I'm sorry to sound so negative – but it'll be of the man Hill saw on a Durham train, miles from any of our crime scenes, who may or may not have anything to do with our enquiry. We can hardly lock him up for leering at a fellow passenger, can we? Even if it is our guy, we need something to tie him to one of these women and, so far, we have zilch. The guy we're looking for has struck on both sides of the Tyne, in the countryside and at the coast. He's killing young and old. And, more to the point, he's mobile—'

'Am I arguing?'

'No, but we've extrapolated hundreds of hours of CCTV data from in and around the crime scenes and come up with Jack shit. We assume he has a car but have no idea what type because the slimy bastard also uses public transport. If he has access to a company pool car, I'm betting he takes a different one each time he strikes. I have no doubt we'll catch him, and I think he has something to prove, but we're no further forward in finding out what his motivation is than we are locating him. No wonder Sharpe grabbed his money and ran. Right now, I feel like doing the same.'

'Wow, you are tired—'

'Aren't you?'

'I'm allowed, I'm older than you.'

Frankie smiled. Her rant was over.

Dick had always been her sounding board. Right now, his eyes were on her computer screen. 'Need a hand?'

'No, you get off before your lass reports you missing.'

'She won't notice. We've got the grandkids for a sleepover.' He pointed at her monitor, more specifically at the blown-up images of the third crime scene she'd been studying. 'Looking for something in particular?'

'Just looking.' She felt guilty being so vague.

He stood up. 'Don't stay too late. There won't be any extra zeros on your payslip.'

She smiled. 'Get out of here and kiss your grandkids for me.'

'OK, see you tomorrow.'

Frankie watched him leave, hoping that David would knock off too. His office light was still on and she worried that he was leaving his nephew too often to his own devices. He couldn't help the lad get over his father's death remotely. On top of that, he was taking the investigation more person- ally than perhaps he should, burying himself in work as a diversion from a complicated home life, pushing himself to the extent that she feared he might crack.

On the back of losing Jane, his brother's sudden death had hit him hard. And when Ben turned up, begging for a place to stay, his timing couldn't have been worse. Deep down, David still blamed his nephew for Luke's death. The lad had been admitted to hospital, having collapsed after a heavy session of drugs and booze. Luke was on his way to collect him when a lorry wiped him out. Unable to forgive Ben, David rejected him outright initially, which angered Frankie to the point of insubordination. Consequently, their working relationship had taken a dive. It was on an even keel now that David had seen sense, but he wasn't making a lot of effort at home as far as she could tell.

With that worrying thought lingering, she called Ben, one eye on David's office door. Frankie had become close to the teenager. Closer, it had to be said, than his uncle. The call went to voicemail, so she sent a text: *Everything OK?*

An immediate reply: *Not sure.*

Anything I need to know?

Depends.

On what? Stop being cryptic.

Has David eaten?

You cooking?

As if.

Then why ask?

I just scoffed the entire contents of his fridge. ☺

You're in trouble, mister. xx

Frankie chuckled to herself. Ben was challenging, but there was no bad in him. Physically, he reminded her of someone, but she couldn't for the life of her think who. She put down her mobile, her attention straying back to her computer screen. Clicking through the stills, she studied each one, finding nothing out of the ordinary at the third crime scene and she'd already visited the fourth. The more she thought about it, the more convinced she became that she had to go in person. There was simply no substitute for scene visits.

29

Frankie texted her father before she left the office. There was food on tap when she arrived at her parents' home, a home-made cottage pie – Frankie's favourite dish and her mother's speciality – left warming in the oven, accompanied by fresh vegetables from her granddad's allotment. As she tucked in, she thought of David's empty fridge, Ben's text bringing a smile to her face. Her boss wouldn't go hungry. She'd tipped him off before heading home, principally to avoid another row between him and his nephew, partly because he deserved a hearty meal after the shift he'd put in.

When she'd finished eating, she thanked her mum, took a shower and put on her PJs, her thoughts immediately return-ing to work. Having come late to the investigation – she'd yet to visit the scene of Margaret Robson's death – she had some reading to do before she turned in. Like all the victims, Margaret was a high-profile figure who worked in North Ty-neside, the co-founder of an international, ground-breaking research organisation involved in the growth of human stem cells.

Such a waste of talent.

This had been a woman trying to make a difference.

Frankie spent an hour reading up on her. She'd lived in Morpeth, a bustling, historic market town around twenty miles from Middle Earth. Many of the stills Frankie had ex-amined before she left the incident room were replicated in the file. Despite her best efforts, she hadn't been able to find an Odin stone on digital or hard copy images, or anything resembling one, placed on or near the body. It made her think of the second victim, David's unexpected find and whether it had any evidential value.

David sat on the sofa, turning his Odin stone over and over in his hand, his mind on the two locked in his drawer back at base. He'd already checked the evidence log and there were no stones of any description mentioned there. Like Frankie, he was keen to check out crime scenes three and four to see if any more could be found. She was right though, his discovery in the graveyard at Boldon was probably coincidental and wouldn't lead anywhere.

On the other side of the room, Ben had his earphones in listening to music so that David could work, a consideration he appreciated. An hour ago, the teenager had been suitably contrite for having cleared the fridge, until his eyes homed in on the carry-out in his uncle's hand. Frankie had been his Get Out of Jail card. Guessing that Ben would have room for more nosh, David had brought enough for two. For the first time in a fortnight, they'd sat down and eaten together, out of cartons their joint ancestor would never have approved of. David was an early riser, Ben the exact opposite. If eating required two people to be present, they'd have starved by now.

Taking his nephew in was history repeating itself, a big deal for both of them, but it was the least David could do for his late brother's child. For the first time since Ben had arrived, David had enjoyed his company over a beer, the odd joke, conversation that didn't involve work, although the lad continually asked about it, interested in what it was like being a cop.

Right now, it was heavy going.

Ben was growing on David. Arriving home to an empty house hadn't been easy since he'd returned to Northumberland, so accustomed was he to the buzz of London. He lived alone there too, though had never once felt isolated like he did now. He had mates, colleagues, a multi-cultural city on his doorstep, the whole wide world represented there. Pauperhaugh was different, a tiny village in the back of beyond, parochial in attitude, with few opportunities to engage with others, especially for the young. He worried that Ben would lack the stimulation of his peers if he stayed too long.

Closing the file on Margaret, Frankie reached into her bag and pulled out the one concerning Alison Brody, the second victim. Leafing through it reminded her of Boldon Cemetery and David's contention that Sharpe had missed vital clues. Her tired eyes skipped through the pages, searching for peculiarities. Alison was thirty-four, a corporate events organiser with her own company: local to the village, unmarried, childless. She was fiercely ambitious, exactly like the other victims.

'Was Alison Brody known at the golf club?' her father asked from over her shoulder. He'd crept up behind her without making a sound. He was checking up on her, poking his nose in where it didn't belong, no doubt hoping to offer the benefit of thirty years in the job, mostly as a detective.

Frankie closed the file without looking round. 'Go away, Dad. You said I could use your den tonight.'

'Don't be like that, I might be able to help.'

'You can. Go and dry the dishes for Mum.'

'That's not quite what I had in mind.' He meant well.

Frankie stifled a grin and kept her head down as he tried to coax her into involving him. Finally, she swung round to face him. 'You don't give up, do you? Why not go the whole hog, phone Granddad and ask him over? We could create a makeshift incident room. He can bring takeaway and we can discuss the case over a couple of pints and a chicken vindaloo, then have a farting competition. The guys in the office love that.'

'Y'know, that's not a bad idea!' He took his mobile from his pocket.

'Don't you dare,' she warned. 'The last thing I need is a family get-together.'

'Even me?'

'Especially you.'

He knew she didn't mean it.

He was her father, but also her mentor, best friend and confidant. Policing had been his life. Thanks to him, she had a wise head on her young shoulders, giving her the edge over her contemporaries when she chose to follow him into the job. Having his counsel when times were rough meant the world to her. He'd always been able to lift her from the doldrums. As a kid, if she got sad or in a strop, he'd make a joke and she'd collapse in a fit of giggles. The Murder Investigation Team had been humourless lately, but in his special man pad, even after the day to end all days, Frankie felt her tension melt away.

Would it hurt to let him in?

He glanced at the station clock on the wall as it clicked forward a notch, a retirement present her mum had bought in RE, a retro shop in the Tyne Valley, an in-joke because he now had time on his hands and would never again be at its beck and call. Frankie followed his gaze. It was gone ten.

'David would raise hell if he knew you were working at this hour,' he said.

'Yeah, like he won't be doing the exact same thing.'

David studied the notes he'd made before leaving the office. He'd read them several times already and it had taken him nowhere – except back to where he started. Every murder was a tragedy, but the fact that the victims were all successful meant something to the killer. Frankie thought so too. Her voice arrived in his head, words tripping off her tongue in a tone of frustration and anger: 'It's definitely their status that is getting up his nose. Ambitious high-flyers, all of them. That's what he can't cope with.' And then she'd asked the question: 'Why?'

If only he had an answer to give.

The offender was savvy. Apart from the stones David had found – the significance of which was still to be determined and amounted to a hunch at best – he'd left no clues. He'd been spotted, that much was true, but he'd been careful, keeping his head low, cancelling out any chance of using facial recognition to identify him. Detectives required an image for comparison and they didn't have one. David couldn't be sure that the man Hill had seen was the same man he was looking for. He was aware of research at Cambridge University that touted the possibility of identifying offenders under hats or through scarves. Biometric surveillance testing was a new innovation, but results fell woefully short of being able to convince a jury in a court of law.

Again, he'd gone full circle. What was it about the victims the offender had a grouse with: their money, their profile within the community, their notoriety? Maybe he was just in-sanely jealous – could it be that simple? – or down-trodden, under the thumb of someone he'd come to despise. David had put out an action to find out if his victims were part of an entrepreneurial group of women who met up on a regular basis. His team had trawled the internet, carrying out count-less enquiries without finding a link between them, beyond the fact that they were killed by the same man. It stood to reason that women not in that demographic were less at risk than those who were. That thought did nothing to relieve the intense pressure he was feeling.

'Why don't you knock it on the head,' her father said. 'You look worn out, love.'

'Yeah, well I have a lot on my plate.'

'Then let me help.' Her dad put on his best begging face. 'Was Alison known at the golf club?' he repeated.

172

'No.' She gave him a pointed look. 'Happy now?'

He pulled up a chair and sat down uninvited. She couldn't fault him on effort and he'd done his homework. 'The club is adjacent to the crime scene, isn't it?' The question was rhetorical. He knew the area like the back of his hand. 'It would've been treated as part of the house-to-house—'

'Of course!' She cut him off. 'But the outside team soon established that she wasn't an employee, known to members, committee or staff, assuming everyone interviewed told the truth. There's no suggestion that they didn't.'

'But did the house-to-house team enquire further?' He raised an eyebrow, an accusation almost. 'You know the score. Potential witnesses only answer the questions put to them.' He pointed at the file in front of her. 'Mind if I take a squint at Sharpe's pro forma?' He put a hand out in readiness to receive it. 'Oh c'mon, it's hardly Top Secret. It's not as if I've never seen one before.'

She searched the file and passed the document over. Discretion had always been her father's watchword and she'd been staring at the file contents for hours. Fresh eyes might spot something she'd missed. What harm could it do?

He speed-read the document, then looked up. 'A bit brief, isn't it? There are no questions here relating to Alison's company.'

'Yes, I noticed that too. I'll have a word with David when I get in tomorrow.' She could see he wasn't happy with her response and felt compelled to offer more. 'References to the golf club are sketchy, I admit. The file contains a list of staff and members. Alison isn't on it—'

'She wasn't known by *anyone* at the club?'

'Not according to this.' She tapped the file. 'For what it's worth, I find that odd too. Given her profession as a corporate events organiser, the club's reputation as a high-end sports venue, the fact that she lived on the doorstep practically, the house-to-house team should've examined this in much greater

173

detail to see if she was known in a professional capacity.'

'That's one of the first questions they should've asked. What kind of Mickey Mouse outfit were they running at Middle Earth?'

David was like a sponge, able to absorb huge amounts of information. That didn't mean it wouldn't take weeks to get properly up to speed on the three cases he'd inherited from Sharpe. Without the benefit of attending the first three crime scenes with the bodies in situ, raising actions and following up on specific enquiries in the crucial first few hours of those murder investigations, he was working on hearsay and what had been logged in the system without knowing if it was factually correct. That wouldn't do: Catherine Bennett, Alison Brody and Margaret Robson deserved better.

David drew in a breath.

Frankie was wrestling with the very same issue. This was part of their problem, why they had struggled to find their feet. In an ideal world, they would have put their heads together, consulted over staff, assembled the best team for the job – a dedicated group of detectives who'd cross-reference every scrap of information arriving in the incident room. As it was, they had been forced to rely on a statement reader, a male detective pushing forty, whom neither of them had met before. It was his job to check for inconsistencies in evidence as statements came in. Fortunately, Frankie had been able to vouch for the receiver, a female detective trained by her father early in her career. She was the office anchor in the pressure-cooker environment of the incident room. David knew of her reputation before he took on the job of SIO.

Frankie's dad apologised for taking a pop at her. 'Was an action issued to scrutinise Alison Brody's company business?'

Frankie nodded. 'It's marked as complete.'

'What were the parameters?'

'All company contacts, staffing and clients, for three months leading up to her death. Alison had been working in the south of England. There was nothing on her books locally. It was put in for referral the day Margaret Robson was found dead. At that point, I imagine all hell broke loose—'

'Three months?' He was shaking his head. 'That's not long enough.'

'I agree.'

'The action was shelved?'

'As I said, they had other priorities.'

'None greater than conducting a comprehensive house-to-house. If I'd been the SIO—'

'Well you're not, Dad, so stop carping.'

'But Alison lived streets away from where her body was found. In my book, that should've taken precedence. She was also well placed to organise events at the club. This shoddy work surprises me. What was Sharpe thinking? He should've been on it like a rash. He was always meticulous.'

'Not this time. According to David, he had his head up his arse. Long story short, his missus left him for a toy boy with a CRO number as long as your arm. He was juggling more balls than he could reasonably keep in the air. He'd gone downhill and wasn't the man you knew.'

'I heard a rumour.'

'Well it's true.'

Her father wouldn't let it go. 'If Alison was local, surely *someone* knew her.'

'Not necessarily. She hadn't lived in Boldon long. If she was anything like me, she may not have been in the habit of telling people where she lived. If they have any sense, most single women who live alone don't share personal information. Considering what's going on across the force area, can you blame them?'

'It's not a bad strategy to adopt.'

'No, and why should she tell? My neighbours don't know

me from Adam and vice versa. I swear they think I'm the pizza delivery girl.'

He laughed at the image of her arriving at her apartment with her dinner in a box more often than she should. There was something else bugging him. It took a moment to rise to the surface. 'Are you going to wait till morning to call the club, or take the initiative?'

'Put like that, you leave me no choice.'

'That's my girl.'

'Stop it. I'm not four years old.'

Looking her up and down, he pointed at the teddy bear pattern on her pyjamas. 'I'll get you a nightcap . . . You want milk or whisky?'

'Neither.' She grinned. 'I'm fine. You get off.'

'I better had. After hanging one on at her reunion party till three a.m., your mum has turned in early. I promised not to wake her on my way to bed.'

'Watch the fifth step. It still creaks.'

Her father smiled.

That step had caught Frankie out once or twice when she was a teenager creeping in way past her curfew. After what happened to Joanna, her parents were understandably cautious and never slept until they knew she had made it home safely. Frankie sensed her father's reluctance to leave, but he rose to his feet, bending to kiss her on the forehead.

'Sleep tight, Detective.'

'You too, Dad. And thanks.'

'For what?'

'Listening . . . I'll make that call and follow you up.'

She could sleep on a clothesline if she had to. Another kiss and she watched him go. As the door closed behind him, she lifted her mobile from her bag, called the club and asked to be put through to the club secretary. She was told it would take a few minutes to locate him.

As she waited, Frankie glanced at the shelf above her head.

Joanna stared back at her, a photograph taken on her fifteenth birthday. A few months later she was dead. A quarter of a century on and Frankie still wasn't over it. Her father was right. She never would be, not until the perpetrator was found. The investigation had been archived – it would never be closed – and yet the likelihood of a prosecution was a pipedream. That fact alone was driving her, motivating her to solve her current case. She couldn't live with herself if she let the victims down.

A voice in her ear.

'Hello? This is the club captain. Can I help? You've missed our secretary, I'm afraid.'

'Then maybe you can help.'

'I'll do my best.'

'I'm sorry to disturb you, sir.' Frankie swivelled her chair around to face the other way, turning her back on Joanna's smiley eyes. It was impossible to concentrate with her in full view. 'My name is DS Oliver, Northumbria Police, Murder Investigation Team. I have a few questions for you and I'm afraid they can't wait.'

'I'm sure you wouldn't have called at such a late hour if it could.' The man sounded lovely, if a little taken aback with her ID. 'You are aware that we already had several visits from your colleagues? The police were crawling all over us after . . .' He cut short his sentence. Many people tripped over the word murder.

'Yes, and I apologise for any inconvenience.'

'No need. We were as devastated to learn of that young woman's death as anyone. Our members were shocked and saddened by it, keen to assist in any way they could. It shook the whole community, I can tell you. Incidents of that nature don't happen in a village like ours.'

'Is now a good time to talk? If not, could you possibly spare a few minutes in the morning?'

'Ask your questions, DS Oliver. I'll do what I can.'

'I'd like to know who handles your corporate events.'

'Oh?' He was understandably wary.

Frankie gave him a push. 'It is relevant to our enquiries, sir. For obvious reasons, I'm unable to say why. You'll have to trust me on that.'

'Fair enough, but I'd have to check this with our admin staff. We don't always use the same company, I know that much. I'm involved in the initial stages of planning, but then it's over to them. We usually make it known that we're running an event, be it a charity fundraiser, bespoke golf event, open day or whatever. We don't have the staff to handle this ourselves.'

'It goes out to tender?'

'It has to. Our events invariably require specialist equipment. There's a whole raft of things to consider. We choose the package that best fits our requirements, not necessarily the cheapest, if you get my drift.'

'Are you able to recall who you've used in the past year?'

'Not offhand, but I can get the information. Can I call you in the morning?'

Frankie grimaced. 'I'd appreciate that but, from memory, have you ever used a company called Results Global Event Management?'

'That rings a bell, but I'll need to confirm it with our admin staff.'

'Yes, of course.' She gave him her personal number. 'I look forward to hearing from you. Thanks for your help.'

30

Frankie lifted her mobile to her ear and mentally crossed her fingers. The number on her home screen was not one she recognised and she was hoping it was the call she'd been waiting for since arriving in the incident room at seven a.m. It was now ten thirty. The club captain she'd spoken to less than twelve hours ago came on the line. He confirmed that Boldon Golf Club had used Alison Brody's company to stage a special three-day challenge event. She almost yelped.

'When was this, sir?'

'Four months ago.'

'Could you email the information?'

'Certainly, if it's of any use.' He was fishing.

'The sooner the better . . . I can't tell you how important this is to us.' Neither could she tell him how keen she was to get off the phone. 'Thanks for responding so quickly.'

Reeling off her address, Frankie said she'd be in touch.

Hanging up, she dragged an A4 pad towards her, keen to jot down her thoughts. Her mind was racing, the conversation having produced a mixture of emotions: anger over Sharpe's obvious cock-up with the house-to-house forms, but excitement too. What she'd been told had set off a chain reaction in her head, adding weight to a theory that she and David had been stewing over for a while.

'Frank?' he called out from Abbott's desk. 'Something I should know about?'

She looked up to find the two men staring at her, other detectives following their lead, all eyes turned in her direction. David had been talking to Abbott when the call came in. Shoulder to shoulder, they approached her desk, lured by thoughts of an imminent breakthrough in the case. Frankie wasn't going to disappoint them, but she wasn't prepared to tell all with the world and his wife looking on.

'Can you give me a few minutes, guv?'

'Sure.' David led Abbott away, glancing back at her.

Ignoring his curiosity, she carried on scribbling.

Ten minutes later, she tapped on his office door and he beckoned her in. Out of politeness, Dick Abbott rose to his feet. Though female police officers were on equal terms, he was old school, always held the door open, stood up if she needed a seat. He was and always had been such a gent. David was waiting for her to spill, eyes firmly focused on the papers in her hand.

'OK if I stick around?' Dick said.

'Yeah, you need to hear this.' Keeping the Odin stones from him was one thing, but Frankie needed him in on this new intelligence. If what she had in mind panned out, he had work to do.

'The floor is yours,' David said.

'Last night I had a good look at the house-to-house file on Alison Brody. It was thin, guv. Believe it or not, the pro forma didn't include her professional profile at all, so I took the liberty of calling Boldon Golf Club and asking if they had ever used Results Global Event Management.'

'And had they?'

'Yes. While I was waiting for them to get back to me this morning, I checked out the company website. It's generic, guv. You know the type: "We are a bespoke, international events company with a dedicated team offering an exceptional service, coast-to-coast, leader and innovator . . ." blah blah. Nowhere on the site is Alison's name mentioned. When I asked the club captain who handled the Boldon event, he gave the name Trisha Conway. She's a freelance events director, brought in to oversee operations.'

David was on the edge of his seat.

'That explains how no one knew Alison,' Frankie continued. 'But it doesn't mean that she wasn't on site at some point during the event. I tried to contact Conway, but the call went straight to voicemail. Hopefully she'll call me back when she picks up the message. By the way, I haven't enlightened club officials that Alison has any connection whatsoever with Results Global, though I'm sure the man I spoke to will have worked that out by now. When I was talking to him last night, he reeled off a list of things the club require when they run a corporate event. They're too big to be dealt with in-house. In a matter of seconds, he'd handed me, or should I say us, a long list of potential suspects. So long, I almost groaned.'

'I'm not following,' David said.

'When I got off the phone, it suddenly occurred to me that each of our victims were handling a whole host of staff. I made a list, in the order they were killed, and a note of the people they might conceivably have come across in the course of their working lives. It's not exhaustive, these are just my thoughts, but you'll get the gist. I imagine the lists will be a lot longer than this.' She passed it to him.

1. CATHERINE BENNETT (28) Blyth victim. Talk-show host and after-dinner speaker. Contacts: media staff, researchers, producers, photographic and technical staff.
2. ALISON BRODY (34) Boldon victim. Corporate events organiser. Contacts: marquee staff, security, inside and outside lighting, insurance, catering staff.
3. MARGARET ROBSON (59) Morpeth victim. Co-founder of medical research organisation: university bods, scientists, medical and lab staff.
4. JOANNA COSGROVE (37) Stocksfield victim. Hot-shot criminal lawyer: junior solicitors, legal secretaries, judiciary, offenders.

David looked up. 'And you think that our man is one of these?'

'It's a longshot, I know, but worth considering.'

Dick's face was a picture. 'You think one of the victims was his target but he knocked off the rest to queer our pitch and make it more difficult to find him?'

'It's a possibility that he may work for one of them, yes. I know you don't want to hear it, but every one of their employees or associates could potentially be a suspect. We all agree that he's killing for a reason and that he can't handle their success. Try as I might, I can think of no other reason why he's picking them off otherwise. He's inactive now – maybe Joanna was his target and he was building up to her.'

'He's been inactive before,' David reminded her.

'I know and I think Sharpe made the mistake of thinking the killing was over. I can only hope there's no one else out there we're not aware of. As I said, our victims represent everything he loathes in women.'

'The team did a background check on the victims' associates. Who the fuck was handling Alison Brody?'

Her expression was enough of an answer.

David exploded. 'I'll kill the bastard.'

There was a knock at the door.

DC Mitchell entered. He'd heard the SIO's rant from beyond the office door and looked a little cautious. 'Guv, sorry to interrupt. Belinda Wells is on the phone. Local journalist. She wants to interview Northumbria's latest detective duo. Her words, not mine.'

'Tell her to sod off. This is not a good time.'

'That's what I told her.' He reached for the door.

'Hold on, Mitch.' Frankie turned to face David, her colleagues looking on. 'Don't let's be too hasty here, guv. This could work to our advantage. Wells is the one who broke the story about The Sleeper. She wants something from us. And we want something from her, don't we?'

David gave Mitch the nod to set up a meeting.

31

The journalist was waiting at the rendezvous point, a cocktail bar in the city centre. She'd met Frankie there once or twice with a view to exchanging information with general CID. The thirst for an in was greater than ever now that Frankie had moved into the Murder Investigation Team. On the way into town, she hadn't stopped talking, telling David that Wells once worked for a decent broadsheet. She was a serious journalist who'd been ousted by an editor who favoured younger, hungrier, eminently more biddable reporters coming up behind her.

'Frankie—'

'Don't get me wrong . . .' Frankie was on a roll, ignoring David's attempt to interrupt or dissuade her from this course of action. 'Wells has lost none of her edge or ambition. She's very keen to establish a rapport with us. Her invitation to meet up is nothing but a ruse. She's not interested in us per se. It's what we can give her that prompted her call. I'm not saying that a relationship with the press can't work for us. It can—'

'Only if we play our cards right,' David warned.

'We need a name,' she reminded him.

'And we'll get one. She'll dig her heels in and we'll get fuck-all if we go in hard.' He gave her the eyes, a clear message that he intended to take the lead and wanted no interruptions. A combative stance wasn't going to work. 'Trust me on this. With this maniac on the loose, we can't afford to put a foot wrong. That said, I think you're right about Wells. She could be of use to us if we want to share details that might draw out the offender, so keep it buttoned.'

Smiling, Frankie pressed a forefinger to her lips.

Revolution was an old bank conversion on Collingwood Street. It had retained its ornate ceilings and marble pillars, symbols of wealth, clues to the successful financial institution it once was. At the bar, Frankie ordered two espressos, then pointed Wells out to the man behind the counter. 'And whatever the lady in red is having.'

'Daiquiri,' the barman said. 'I'll bring them over.'

She held up a twenty. 'Is this enough?'

He nodded a yes.

Placing the note on the bar, Frankie told him to keep the change – not that there would be much left over – and led her guv'nor across the room. Wells was sitting away from the other customers where they could have a confidential conversation without being overheard. Leather-clad booths around the outside of the room afforded a level of privacy for doing business with the cops.

Frankie took a seat on one side of her, David on the other.

'Belinda.' He smiled as he shuffled in beside her. 'Nice to see you again.'

'David Stone.' The woman extended a hand of slender fingers, the skin thin and wrinkled. 'Congratulations on your appointment. You're back where you belong.'

'And so are you.'

'You two know each other?' Frankie glared at David. 'You never said.'

'I couldn't get a word in edgeways.'

David gave the journalist a firm handshake. A strawberry daiquiri on the table matched the colour of her lipstick, a generous pouty mouth her best asset. The woman was pushing sixty, more attractive than pretty. Fully made up, she hadn't managed to hide a lined complexion brought on by heavy smoking. The smell on her clothing had always made him slightly nauseous but today it was missing. She'd finally given up.

The barman arrived with their drinks.

The SIO waited for him to move away before speaking. 'We're busy, so I'll get straight to the point. I'd love to work with you, if that's what you're after, so long as it's mutually beneficial. Let me make myself clear. Whoever Frankie and I choose to liaise with in the press must have our best interests at heart. So, let's have our meeting and see how that pans out.'

Wells nodded. 'Works for me.'

'First, we don't want anything made public that we're not happy with. We need someone of integrity and you happen to fit the bill. You're a pro who knows the score and we stand or fall by our results. Anything that gets in the way of that isn't going to work for us.'

The journalist took a sip of her drink, eyeing David over the rim of her glass. His background in the Metropolitan Police wasn't news to her and he owed her on that score. She was aware that he was no pushover.

'You already know what we're up against,' he said. 'This is a big job, one we need to resolve quickly. There must be an element of trust between us before we can proceed.'

'I'd expect nothing less.'

'I know I can rely on you, but Frankie here needs proof.'

Wells knew what was coming.

'You've already queered our pitch publishing details that ought not to be in the public domain,' David said. 'That worries me. Who coined the phrase The Sleeper?'

'That would be me.' Wells didn't try and deny it.

'And what prompted that?' Frankie couldn't help herself.

'You expect me to give up my snout?' Wells scoffed. 'C'mon, you know better than to ask.'

'We need to know where it came from,' David said. 'The way I see it, you've been talking to the offender or someone on my team. That's not on. In future, if you want information on this or any other investigation, you come to me or Frankie, not some arsehole who wants to shout their mouth off to make him or herself look good. As a gesture of goodwill, I need you to break your unwritten code of ethics and divulge your source.'

Wells didn't budge. 'No can do.'

'Then we have nothing more to discuss.' David stood up, sucked in a breath, disappointment showing on his face. 'Frank, we're out of here.'

Wells looked up at him. 'Is that it?'

He eyeballed her. 'That's it.'

'No further discussion or negotiation?'

'We don't have time to play mind games, Belinda. Enjoy your daiquiri. It'll be the last we pay for.'

'David . . . sit down. I believe two-way street is the accepted phrase.' Wells' grin exposed good teeth. Implants that probably cost half his annual salary. 'It would be insane to give you what I've got unless there's something in it for me.'

'Who was it, Belinda?'

Frankie crossed her arms and waited. She was impressed with her guv'nor's direct approach. He understood what was required in delicate situations like these. Transactional analysis was the name of the game and he was in the driving seat. Wells had made the initial overture, not the other way around. She'd tipped her hand and he was determining how far he could reasonably push her. If she wasn't prepared to trade, they wouldn't be sitting here, and if she didn't negotiate a deal with him, someone else sure as hell would.

'Make your argument,' Wells said. 'I'm listening.'

David sat down. 'Don't throw away an open line to the top on some piece of shit who's not and never will be in the know. Frankie and I can make it worth your while, on our terms and timescale obviously. I'll be straight with you. You have one chance to buy yourself an exclusive if, and I do mean *if*, you play ball now.'

Wells glanced across the bar, considering her options,

weighing up the pros and cons before turning to face him. 'If it gets out that I'm not trustworthy, no informer will ever talk to me. You see my problem?'

'That's a fair comment.' It was time to level with her. 'Listen, there are two scenarios in play here. One: a very dangerous man – who will kill again and has already devastated the lives of four families – has been in touch with you. Two: the leak came from one of our own. Either way, I need a name. If it's the former, I know you're the kind of woman who'll do her civic duty, irrespective of the consequences. You've done it before. In any event, he'll have given you a dodgy name. If the latter, I've got you covered. I'm not interested in having the leak in my team sacked, just getting him the hell out of my incident room.'

There was a beat of time as Wells considered her options. She appeared in two minds, unsure of which way to jump. It seemed to take forever for her to respond. She hadn't taken her eyes off David. 'And if he gives me grief?'

'He won't.'

'He might.'

'Then I'll personally see to it that he loses far more than his place on my team.'

'What's in it for me?'

'If you stick with us, you'll get the legitimate story, the inside story, not just now but in the future – and you'll get it first. The Met didn't give you that. I will. You have my word on it. With us onside, you won't need to go scratching in pubs for information. The nationals will be green with envy, if not banging on your door with job offers.'

'I need more than that' – she quoted him – '"as a gesture of goodwill" and off the record.'

'Yeah, right!' Frankie exploded, unable to hide her disgust. 'Will you listen to yourself? I'll spell it out, shall I? Four women are dead. More are in danger. What kind of woman would sit back and do nothing when they could help?'

David eyeballed her: *Keep your voice down and stay out of this.*

Wells was holding her own. 'How do I know you won't take the name and shaft me?'

'When have I ever broken a promise to you?' David fired off another round. 'And since when did you turn into such a cynic?' Wells didn't answer but he had her attention. 'What on earth happened to you? Why are you dishing the dirt on us, giving this monster what he craves? Our lives are difficult enough already and it's not your style. You want honesty? OK, here it comes. We have a four-hander and we're nowhere, but I'm guessing you know that already. Your newspaper gave Sharpe a hard time. He made mistakes, but so have you. He opted out and you kept going. You gave the killer a label. You know as well as I do that he'll be loving the notoriety. Your paper is culpable and you along with it.'

Wells had to think about that one. 'What do you really want, David?'

'We're the good guys, remember? My skill is picking the right team, people who can work together for the good of my community. You're an investigative journalist, second to none, a woman of conscience . . . At least you used to be. I need someone who can flush out the bad guys covertly. That's what drives you. Tell me I'm wrong.' He paused. 'I need someone on our side. I think you are that reporter. In short, I want you.'

'Bullshit! You want that name.'

'Yes, I do, but I'm asking you to work with us. Frankie just told you what's at stake. You have a voice you can use to turn this around, put a positive spin on things and reassure the women of this county that we're working hard to protect them. We are, in case you're in any doubt. We will get this maniac and when we do . . .' He let the sentence trail off.

'That was quite a speech.'

'It was a plea. Are you with us?'

Their eyes locked.

Wells hesitated. 'I tried it on with DC Mitchell—'

'What?' A look of horror crossed Frankie's face. Of all the names she could have come up with, his was not on the list.

'Don't panic!' The journalist glanced at Frankie, then at Stone. 'He told me, in no uncertain terms, to fuck off. The name you want is Dunne.'

'And dusted,' Frankie whispered under her breath. 'You approached him?'

'No, he called me, shortly after I spoke to Mitchell. Maybe the rookie told someone in the office about our conversation, or Dunne overheard him on the phone. We met up that evening. We sat here, in this very seat, as it happens.'

'You have a tape of the conversation?' David asked.

'What do you think?'

'Hang on to it,' he said.

'How much did it cost?' Frankie asked.

'Couple of pints. He's a pussycat when you get to know him.'

Frankie shook her head. 'A slug is what he is.'

Ten minutes later, the detectives shook hands with Wells and stood up to leave. They had got what they had come for and were keen to get back.

32

To keep everything open and above board, David made extensive notes on his discussion with Wells. When the time was right, he intended to keep his word and give her something she alone could run with. In return, she'd agreed that he could approve the wording for whatever gem he wanted to share with the public and would hold the line until he gave the go-ahead for its release.

Frankie had given him earache on the way back from the meeting, believing that he'd said too much. David knew different. All he'd said about Wells was true. She was a brilliant journalist. What's more, they had history. When his Met colleague was shot dead in her own home, Wells saw red. She'd put together a comprehensive dossier on the man who killed her and handed it to police in exchange for an exclusive. It was her doggedness that eventually led to his arrest, detention and subsequent life sentence – a last-ditch attempt to keep her job in the south of England. Then the Met reneged on the deal and she was out on her ear.

Wells had never once mentioned rumours circulating about David and Jane. She could have made their relationship into a sleazy soap opera to titillate her readership. She was better than that, which was why he trusted her. Investigative journalists could go places where he could not, infiltrating organisations, interviewing anyone they chose, without being hog-tied by rules and regulations. If he could cultivate a relationship with Wells, she'd be an asset to the MIT. As far as David was concerned, she was the real deal. In time, Frankie would think so too.

A knocking sound drew his attention from his notes.

Dunne was loitering outside. Taking Stone's interest as his

cue to enter, the pathetic excuse for a detective pushed open the door. 'Guv, you wanted to see me?'

'Give me a second.'

The DS closed the door and approached Stone's desk.

The SIO finished scribbling, closed his notebook and slowly pulled a personnel file towards him. Now he had Dunne in his office, he wanted to make him sweat. Frankie wouldn't be far away. She'd be standing guard, under strict instructions to keep the rest of the team at bay. This was something the DCI needed to do alone.

Dunne pulled out a chair.

Stone glared at him. 'Did I invite you to sit?'

'Is there a problem?'

'On the contrary, things are looking up.' Stone kept his cool, glancing again at the personnel record on his desk. He flicked a few pages, leaving the document wide open, Dunne's mugshot clearly visible on the inside front cover.

The DS recognised it immediately.

The SIO tapped the file. 'Exemplary conduct, it says here.'

'What can I say?' A shrug from Dunne. 'I'm good at my job.'

'Is that right?' Stone narrowed his eyes. 'The problem is, that description flies in the face of everything I know about you. I'm asking myself what has changed. You've made it plain that you prefer Sharpe's methods to mine. I can live with that. What I'm finding more difficult is your grandstanding antics in front of your pals.'

Dunne didn't flinch. He just stood there: out-of-line, untouchable, disrespectful – a direct challenge to the authority of his SIO. Knowing that he was facing a detective trying to undermine the investigation, the man who'd handed the killer a label – and may even have put women's lives at risk – Stone was tempted to leap across his desk and deck the bastard, but he knew Dunne would like nothing more. It didn't get more serious than an assault on a fellow officer. Maybe that was what he was after.

He wouldn't get his way.

A face-off: senior officer to subordinate. 'If it's me you have a problem with, spit it out,' Stone said. 'I'm not unreasonable. Nor am I oversensitive to criticism. I assume you have an explanation. This is your opportunity to voice it.' He paused, sat back in his chair, cupping his hands behind his head. 'No? OK, I'll keep this brief—'

'If this is about my spat with Oliver?'

'It's not, though that also requires an explanation. What did you say to make her lose her rag?'

'Nothing.'

'Nothing. Hmm . . . OK, we'll leave it there then. For now, anyway . . .' The DS visibly relaxed, a smirk developing. He turned to leave, thinking he was off the hook. He wasn't – David hadn't even begun. 'You're not dismissed,' he barked.

Dunne turned on his heel, retraced his steps.

There was no apology.

'You may not have anything to say, but I have plenty,' Stone said. 'Prior to my arrival, you were given the job of checking victim associates, business and private, on Alison Brody. Is that correct?'

'And?' Dunne's arrogance knew no bounds.

'Remind me how far back your guv'nor asked you to go?'

'Three months.'

'And yet you only managed two before you put the action in for referral.'

'There was a reason for that.'

'Which was?'

'A second victim had been found and—'

David cut him off. 'I'm fully aware of that. Understandable for a day, or even two, but you must've known that Sharpe never signed off on the referral and *you* never continued with the action or raised the issue again. Why was that? Did you get bored with it?'

'No, sir.'

It was the first time since Dunne had entered the room that he'd acknowledged Stone's rank or addressed him correctly. His eyes found the floor, his weight shifting from one foot to another. He knew he was in trouble.

'Was it perhaps beneath your pay grade?'

'No, sir.'

'Now listen carefully – I'd hate you to get this wrong. Clear your desk. Dick Abbott is taking over your role here permanently and Superintendent Gale is expecting you in general CID first thing in the morning.'

'You can't do that!'

'I just did.'

Dunne laughed in his face. 'For slinging mud at Oliver and not completing a job in the middle of a multi-murder investigation? You're having a laugh . . . sir. That'll never stick—'

'But the other, more serious matter, will.'

'What other matter?' Dunne almost choked on his words. He put his hands behind his back, squaring his shoulders, shifting his stance, his bravado deserting him. He was practically standing to attention.

'Discreditable conduct. You should choose your drinking buddies more wisely, DS Dunne.' Stone watched the colour drain from the detective sergeant's face and went in for the kill. 'I have conclusive proof that you were the leak from this office. There's no place for a bigmouth on my team . . . as of now, your HOLMES authorisation is no longer valid. Now get out of my sight.'

33

Dunne pushed past Frankie as he strode into the incident room, swearing loudly, drawing the attention of the whole team. He made his way across the room to the printer, picked up a carton of A4 paper, tipping the lot out on the floor. Back at his desk, he searched his drawers, pulling out personal items, dumping them in the empty box. Enquiries from his entourage went unanswered. They were gobsmacked, unable to comprehend what had gone down in the SIO's office and Dunne was saying nowt. He'd hardly admit to the reason for his sudden departure. Mates or no mates, they wouldn't forgive that.

Frankie caught Abbott's eye. 'Dick, the guv'nor wants to see you.'

Abbott pushed his chair away from his desk and disappeared.

'Congratulations, Dick. Your MIT secondment has been made permanent with immediate effect. I won't go into all the whys and wherefores . . .' David paused, reconsidering. It wasn't fair to keep Abbott in the dark if he was replacing another member of the MIT. 'On second thoughts I will,' he said. 'But this is for your ears only. Dunne was the leak and is no longer welcome here. He's out. You're in.'

For a split second, Abbott was stunned into silence. 'Is that official? I assume you've squared it with the head of CID—'

'In a manner of speaking . . . Incompatibility is all he needs to know.'

'Bright won't buy that, guv. He'll know something's up.'

'He might well do, but my guess is he won't ask a question he doesn't want the answer to. He has too much on to bother with personal trivia – and so do we.'

'It's just . . . well, not to put too fine a point on it, I don't want to get my hopes up if there's any doubt.'

'There's not.' David smiled. 'You're safe to tell the missus. There's an email in Bright's inbox informing him that you're taking over and, if he should ask any awkward questions, I'll deal with it when the time comes, assuming you're in agreement.'

'Guv, I don't know what to say.'

'A simple yes will do.'

Dick beamed a thank you and leaned across the SIO's desk to shake on it.

'Excellent,' David said. 'You deserve the opportunity. Frankie and I are delighted to have you on board. Forthwith, you have one priority. I want you to go over Dunne's actions – all of them – and report back. Start with Alison Brody. There's unfinished business there that needs an expert eye. Frankie will fill you in on the details. Let me know what gives.'

'Yes, guv.'

'Dick, if you hear rumblings of nepotism, feel free to refer the doubters to me. Dunne's departure is about leaking confidential information. It has nothing whatsoever to do with winding Frankie up. And, while we're on the subject, is there anything you want to tell me about that?'

Abbott clammed up. 'No, guv.'

'You heard what he said to her, didn't you?'

'I did, yes.' The DS was suddenly uncomfortable.

'What was it?' When his newest recruit failed to enlighten him, David gave him a push. 'Listen, your loyalty to Frank is commendable, your hesitation perfectly understandable. I'm aware that I'm putting you between a rock and a hard place, but I need a straight answer. Frankie is a valuable member of this team. If she wasn't important, to both of us, I wouldn't ask. She needs support right now and it would help if I knew why.'

'Guv, may I?' Dick pointed to the computer monitor on the SIO's desk, then walked around to where he was sitting. 'I need you to log on to HOLMES, guv. My authorisation won't let me in to what you require.'

Intrigued, David logged on, then moved aside, allowing him to access the system. He tapped a few keys, calling up a file: Joanna Oliver. When David read the name, he felt his stomach lurch. Abbott was still typing but David's focus was elsewhere, his mind scrolling through the past few weeks. Everything now made sense. Little did he know there was worse to come. A statement popped up on screen. The contents of that document took his breath clean away.

I am Detective Inspector Frank Oliver, Northumbria Police. At 23.05 on Friday, 12 June 1992 I was the on-call DI for the force area. I was called to an incident at Park Terrace, Southwick, Sunderland, described as a fatal stabbing of a young woman. On arrival at the scene, I was shown to the body by PC Stuart Wright. On further examination, I found that the young woman was my fifteen-year-old daughter, Joanna Oliver. At this time, I made formal identification. Joanna's date of birth is 16 March 1977. I left the scene and contacted senior supervision. I was informed that I could take no further part in the investigation and withdrew.

David closed his eyes, rubbing at his forehead as everything fell into place. Frankie's reaction at the crime scene; her argumentative attitude with the pathologist at the morgue; her blow-up with Dunne in the incident room just beyond his office door; but most important of all, her inability to share even the briefest details.

'Obviously, you just found that,' Abbott said.

'Understood.' David looked at him, trying to recall Frankie's argument with Dunne, then spat out a question: 'What the fuck did Dunne say to her? I thought he was slagging off her detection rate.'

Abbott shook his head. 'It was her father's track record he was ranting on about. He said it was unimpressive. When he mentioned Joanna, I didn't twig that he meant her sister, not victim number four. It wasn't until later that I realised he was alluding to the fact that her father couldn't solve his own daughter's murder. I'm sorry, guv. I should have brought it to you sooner.'

'Well, you've done it now. Thanks, you can go.'

As the door swung open in a wide arc, David caught sight of Frankie approaching Mitchell's desk, a spring in her step, fully focused on her work. His eyes followed her. As she moved out of his eyeline, he slammed his fist on the desk. How on earth did she keep going?

34

'DC Mitchell, can I have a word?' Frankie waited for the detective constable to look up. Having witnessed Dunne's sudden departure and noticed Abbott's lengthy interview with the SIO, her formality had Mitch baffled. He searched her face trying to read her expression. She gave nothing away. 'Not here,' she said. 'The statement reader's office is free. We'll use that.'

She moved towards it with Mitch on her tail.

'Shut the door,' she said, taking a seat. The office was soulless, no windows to distract the man whose office they were using. It was a tiny room with one desk, one chair and statements piled high on every available surface. How he could sit day after long day in that environment was a mystery to Frankie.

She caught Mitch's eye. 'It has come to my attention that you've been talking to the press.'

He looked ruffled. 'Has Wells made a complaint?'

Frankie threw her hands up, a gesture of incredulity. 'No, no, no! How many times have I told you, never ever volunteer information? The fact that you asked the question sounds to me like she has grounds, wouldn't you say?'

'Yes, Sarge. I wasn't very pleasant to her, that's all.'

'Are you nuts? What did I just say?' She bit her lip. 'Have I taught you nothing?'

Mitchell apologised. 'You know me – too honest for my own good.'

His joke fell flat.

'This is no laughing matter, DC Mitchell. Now, would you be good enough to explain the extent of the connection between yourself and Belinda Wells. And, while you're at it, you can tell me why, as your direct supervision, I knew sod-all about it?'

'What?' Mitchell panicked. 'I'm not the leak!'

'This isn't about the leak.'

'Oh . . .' He relaxed. 'It was nothing, Sarge. I swear. There is no connection between us. I've only spoken to her twice, the second time this morning, which you already know about. I—'

'And the first time?' Frankie watched his Adam's apple slide up and down his gullet. He didn't want to answer and she knew why. 'Do I have to remind you that your appraisal is due soon? What did she want?'

Mitchell cleared his throat. 'She wanted me to be her snout.'

'And what was your response?'

'I told her it wasn't my style.'

'I think not.' Frankie gave him the eagle eye. 'An approach of this nature should have been reported immediately. You know why? Because, if the shit ever hits the fan, you're covered. You told a member of the press to fuck off, isn't that the truth of it? In case you didn't know, that's conduct unbecoming an officer. I should take this to the SIO.'

His mouth fell open. 'Do you have to?'

'Depends on the explanation you have to offer in your defence.'

'Only that she was quite persistent.'

The door opened and the SIO walked in. 'Frankie?'

Mitchell almost buckled. Then, to Frankie's surprise and amusement, he lifted his chin and, without prompting, uttered a damning confession to their boss. 'I should've told you about it, guv. I realise that now. Please accept my profound apology. It won't happen again.'

Realising that Frankie had been faking her displeasure, David played along. 'Well, I can't say I'm happy about it, but the least said, the better.' He eyeballed Mitchell. 'Lucky for you, I've had my fill of personnel issues today, so we'll consider the subject closed. If anyone else approaches you, give us a shout, man. Don't keep it to yourself.'

Mitchell blew out a breath. 'Thank you, sir.'

Stone left them to it, a smile on his face as he turned away.

'Looks like you've won yourself some brownie points,' Frankie said, a twinkle in her eye. 'Your appraisal is safe, Mitch. But, for crying out loud, work on your volunteering routine before the next one. It's shite. Less is more. That's the key.' Finally, the young DC twigged that she'd been winding him up all along.

35

The SIO was keen to visit scenes three and four. Without saying why, he instructed the team that he and Frankie would be unavailable for the rest of the day. Dick Abbott was more than capable of holding the evening briefing if they didn't get back by six o'clock. Besides, in the privacy of David's office, he'd shown his colours and earned the right to take charge of the MIT.

Heading for his car with Frankie in tow, David tried and failed to get her father's statement out of his head. He'd known coppers turn up to the scene of accidents to discover that a family member was a casualty, even a fatality, but he couldn't imagine anything worse than coming across a murdered child. It was just as well Dunne had left the building. Had the DS still been there when David finished talking to Dick, he'd have taken a swing at him and now he regretted holding Frankie back.

As he headed south, towards the River Tyne, she glanced at him.

'I thought we were going north.'

'It'll be quicker if we visit Stocksfield first. It's more familiar, for a start. Apart from CSI photography, the Morpeth scene is new to us. It'll take longer to examine and it'll be easier to get back to Middle Earth from there.' He checked his watch. 'It's getting on . . . I don't want to get caught in traffic at the arse end of rush hour.'

'Makes sense.' Frankie settled back in her seat.

Twenty minutes later, David parked in the Stocksfield railway station car park. Locking the car, he made off through the side of the metal gate, across the rough ground where Joanna

Cosgrove had been found, Frankie arriving at his shoulder as they reached the sleepers. Several wilting bouquets had been placed on top.

David shook his head. 'I hate all this shit.'

'They're just paying their respects, guv.'

'Then they should go to church.'

'You OK? You seem overly offended by it.'

'I'm fine,' he lied, an image of ribbons and flowers tied to the railings outside Jane's flat arriving in his head, dozens of them, mostly left there by people she didn't know. When did that become a British tradition?

Putting on a pair of nitrile gloves, he moved the flowers off the railway sleepers and out of the way with a view to examining the ground forensically, an area littered with stones, broken pieces of concrete, weeds and moss. Carefully, he felt around the edges of the sleepers, checking the gaps in between each one, in case the Odin stone he was hoping to find had been hidden beneath the victim and then dislodged, either when her body was removed, or in the storm beforehand.

'Nothing,' he mumbled under his breath.

Frankie sighed. 'I assume you checked the exhibits log before we left?'

A nod. 'I did it last night.'

'There were no stones mentioned?'

'None.' Shrugging his shoulders, he moved round to examine the other side of the sleepers. 'We could be chasing rainbows here, Frank. Apologies in advance if I'm wasting precious time.'

'No worries. My dad would be well impressed that you're even looking.'

Mention of Frank Oliver II sent a chill right through him. 'Why's that?'

'He once told me that everything you see is a signpost.'

'A wise man, your dad.'

'David.'

'What?' He looked up.

'That.' Her focus was a graffiti-covered stone slab around three metres away: RIP Joanna. 'Do you think he's been back?'

'Not a chance.'

'It's another reference to the victim being *at rest*.'

'It'll be someone who left the flowers.'

'With a spray can handy?' She had a point.

'Find the can and I might get excited.'

As she took off, David resumed his search. He ached to tell her that he knew about her sister, but he wasn't sure if it would relieve the pressure she was under or add to it. Instead he kept quiet. A few minutes later, her feet arrived by his side.

She never spoke.

Unusual.

'I'm sorry I doubted you,' she said.

Her comment, laced with tension, was too strong to ignore. Again, David looked up. She was staring at a point over his shoulder, an expression of consternation. Taking an evidence bag from her pocket, she approached the crumbling wall behind him. David studied it as he joined her. One item stood out among the debris of fallen masonry: an Odin stone placed carefully on a foundation slab, sheltered inside the gaping hollow.

She reached out for it.

'No!' David grabbed her arm. 'Don't touch it. I want an official photographer out here. One I can trust to keep their mouth shut.'

'Foley's as good as any,' she said.

'Do it.'

Frankie made the call.

36

Job done, Foley was told to retain the photographs in a mis-
cellaneous file. 'Log the stone under confidential cover in the
exhibits room. Mark it with my name and tell no one,' David
warned. 'I want it contained in a box so it can't be viewed.'

'Consider it done,' Foley said.

'What time do you knock off?'

'Not for a while yet, guv.'

'Put yourself on standby, we might need you again.'

'I'll be waiting.' Foley was already heading off.

On the way to Morpeth, they crossed the River Blyth, reminding them of the first Odin stone they had found on the town's
beach promenade. They took the B1337, arriving at the crime
scene within ten minutes of leaving the A1, the UK's longest
road linking the capital with Edinburgh.

'Three scenes down, one to go,' Frankie said.

David nodded. 'Don't get too excited. We still don't know
what the bloody hell they mean. If anything.'

They walked the route Margaret Robson had taken on the
night she was murdered, starting at the marketplace. Outside
Rutherford's department store, on the main shopping thor-
oughfare, Frankie stopped walking. 'She was last seen alive
here. The witness knew her well. They had a chat for a minute
or two, then Margaret walked that way, heading home.'

'Show me,' David said.

Frankie led the way, turning right off Bridge Street into Old
Gaol Yard. 'Margaret was in the habit of using this cut. The
witness saw her enter the yard.' She pointed ahead to an old
iron footbridge that crossed the River Wansbeck. The detectives walked on, entering the footbridge through a cast-iron

archway that held an old-fashioned lamp in the centre at the top.

They came to a stop in the middle.

In the glare of full sun, Frankie put on her sunglasses and David followed suit. The view from Chantry Bridge was stunning in both directions: Oliver's Mill fish pass upstream, built to ease the way for salmon and sea trout over a steep weir; St George's United Reform church on the north bank; to the east of the bridge, which they had driven across to access the town, a road bridge named after Scottish civil engineer Thomas Telford, built in collaboration with architect John Dobson, one of North Shields' most famous sons.

'Jesus!' Frankie whispered under her breath.

'What?'

She turned, her expression blank.

'You said "Jesus" – I assume you weren't praying.'

She peered over the railing onto the footpath below, a grim reminder of her sister's fate. It psyched her out. She glanced at the church spire before turning back to face him. Maybe a prayer for the victim wasn't such a bad idea. 'I was thinking how calm and picturesque it is here. He's sullied it, David.' She covered her unease with a question. 'Notice anything?'

'What am I looking for?'

She pointed to a block of flats in the distance, the sun glinting off windows with a view of the weir. 'There's a direct line of sight from Rae and Andrea's flat. When I read up on the case, I thought there would be.' She grabbed his upper arm, steering him in the other direction, away from the town. They crossed the river. On the left-hand side of the bridge's medieval abutments, a gap in the stonework afforded entry onto the riverside.

Frankie came to a halt. 'C'mon, it's down here.'

A few steps led down to a cracked concrete path which disappeared under Telford Bridge. To the left of the path, the grass petered out onto a sandy beach close to the water's edge.

The area was fringed by long grasses and weeds, part of which was fenced off to stop small children falling in the river.

'These cases are beginning to merge into one,' David said. 'Remind me, was Margaret on the grass or the sand?'

'Half and half. No staging.'

Frankie accessed images on her phone to show him the exact location where the body had been found. They climbed down to the riverside path and began a thorough search of the area. In each case where an Odin stone had been found, it was within a yard or two of the body.

An hour later, exhausted by the heat and frustrated at having found nothing, Frankie went back up on to the bridge for a bird's-eye view. When David looked up at her, she shook her head. He wasn't happy. He spoke as she descended the steps and made her way towards him.

'We're wasting our time here, Frank. This is a popular spot for kids and dog walkers. If there was an Odin stone here, it's long gone.'

'You want me to call out the CSIs to do a proper fingertip search?'

'No, let's knock it on the head. I need a pit stop.'

The Joiner's Arms was the closest pub. David told Frankie that he'd had no time to shop and couldn't face the thought of another takeaway. Ben had no wheels, and less money. There was no chance he'd managed to fill the fridge. The detectives chose to eat outside on a picnic bench, neither making much conversation until they were done. The grub was excellent, a lot better than either had expected. Frankie pushed her plate away and picked up her drink.

'It seems that your nan was wrong about the power of the stones.'

'Looks like it.'

'Do people really believe in that stuff?'

'She did . . . and if we'd found one today, I'd think the

killer did too.' David put his elbow on the table, supporting his chin with the heel of his hand, his disappointment clearly visible. 'I've been thinking about her a lot lately.'

'You're bound to. You're living in her house.'

'My house now,' he corrected her.

Frankie wiped a film of sweat from her brow. 'How's the refurb coming along?'

'So-so. Ben called earlier. The plumber finally came back.'

'That must be a relief.' She'd stayed over with him shortly after Luke died and took the coldest shower she'd ever had the next morning, pipes banging, water spluttering from the shower head – not to be recommended. Remembering the torture chamber he called a bathroom, Frankie almost shivered.

David had gone quiet.

'Cheer up. It was always a longshot.' She changed tack. 'Did your nan ever talk about the stones?'

David nodded. 'Luke and I were in a right state when my parents died. I was six, he was eight. The first night we stayed over at her place, she put us in her lumpy old bed – there was only one – soothing us, reassuring us that everything was going to be all right, telling us that we'd live with her from that point on. It never occurred to us where *she* was going to sleep.'

'Acting as surrogate parents to two small boys can't have been easy.'

'No, but she insisted. She said our parents would want us to stick together and we weren't going to disappoint them.' Frankie could see what it meant for him to offload. She'd done a bit of that herself lately and allowed him to talk without interruption. 'She tucked us up with a hot-water bottle and sat with us for a while. When she finally stood up to go, I watched her fold our clothes into a neat pile, then thread the stone with string and hang it over the bedstead before she turned out the light. I didn't know what it was until I quizzed her the next morning.'

'Fuck!' The expletive escaped unbidden, drawing the attention of others.

His words had sent Frankie back to her bird's-eye view from Chantry Bridge an hour ago, and further still to the research she'd carried out in the incident room shortly after the second Odin stone was found. 'We knew you could hang them up, David. So *why* in God's name have we been looking on the ground?'

As he paid up, Frankie broke into a run.

Nothing had drawn her eye from the bridge, although she'd scanned the ground for the colour blue – the ligature. The scene had been processed by her CSI colleagues, but since Margaret's death, violent storms had battered the county, sending debris flying in all directions. She'd been hoping to get lucky. She hadn't. No colour other than blue would've alerted her, although now she came to think of it, she felt sure she'd seen a flash of red, exposed when the wind blew through trees close to the riverbank. Berries, she assumed.

What if she was wrong?

David arrived by her side, breathing heavily.

'There!' she pointed.

About eight feet from the ground, a tiny stone dangled from a tree branch on a thin red ribbon, placed there deliberately. Her guv'nor was already on the blower to Foley. This had to be a calling card.

37

He pulled his laptop towards him, logged on and opened up Safari. Surfing the net always relaxed him. There was something infinitely satisfying about a tool that produced such quick results. It took no time to find suitable victims: police officers commended publicly for outstanding contribution; those who'd rescued people from harm: drownings, house fires, RTAs. You name it, they'd done it, putting their lives on the line in the process, above and beyond a duty call. All very publicly spirited, so fucking right on he almost threw up.

Stand by your beds, ladies.

He'd spent hours on research, consulting web pages of interest, ruling out the dross. The first female officer he found during this session was top brass, a woman at the back of the queue when looks were handed out, not the most attractive he'd ever seen, but that was no barrier in the whole scheme of things. No, he decided. She might be higher up the food chain, but she lacked the attitude he was after. He was only interested in kickass females. Opinionated was the attribute he most loathed in the fairer sex. He scanned more pages, adding several to a growing reading list – none of whom were direct hits – stopping only to order a Chinese takeaway.

A man on a mission had to eat.

When the delivery girl left, he put his feet up and tucked in, continuing to explore his options, his master plan taking shape, in his head if not on paper. The new SIO was clueless, the so-called cream of the Met he'd heard so much about, the Northern Rock. Gaining this man's attention was proving difficult. His new scheme was the right way to go, he was sure of that, but his search went on, requiring vigilance and careful selection. He had one chance to get it right.

Since the idea first occurred, it had taken up every second of his time. According to Steph, patience was a quality she admired, one she clearly didn't associate with him. The bitch was as wrong about that as she was about him. Hadn't he demonstrated that he was more motivated than ever? The kind of guy who would and could carry out an operation on a grand scale in order to attract her attention.

Concentrate on what's important.

He'd done OK so far, except how was that good enough? OK was adequate, tolerable, average, words she'd used so frequently it had prompted him to show her what he was made of, even though it was unlikely to bring about her admiration or put his life back on an even keel. Angered that her seal of approval mattered, he threw his takeaway carton across the room, and moved the cursor, clicking frantically at another tab . . .

And another . . .

And another.

Headline: *Female Detective to receive Queen's Police Medal.* A QPM was impressive. This one had been in the job for years, was well thought of, the kind of officer others aspired to emulate. She'd worked her way up through the ranks, the whole of her service completed in Northumbria. She'd been influential in setting up victim support initiatives, liaising with Rape Crisis and similar agencies.

Boring.

He jabbed at the backspace key, opening up a web page saved to his favourites. He wasn't going to rush this. Selection was key. He needed someone local, that much was true, but a woman with a much higher profile, a recognisable female in the force, someone connected . . .

Headline: *Police Chief commended for professionalism and*

dedication. An officer engaged in community policing, who'd taken police into classrooms to teach kids good citizenship and share safety initiatives, warning of the dangers to avoid, online and in the real world.

Fuck no!

It was easier ruling them out than in.

Backspace.

Headline: *Officer Injured in the Line of Duty*. Whoa! No medals, but a candidate nevertheless: a force favourite, a poster girl who had a lot going for her. He'd seen this one in the flesh. She was slim in stature, a necessary prerequisite if he was to take her out. He thought he would be able to handle her but then he might not . . . On second thoughts, a change of direction and a different modus operandi would minimise the risk. A ligature was fraught with danger when dealing with a pro, a knife too. Though he enjoyed getting up close and personal, it wasn't practical going forward, something he couldn't afford with a woman like this.

A firearm?

Hmm . . .

Less complicated . . . and a damned sight more achievable. It would put distance between him and his prey. He could scope out a vantage point with an easy escape route and draw his target to him. Shouldn't be too difficult if he used his nous and planned it properly. The downside hit him then: a gunshot would draw unwanted attention and jeopardise his freedom. And there was one other thing: MIT detectives might not attribute a change in MO to him, which would defeat the object. Would that be so bad?

Yes, it fucking would.

The whole point of the exercise was to create mayhem. Enable a situation where he could finally take some credit. The Odin stones – his badge of honour – would take care of that, except they hadn't yet been found, or if they had, they'd not made an appearance in the press. As he scrolled further down the page, his eyes seized upon a photograph of DCI Stone, next to him, the female officer with the necessary credentials. Yes! She was so much more than a definite maybe. He'd finally hit the jackpot.

38

Frankie was totally exhausted. By the time Foley left the Morpeth scene, it was getting dark and the briefing at Middle Earth was over. Abbott had told the SIO that the team were packing up, so David suggested to Frankie that they head to his cottage twelve miles away to regroup and talk about where to go next. When he drew up outside, the lights were on in the living room. They could see Ben through the window, standing on a ladder, scraping walls.

David glanced at Frankie, narrowing his eyes. 'Did he know we were coming?'

She snapped her head around. 'No! Give the kid a break, why don't you?'

'I've given him a damned sight more than that, Frank.'

She softened. 'You've done the right thing, boss.'

'I know, but this village is no place for a kid like Ben.' He pointed along the empty lane to drive home his point. 'As you can see, there's not a soul around half the time.'

'It didn't do you any harm.'

'No, but I left as soon as I was old enough to go it alone. Besides, I had Luke to keep me company and my nan didn't work. You and I are on the go, twelve, fourteen hours a day. It's not fair on Ben.' He flicked his eyes towards the house. 'As you can see, he's bored witless when he's not at university. I caught him cleaning the shower this morning. Thought I was seeing things.' David laughed. 'Actually, I'm considering getting him some wheels. A car would give him independence.'

'That's a lovely idea.'

He gave her side-eyes. 'You forgot to tell me it was expensive being a dad.'

She threw him a wide smile as they got out of the car. He

was being ironic. 'Dad' wasn't a word he'd ever associated with what he was offering his nephew, but that's exactly what he'd become, despite his reservations. It was a stopgap, nothing more, but it was exactly what he needed, what they both needed in their lives right now.

Ben climbed down from the ladder as they entered the living room, face and clothing covered in plaster dust. 'I hope neither of you wants a shower. The plumber's been and we have no hot water until tomorrow afternoon. He reckons the bathroom will be finished at the weekend, tiling an' all.'

'Showers are the least of our worries.' David pointed at scraps of wallpaper sticking to his hair. 'And maybe you should have thought of that before you decided to take on the DIY.'

'Oh, I'll be all right. The old lady next door said I'm welcome to use her facilities anytime.'

'You know the neighbours?' David was genuinely astonished.

Ben nodded. 'I helped her in with her shopping a few times. Her husband gave me fresh hen's eggs and cooking apples from their garden. They taste a bit sour though.'

'They're not for eating, you daft sod. The word "cooking" was a clue.'

Frankie laughed out loud. 'I'll make some tea.'

When Ben had finished stripping the wall, David lit the fire. Even in summer, the north-facing cottage was cold and Ben had the windows open. He disappeared next door to get cleaned up, giving his uncle and Frankie the opportunity to talk shop. They talked briefly about the Odin stones – a full house at all four crime scenes, but there were more pressing matters to discuss. With Dunne gone, David had a decision to make regarding the rest of the team. He couldn't keep the discovery of the stones a secret for ever, but neither could he afford to lose the knowledge and expertise of detectives who'd been involved in his investigation from the outset.

'You can't replace the whole team,' Frankie said.

'Don't you think I know that?'

'Has anyone requested a transfer?'

'Not yet.'

'There you go then. You have no choice but to keep them on. Pam Bond is solid.' Frankie was talking about the receiver. 'She's great at her job and validated by my old man. If that's good enough for me, it should be good enough for you. He didn't pin that badge on many. You have no worries on that score. Besides, Dick seemed to think the briefing had gone well. I'm sure he'd have said if there had been a hint of bad feeling.'

'It's not the receiver I'm concerned about, it's the statement reader. I need him onside and I'm not sure how close he is to Dunne.'

'Dunne's an arsehole . . .' She got up to throw another log on the fire. 'They're probably keen to see the back of him.'

'Are you talking about me?'

Frankie turned her head.

Ben was standing in the doorway, freshly showered, with wet hair and clean clothes on after his visit next door. It was clear from the hurt expression on his face that he'd only heard the last part of her sentence.

'No, you idiot. We have a few staffing issues.'

Ben wasn't sure what to believe.

Horrified, Frankie glanced at her boss. 'David, tell him!'

'She's right, Ben. It wasn't about you.'

Frankie had already switched her attention to the teenager in the doorway. 'Ben, we're friends. You know that if I had something to say, I'd say it to your face.'

'Fine, whatever.' Briefly, the lad's gaze fell on the coffee table, then switched to his uncle. 'I thought you'd given that to me.'

He was referring to the Odin stone David had been playing

with subconsciously ever since he'd arrived home – the one he'd had in his possession ever since he was a kid – an action not lost on Frankie. She loved the idea that he'd pass the keepsake to the next generation, a tradition her own family were keen on. It was especially important, because Ben was David's only living relative.

Warmed by his generosity, Frankie caught his eye. 'I thought you didn't believe in all that shite.'

'I don't,' he bit back.

'Yeah right.'

He blushed, sending her a non-verbal warning to drop the subject.

Ben pulled a face. He was confused, and rightly so. He had no idea what they were on about and his uncle had no intention of filling him in. Stones like the one David had replaced on the table were hot news only three people in the world were aware of: himself, Frankie and Foley – four if he counted the offender. Tomorrow, he intended to share the story of their discovery with his team. Until then, it must remain confidential.

39

Frankie looked over her shoulder as someone knocked on David's office door. The statement reader and two detectives entered from the incident room. A delegation in a closed office signalled trouble. Frankie wondered what they were up to and was surprised when the most senior of the three asked her to step outside a moment, so he could talk privately to the SIO. David nodded a dismissal. After their conversation about staffing last night, and under the impression that he'd summoned them for a dressing down that could only take place out of her hearing, Frankie left the room immediately. Whatever the story, it didn't involve her.

'You have five minutes,' David said as the door closed behind her. 'We have serious work to do this morning.'

The statement reader was the mouthpiece. 'Sir, what Dunne said to Frankie wasn't on. He's always been a bully and we were disgusted by it. If you want to know what it was—'

'That won't be necessary,' David said.

'Did she tell you?'

'No, she never said a thing. And for your information, just in case any of you are taking a punt at why he was given the push, it was unconnected. When I'm ready, I'll fill you in on the details and not before. For the time being, let's just say that his departure was timely and draw a line under it.'

'Yes, sir.' If the statement reader knew what had gone down, he had the sense not to voice an opinion.

David wanted to know which way the wind was blowing before making the disclosure. 'Do I have your full support?' he asked. 'Because if not, feel free to walk. I have something of real value to discuss this morning and I have neither the time nor the inclination to work with people I can't trust.'

'We're right behind you, guv.'

The two detectives confirmed it.

'Good.' David checked his watch: 9.50 a.m. 'There'll be a briefing in ten. Get your shit together and tell the others to do the same.'

As they walked out, Frankie walked in. 'Problem?'

'No. They came cap in hand.'

'Blimey! That is good news. Did you tell them about Dunne?'

'I thought I'd leave that to you.' David grinned.

All conversations ended as they walked out of his office into the incident room ten minutes later. Without the disrupting influence of Dunne, the Murder Investigation Team were a different bunch entirely. Even those who hadn't been part of the delegation in Stone's office earlier could sense that he had something new to communicate. Before that, he asked for an update on the evening briefing that he and Frankie had missed the night before. He listened carefully, then asked if there was any news on the e-fit.

DC Mitchell showed a hand. 'No, guv. Hill is away on business. She's back the day after tomorrow and has agreed to meet the operator at the first available opportunity.'

'She's aware of the urgency?'

'Yes, guv.'

'OK, pay attention then. DS Oliver has some important news to share.'

Frankie stood up. 'As you know, the governor and I have now had the opportunity to visit all four crime scenes. This is an odd one, so listen carefully. When we were at Blyth, the boss picked up an Odin stone. For those of you who don't know what that is, I'll explain in a moment. The guv'nor thought nothing of it but pocketed the item because of a personal connection – lucky for us. I say lucky, because we later visited the second crime scene and, lo and behold, we

218

found another.' With a remote, Frankie brought up images of all four stones on a smart TV, the last two in situ. 'The Blyth stone hadn't triggered an immediate reaction because it was found on the north-east coast, exactly where you'd expect to find stones like that, but inland at Boldon rang alarm bells. It was bagged and labelled in case it had any evidential value. We then visited Stocksfield and found another, placed deliberately inside part of a retaining wall that was crumbling away. We had it photographed by a CSI photographer. Lastly, you guessed it, we found yet another hanging from a tree at the Morpeth scene. Again, this was photographed and all four are now retained in evidence under confidential cover.'

Good and bad vibes travelled around the room.

Frankie paused to explain, for the benefit of those unfamiliar with the stones, what they symbolised. 'In addition, at Joanna's post-mortem, we were told that none of the victims had injuries associated with having fallen to the ground after strangulation. The pathologist said, quote "It's as if they were laid down with care after death, as you or I might handle a child who'd fallen asleep," unquote.'

Glances were exchanged. It was obvious to David that the team weren't yet on board, but they were intrigued – more importantly, they were listening. 'I'll be honest,' he said. 'Frankie and I have no idea what this means, only that it's of significance to the person we're looking for.'

Frankie glanced in his direction: *OK to carry on?*

His nod was her cue to begin.

'Now then, thanks to DS Dunne, the moniker The Sleeper made its way into the press. That's not only unfortunate, it's criminal, because there is a sleep connection here.' She paused, making sure she still had everyone's attention. 'Catherine Bennett's body was left on its side, in a foetal position, Alison Brody was deposited within the boundary of a cemetery plot. Take a look at this . . .' She pressed a button on the remote. The screen changed, showing the cross she'd found close by.

'This ornate engraving is marked on a commemorative cross adjacent to her body ... .'

At Rest.

Frankie didn't stop for breath. 'Margaret Robson was killed within yards of a church.' The screen changed again, an image of the Morpeth crime scene, St George's church spire visible in the background. 'And last but not least, Joanna Cosgrove was laid out on sleepers.' Another image popped up on screen: *RIP.* 'These three letters were spray-painted on a slab at the site of her murder, graffiti put there after the scene was processed. The slab has been uplifted and the paint will be examined.'

'Too right,' someone said. 'Who pays their respects with a can?'

'Precisely.' Frankie and the SIO exchanged a look. 'We can't be sure, but we suspect that the offender may have revisited the scene.'

There was a beat of time before anyone spoke.

'Sounds like he's playing God,' the statement reader said. 'Wouldn't be the first time. Remember that case a while back, the guy who left prayer cards at the scenes?'

'Forster?' Mitch said.

'Yeah, that's him.'

'He's in prison,' Frankie said. 'I checked.'

'Our guy is just as much a weirdo . . .' Abbott's phone bleeped an incoming text. He went for his pocket, apologising for not switching it to silent for the briefing. 'I mean, whoever heard of anyone killing and then protecting his "sleeping" victims from harm?'

'That's the kind of twisted logic we're up against,' David said. 'If he has returned to the fourth scene, Frankie and I will check the rest to see if he's been back there. Be warned. None of what we've told you leaves this room. Without a doubt, this arsehole will be scrutinising the papers. We don't tip him off that we're on to this. Mitch, contact the police research unit. Find out if there's ever been a run of offences connected with mythical stones or anything like it.' He scanned the room. 'Any comments?'

There were none forthcoming.

The team were stumped.

40

Abbott gave David the eye as he left the incident room. That text must've been important. He had something to say that he didn't want to mention without discussing it with the SIO first. David hung back, telling Frankie he'd catch up with her in the car park, head-pointing Dick towards his office.

'What's up?' David closed the door and remained standing. He didn't have time to hang around.

'We got the forensic report in for Margaret Robson's clothing and possessions, guv. A tiny amount of waxy substance was discovered on her handbag, similar to the stuff Collingwood found under Joanna's fingernails. Our offender got sloppy . . . And that's not all . . . Attached to the sample, there are minute traces of fingerprint ink.'

'You're kidding me!'

'I'm afraid not.'

The detectives were excited and horrified in equal measure.

'Maybe the ink came from an offender recently processed,' Abbott suggested.

'I bloody hope so.' David was way ahead of him. 'Check the system for the usual suspects, Dick. Find out if anyone with a similar MO or record of serious violence against women has been fingerprinted by our force in the week before Margaret was found dead. You know what to do.'

'The alternative—'

'Is not something I want to contemplate.' David cut him off. He took a moment to gather his thoughts. 'It might be wise to run Margaret's name too. See if she's been anywhere near a police station recently. Failing that, talk to her family or close associates to see if they have. Can we ID the origins of the wax?'

'They're looking into it. I asked them to hurry.'

'Good man. Can you and Mitch work the weekend?'

'I can – and Mitch will do cartwheels to impress you. He's after a permanent posting.'

'And he might get one at this rate. Let's get to the bottom of this before we share it with the team.'

'Jesus!' Frankie was staring at newly painted RIP letters scrawled artistically on the derelict battery observation post, just off the promenade at Blyth beach, proof that, since their last visit, the perpetrator had returned. This scrawl of graffiti was bigger than the one found at Stocksfield station. Then again, he had a larger concrete canvas on which to make his point – whatever his point was.

David heard Frankie's frustration, loud and clear. He'd seen what she'd seen, but didn't react. He was too busy stewing over his conversation with Abbott, wondering if the fingerprint ink had come from an offender or a serving officer. An unsettling thought . . . but no less disconcerting than the expression currently occupying the face of his perturbed colleague.

Frankie swung round, and round again, scanning the foreground, then the horizon, her body rigid, her expression intense, sharp eyes flitting from place to place. She seemed to shiver, as if a ghost had walked up and tapped her on the shoulder, a reaction so strong it had him wondering if she was not actually in the present, but in another time, at a different location, a quarter of a century in her past. This was no time to disclose what he knew of her sister's fate.

He bottled it. 'You OK?'

Another shiver, a quick nod.

'Frank, you're not . . .' He searched her face. 'What's wrong?'

'Nothing . . .' She waved away his concern. 'I just had the oddest feeling that I was being watched.'

*

A visit to Boldon Cemetery and the Morpeth riverside produced the same troubling results, graphic RIP signs taunting them, like the one-finger salute: *Don't underestimate me*. They had been to Morpeth only hours ago and yet the offender had snuck in after them, probably in the dead of night, to paint a large sign, three feet across, on the underside of the beautiful Telford Bridge.

'This fucker is laughing at us,' David said. 'I want CSIs out, paint samples taken at each crime scene. Action it, Frank.'

She was already on the phone.

41

Intense and painstaking work by Abbott had taken him nowhere. He was jaded, unusual for him, his energy sapped by
the complexity and sheer number of enquiries he'd managed
to process over the weekend. 'I've trawled the database as you
suggested. There was no one with the level of violence picked
up in the time frame you gave me.'

David let out a big sigh. 'None?'

Abbott shook his head. 'Well, there were two domestic
incidents. Both of the offenders are on remand in Durham
prison, I checked. Which rules them out for Joanna Cosgrove's murder. I could go further afield, boss.'

'Raise an action to include neighbouring forces.'

'Will do.'

'Any luck with Margaret?'

'I'm sorry, guv. There's no evidence that she's ever seen the
inside of a police station, much less been processed in one.
Mitch and I interviewed her family and close friends, some
personally, some on FaceTime, others on Skype.' When it
came to policing, there was no substitute for seeing the whites
of a person's eyes. 'We cross-checked every name in her address book against the system. No joy, I'm afraid. Chances are,
the fingerprint ink found on her bag came from contact with
the sicko who ended her life.'

It was the obvious conclusion to draw.

David raised the possibility that the killer could be one
of their own, but his theory incensed Frankie. She'd been a
copper for as long as he had and was fiercely loyal to her
Northumbria colleagues. When Abbott sided with the
guv'nor, backing his point of view, she ceased ranting . . . but
not for long. The conversation was awkward, for all of them,

especially so for Dick. It must've been startlingly obvious to him that such a difference of opinion between lead detectives would cause friction in their professional partnership. If not stamped on quickly, it had the potential to alter the dynamics of the team.

The SIO had read his mind . . .

'Dick, can you give us a minute?' As Abbott got up and left the room, David steered Frankie in another direction. 'We need that e-fit,' he said. 'When is Hill coming in?'

'End of the week.' Her voice was softer than before.

He tensed. 'I thought she was due in today.'

'Not any more . . . Her daughter rang in on her behalf. The conference Hill attended had a serious outbreak of the norovirus. They've been falling like ninepins, apparently. Hill went down with it overnight. She's unable to travel. Presently, she's holed up in a London hotel room, spewing her guts out, unable to stand. We can't offload the job to the Met either. She's highly contagious and will be for a few days yet. She's booked a train for Wednesday. I wouldn't hold your breath.'

'Damn it!' David's head went down, physically and metaphorically.

'I'm sure she'd rather be here than where she is right now.' Frankie waited for him to look up before taking another pop at his unnerving supposition that the offender might be found within their ranks. 'Tell me you don't really believe that we're looking for a copper. In every UK force there are arseholes unfit to hold office – Dunne is a case in point – but there's a world of difference between leaking information and killing four women. I can't even bear to give it houseroom.'

'Me either, but it's not something we can afford to ignore. If that's how it turns out, we can only hope he's not local, though I'm inclined to think that he probably is, or from a force bordering ours, someone who knows the area well. Whoever he is, he's running rings round us.'

'Tell me something I don't know.' Frankie's tone was sour.

'OK, I will . . .' David drew in a breath, frustrated with her negativity, counting on his fingers to make relevant points. 'One: there's no established pattern to these killings. Yes, the victims are all women of a similar status, but some are young, some middle-aged, and there's no physical similarity, so he's not choosing lookalikes. Two: there's no geographical link, which means he's smart enough to have us running all over the force area chasing our tails. Three: the murders were committed on different days of the week, at different times of day, which makes sense if we're hunting someone working shifts. Four: that fingerprint ink is a clear indicator that it was someone who has or had access to a police station. We now know, or think we know, that it wasn't anyone who was locked up before Margaret Robson died who also has a propensity for violence. Nor was it her or anyone she knows. Dick just said so—'

'Five . . .' she mimicked him. 'Who's to say it isn't some mug punter who was locked up for something else? Someone who's never been convicted of violence? How many offenders have we processed in our force area since these killings began? They'll all have traces of print ink on their person. Even those arrogant enough to think that they can kill and get away with it slip up. Prisons are full of them.'

'I don't disagree with you but, if that were true, where do you propose we start looking? Equally, it could be someone close to home—'

Frankie ignored that as if he'd never said it. 'Six: he's made mistakes. What self-respecting copper would do that?'

'C'mon, Frank. Look me in the eye and tell me you don't think he's in the know.'

She looked away.

David gave her a shove. 'Are you suggesting that he returned to the crime scenes on the off-chance that we weren't watching them? He *knows* we're not – in my opinion, another pointer to him being an insider, whether you like it or not.

The more we dig, the stronger the notion of a shift-worker comes into my head. He fits the profile—'

'What profile?' Her words were laced with contempt. 'Did you ever consider that he could just be on the dole?'

'With the forensic awareness of a copper?'

'Hardly. He left a clue the size of Texas on Margaret Robson's bag.'

'There's no such thing as the perfect murder, you know that.'

'Oh really?' she bit back. 'There are thousands of killers walking around out there who've never been brought to book, thousands of victims who never got justice. Happy endings are for crime fiction, guv. So don't patronise me! He can't get away with this. I won't let him.'

Realising what he'd just said, and that her sister's murder had never been solved, David felt like a prize shit and tried not to show it. Frankie's eyes were moist. For a moment, he thought she might lose her composure and break down. They had fought before, had many difficult conversations since they had teamed up, some of them soul-searching. This one was the pits. He wanted to comfort her, tell her that he knew her secret, but she was in no mood for a deep and meaningful. She'd pull up the shutters, blocking any attempt to console her.

He recognised the signs.

Instead, he lowered his voice, and with it the temperature, mind back on the job. 'I'm just trying to understand how it's possible that he's alluded us for so long, Frankie. Can you at least consider the possibility that it could be a copper or a civilian who works with us? We need answers. We're in the firing line here.'

The exchange went on for another five minutes. David reinforcing the fact that they couldn't overlook the possibility that the serial killer they were dealing with was hiding in plain sight, that he would look and act normal, that it was a fallacy to suggest that he was somehow deranged, Frankie countering his arguments, turning up the heat.

'You've changed your tune,' she scoffed.

'Excuse me?'

'You were the one calling him a maniac—'

'Turn of phrase and you know it. The truth of it is he's probably as sane as you and me.' He pulled a crazy face, making her laugh out loud, then drove home his point that serial killers were unlike the fictional characters dreamt up by Hollywood screenwriters to titillate viewers, but something else entirely. 'We can't afford to buy into that stereotype. We should be concentrating on the attention-seeking behaviour of the man we're dealing with, whether or not he's ever pulled on a uniform.'

Finally, she capitulated.

'Sometimes, I hate this job!'

42

'Are we speaking then?' David said as they left the incident room for their second office – a long stretch of sandy beach a short drive away, nowhere near Blyth. They'd had their fill of that coastal town recently and hadn't seen each other for hours. While he'd been updating the head of CID, Frankie had been liaising with Mitch, trawling through information supplied by the police research unit. There was plenty to look at: intelligence on the occult, witches' covens, devil worship even, but nothing appertaining to mythical stones. Bug-eyed, she required fresh sea air and thinking time. He needed to lift her spirits. 'It'll be awkward if we're not the best of friends by close of play.'

A sideways glance. 'Why's that then?'

'I'm invited for supper. Your dad called.'

'He did?' Frankie stopped walking and rolled her eyes. 'The two of you in one room is all I bloody need.'

'It'll be fun!'

'It'll be *Mastermind* and you'll be in the chair, two minutes on your specialist subject: the murder of four women in the Northumbria force. I'll cancel. My old man will understand.'

David fell silent as she made the call. She was right though. If her father cottoned on to the idea that a copper might be responsible for the recent spate of murders, he might be tempted to stick his oar in. It was in his blood, as much as it was theirs. When David accepted the invitation, he'd done so for her, but maybe a visit to the Oliver house wasn't such a good idea.

She ended the call, pocketing her phone.

'Sorted.' She'd told her father that something had come up. 'Was he disappointed?'

'You could say that.' She was smiling as she said it.

They walked along the promenade for a few minutes, then down the footpath onto the beach. In half an hour, it would be high tide. Out to sea, dark clouds threatened rain, but it hadn't put off northerners from having fun. Under his grandfather's guidance, a little boy was flying a *Despicable Me* kite, struggling to keep it airborne. Two smaller children squealed with delight every time he managed to launch it. As the detectives stood watching, David's phone rang.

'Belinda!' Putting the phone on speaker so Frankie could listen in, he thanked the journalist for keeping her word. She'd lifted the profile of the police effort in the press considerably, lessening the focus on The Sleeper. 'I'm betting he won't like that,' he told her. 'And that's exactly what we're after. How are you?'

'Fine,' Wells said. 'How are you getting on?'

'We're making progress.' He didn't elaborate.

'I see Dunne is history.'

The two detectives exchanged a worried look.

'He's giving you grief?' David asked.

'On the contrary . . .' There was levity in Wells' voice. 'Whatever you said to him did the trick. I've not heard a peep out of him since you and I spoke.'

'Then how—'

'When I said I'd help, it didn't mean I wouldn't spy. Don't panic, David. My information came from legitimate sources at HQ, not from anyone close to you. Where are you anyhow? Sounds like you're in a wind tunnel.'

'Taking a walk to clear my head.'

'That must be quite a development.' Wells was fishing.

'We're working on it.'

'Can you share?' she asked.

'Only in general terms.'

'Fair enough.' She listened patiently as he explained what he had in mind. 'When do you want it printed?'

231

'Yesterday,' David said.

'Consider it done.'

'Oh, there is one other thing you could do for me . . . nothing to do with the investigation, it's personal.'

'You're into older women? Outstanding!' she laughed.

David grimaced, a pair of pouting strawberry-coloured lips flashing before his eyes. 'You'd be quite a catch for any man, Belinda, but I'm not in the market at the moment. I'll be sure to let you know if that changes.' David looked on as Frankie stuck her fingers down her throat. Working hard to suppress a full-on belly laugh, he went back to Wells. 'I'm too busy chasing villains and trying to look after a bereaved nephew. Any chance you have an opening for an intern? He's a journalism student at Newcastle Uni.'

'Sorry, my inner Good Samaritan is all used up.'

'Right . . . No problem. I shouldn't have asked. I know how busy you are. I just thought he could shadow you, he'd learn a lot and it would take his mind off his dad. My brother was killed in an RTA recently. I'd like to give the lad something to do until his course restarts in September.'

'You always could twist women round your little finger.'

Frankie's right eyebrow turned into a big question mark: *You can? That's news to me.*

David smiled a coy reply: *There's a lot you don't know about me.*

Wells' keen sense of humour had lifted the mood of his 2ic and for that David was grateful. He couldn't say that she was yet back to her old self, but she was getting there. It was good to see. Frankie might lose her rag from time to time, but the thing he most loved about her was her ability to bounce back. She'd have her say and be done with it. She wasn't one to hold a grudge.

'What's his name?' Wells asked.

'Ben.'

'How old?'

232

'Eighteen.'

'OK, send him my way. Maybe he's in the market for a new squeeze if you're not.' Another laugh.

David ignored the quip and high-fived Frankie. 'I'll drop him off in the morning.'

Frankie didn't verbalise her admiration for David's efforts on Ben's behalf. She was too choked for words, pride filling her up as he thanked Wells. Ending the call, he made another, giving his nephew the good news. Whatever Ben's response, it pleased David no end and delighted her. In his private life at least, things were looking up.

She ducked as the kite plummeted, hitting the sand yards away. The tide was creeping up the beach, crashing in, foaming and curling, a fine spray of seawater kissing her skin. A walk here – in any weather and in any season – was stimulating, allowing her to think more clearly away from the mayhem of the incident room, constant interruptions and office politics, the latter constantly on her mind.

'Is something bothering you?' David asked.

Her mood changed in a flash. 'Apart from the fact that we haven't made an arrest, you mean?'

'We're making progress, Frank. The team can sense it. It'll spur them on to close the case.'

'We're a long way from that,' she warned.

'We'll get there if we keep the faith.'

Frankie was nodding. 'For what it's worth, you did the right thing playing it safe. Leaving the Odin stones under confidential cover was a good move. And by sharing the information internally, it must be glaringly obvious to those we inherited from Sharpe that you've made a conscious decision to trust them now that Dunne is out of the way. They're joining the dots though, David. They've already worked out that you have reason to doubt others within the wider force.'

Before he could answer, his phone rang again. This time it was Abbott and, once again, he allowed her to listen in case she needed to hear what he had to say. As it turned out, she did . . .

'Guv, we've had word on the waxy substance found on Margaret's bag. It's a proprietary mixture of micro and technical waterproof shield, the type used on low-quality wax jackets you can buy on any market stall. Put it this way, we're not talking Barbour.'

'Not a copper then?' Frankie said.

David ignored the dig.

'I can't make my mind up if our man is clever or the exact opposite,' Abbott added. 'On the one hand, the jacket was a good bet: easily washed down; the garment of choice for the county set, dark in colour, not unusual in any way that would draw attention, or if seen by the likes of Annie; unlikely to snag on anything if his victims put up a fight, not that any of the poor sods had a chance.'

'Apart from Joanna,' David reminded him.

'Yes, apart from her. Lab staff are certain that the wax under her fingernails is the same type, guv. He should've done more homework on the type of clothing to wear on his killing spree.'

David thought for a moment. 'This is a long shot, a job for Mitch. Tell him I want every custody sergeant in the force to check property and photographs going back three months and not to put it in for referral without checking with me first. Let's see who's been brought in lately sporting a cheap wax jacket.'

Abbott was gone.

43

By eight o'clock in the evening there were ten times the number of ongoing actions than there had been that morning. It had taken longer than Frankie had hoped but the investigation had finally stepped up a gear. The mood among her colleagues had lifted. There was a real buzz in the office: telephones rang off the hook; radio chatter increased and there was a palpable urgency among the murder detectives under her command. She left the incident room more buoyed than when she'd arrived. That euphoria didn't last. As she walked towards her car, that same feeling of being under surveillance she'd experienced earlier in the day was like a stab between her shoulder blades. Unease crept over her, a physical sensation, so strong it lifted the hairs on the back of her neck and made her swing round to check if anyone was there, heart kicking a hole in her chest. A tall figure was striding across the car park at a fast pace: *Andrea*. Frankie exhaled, annoyed with herself for being spooked for no reason.

His eyes homed in on her. Female coppers, like their male counterparts, had an arrogance about them: the way they clocked a room, alert to anything out of the ordinary; the way they walked, smug and egotistical, like they owned the goddamn world; the way they spouted their opinions on every issue, whether or not their audience was listening or even interested.

Did she have a point of view on early death? he wondered.

A grin spread across his face as he watched her in conversation with her sister-in-law. A smidgeon of tension there, he thought. A minor disagreement? Girly squabble most likely. Unusual. This bunch was tighter than most, and for good reason, which is why he'd chosen her. On so many levels, she was the perfect nominee, from a celebrated family, connected through the generations in a way that no other relatives were. Offing her would have spectacular results, causing ripples that would reach the capital, creating headlines no SIO could afford to ignore.

Steph would be well impressed.

'Frankie, what's wrong? No, cancel that, I know what it is.' Andrea seemed genuinely concerned and, if Frankie was reading her right, more than a little miffed. She didn't hold back. 'Do you know how worried your dad is about you? How worried we all are? Except your mum. Her head is . . . well, I haven't a clue where her head is half the time, but then that's nothing new. I've never been able to work her out.'

'The feeling is mutual.' Frankie's joke fell flat.

'Well, she may not have noticed that you've gone walk-about, but the rest of us have. You're pushing us out and it has to stop. You've been out of sorts for days. We've all noticed it. You've not returned my calls and texts. You turned down an invitation to supper, and Rae – you remember her don't you: drop-dead gorgeous, blue eyes, five two, your big sister? – has left countless voicemail messages that have also gone unanswered.'

'I've been busy.'

'And I have to sleep with her, which has felt like sharing a sack with a couple of ferrets the last few nights. Unlike you, I don't drive a desk. I'm mobile in a Traffic car, which means I need my kip and, right now I'm wasted, so why don't you stop giving us all the run-around, eh?'

'I'm not!' Frankie lied. 'David and I have a lot on. We're running a four-hander, in case you haven't noticed.' She peered into the darkness, scanning the car park for . . . she didn't know what.

'Too busy for us?'

Frankie snapped her head around. 'At the moment, yes. I haven't got time to fart around playing happy families while innocent women are dying left, right and centre. I would have thought you of all people would be applauding, not giving me grief.' Her attention drifted from car to car, to the shadowy area at the back door of the station, the entry and exit gate and beyond the barrier to the street. Nothing. She relaxed, her heart rate returning to normal. 'Dad sent you to hold my hand, is that it?'

'What if he did?'

'He should butt out of my business—'

'That's not fair, Frank. You went to him, remember?'

In Frankie's peripheral vision, she was conscious of movement over Andrea's shoulder. Once more, she peered into the darkness, checking the area warily, trying and failing to hide her preoccupation with what or who might be lurking there and found nothing beyond what she would expect to see.

Andrea was still giving her what for, but David's words were louder: *the killer we're dealing with is hiding in plain sight.* Her anxiety increased, an impression that there was someone close by, a ghost invisible to the naked eye. She couldn't tell Andrea; she'd sound like a nutcase if she did and get earache for her trouble. On Blyth beach, she'd had that same sensation of being watched and shrugged it off, blaming it on the stress of the case, lost sleep, the sheer volume of work currently on her desk, but the feeling that she was under observation was stronger now than ever before.

Across the car park, his target glared at her sister-in-law, her mouth going twenty to the dozen. She was fiery this one. It wouldn't be easy to catch her off-guard. She'd been a copper for the best part of fifteen years. With her present work commitments, he could see no easy way of luring her away from the safety of others . . . not for long anyway. More often than not, she was double-crewed. A minor dilemma, but one he couldn't ignore.

She'd kick the living shit out of him if he got too close.

Presently, she was stationary, but he couldn't do her now with the other bitch in the way. He couldn't do her in her car either. That might have been possible if he'd snuck in there while she wasn't looking but, while he had a legitimate excuse for being in the area, that would be a risk too far, even for him.

His agitation grew.

Headlights.

He slid down in the seat of his vehicle as a Traffic car arrived, a flash of lights to a colleague who was heading the other way, its main beam illuminating the car park. Waiting for it to pass, he got out of his car and made off through the secure car park, wending his way through private cars and service vehicles adorned with force insignia and out of sight. He'd bide his time. No rush. A last glance over his shoulder. The two women were friends now. Or were they? It tickled him to think that it might be their last conversation.

'Fine!' Andrea said. 'Ignore me, why don't you?'

Frankie turned to face her. 'I'm not!'

'What the fuck is wrong with you? You're jumpy . . .'

'Don't talk crap.' More movement across the car park, a growing sense of alarm. Ignoring the black looks of her sister-in law, Frankie searched her pockets, swearing under her breath when she didn't find what she was after, an item every woman needed: security against those who might do them harm.

'Come for a drink,' Andrea said. 'We need to talk and you're going to tell me what is going through that head of yours.'

'I can't,' Frankie said. 'I've got to go.'

'I thought you were finished for the day.'

'I am. I left my phone on my desk.'

'I'll wait.'

'No. Look, you're right, I'm exhausted. I need to get a reasonably early night. Alcohol keeps me awake. Seven hours sleep, I'll be as right as rain—'

'No, you won't. Frank, I think you should see a counsellor. It helped you once—'

'Take a hike! And while you're at it, get your nose the hell out of my business and keep your opinions to yourself. If you go to blabbing to David, I'll never forgive you. I mean it, Andy. Never!'

Before she could respond, Frankie turned on her heels and fled, tears pricking the back of her eyes as she marched off without a backward glance. She didn't dare look over her shoulder, convinced that if she did there would be two pairs of eyes, not one, staring back at her.

Keying in the combination to gain access to the building, she heard the lock click and yanked the door open with enough force to snap it from its hinges. Sucking in a breath, she sized up the dark car park through the security glass, suddenly aware that in her rush to get inside she may have left Andrea vulnerable. She needn't have worried. Her car was on the move.

Frankie raced upstairs to the major incident room. Two civilians passed her in the corridor wishing her goodnight as they left for the day. The night was anything but good. She wanted to grab her phone and get out of there. She pushed on through a set of double doors, head down so she didn't have to engage with anyone else.

Almost there.

'Frances!'

Startled by the use of her proper name – no one ever called her that – Frankie raised her head. 'Sir?' She came to a stop. 'How are you? I heard you were living the high life in the South of France.'

'You heard right. This is a fleeting visit. Thought while I

was here I'd check in on my replacement.'

Living overseas had done nothing for the former DCI. Sharpe looked like a broken man. He had no tan to speak of. His hair was greyer, his face thinner than she remembered. Unsurprising, she supposed. In their line of work, divorce was an occupational hazard, shattering the lives of many. Some detectives never got over it. Standing in the dim corridor, Sharpe was a shadow of the man he used to be. She began to wonder if he was now regretting his decision to put his ticket in, as some coppers did, including her father. Despite a rough day, a tough year, she couldn't imagine her life outside of the job and chose not to think too far ahead.

'Once a copper, eh?' She smiled.

'Is he around?'

'No, I'm afraid, like Mr Presley, DCI Stone has left the building.'

She could smell alcohol on Sharpe's breath. Then, in a moment of clarity, her sympathy for him disappeared, replaced by a much darker emotion as David's voice arrived unbidden: *Can you at least consider the possibility that it could be a copper?* Frankie was instantly on alert. What was Sharpe doing here? The door to the incident room stood ajar. Had he been in there, poking around?

'Are you OK, Frances?'

'Fine,' she lied. 'Why wouldn't I be?'

She didn't want to acknowledge what was going through her head. The idea that she might be standing face to face with a quadruple killer in the place she felt most safe was as bizarre as it was frightening. Was it the heat of *his* eyes she'd felt when she was arguing with Andrea in the car park? Had he been watching her from above? Had he decided to make his getaway when he saw her turn back towards the building.

'How's Stone doing?' he asked.

She cleared her throat. 'Great.'

'And the case?'

'Not so great.' Frankie didn't expand on her answer. Did Sharpe already know? Had he flicked through David's policy book, had eyes on the murder wall or scanned the papers on her desk? Was he looking for confidential information that only an SIO should know?

'Congratulations on your appointment,' he said.

'Thank you, sir.'

He held out a hand. 'Good to see you.'

She cringed as she shook it. 'You too.'

She watched him walk away, then pushed open the door to the incident room, grabbing her phone and the pepper spray she'd hidden in her desk drawer, then made her way back to her car and drove away, checking her rear-view mirror every now and then. Paranoid she may be, but she was taking no chances.

She keyed David's number.

He picked up immediately.

'Guess who I've just seen?'

44

With both hands full, Frankie bummed her way through David's office door and kicked it shut with her foot. She placed a coffee and a fresh chocolate croissant on his desk. His eyes never left the newspaper he was reading, neither did he thank her for the unexpected breakfast treat she'd paid for out of her own pocket as she plonked her body down in the seat opposite, on starter's orders for a crucial head-to-head. 'Morning, Frankie,' she said for his benefit, taking the lid off her latte to let it cool, trying to prompt him into conversation. When nothing came back she added: 'David, put your newspaper down. We need to talk about Sharpe.'

Now he looked at her – really looked at her – his expression inscrutable. This was not what she expected. It certainly wasn't the attitude of someone gagging to make an arrest or even talk about the possibility, or anything else she'd raised with him last night. It took a while for him to speak.

'He scared you, didn't he?'

That was an understatement, but she chose not to confirm it. Her voice had given her away when she'd rung him from the car. She was aware of that. He'd listened carefully and then told her to calm down and go home. They would discuss it first thing. She took his advice to sleep on it and didn't argue. And yet, now was 'first thing' but when she came in a moment ago, he'd not so much as raised his head or acknowledged her arrival.

'Frank, you've been working hard. We all have. It was late—'

She gave him hard eyes. 'What's that got to do with anything?'

The feeling of being sold out was instantaneous. The

thought that Andrea might have repeated the conversation they had in the car park to her boss was inconceivable. It would damage her, at the very least make David wary of taking her seriously. Despite his undoubted respect for women, he obviously didn't understand what it felt like to be one in mortal danger. The fact that she was a police officer didn't make her immune to fear. Unconsciously, she slipped a hand into her pocket. The pepper spray was still there. She was trained to take down an offender if she had to, even a much larger, stronger man, but the rage of someone capable of overpowering and killing four innocent females was unpredictable in extreme. He could have killed her before she had a chance to raise the alarm.

'Well, you needn't have worried,' he said. 'Sharpe flew back to the UK for Duncan Carr's funeral—'

'You've spoken to him?'

'No, I asked around. That's what I do, I'm a detective.'

'And so am I.' She was cut by his remark.

'I rang your dad to confirm it, Frank. He was there all afternoon with dozens of witnesses.'

'That's it? You're writing his appearance off, just like that?' Frankie had hardly slept for thinking about her experience last night. She felt a shiver down her back. For a moment, she was back in that dim corridor trying to keep her head, doing her level best to second-guess Sharpe's next move, attempting to breathe.

'Frank, you sounded spooked on the phone. You've gone from an out-and-out refusal to believe that a cop was responsible for the cases we're investigating, to making wild accusations about a former senior detective without any proof or credible explanation. He has a legitimate excuse for being in the country—'

'A convenient one,' she said.

'From what you told me last night, he also had a perfectly reasonable excuse for being in this building.'

'Did he contact you and say he was coming in?'

'No, but—'

'There you go then. He was here, David. Right here, possibly even in this room. Doesn't that bother you? It should. I happen to know he didn't come in through the front door. I checked with the front desk after we spoke on the phone. Which means he accessed the building via the back door with no authority to do so. You need to change the combination code.'

'I will, but Sharpe worked here for years. He probably did it without thinking. It's irregular, I agree, but not a serious offence—'

'That rather depends on his intention. Technically, it's a burglary, not something to be overlooked.'

'I'm not prepared to hang him out to dry on the basis of that.'

'Will you listen to yourself! We know that he was in the area for the first three murders. We know that he never caught, or even came close to catching the criminal we're after. Have you ever asked yourself why a man of his stature was so incompetent, why he gave up and moved abroad? David, he was in charge! Well placed to investigate as he saw fit. We don't know where he was when Joanna Cosgrove died, but it needs investigating. Aren't you even a tad concerned?'

'I'll look into it.'

It was a dismissal. As far as he was concerned, the matter was closed. Stunned by his apathy, Frankie wanted to leap across his desk, grab him by the lapels and shake some sense into him. Instead, she restrained herself, trying hard not to show her disappointment. This was big – potentially huge – and yet he wasn't remotely interested, let alone excited. In her mind, there could only be one reason.

She had to know.

She studied him as she spoke. 'I saw Andrea last night.'

'Is that relevant?'

'I don't know, you tell me. She was waiting for me when I left work, wanting to know why we'd cancelled supper with my old man. I told her the same as I told him. Thought I'd throw that out there, in case she asks. When you're making up the truth, it needs to be consistent, guv.'

Not a flicker.

He went back to his newspaper.

Frankie stayed put and tried again, taking a bite of her croissant as if she'd accepted his bullshit or even agreed with it. It nearly choked her. She continued with her ruse, trying to find out if he'd spoken to Andrea. 'Naturally, I was blamed for being a killjoy. Andrea and Rea were also invited but when told that we weren't going to make it, they pulled out too. It made sense to put it off until we could all be there, I suppose. Anyway, she sends her best.'

'That's nice.'

Frankie was sick of looking at the top of his head. 'Yeah, and Theresa May doubled our salaries with immediate effect and pledged to reinstate all the officers we've lost.'

He glanced up from the newsprint. 'Sorry, I didn't get that.'

'That's because you weren't listening. You haven't been listening since I walked in. What is wrong with you?'

'This.' He slid the paper across his desk, his face set in a scowl.

Frankie speed read the column Wells had put together, skipping over the front page to a paragraph he'd ringed in red.

According to a press official, there have been major developments into the deaths of four women in the Northumbria force area. The SIO, Detective Chief Inspector David Stone, declined to elaborate on the nature or extent of his enquiries. What we do know is that further examination of all four scenes have been carried out and that samples are now being processed forensically. The police are hoping that these and other tests will lead to the identity and apprehension of the person responsible.

Handing the paper back, she held on to her anger. 'That's what you wanted, isn't it?'

'Word for word, but I hope we haven't set ourselves up to fail.'

'We? I had nowt to do with it.' Frankie watched him closely, her head dipped on one side. 'Did you get out of bed the wrong side, David? It seems there's no pleasing you today. This is exactly what we planned. It was a good idea yesterday and it still is. I really hope that your suspicions are incorrect but, if we are looking for someone close to home, we need to keep an eye on the confidential cover file in case anyone tries to access it. That's top priority, hourly checks from this point on. And, if my opinion still counts, there is no one closer to home than your predecessor.'

Her phone rang, a number not in her address book.

'I have to take this.' She didn't wait for his consent. 'DS Oliver.'

'Good morning. My name is Trisha Conway. I'm a freelance events director. I gather you want to talk to me about some work I did at Boldon Golf Club a few months back.'

'I do indeed.' Frankie was on the verge of adding *'You took your time and now it's inconvenient,'* but managed to hold back. A half-assed apology was in the process of delivery . . .

'. . . for not getting in touch sooner. I've been directing operations in Barcelona over the weekend and just picked up your message. Is there any chance we can meet today? I'm flying to Stavanger in the morning – unless you want to meet at the airport early doors for a quick chat? That would work for me. I'll be kicking my heels for an hour or so.'

'What time is your flight?'

'Eleven fifteen.'

Frankie made a quick calculation: Conway would have to go through security a good while beforehand, ruling out Frankie's attendance at the morning briefing and she wasn't having that. Things were beginning to get interesting. She wasn't finished with Sharpe yet.

Trish Conway lived in an executive Baltic Quay apartment on the Gateshead side of the Tyne, a property with panoramic views of Newcastle's iconic bridges, within easy reach of bars, restaurants and the many cultural venues to be found in and around the city centre, two of the best – the Sage Gateshead and the Baltic Centre for Contemporary Art – literally on her doorstep.

The interior of the apartment was smart, a little minimalist for Frankie's liking, but with a wow factor similar to that of her own frontline apartment overlooking the North Sea. Not that she'd had time to enjoy it lately, so brief had been her visits home. Late nights, early mornings and sleepovers at her parents' home had put paid to that. Work took precedence . . . always.

As she sat down in the open-plan living room, Frankie studied the woman she'd come to see. She was around forty years old, slender with olive skin and hair tied back in a ponytail. Dark eyes stared out from behind a pair of glamorous black-framed glasses. Conway had impeccable taste in clothes and jewellery. She knew what suited her and it showed. For someone just in from Barcelona, she was super smart, showing no sign of travel fatigue. She already knew why the police wanted to speak to her.

'How can I help you? As I told your DC when he called, I've done no events for Alison Brody for a couple of months, the last one being a corporate affair at Boldon Golf Club.'

'That's the one of interest to us. Was Alison hands-on? I only ask because no one at the club seems to know her.'

'She only made one visit as I recall.'

One was all it took.

'Let me ask you something. What was she like? As a person, I mean.' Frankie was trying to establish if she was the type to

247

stop and chat, or someone who just got on with what they had to do and took little notice of those around her – a bit like David this morning.

'I worked for her,' Conway said.

'That's not what I asked.' Frankie gave her a push. 'It's easier if I don't have to guess, Trish.'

'You want the honest answer or the polite one?'

The DS wanted the truth. 'You didn't like her?'

'I didn't dislike her, as such. She was a very busy woman with multiple projects going on simultaneously. Our relationship was steady. She had a great business brain but – how can I put this? – warmth and hospitality were not her best assets. She wasn't the type many warmed to.'

Frankie wanted more.

Realising this, Conway supplied it. 'Look, Alison could be a loudmouth on occasions, not just with me, with everyone. If she saw an opportunity, she went for it, no holds barred. If she wanted something done, it had to happen right away. She had little patience. What happened to her is appalling, no one deserves to die like that, but she rubbed many up the wrong way. Had it not been for the fact that her death has been linked with three others, it wouldn't surprise me if someone wanted to shut her up for good.'

Frankie remembered her conversation with David and the list she'd produced when she was trying to convince him that it was the victims' success the offender despised enough to kill them. As an ambitious woman herself, she knew only too well what it was like to fight for equality in a male-dominated environment. She'd seen other females try to emulate men in order to reach the next rank, taking on their characteristics, swearing and shouting to get their own way. If Alison Brody had fallen into this trap, could it be that Catherine Bennett, Margaret Robson and Joanna Cosgrove had too? It had Frankie wondering if it wasn't their achievements that got them killed, but perhaps their direct approach to men who worked for them, or even those who didn't. On social media, even a hint of feminism was enough to get some going, the backlash ranging from snide put-downs to death threats. Equality was a world away.

'She'd made enemies?' Frankie said.

'Put it this way, she had few friends.'

Frankie valued Conway's honestly. If it had been a man slagging off a successful woman, she might have taken less notice, but coming from an equally ambitious female, it sounded odd. Not all women appreciated the accomplishments of their peers, but most did, celebrating their success, applauding them for it. Come to think of it, this was the first time anyone had disrespected one of the victims. If anything, the opposite was true – and this wasn't unusual. Even if a murder victim was a complete and utter waste of space with a long criminal record, their pals, sweethearts and relatives would never slag them off. Forgetting their failings, acts of violence or long terms of imprisonment, the platitudes would come spilling out: they were mint; wouldn't hurt a fly; salt of the earth; they'd do owt for anyone.

'Was Alison's highhandedness directed at anyone in particular?' she asked.

'I couldn't say. I'm freelance. Alison and I had limited contact.'

'What about at the Boldon job?'

'Not that I can recall, though she was a bit short with club staff when we had to wait for your lot to turn up because someone had broken in and stolen some of our expensive kit. To say she was furious was an understatement.'

'"Your lot?"' Conway's words hit Frankie like a brick.

45

David had made his play in the press – with help from Belinda Wells – but was now feeling under pressure to deliver good news to the head of CID and the general public. From the outset, the offender had been one step ahead – that situation had to change – and, though David was confident that Detective Chief Superintendent Bright had his back, as Senior Investigating Officer he was also aware that he'd stand or fall by his results – and, by association, so would his 2ic. Frankie had a point about Sharpe, and it worried David, but it needed careful handling, a foot-off-the-pedal approach, not the in-your-face Frankie Oliver method. Enthusiasm was one thing, but sometimes there was no stopping her and he was forced to rein her in. That didn't stop him feeling guilty for stamping his size tens all over her theory. In his opinion, Sharpe was an unlikely suspect, but as soon as Frankie materialised he'd reassure her that he was taking it seriously and would ask her to investigate.

A job in the MIT had always been her dream, a chance to emulate her father and grandfather. It meant everything to her. She had the potential to make SIO herself one day. David intended to help her make the most of it. She could play at it in front of the squad, but she wasn't ready yet. They had an understanding: in the MIR, she had his back; behind closed doors, she could speak her mind. She excelled in that and she'd be no good to him otherwise, but there were so many other considerations . . .

SIOs had to think about finance, manpower, media, operational need, the reputation of the force and a raft of other things. Frankie only had to think of the lock-up. Last night, she'd come up with something fresh, something that may or may not be valid, but was certain to generate new lines of enquiry. Still, it was his job to prioritise, to think laterally. As he checked back through his notes, looking for inspiration, the youngest victim kept popping into his head. He hadn't lost sight of the fact that Catherine Bennett, the high-profile and semi-famous talk-show host, would not have been recognisable when she took her last walk on the promenade where she met her death.

Blyth.

David sat back contemplating, hands behind his head, eyes straying to the force area map on his office wall. He got up to consult it. Unless you'd lost your way, the town was not a place you'd come across by accident. Its position on the north-east coast meant that, unless you were heading there specifically, you wouldn't travel through it to get anywhere else. Blyth was also the scene of the first murder, the most significant for an offender on a mission. Assuming he hadn't killed before, there would've been first-time nerves. Familiarity with the scene would be an essential ingredient, as would an escape route if things went wrong.

The more David thought about this, the more convinced he became that concentrating his efforts on Blyth had merit. Together with his suspicion that the enemy was within, rather than without, he decided on a plan of action that might well bear fruit. Turning away from the map, he walked to the door, peering out into the incident room through the internal window, his gaze travelling around the room. There was no office banter going on. The statement reader's office door was firmly shut, blinds drawn. Abbott had his head down working through Dunne's actions; Mitch was flat out too, checking on Sharpe as well as collating a list of offenders recently arrested whose property included a wax jacket; the rest of the team were similarly engaged, especially the receiver following the latest press announcement. David glanced at his watch. Frankie wasn't yet back from seeing Conway.

What the hell was keeping her?

He'd tailed her for around half an hour, allowing two-car cover to be on the safe side, careful not to get too close. By their very nature, police officers were surveillance-savvy and he was betting that she would be on the alert. In his mind, there was nothing surer. When he'd seen her last night, she was distracted but he couldn't count on that being the case today. Hitching his haversack onto his shoulders, he was careful not to look at her directly as he got out of his vehicle ready to make his move. Aware that he couldn't afford to put a foot wrong, he turned the other way, then came to a stop within touching distance, watching her reflection through the window of a riverside restaurant. Pretending he was taking a photo through the window, he pressed the reverse button, tempted to snap a selfie, except he wasn't that daft. Instead, he captured one of her over his shoulder. Maybe he'd send the image to her boss.

Fucking class.

That would really put the wind up him.

She appeared in no particular hurry to get to her destination, wherever that was. It excited him that she was out in the open, on her own where he could get at her. He had the means and had waited patiently for an opportunity. His method was slightly out of the ordinary, not entirely unheard of, but one that would not only catch the imagination of local people, it would leave the SIO reeling.

As his target moved away from her vehicle, his excitement grew. He set off in pursuit, observing her closely, yet keeping his distance, in case she should glance over her shoulder and recognise him. He didn't doubt for one minute that she possessed certain attributes, skills in problem-solving that equipped her to do her job, but then so did he . . . whether or not the bitch he was trying to impress recognised it.

He chuckled as a thought occurred to him, a conversation he remembered from a while back. Steph was spouting forth, informing others that you could tell from an early age if a kid would be a leader or a follower. Another dig at him, he supposed.

He was done with her.

Up ahead, his target stopped to answer her phone. A quick word with the caller, then she hung up, making off down the road, head held high, shoulders back. Her swagger annoyed him, learned behaviour, he assumed, something that came from within. Whether or not it was down to parental influence or something else he wasn't qualified to say, and neither did he care. That claptrap didn't interest him. He may not come across as a leader to some, but what did they know? His job had gone down the pan but whose fault was that? Did he even care? He was major-league now, supremely confident in his ability, his name in the headlines. This, he decided, would be his penultimate killing – then he'd be ready for Steph.

46

Ideally, David would have liaised with Frankie before ordering a trawl of records to include serving/retired coppers and
civilian personnel who lived in, or had strong connections to,
the Blyth area, now or in the past. Sharpe would be included
in those parameters, though that was a job for Frankie and
her alone. A man's reputation was at stake. It was a big ask for
one person, but what the hell? Frankie had nothing to lose
and everything to gain if she was right. They had agreed that
if they were dealing with a copper – a matter that was still
open to debate despite her alarming encounter with Sharpe
– an officer from their own force was their best guess. Failing
that, Durham and Cumbria were worth a look, someone able
to travel in and out of the area with ease, an individual who
perhaps knew the seaside town well – anyone with a link to
processing offenders through the system and/or with a penchant for myth and legend.

David had to act – and he had to do it now.

He picked up his internal phone. 'Pam, I can see you're
busy, but can you step into my office a moment?' The SIO
checked his watch as he waited. Frankie had been gone a
while, far longer than he'd anticipated. It wasn't like her to
go AWOL and he wondered what Trish Conway had said that
was so interesting. Unless his 2ic had gone off to lick her
wounds. He was about to call her when a knock drew his
attention.

The door opened and Pam Bond walked in. She was a tall
woman, around six three, a detective sergeant who stood
head and shoulders above most of her colleagues, male or
female. Nicknamed 007, hers was a pivotal role. Every piece
of information that came into the incident room passed

across her desk: documents, press cuttings, photographs, CSI reports, telephone messages, the lot. Consequently, she knew more about the investigation than anyone, including him.

'You wanted to see me, guv?'

David nodded. 'Sit down and take the weight off.'

'I'm happy standing.' She looked unsure.

'Relax. You're not about to receive your marching orders. You've worked for Sharpe for three years and I'd like to pick your brains. The team are stretched and I'm considering asking for someone to give us a hand. Doesn't need to be an officer who knows much about the case, in fact it's probably better if they don't, but I need someone who can keep their mouth shut.'

Her concern turned to intrigue. 'What kind of job is it?'

'A sensitive one that requires research into our HR system.' He didn't elaborate further. The least said the better.

'We have an aide who'd be perfect,' Pam said. 'She's been on extended leave of absence—'

'Indira Sharma?'

'That's her, though she prefers Indi, guv. She's looking forward to meeting you and is due back at work tomorrow. I happen to know she's around. I'll get her to come in now if it's urgent.'

'What's she like?'

'She's a flyer. Before she went on leave she spent time on secondment in personnel. She also has Professional Standards and HR knowledge.' Pam grinned. 'She'll know more about us than we do.'

'She's discreet?'

'And ambitious. I'd be more than happy to recommend her but I'm wondering why you're not giving this to Frankie. I know she's got a lot on but there's no one better in my opinion. Indi is good, reliable too, but Frankie can knock spots off her. And, in case you're in any doubt, it's not because we know each other, or because of my close relationship with her father.'

'The thought never crossed my mind.' Pam was preaching to the converted. If David wanted such an important job doing, he need look no further than his 2ic, except she had a job to do on Sharpe that, for now, he wanted to keep under the radar. 'Frankie's out and about. You haven't heard from her, have you?'

A shake of the head. 'No, sir.'

'Me either.' His mobile bleeped an incoming text. He lifted the device from his desk, a raised eyebrow. 'Speak of the devil . . .' He pointed at the chair Frankie had occupied earlier. 'Don't go away.'

Pam sat down to wait, crossing the longest legs he'd ever seen on a woman. He accessed the text, a message that was short and to the point. Frankie never wasted words when she had something to say – especially when she was pissed off.

Held up. Flat tyre. Any chance you can pick me up?

David keyed a reply: *Not a hope in hell.*

No worries. I'll think of something. Failing that I'll grab a cab.

Everything OK?

Hunky-dory.

Anything I need to know?

Making a few enquiries, then I'll fill you in. Back soon.

She was gone.

David glanced at 007, a frown developing. Not about anything she'd said. Pam was pushing against an open door telling him that Frankie was the best detective to help him out, but the job he wanted doing was too important to farm out to an aide he'd never met before, even if she came highly recommended.

Needs must.

'Something bothering you, guv?'

'No.'

Stone wasn't telling the truth. Deep down in the pit of his stomach, he felt tension building. One time when Frankie had gone off to do something, without telling him where she was going, she'd come a cropper. She'd promised never to do it again and yet she had, several times, and would continue to do so. Maverick tendencies were in her DNA. He'd been forced to let it go. If he fussed over a detective of her stature, she'd resent him for being over-protective. She knew her own mind. He had little choice but to trust her instincts. He only hoped she wasn't flying solo, putting herself at risk.

Pam was staring at him. 'Is there anything else, sir?'

'No, you carry on. You've been extremely helpful.'

'Shall I call Indi?'

'No, it can wait until she's back tomorrow. But as soon as Frankie arrives, show her in.'

'You're making the right choice, sir.'

'Thanks.'

As she left the office, David wondered whether he should down tools and go pick Frankie up. He really didn't have the time. Bright had indicated his intention to call in at Middle Earth and would expect to see him there. As if by magic, Frankie's voice came over the radio. Instead of leaving his desk, David listened into the chat on the wire.

'*Mike 2151: I have an urgent enquiry to make. Any mobile units near the Sage available to pick me up?*'

No response.

'*Mike 2151: Any Traffic units able to assist?*'

'*Mike 7003: Traffic units tied up. Say where and I'll come down and confer.*'

David smiled. Mike 7003 was Andrea's collar number. She'd gone to Frankie's rescue . . . and not for the first time, saving him a job, putting his mind at rest. They would both be back in time for lunch.

47

Within minutes of responding to a shout-out, Andrea arrived at the rendezvous on the south side of the Tyne as arranged. As a Traffic officer supervising a large team, she was single-crewed, ready to respond to a fluid situation. That was the nature of her job. Given their row last night, the meeting was bound to be awkward. Frankie wasn't sure she wanted to see Andrea but was nevertheless grateful that she'd taken the time and trouble to bail her out.

The smile didn't quite make it to Frankie's lips. Everything Andrea had said in the station car park about her failure to play nice with their family was true, but she had no right to suggest that *she* should see a shrink, even less to run off at the mouth to David – if that's what she'd done – no matter how well-intentioned.

Their friendship would withstand this small blip.

Still, Frankie had to know.

Taking a deep breath, she leaned on the open window of the Traffic car, intent on clearing the air. She locked eyes with her sister-in-law, aware that if she was asked a direct question Andrea would never lie to her. 'Have you spoken to David?'

'Frank, you know me better than that.'

'Sorry, I had to ask.'

'You did?' Andrea narrowed her eyes, got out and locked her car, friends again. 'What's going on? Sounded like you were in a hurry.'

'I am. I've just had an illuminating conversation with a witness. I was about to investigate, but some arsehole slashed the front tyres on my pool car.'

'Kids?'

Frankie shrugged. 'No idea. I didn't see.'

She had to work hard not to give away her anxiety.

'I'll get the low-loader down to uplift it.' Andrea made the call and then turned off her radio. They stood for a moment, taking in the view, people-watching. Frankie glanced at her watch. 'I have a few enquiries to make that can't wait. Can you spare an hour or two to chauffer me around and drop me back at base? I need to update David.'

Andrea grinned. 'The rate we're going, it might be the only way we get to speak to one another for weeks.' She thumbed towards her car. 'Jump in. There's an espresso on the dash. You look like you need it. I'm—' Andrea hit the deck, a projectile striking her body with such ferocity, she hadn't known what hit her. For a split second, Frankie froze, staring at her crumpled shape on the pavement, a low moan coming from Andrea's mouth as she looked down at the crossbow bolt sticking out of her chest.

'Ohmigod!' a woman screamed.

Frankie wasn't sure if it had been her own voice she'd heard or someone else's, an image of Sharpe's gaunt face arriving in her head. There was a moment of silence, before someone started wailing. *Jesus! Did you see that?* Another female voice . . . *Shit! Someone shot a copper.* Having witnessed Andrea go down, the young woman's face was sheet-white. *What the fuck? She's bleeding!* The female standing next to her was shaking uncontrollably, unsure whether to run for it or remain where she was. *Did anyone see what happened?* Her eyes searched the surrounding area, eventually finding Frankie's. *She's in a bad way. Do something!*

Frankie wanted to tell them all to shut the fuck up. She had a split-second decision to make: stem the blood or call an ambulance? Working quickly, she sank to her knees, took off her jacket and wrapped the garment around the bolt, making sure not to touch it so as not to contaminate evidence. She held it there, while at the same time trying to offer reassurance and estimate where the shot had come from.

She'd be no use to Andrea if she went down too.

Her eyes were everywhere: Baltic Square was heaving and, to her left, a queue of folks waited at a bus stop. A group of tourists rode towards Keelman's Way on the C2C cycle route, unaware of the drama taking place yards away. On higher ground, dark shapes on the horizon looked down from the Sage car park. With the sun behind them, Frankie couldn't see faces, or discern if they were focused on the Millennium Bridge being raised or watching her. On the lower tier, a busy car park was hiding God knows what.

A growing huddle of bystanders were gawping, spooking Andrea, panicking her.

An older male stammered, his expression one of abject horror: *Poor lass, I hope she makes it.*

Turning back to Andrea, Frankie put pressure on the wound to stem blood that was changing her white uniform shirt red. It wasn't so long ago that the boot was on the other foot, Andrea rescuing her from a deranged killer hell-bent on taking her out. In a flash of clarity, Frankie knew exactly what David had gone through with Jane.

She was choking back tears.

'I'm fine, Frank . . .' Andrea coughed, her breath shallow. 'Go!'

'Not on your life! We'll get him, but I'm not leaving you.'

Andrea was not fine. And neither, it had to be said, was Frankie. Slimy warm blood seeped through her fingers. She felt her stomach heave.

A middle-aged man approached. 'Want a hand?'

'Are you a doctor?'

'No.'

'Then step away.'

Frankie pressed down on Andrea's wound.

Unclipping her radio, Frankie pulled it to her mouth: 'Mike 2151 to Control. Officer down outside the Baltic Kitchen, South Shore Road, Gateshead. Assistance and an ambulance required. Tango 7003 has sustained a crossbow bolt through upper left chest. She's conscious but bleeding badly. Any officers north and south of the river to make their way to my location.'

'ANPR,' Andrea whispered, her breath ragged.

'Butt out!' Frankie said. 'This is my investigation, not yours, Inspector.'

She and Andrea had ribbed each other mercilessly since training school, one-upmanship always on the agenda, every opportunity to go one better. Squeezing Andrea's hand, not knowing whether to laugh or cry at her bravery, Frankie kept talking, ordering live feeds on Automatic Number Plate Recognition as Andrea had suggested . . . 'And CCTV to be monitored on both sides of the Tyne to see if we have a runner. The Millennium Bridge is raised and closed to pedestrian traffic. I want it left that way and a PolSA team here ASAP.' She placed Andrea's radio on the pavement. The crowd were closing in. 'Unless you are medical personnel, move back!'

Some onlookers were too shocked to move, others taking photos. While that would appear disgusting to some, it might help her ID the offender if he was still on the Quayside, or even in the crowd. A shiver ran down Frankie's spine as she asked anyone who'd taken photographs within the last half hour to keep hold of them and contact police.

'Did anyone see anything?' she yelled.

People were shaking their heads, but one man stepped forward. 'I saw someone run that way.' He pointed east, a hysterical girlfriend clinging to his arm. 'I don't know if he's your guy. He just daubed the pavement with graffiti and fled.'

Frankie's heart sank. 'Show me.'

As the crowd parted she saw the letters RIP spray-painted on the pavement. More than one pair of feet had trodden on the killer's signature, probably not his. 'I'll lock up anyone who stands on that graffiti. This is a crime scene . . .' She pointed at the witness. 'You stay put. The rest of you, move away!' Her eyes were back on the witness. 'Can you describe him?'

'I hardly saw him,' he said. 'He was running like a whippet, that way.' He thumbed over his shoulder. 'Guys his age all look the same to me.' He pointed at the cynical epitaph on the ground. 'This is a sick joke, surely.' His focus switched to Andrea. 'Is she going to be OK?'

Frankie didn't answer . . .

She didn't know.

At her request, the witness continued to describe what he'd seen and precisely in which direction the offender ran off. Frankie followed his gaze to the private car park to the Baltic Quay apartment block where she'd interviewed Conway, telling him to write down or talk the description into his phone in as much detail as possible. As he took out his mobile, she felt Andrea's hand lose its grip on hers.

'Andy, hold on . . . help is on its way.'

Her attempt at speech was hardly audible. Andrea was sweating and confused. Rapid blood loss did that to people. She looked pale and cold, despite the warm weather, but this was no time for Frankie to lose her bottle.

Focus!

Lifting the radio from the tarmac, she pressed the transmit button: 'Mike 2151 to Control: We have a runner, youngish, fit, dark clothing, dark glasses, carrying a black haversack, wearing a beanie hat, approximately five eight according to the witness. Last seen heading on foot in the direction of the flats to the south-east of the Baltic Flour Mill. Newcastle and Gateshead units, make your way to that location, one of you to the Sage Music Centre car park in case he doubled back. We need eyes on this man and stop and search. He may be armed. Approach with caution. I want firearms and SOCO here now!'

'Control: That's received. Ambulance deployed to your location.'

'ETA?'

'Three minutes.'

Frankie hoped it would be less. Either way, it would be the longest three minutes of her life. There was no doubt in her mind that every police officer and ambulance crew would be racing to the scene. Her training had equipped her for most things. Relaying information concisely was vital, giving the emergency services half a chance to save a life, police the opportunity to catch an offender on the run before he had the chance to go to ground.

Think!

'Mike 2151 to Control: Advise medics, one crossbow bolt below the left collarbone, casualty losing consciousness.' The eyewitness turned to leave. 'Sir, please remain until my colleagues get here.'

'What can I do?' He didn't seem sure that he wanted to help.

'Yeah, hang on . . .' Frankie searched Andrea's trouser pocket, located her keys and threw them at him. 'Grab the first-aid kit, the defibrillator and a stab-proof vest. Everyone else, move back! Give us some room here.'

Her radio burst into life: 'Control to 2151 . . . Urgent talk through request from 7125, now en route to your location.'

Frankie took a deep breath. 'Go ahead 7125.'

David didn't fuck about with collar numbers. 'Is this our man?'

A sob left Frankie's throat. 'Graffiti drawn on the pavement would suggest so, guv. It's not who I thought it might be. Too young.' He would know who she meant without spelling it out. 'You can add attempted murder to your charge sheet, a deliberate attempt to take Andrea down . . .' Her voice broke. 'I didn't see the shooter, but the bolt probably came from the upper tier of South Shore Road car park.'

'If he used a crossbow, you're not looking very far,' David said. 'Keep your head down.'

263

Frankie received his message loud and clear. What he was saying, and yet not saying, was that the shooter might take another shot, or that she, rather than Andrea, might have been the target. The witness was back with everything she'd asked for and two stab-proof vests.

'Hold on, guv.' She asked the witness to put one jacket on and search the bag for absorbent wadding or bandages, anything that would soak up blood. He held them out to her. 'Ever wanted to wear one of those?' She pointed to his stab-proof vest and could see that he had. He seemed to be standing straighter, taller, his chance to play the hero. 'Try and persuade the crowd to take cover inside the Baltic and remain there until my crew arrive.'

He was gone, a confident voice, an air of authority, controlling the crowd as best he could. Sirens were getting closer . . . Replacing her blood-soaked jacket with the wadding, Frankie laid the remaining Kevlar vest on top of Andrea, her sole priority to keep her alive. She only had the witness's word that the shooter had left the scene. If he took another shot it would be curtains for one of them.

Frankie hadn't time to indulge those unsettling thoughts. There was a lot of chatter on the radio as officers converged on her position. A PC arrived on the scene. She shouted to her: 'Get your tape out. I want a cordon from the doors of the Sage down to the riverside, likewise from the rear of the Baltic. When you get support, take details of any potential witnesses and clear the area. Keep me posted.'

'Mike 7125 to 2151. There's an accident on the Coast Road. Anything I can do from here?'

Right now, that was the least of Frankie's worries. If she set eyes on David, and he on her, they might struggle to keep it together. 'Is India 99 in the air, guv?'

'Negative. It's on another job. The ambulance will be quicker. It'll be with you in seconds. Police launch also on its way.'

Frankie repeated the description as more officers joined the hunt. 'Check the bus terminus, Baltic and surrounding flats, retain all CCTV and make sure the description of the suspect is circulated widely.' She looked over her shoulder as paramedics jumped out with vital equipment, then turned back to Andrea. After a super-human effort to stay awake, she'd finally lost consciousness.

48

He was home and dry. Crossbow disposed of, he drove up the ramp into Gateshead nick and parked up. As he headed inside the depressing building, others ran in the opposite direction, as if they were on fire, responding to a request from DS Frankie Oliver to flood the area with bodies and apprehend a suspect who'd shot a Traffic cop on South Shore Road.

No shit!

Jill, the chubby female civilian at the front desk looked up as he entered. Her smile was reciprocated, a wink for good measure. He'd always had a way with women, Steph the only one who could be described as the exception. Still, he couldn't have everything. In any case, in a personality contest, he'd win hands down.

'Have you heard?' Jill's voice was a little croaky.

He couldn't imagine why.

'Yeah,' he said. 'Hard not to.'

'Is she going to live?'

He waggled his hand from side to side: touch and go.

'I'd love to chat,' he said, 'but I need to check in with my unit. Mind if I use your phone?' He held up his mobile, grimacing at the mousy blonde. 'My boss won't be at all happy. Battery died at the worst possible moment.' He didn't tell her that the device was switched off and had been since an opportunity dropped into his lap, or that it was part of his game plan to cover the bases.

He parked his butt in the front office, put his feet up on a chair, helping himself to a sweet from an open packet someone had abandoned on their desk. Mm . . . his favourite. You never knew what you were getting with a bag of Revels. Popping it into his mouth, he thought about his good fortune.

When he rose this morning, in his wildest dreams he could never have imagined that she'd offer herself up as a victim in a place where he could literally take the high ground, a chance to pick her off with ease. He was driving south across the Tyne Bridge when a voice he recognised came over the radio, a short radio transmission from DS Frankie Oliver asking for assistance. Traffic cop, Inspector Andrea McGovern, responded almost immediately. And then he'd punched the air when Oliver pinpointed the rendezvous.

Some things were just meant to be.

Once in position, he'd lined up his target, ready to take his shot. He'd noticed that they were friends now, not like last night. Two officers who shared the same family connections was like scoring a double whammy. The incident was sure to be headline news. Stories involving cops always made the nationals, the TV too.

Stephanie Craven would be next.

A warm feeling washed over him as he dialled her number and waited for her to pick up. Momentarily, he thought she was going to ignore the call, but then the dialling tone stopped and she came on the line.

'Craven.' Her delivery needed work.

'Boss . . .' She hated him calling her that. 'Thought I'd—'

'Where the hell have you been?' She cut him off, her tone derisory as always. Spiteful cow. 'Have you heard what's going down on Gateshead Quayside?'

'It would be hard not to.'

'And you didn't think to call in?'

He sidestepped the question. 'Terrible news. You want me down there?'

'I asked you a question! I've been trying to contact you for the past half hour.'

'On the radio?' He already knew the answer to that. Following his intervention, a call had gone out force-wide to desist using radio communication unless the call was urgent.

Par for the course when a big operation was underway.

'I couldn't get a look in,' she barked. 'Why didn't you answer your mobile?'

'I was driving.' It was always a fucking interrogation with her. He kept his tone polite, rolled his eyes at Jill, letting her know that he was getting earache from the woman on the other end. 'My phone died, boss.'

'Are you kidding me? How many times have I told you that you are on call 24/7, that you are contactable day and night? I can't be doing with slackers on my team. Consider this a verbal warning. You'll be out on your ear unless you up your game . . .'

Hadn't he just done that?

Suppressing a giggle, he winked at Jill, tuning Steph out, though it pleased him greatly that she'd been in touch. It meant she wanted to deploy him to the scene, which suited him perfectly. Involvement in a major incident was all he'd ever wanted. All he'd ever dreamed of since his university days. Now he was right in the thick of it, not only metaphorically. It looked like he'd finally get his way.

49

On Frankie's instruction, Stone had changed direction, meeting her at the Royal Victoria Infirmary. Ordinarily, Andrea would have been taken to the Northumbria Specialist Emergency Care Hospital at Cramlington but, in view of her condition, the height of rush-hour and medical emergencies elsewhere – a decision had been made to get her to the nearest major trauma centre. She was alive, in surgery now, but Frankie had gone to hell and back in the past hour or so. She was really shaken up.

David placed a steadying hand on her shoulder.

She glanced at up him, smears of dried blood on her left cheek and forehead, eyes red raw. She'd lost it once medics had taken Andrea into their care and seemed eaten up with guilt. When she spoke, her voice was croaky and small, like a child's: 'I ask too much of people, David. I could've taken a taxi. She wouldn't have been there if it hadn't been for me.'

'Don't torture yourself. You couldn't have predicted this. We had no information that he'd come for one of us. None. You did good, Frank . . . better than good.' It went without saying that today's incident was the worst attack on a Northumbria Traffic officer since 2010 when PC David Rathband was maimed by criminal sociopath Raoul Moat with a sawn-off shotgun shortly after his release from Durham prison. Because both victim and perpetrator were now dead, the SIO held back from making the comparison. 'The team and I are very proud of you,' he said. 'As will your family be—'

'Except Rae, you mean!'

'Yeah, like you meant it to happen.'

Frankie had sent a car to collect her sister from work and bring her to the hospital. As Andrea's civil partner, Rae was legally her next of kin. Frankie checked her watch. 'She'll be here soon. What am I going to say to her?'

'Your actions saved Andrea's life, no question. If you don't tell her that, I will.'

Frankie looked down at her bloodstained hands, shoved them in her pockets and shut her eyes tightly, blowing out her cheeks, trying to control her emotions before having to face her sister. Seeing how distressed she was, David tried his best to lift her, but she was trembling uncontrollably, not hearing or even listening, eyes peeled to the door in front of them, imagination in overdrive, wondering what might be happening in the operating theatre.

Someone burst through a door behind them. They turned to find her father arriving from the corridor. He embraced his daughter for what, to her, seemed like an age. Offering words of comfort, he stepped away and shook hands with David. 'This is becoming a regular occurrence,' he said. There was no smile on his face. The first time the two men had met was on a hospital ward, Frankie the casualty on that occasion. He didn't hang around. 'What's the prognosis?'

David hesitated, trying to formulate words that wouldn't add to their distress. 'She was lucky, Frank. She's lost a lot of blood but the bolt missed her heart. She's not out of the woods yet. There's no nice way of saying this . . . but it has an expandable blade that only opens once it hits its target, designed to cause maximum damage . . .'

Frankie shuddered.

Her father gave her another hug, his focus remaining on the SIO.

David carried on. 'It's going to be a difficult few hours. We were warned that there could be complications, but the surgeon seems fairly confident . . .' The sentence died in his throat.

Frank Snr didn't delve any further. He was experienced enough to know that David was in no position to offer guarantees. They both knew his daughter-in-law was tough. She'd be fighting tooth and nail to live. Instead, Frankie's father did what most coppers would in situations like these, he focused on the incident, firing off a series of statements and questions as if he were still in post.

'Crossbows are heavy,' he said. 'It's hard to run with such a weight on your back, assuming he took it with him?'

'That's his MO, Dad.' Frankie's expression was cynical. 'Besides, there are lightweight models on the net for thirty quid, available to any dickhead wanting to purchase one. And, let's face it, we don't know how fit he is, although the witness said he can run like Usain Bolt.' The word 'Bolt' made her shudder. 'Otherwise, we know fuck-all about him.'

'How in God's name did he get away with so many boots on the ground?' her father asked in a way that sounded like an accusation.

'That would be my fault,' Frankie said.

'Like hell it was!' David jumped to her defence. 'You stayed with Andrea. What other choice did you have? If you'd left her, we might now be standing in the morgue.' He met her father's gaze. 'Don't listen to her, Frank. She did an amazing job, if only she'd realise it. If it hadn't been for her one-woman show on the Quayside, we'd have been nowhere. As it is, we know he took his shot from the upper tier of the South Shore Road car park, among other things.'

'He was seen?'

'By a Japanese tourist from the north side of the river. There's not a copper in the force – on or off duty – who hasn't rung in to offer to help. We've got it nailed down and we have Frankie to thank for it.'

'That goes without saying . . .' Her father wrapped his arm around his daughter's shoulders, addressing them both. 'Are you going to tell me what I'm missing here? I've been given the heads up in general terms but there's stuff I still don't know.'

'And that's the way we want it to stay.' Frankie shrugged herself free of his grip. She didn't want him to know the gory details. He'd already been there.

'You don't want my insight?' he said.

'No.' Even in her own head, she sounded defensive.

Her rejection had no effect on him. 'C'mon, I wasn't born yesterday. How in God's name did he know that Andrea was on the Quayside?' He answered his own question. 'He either followed her, in which case ANPR should pick him up, or he's party to radio communications. Which is it?'

David levelled with him. 'Andrea may not have been his target, Frank.'

'Same difference. She's family and I want this fucker found.'

'We all do.' David turned to face Frankie. 'What were you doing just before Andrea was hit?'

'I'd asked her to give me a lift. We were about to leave the riverside. She stepped towards her car and then went down like a bag of hammers—'

'I'm not sure what the optimum shooting range is with a crossbow,' her father said. 'But I do know that if the bolt isn't loaded properly, it can miss the target. Whoever you're dealing with wants maximum exposure. He's left us a message, guys: Catch me if you can.'

'You could be right,' David said. 'He's been forced to change method. He's not stupid. If he's one of us, he wouldn't risk getting into close combat with a cop, whoever his intended target was. He may have bought his weapon recently. Once they get that bolt out of Andrea's chest, it should give us a hint at the type of crossbow used. I've got feelers out with the National Crossbow Federation. Once we have more information to hand, we'll be able to check on provenance and maybe pick him up.' He turned his attention to Frankie. 'Until we do, you should stay at your dad's house. Take a few days off.'

'Not a chance . . . I'm going nowhere.'

'David's right, love. Don't be too hasty.'

'I'm not sending you home,' David added. 'I wouldn't dream of it, but the shock will hit you hard when it comes. I've been there, remember.' He stalled momentarily, considered an explanation for the benefit of her father, then decided against. This was not about Jane any more, or Joanna Oliver, it was about Andrea and Frankie and what they had both been through. He turned to look at Frankie. 'Just know that the opportunity is there if you want it.'

'I don't!' She glared at him, ran a bloody hand through her hair. 'You're not putting me on the bench, I've earned the right to be involved. Do you seriously think I could go home and put my feet up while that arsehole is out there? I want him off the streets and in a cell. You of all people should know that I won't rest until we get him. I don't need your protection.'

'The hell you don't,' her father said. 'It's my house or a safe house. Take your pick.'

Frankie rounded on her father. 'For God's sake. I'm a police officer! Don't treat me like a five-year-old.'

'Then stop acting like one and take my advice.'

'David, tell him!' It was a plea almost. 'I'm perfectly capable of looking after myself.'

'Frankie, be reasonable. Your dad's right. You could be in grave danger.'

'Yeah, and I could be hit by a bus crossing the road unless I take the necessary precautions, which I will. I'm not stupid.'

'Then come home, just for a day or two. What harm will it do?' Her father switched his attention to David. 'I can see her point of view about working though, David. Given the same set of circumstances, I wouldn't want to stay home either. I'm happy to ride shotgun. I'll drive her in in the morning and pick her up when she's ready to leave. How's that? If she argues, I'll cuff her to her bedpost.'

Frankie laughed and then started crying.

'Do we have a deal?' David asked her. 'If he's a copper, he might know where you live—'

'He's not a detective!' she exploded. 'If Trish Conway's intel can be relied upon, he's a uniform or a CSI.'

The two men looked at one another – both stumped.

50

David dropped his car keys in an empty fruit bowl on the kitchen bench, opened the fridge door and pulled out a carton of milk. It smelled rank. He tipped the rest of the lumpy liquid down the sink, grabbed a beer and opened the bread bin. Dropping two curled-up slices of stale bread into the toaster, he waited for it to pop up, slapped a thick layer of butter on top and took it into the living room, lighting the fire before he sat down to eat. He was about to turn on the TV when headlights took his attention. A car drew up outside. Seconds later, he heard a key in the lock.

Ben arrived in the room with Wells in tow, an accusatory expression on her face.

'Shit!' David palmed his brow. 'I forgot to pick him up.'

'You don't say.' The journalist gave a wry smile, then added a rebuke. 'Be honest, David. You never gave him a thought. I hope you know he'll be scarred for life.'

David offered an apology to his nephew. 'I'm hopeless at this parenting business—'

'Not according to the Boy Wonder,' Wells interrupted. 'He said you're a lot of fun. Can't see it myself, but I'll take his word for it.'

Ben chuckled.

David did too. It pleased him to learn that his nephew had spoken of him in positive terms. Looking after his brother's child, or one of his own, hadn't been on his bucket list. Still wasn't, though he'd keep that to himself. On the one hand, he liked having Ben around; on the other, he longed for his old life where he could come and go at will, stay out all night if he so wished, bring friends home without thinking about it. And yes, there had been periods when he'd not given the lad a second thought because his focus was elsewhere.

'Thanks for bringing him home,' he said.

'Oh,' Wells said. 'I love driving in the back of beyond on pitch-black roads after a long shift. It was that or contact social services . . . or take him to my place, but that might have been inappropriate on his first day in the office. I normally wait at least a week.' A pair of smiley eyes met David's, reminding him of their playful conversation about being in the market for a new squeeze. She had a colourful reputation where men were concerned, not all of them her own age. 'He's going to need a set of wheels living here, don't you think? Especially if he's working with me.'

'It's on the list.'

'It is? Class!' Ben gave Wells a winning smile.

She winked at him, then turned to face David. 'How's Andrea doing?'

'She's alive. It's too early to tell what damage was done.'

'And Frankie?' Ben asked.

'Bearing up.'

'I'll give her a call.' Ben pulled out his mobile.

'I'd wait till morning,' David said. 'She's knackered.'

'Understandably,' Wells said. 'She's had a tough day. We all have.'

Ben returned the phone to his pocket.

It was obvious that Wells had hit it off with him, but David was tired, not ready for conversation, polite or any other kind. Had it not been for the gravity of the situation he was handling, the fact that Ben knew Andrea personally, his nephew would no doubt have shown his appreciation for shadowing Wells on the most newsworthy day in recent history, albeit a sad one. David could tell from the lad's expression that it had been an amazing experience he was desperate to share.

When the journalist made no move to leave, David glanced at the pathetic remains of his toast on the coffee table, then at Ben. 'I wish you'd said you were bringing Belinda home. I can't feed either of you.'

Wells held up a stiff brown paper bag. 'We came equipped.'

They ate their takeaway like vultures, straight from the cartons in which it had arrived. For David, it was like being back in the incident room, no time for good manners or pleasantries, no need to lay a table. A knee and a fork each, salt, pepper and a bit of kitchen roll was all that was required. When they'd finished eating, he dumped the rubbish in the trash and found his guests whispering conspiratorially when he returned to the living room.

'Anything I need to know?' he said.

Wells raised an enquiring eyebrow. 'We were thinking the very same thing. Your nephew is no slouch. A born hack, I'd say.'

Ben was blushing.

'And, before you ask . . .' Wells eyed David across the room. 'My new protégé has been made aware that when he's working for me, whatever happens in the office, stays there—'

'She has more rules and regs than you'll find in the police handbook,' Ben quipped. 'For a moment, I thought she was going to ask me to sign the Official Secrets Act.'

Wells laughed. 'That won't be necessary now we've come to an arrangement.'

'I'm almost frightened to ask.' David shifted his focus to his nephew. 'Just how much do you know?'

'Only that you're heading for a showdown with someone closely connected to the police and that it's highly confidential.'

David rolled his eyes: Only!

'See,' Wells said. 'He's a natural. Absolutely nothing gets past him.' She could see that David was uncomfortable discussing confidential information in his nephew's presence and it prompted her to regard him with a pointed look. 'It was your idea to take him on, David. I trust him. Question is, do you?'

David glanced at Ben. 'Your dad was always discreet.'

'Like father, like son,' Ben said.

'That's as may be – and I won't deny that I have reservations, particularly in a case as serious as this one – but I'm prepared to give you latitude. Belinda's judgement is good enough for me. Don't let her down.'

'I won't, I promise.'

'Cross me once and you're on your bike,' Wells stressed. 'And know this: you'll never get a job in the industry if you come unstuck. Do right by me – more importantly, by David – and there might be a future for you at the paper one day if you want it.'

'Thanks for the vote of confidence. I really appreciate that . . .' He paused. 'But I'm considering my options.'

'Since when?' Stone and Wells said together.

Unable to hide his surprise, David added: 'You don't get an offer like that every day.'

The lad tested the water to see what reaction he might get. 'After what I saw today, I'm tempted to dump my course and join the police.'

David shot him down. 'Don't do it!'

'You did!'

'Yeah,' Wells said. 'And look at him. You want to end up like that before you turn forty? I'd stick with journalism if I were you, son. We have more fun.'

Ben laughed.

David had meant what he'd said to Ben, today anyway. In reality, the SIO wanted no other job than policing. The idea that his nephew might follow in his footsteps – as Frankie had her father and grandfather before that – gratified him. Still, he fired off a warning, driving Wells' point home . . .

'Belinda's right. You should heed her warning if you're serious about journalism. And, should you ever be daft enough to consider a career on the force, the same goes. Blot your copybook now and I'll see to it that you can't go there either.

There's too much at stake to go shooting your mouth off.'

'I get it, OK?' Ben's hands were up. Keen to take the focus off his potential job prospects, he moved on, busting to share his day. 'You should've seen Belinda today, Dave. She was amazing. We interviewed loads of witnesses, people who were there when Andrea went down.'

'This is not a game,' David warned. 'She could've died today. She still might.'

'Yeah, sorry. I didn't mean—'

'Relax. I know what you meant. And I'm not trying to curb your enthusiasm, but this case just got personal, for Frankie in particular, so bear that in mind when you talk to her.' He glanced at Wells. 'I'm sure he told you how close Frankie is to Andrea. They joined together. They're sisters-in-law. Inseparable.'

Wells nodded. 'Must've been an awful shock for her.'

She didn't know the half of it.

Ben was off again, stimulated by the day's events, excitement taking over. 'It was so easy to find witnesses and make them talk. Belinda really knows how to turn the screw.'

'You didn't do so bad yourself,' Wells said.

'I did nothing.'

'Don't listen to him,' she said. 'He's been like a dog on heat monitoring social media. By the way, he found stuff you might not want in the public domain.' She glanced at Ben. 'Will you tell him, or will I?'

'Take a look at the hashtag #BalticShooting on Twitter,' Ben said. 'It's all there, laid out in a hundred and forty-character chunks. There are some distressing images on there of Frankie and Andrea you might want taken down.'

'Thanks for the heads-up. I'll pass that on to my team . . .' David lifted his beer, toasting his nephew, trying to hide his discomfort. The person who shot Andrea would be loving it. 'You did good, Ben. Keep an eye on that feed.'

'Looking for what?' Ben was on the edge of his seat.

'Users who won't let it drop. Anyone who contributes a lot to the discussion or seems like they're in the know. Those who make odd comments you might think worthy of further investigation. Our social media team will be monitoring it too, but they're mostly dinosaurs. You might pick up something we miss. The more eyes the better. Bear in mind that the person we're looking for may have signed up recently. He's a narcissist. If he thinks he's the centre of attention, he won't be able to help himself.'

'That's what Belinda said.'

'Did she?' David chuckled. 'She'd make a good SIO.'

Ben continued: 'Investigators were all over the crime scene. I've never seen so many cops in one place. Crime scene investigators were scraping paint off the pavement looking for clues.'

'And did they find any?'

'Hey!' Wells cut in. 'Don't take the piss. He's been busy. He knows a thing or two about graffiti. Go on, tell him, Ben.'

'Tell me what?'

Ben looked at his uncle, proud that he was being invited to contribute to such an important discussion. 'Belinda and I visited the crime scenes today. The graffiti was OK, but it was amateurish, by any standard. Put it this way, he was no Banksy. I know the offender fled today's scene in a hurry, but a genuine artist would never be able to resist attaching a signature to any piece of shit. They're so quick. I know, I've watched them do it. If my opinion counts, you're not looking for a pro.'

51

At Middle Earth, the mood was grim, despite the good news that Andrea had survived her surgery and would live. Every member of the team approached Frankie as she entered the office, showing solidarity, offering sympathy, vowing to up their game, no overtime payments required. Removing his 2ic from the incident room, saving her from more empathy than she could possibly cope with, David pointed at the chair on the opposite side of his desk, keen to discuss the theory she'd offered the previous evening, but first . . .

'Take the weight off, Frank. How is Andrea?'

'I popped in to see her on my way here.' The tired DS dropped into a chair, baggy eyes staring back at him. 'Rae stayed with her all night. They're both exhausted but relieved that it wasn't worse than it is. You know what Andy's like. It'll take more than a bolt through the chest to stop her. She'll not be playing golf for a while – or driving, sadly. She saw nothing untoward before she went down. I said you'd be in to see her later. She knows the score.'

'Can *you* recall what happened just before she was hit?'

'Of course. I wasn't hit, was I? We were just chatting, as you do. It was a gorgeous day, loads of folks on the quaysides north and south of the river. We were about to get into her traffic car. She turned towards it and that was it. Next thing I knew she was flat on her back.' Frankie paused, a dark expression arriving. 'You may be right, David. I think he *was* after me. He knows my history. Who better to target than an Oliver?'

'Or he was targeting Andrea just because he can. Sending a message that he's close and can get to Northumbria's finest, whenever the mood takes him.'

'I suppose.' Frankie combed her hair with her hand. 'I didn't sleep a wink last night. Not because I might be on his hit list – that's the least of my worries with my old man shadowing me,' she snorted. 'He actually asked me to put on Kevlar to walk from the front door to the car this morning. It must be all of three steps. Can you believe that?' David was about to say something nice but she batted it away. 'I'm not making light of it. I won't lie to you and say I'm not afraid. I'm fucking petrified, if you want the truth, especially since our man has changed his weapon of choice, but what scares me most is the fact that adversity seems to follow my family around. Put it this way, we're not the luckiest on the planet . . .' She clammed up – as if she'd suddenly realised that she'd said too much. She corrected herself. 'I mean, first me, now Andy. Who'll be next?'

'Frankie, there's no need to pretend.'

She drew in a sharp breath. 'About what?'

'I know what happened to Joanna . . . your Joanna.'

Frankie met his gaze defiantly across the desk but didn't ask how he found out or even how long he'd known. Maybe it wasn't important now. Maybe it was enough to know that she didn't have to hide it any more.

He dropped his head on one side. 'Why didn't you tell me?'

'Why didn't you?' she bit back.

'Because I'm an idiot . . . And because I didn't know how you'd take it.'

'Dead men's shoes?'

'Something like that. And when I got to know you, we got on so well and there never seemed the right time to offload. The longer it went on, the harder it became. It's not easy, is it?'

'I've never been able to talk about Jo.'

'To anyone?'

'Only my dad . . .' She stalled, lost in a memory. 'Do you also know he was first on the scene?'

David nodded.

Frankie went quiet.

He gave her a moment.

It took a while for her to look at him, even longer for her to speak. 'You would have loved Joanna. She was funny and bright, but tested Mum and Dad, defying their curfew, generally pushing the boundaries. If you thought Ben was difficult, think again. Jo went out to meet a friend one night and never came home. I miss her so much . . .' A tear dropped on to her cheek. She wiped it away, eyes on her boss. 'Well,' she said. 'That got the party started.'

And suddenly David understood why she'd been so vociferous when he'd rejected Ben after Luke died, why it was so important to her that he offer the lad a helping hand, even though she hadn't known him that well. David remembered her yelling at the top of her voice, trying to persuade him that teenagers were hard-wired to clash with parents. Ben had lost both of his. He'd reached out after his father died, that much was true, but with the arrogance of youth, unwilling to give an inch.

David changed the subject, safer ground for both of them. 'You said last night that you had a theory that we're looking for a uniform or CSI. Are you ready to tell me what you were driving that?'

'If you recall, I tried last night.'

'It was neither the time nor the place—'

'Because my dad was there?'

'No. Because . . . because I have a heart.'

'Oh please! I don't know which is worse, you or him. Look, I appreciate your concern, I do, but give me credit. I can cope, OK? I'm a copper.'

'And Andrea is your sister-in-law—'

'So what?' She glared at him. 'Hey! If you don't think I'm up to the job, just say so.'

'Did I say that?'

'You didn't have to. It may as well be written across your

forehead.' She lifted a hand, fending off his attempt to make her see sense, her face burning with rage. 'Can we stop pissing about and get on with it? If we're going to get on top of this, you need my insight – or should I say Trish Conway's.' She relayed her interview with Conway, telling him about the burglary that had taken place in the run-up to Boldon Golf Club's corporate event; Alison Brody's reaction to it; her angry exchange with club staff over the delay in calling in the police and the length of time it took them to arrive.

David listened intently.

'I checked the log, guv. No detectives were involved at the scene of the burglary at any point. In my book, that rules them out. If Dunne had done his job, we'd have picked up on it. He should have flagged it up when carrying out his enquiries into Alison's death. If he had, it would have made its way into the system. By the way, he's bad-mouthing us to others.'

'What's done is done, Frank—'

'It doesn't make it any less galling.'

'No, it doesn't, but there's no point dwelling on his failings, even if, potentially, they may have cost a life. Hopefully he'll work that out all by himself and will have to live with it for the rest of his days. On top of that, he's lost his status as a murder detective and will never recover from it. He's a car crash waiting to happen. Rest assured, Professional Standards will be knocking on his door by close of play.'

That seemed to satisfy Frankie, but on the subject of Trish Conway, she had more to give. 'According to Conway, Alison was an arrogant, self-opinionated shouty-mouth, a hard-ass, not very pleasant. I made a few calls last night to relatives and colleagues of the other victims.'

'You did what? Didn't I tell you to go home and rest?'

'How could I? Besides, since when did I need permission for a little unpaid overtime?' She moved quickly on. 'Anyway, after a little sensitive persuasion, I got them to open up. Catherine Bennett may have come across the airwaves as a friendly talk show host, but behind the scenes she was not averse to stamping her feet to get what she wanted, in the nicest possible way. The studio crew she worked with referred to her as "the diva". Scientist Margaret Robson was affable, but also a woman who wanted things done right. Nothing wrong with that. There's a pattern here, David. Remember when we interviewed Hill about the man she saw on the train? Her reaction to her daughter's singing was a little OTT, don't you think?'

'I thought so at the time, though she was under a lot of stress.'

'Yes, she was, but didn't she also say there was a mix-up with her ticket? At her own admission, she'd had a run-in with the train guard. It sounded like she had a genuine grievance – it happened to a friend of mine once and he had to pay the full fair, three hundred plus quid for jumping on a delayed train, rather than the one he'd booked – but maybe she said too much for our guy's liking and that's why he gave her such a hard time.'

'Anyone ever tell you you're good at this?'

'Many times.' She managed a smile, though she was far from done. 'Joanna is the only one of our victims that no one has a bad word to say about, but that's unsurprising, given our supposition that she was a spur-of-the-moment choice. She called Joseph Cohen from the train, remember? I couldn't get hold of him to confirm this last night, but I spoke to him this morning. She was voicing an objection on the case they were dealing with. Maybe she was overheard by the man who killed her. Far be it for a woman to have a point of view.'

'Or maybe he just didn't like the look of her,' David offered.

'That's also a possibility. He's hardly rational, is he? Last night proved that. His beef is with women who know their own minds, women prepared to speak out if they have something to say, those who dare to get stuck in and demand their rights in whatever form that takes. I think our man feels or has felt persecuted by a woman in his past and this has led to a hatred of strong women, which I believe is his motivation to kill. This may sound like rampant speculation, but it makes sense to me.' She may as well have underlined it with a thick red pen.

52

If David had been in any doubt when Frankie began joining dots, offering an explanation of how things may have gone down, he wasn't now. She had the uncanny knack of being able to focus her lens on the minutiae of a case to illuminate the truth, but it was nothing more than a starting point. The offender's internal logic may no longer be as ambiguous as it once was, but he was out of control, building up to something sensational. There was only one certainty in play: he intended to kill again.

They had to stop him.

'OK, you've had your say, now it's my turn.' David sat back in his chair, hands behind his head, studying Frankie for a moment or two. He had instructions to pass on that she wasn't going to like, let alone agree with. He decided to recap before parting with them. 'We may have ruled out the detective division if – and it's still a big if – we think it's a serving officer or civilian member of staff. The spray paint won't take us anywhere. You can buy it at multiple outlets right across the region. Even if we had the time to trawl through the CCTV footage in every DIY and department store, which we haven't, what will we find?'

'We have a partial description to go on.'

'C'mon! Annie gave height and build that fits half the male population of the north-east. The witness to the crossbow shooting didn't fare any better, did he? He gave the same physical characteristics, but little else, and the substance found under Joanna's fingernails is all very interesting, but it doesn't help us either. Every Tom, Dick and Harry in Northumberland owns a wax jacket. Some are coppers, some not. We could still be looking at an offender here.'

'I thought you asked Mitch to put the screws on custody sergeants to come up with names of prigs wearing them?'

'I did.'

'It was a sound idea.'

'Yeah, I thought so too.'

'I'm hearing a but.'

David let out a heavy sigh. 'Mitch fed back on that while you were out getting shot at yesterday. The bastards laughed at him. There are so many personal descriptive forms mentioning wax jackets, it'll take him a year to process the list of potential candidates. We have neither the resources nor the time to do it—'

'OK, so how many contenders live in Blyth?' Frankie's enquiring expression demanded an answer.

'One . . . a female who bought her coat on a Sunday market stall in Amble. So where does that leave us? Apart from a tiny trace of fingerprint ink and a bit of wax, the man we're hunting hasn't put a foot wrong.'

'You're a cheerful sod today. Why don't we just throw in the towel and be done with it? Then we can all go home.'

'Not remotely funny.'

'Then what's with the negativity?'

'I'm not being negative!'

'Could've fooled me.' She tried to lift him. 'Hill's e-fit might help us—'

'I very much doubt that. It's easy to alter your appearance these days; wigs, glasses, coloured contact lenses all freely available. When Hill described the weirdo she encountered on the train, a disguise was the first thing I thought of.' David paused to glance at his watch. 'Isn't she due home today? I want her in here and talking this afternoon.'

Frankie rolled her eyes. Hill wasn't coming.

'Not going to happen,' she said. 'Her daughter told Abbott that she's had a relapse. She's been told to stay put and won't be back till Friday, late afternoon. If she's up to it, we may have something to go on at the weekend.'

David's despondency travelled across his desk, landing in Frankie's lap. It was heavier than it should have been. There was something else bothering him. 'What are you not telling me?'

He sidestepped the question. 'Doesn't it worry you that no one else on that train remembers him, even the bloke she claims got in between them, the tall guy she described from seat thirty-nine with the overly large suitcase? Mitch said he was clueless. He has no recollection whatsoever of our suspect.'

'Why would she lie?'

'I'm not saying she lied. I merely make the point that her so-called' – he used his index fingers as inverted commas – '"evidence" hasn't been corroborated by any other traveller.'

'Is that so unusual? Most people walk around with their eyes pinned to their phones these days. God forbid that they would talk to a human in the flesh. And Hill did say the carriage was almost empty by the time he boarded. I reckon that was part of his plan, don't you?'

'Based on what?'

'Think about it. If he's a frequent rail user, he'd be aware that some services terminate at Newcastle, which means he'd know that passengers heading north to Scotland wouldn't be on it. Where better to terrify a vulnerable female traveller than on a late train, in a railway carriage that's practically empty? Men have a very different experience when they're on public transport, David. They're not on the lookout for trouble, whereas women are fine-tuned to potential assault. You could even say we're expecting it. The point I make is that we take notice. Hill saw him, David. I'd lay money on it.'

'I hope you're right.'

'Trust me. He's killed four times – and almost made it five. He's getting more and more audacious and he's changing tactics. He's on a mission. Even with the whole force on high alert, we're pissing in the wind and he knows it. Hill is our best chance to ID him. It isn't an accident that he's managed to avoid detection up to now. He's clever—'

'Then we need to be smarter, more creative.'

'Meaning what?' Frankie waited.

'Meaning unorthodox.'

She leaned forward, perched on the edge of her seat, a mixture of intrigue and worry flooding her face. 'Have you forgotten we have a rule book?'

'Sod that. We need to outmanoeuvre him.'

'And how do you propose to do that?'

'We play him at his own game, bend the rules to our advantage.'

'Bright won't sanction that—'

'Then we don't tell him—'

'Are you crazy? That's professional suicide, for both of us. If he gets wind of any shady dealings, he'll send us packing quicker than we can say P45.'

'Calm down. I'm not proposing anything too serious, but if you want to find a worm you have to get your shovel out. Are you with me or against me, yes or no?'

She didn't answer.

David dropped his gaze. Like it or lump it, it was time to come clean. When he looked up, Frankie had her arms crossed, waiting for a confession. Anticipating a penance, he was tempted to say three Hail Marys before he threw in the grenade. 'When I said, *we* need to be creative, I meant me. You're confined to barracks until we make an arrest.'

Frankie stared at him in disbelief.

'No arguments, Frank. You said yourself that Andrea stepped in front of you just before she took the hit. Whoever was the intended target, we can't afford to take chances. Andrea has two armed officers with her, day and night, who'll not be stood down without my say-so. When she's discharged from hospital, they'll go with her. It would be a dereliction of duty if I didn't protect you too.' Hearing was not the same as listening. David had to find a way to make her see sense. 'Your anger is perfectly understandable. You've worked hard on this case. I hate to ground you now, but you're my responsibility. I'm not about to give this moron a second pop at you.'

'You can't lock me out of the investigation—'

'I'm not. There's plenty for you to do here.'

'An office job while you swan off making your name? I don't think so.'

David could see how angry she was. He looked out of the window, a momentary distraction. Nothing could hurt her more than taking away her opportunity to lock up a killer and bring justice to victims. Putting her on routine enquiries she was overqualified for wasn't going to cut it. He hated pulling rank, but he would if he had to. 'Frankie, c'mon, this is not just about you. Haven't your parents been through enough already? Don't you think you should put them first for once? It's not what I want either, believe me, but I wouldn't forgive myself if anything happened to you.' He head-pointed to the door. 'And neither would that lot.'

'And if I refuse?'

'I could order you to withdraw from the case.'

'Don't bother, I'll quit!'

She stood up, drew her warrant card from her trouser pocket and threw it on the desk.

David knew he was beaten. He could stick with plan A but what would be the point? And the truth was, he needed her. 'Frank, sit down.'

'What for? I have grunt work to do.'

'For fuck's sake, be reasonable. You think I like doing this?' If he didn't give a little, he'd lose her. She was central to the investigation. He wanted her involved. 'Maybe there's a compromise. You're deskbound *unless* you're with me *and* you're prepared to wear protective gear. I promised your old man I'd keep you safe.'

A moment's hesitation, but Frankie knew it was all she had.

She sat down, leaving her warrant card on his desk, a stark reminder, if one were needed, that she wouldn't be pushed around or cosseted. An overreaction, in his view, but understandable. She wasn't ready to play the fearful victim, hiding indoors until the Bogey Man was safely behind bars. That wasn't her style and it would hand the perpetrator the upper hand.

David knew that.

'I'm not proposing a breach of regulations, Frank. What I have in mind is a sting. I want to give our guy a shove to see if I can flush him out.'

'Where has this come from? If I'm allowed to ask.'

'I had a long and interesting chat with Wells last night.'

She bristled. 'Without me?'

'It wasn't planned, I promise you.' David flushed up, shamefaced. 'I forgot to pick Ben up and she brought him home.'

'And I suppose she had insight to offer.'

'They both did.'

Frankie had cottoned on to where he was going. 'You're not seriously suggesting that we share intelligence with a journalist and an inexperienced teenage relative in an investigation of this scale. It's not only mad, it's unethical. There are families to consider: parents, husbands, boyfriends, children. You can't play mind games with a killer in the press without someone getting hurt—'

'You think I fed Wells a line to get the dirt on Dunne?' His eyes never left hers. 'Did we or did we not agree to work with her?'

'Not like this.' The scowl had morphed into a glare.

'I don't expect you to trust her but, for the record, I do.' David reached inside his desk drawer. He handed her some newspaper cuttings from his time in the Metropolitan Police. 'Read those.'

She bristled. 'You've already spoken to her, haven't you?'

'No, I haven't. You're my 2ic. That's why we're having this conversation. Mind you, Wells waits for no man . . . or woman. I told you, she's the real deal. She doesn't need the crumbs from our table. She's got a fucking banquet on hers already. She can leak stuff for us, intelligence we control.'

'Oh, that's big of her.'

David showed his frustration with a sigh. 'Ben rang in, by the way. He doesn't think our man is on Twitter, or if he is, he's keeping his head down. He's still monitoring the #Baltic-Shooting hashtag, but he doesn't think it'll lead anywhere—'

'He's a kid, David! He shouldn't be anywhere near this.'

'I thought you wanted me to encourage him!'

'I do.'

'Then what's your problem?'

'Wanna list?' Frankie pushed her warrant card further across his desk. 'No, David. Find yourself another bagman.' She stood up and turned to leave.

'Oh, your dad and granddad would be so proud, not to mention Andrea—'

She rounded on him, eyes on fire. 'Don't you dare mention them! If you're considering underhand methods, you're not fit to clean their boots.'

'Bollocks.' Now David was angry. His comment was imprudent, out of his mouth before he had time to take it back. In retrospect, there was nothing he could've said that would rile her more. With the gloves off, heads turned towards his office door from the incident room beyond. He dropped his voice. 'You think your old man hasn't pulled a few strokes in his time?'

She ignored the question. 'Give Dunne a call. I'm sure he'd be delighted to cut as many corners as you like, maybe throw in a few idiotic ideas of his own.'

David laughed.

Frankie didn't.

'I know what you're doing, David. This is not about Jane, my sister or Andrea. Nor is it about you or me and whether we get a commendation from the Chief when we resolve this investigation. It's about four brilliant women going about important business, set upon by a freak who can't cope with their success. He's is not attacking them. He's attacking their way of life – and the lives of every female in this region.'

'You think I don't know that?'

She shrugged. 'Look, I want to lock him up as much as you do, but if we go off-piste, we'll play right into his hands. The CPS will hang us out to dry and that fucker will walk. In my book, that's even worse than not apprehending him.' She was welling up. 'They never found the arsehole that killed my sister. He's still out there, David. Have you any idea what that feels like? I will not be held responsible for letting the man we're after slip through the net on a legal technicality, so whatever hare-brained scheme you're planning, I want no part in it.'

'Frankie, stop!' He pushed the warrant card back towards her. 'I'm sorry for what I said. Stop buggering about and help me. I need your expertise more than ever now.'

'And if the wheel comes off?'

He grinned. 'I've got a jack handy.'

She softened slightly.

'Whatever happens will not reflect on you, I promise. I'll take full responsibility . . .' For the first time since she'd entered his office, David felt that he was making headway, but he wasn't there yet. Not even close. 'Can you think of a better way, honestly? And for the record, when I said you were confined to barracks, I wasn't blocking you, just trying to keep you alive. If you'll wear a stab-proof vest, you can come out to play, but first there's something I need you to do. I want you to brief Indira.'

She frowned. 'With what?'

'Your father and Wells both made the jump that an insider

might be responsible for these killings. I don't want to go public with that yet and Wells has agreed not to publish it. I'd rather start a whispering campaign within the force and see where it takes us. I'm hoping it'll trigger a reaction. We're already monitoring the file we left under confidential cover, right? Apart from the MIT, no one knows what it contains. If the offender is a Northumbria employee, he'll be clambering to know what we're hiding. He might take a punt at the Odin stones but he won't know what's in that file until he looks. I'm betting that he won't be able to help himself, so I've ordered a full-blown audit trail. In fact, if anyone tries to access HOLMES who's not working on the enquiry officially, I want a trail on that as well. Ask Abbott to take care of it. I'll be using Indira to leak information.'

'Why her? She has little experience—'

'Which makes her the perfect choice. A loose tongue from a rookie cop isn't unusual. We've all done it to raise our profile in the eyes of others. You can't do it, can you? No one would buy an indiscretion from you. If Indira drops it into conversation when we're not around, we can get the whispering campaign going and take it from there.'

Frankie was shaking her head. 'Our man is not that stupid.'

'How can you be so sure?'

'I'm not, but—'

'Look,' Stone interrupted, 'if he's one of ours he'll know we're struggling. He'll be riding high, getting a kick out of the notoriety, seeking out every snippet of information about him in the public domain. He's never been tested before. Not really. Sharpe was too busy playing "shaft the wife" to do his job properly. Neither of us knows what effect it will have on the perpetrator if we pile on the pressure. If he thinks we're on to him, he might take a peek at that file, just to see how long he has before he needs to make a run for it.'

Frankie picked up her warrant card, the newspaper articles, and left the room.

53

Before she left the station, Frankie checked in with Rae and read through the articles David had given her, and more besides, some including the trial of Jane's murderer and the fallout from that. To say she was impressed with Wells' approach would be a gross understatement. It was her voice that stuck, the tone of someone who cared more for those affected by tragedy than she wanted to sensationalise a story that would sell newspapers. Though Frankie still had reservations about David's plan of action – in relation to Ben in particular – she managed, somehow, to push her concerns to the back of her mind and trust his instinct.

He deserved her loyalty.

Indira arrived at her elbow. 'You wanted to see me, Sarge?'

'Yes,' Frankie stood up, scooping a packet of tabs off the adjoining desk before turning to face Indira. 'Come with me . . .' She handed her a Kevlar vest. 'Put this on. Don't ask questions and whatever you do, don't tell the SIO. Apparently, smoking can be hazardous to your health.'

Abbott was shaking his head, a big smile on his face.

'Did you want something, Dick?'

'Not a thing. Nice to see you haven't lost your sense of humour.'

'We're in the ladies, if anyone asks.'

Outside in the station car park, Frankie lit up and leaned against the wall of the building, one knee bent, foot flat against the brickwork. The cigarette tasted good. Her father would kill her if he knew, but this case was getting to her. No matter how long it took, Frankie intended to find the man responsible.

Indira could no longer bear the silence. 'I didn't know you smoked.'

'I don't.' Frankie blew a smoke ring in the air like a pro, making her laugh. Frankie offered the packet. 'Want one?'

Indira shook her head. 'Bad day?'

'Bad couple of weeks.'

'Anything I can do to ease the pain?'

'As it happens, I need a volunteer.'

Binning her cigarette, Frankie turning her attention to the aide. Physically, they were about the same height. Indira had exquisite skin and bone structure, soft dark eyes beneath high-arched brows, a long straight nose, a hint of pale lipstick. She listened attentively as she was briefed, then took off for the locker room to repair her slap.

Frankie lit up again, enjoying the second hit more than she had the first. By the time she arrived in the office, Indira's Kevlar was gone. She looked like she was heading out to a party. She was keen to assist, brimming with enthusiasm as they left the incident room. To hear her tell it, this was almost an undercover job.

The Wall's End pub was heaving by the time they arrived. Safety in numbers, as far as David was concerned. Frankie had left her protective armour in the car. A few officers from the late shift were seated in their usual corner, swapping stories, a lot of banter and leg-pulling going on, the loudest of them holding court. Right on cue, Indira waved at the group and made her way towards them unprompted, a wide smile on her face. She was quite a character and popular with everyone, a savvy choice.

Frankie watched her strut her stuff, joining in with the raucous behaviour taking place. David got the drinks in, a half of beer for each of them, and something that looked mysteriously like a G&T for Indira which was, in reality, sparkling water with a slice of lime. Tagging on to the company, the SIO remained tight-lipped on the investigation, assuming an air of quiet confidence when met with questions from the group, everyone keen to know the current state of play.

Having drawn a blank with their enquiries, the assembled officers asked after Andrea, telling Frankie to extend their best wishes to her. There was a collection going on at Middle Earth, along with a huge Wonder Woman card that everyone on duty had signed for Frankie to pass on to her.

Indira had managed to squeeze herself in between a young PC and an older officer, her intended target, a man with an excessive hunger for office gossip. Frankie and David hung around for half an hour. He bought a round for everyone, then gave her the nod to leave. She finished her drink and stood up. Grabbing her jacket and bag from the back of her chair, she told the group to enjoy what was left of their evening before the pub called time. It wouldn't close until they wanted to leave.

'You not staying, Sarge?' asked Kevin, a probationary constable.

"Fraid not . . .' She threw him a smile.

Frankie switched her focus. 'Indi, you coming or stopping?'

Indi threw her drink back, feigning reluctance, like she'd rather stay than go – she was playing a blinder.

'Looks like she's got the taste for it now,' someone said.

David seized the opportunity to big her up in front of everyone. 'It's fine, Indi. You stay. You've earned it. Have one for me while you're at it. We couldn't have managed without you.' He scanned the table. 'Will one of you see she gets home?'

Every single hand shot up.

'Windy has reached a new low . . .' the most vocal of the group said as the remaining company settled into the rhythm of normal conversation. He took in Indira's frown, another falsehood. Anyone would think she'd genuinely never heard the nickname. 'You've not met Superintendent Gale?'

'You haven't missed much,' Tony said. 'He's a total waste of space.'

'Bit like you,' someone said.

'I was warned about him,' Indira said. 'Windy by name and by nature, I heard.' She didn't mention that it was Frankie who'd cautioned her, or that she knew that Gale was a mis-ogynist, unpopular with female employees, police or civilian. Not to mention that he was hard on anyone with the surname Oliver due to a run in with Frankie's father early on in his career.

'You heard right,' Tony said.

'Graduate entry?' the sergeant among them snorted. 'No entry, more like. No fucking clue either. Bright put him on standby in case there was any more trouble. Told him all leave was cancelled. He asked, "What for?" You'd think in view of what happened last night he'd have worked that out all by himself. He missed a round of golf and presently has a face resembling my arse. He's a nobber. Take my advice and steer clear.' He stood, picked up his wallet, pointing at Indira's empty glass. 'Another gin?'

'I shouldn't.'

'But you will. Not driving, Stone said.'

'Better not, I've not eaten since midday.' That much was true. 'I'll be pissed if I have another.'

'Get her a double and something to chew on.' Tony would spend anyone's cash but his own. He glanced towards the bar, then at Indira. 'You have a choice: a Scotch egg or a bag of Nobby's Nuts.'

The sergeant looked at her apologetically. 'That's all they have at this time of night. They stop serving food at nine.'

Indira held up her tumbler. 'I'll pass on the Scotch egg.'

The sergeant sloped off to the bar and was back in minutes. Another half an hour into the conversation, the crowd was getting noisy. Indira was acting the fool like everyone else, enjoying the subterfuge. With the SIO and Frankie gone, the chat became smutty, then wound its way back to the attempt on Andrea's life and then, inevitably, to the quadruple murder case.

'Stuff must be happening if Stone and Oliver have gone back to work this late.' The sergeant checked his watch and made a joke: 'Whoever heard of detectives pulling the night shift?'

'Maybe it's Frankie he's pulling,' someone Indira didn't much care for said.

'Fuck off!' Indi showed her displeasure, a derisory look. 'I didn't hear you complaining when you were necking free beer.'

Seeing he'd upset her, he held his hands up in lieu of an apology. 'So, if no romance, what's the story with those two? C'mon, spill. We want the full low-down.'

Indira's expression was coy. 'I really couldn't say.'

'Bollocks,' the sergeant said. 'You're among friends. We're the good guys, remember? All it takes is a nod or a shake of the head . . . Come on, are they getting ready to make an arrest or not?'

'You reckon she can pull it off?' David asked as they let themselves out of the office for the final time and made their way to the car park. He'd stood her father down, saying he'd drop Frankie off to save him coming out.

'Well, Mouth of the Tyne was there, so job done as far as I'm concerned.' Frankie strapped herself in. 'He couldn't keep a secret if his life depended on it. Indi said she'd text me when she gets home. By midday tomorrow, it'll be all over the station. Then we wait . . . Hopefully our man will make his move.'

54

The team were treading water. Stone's plan to draw the offender out from whatever hole he'd crawled into had taken much longer than he, or anyone, anticipated – an agonising wait for all concerned. For the best part of two days, despite her efforts, Frankie had watched every second, minute, hour tick by on the office clock. Her head had gone down. Murder detectives had been grafting hard, but they were battle weary, becoming more and more dispirited as time passed by. The only plus point was that a fifth victim had been avoided – Andrea was making slow but steady progress, which was more than could be said for her sister-in-law.

Frankie had begun to imagine that the Odin stones in the exhibits room had a new myth attached to them; that under lock and key, deep in the bowels of the station, their so-called protective quality had morphed into the exact opposite – something sinister and destructive – or that if she walked downstairs to check on them they'd be gone. Like David, she was a disbeliever in rituals and witchcraft but, the feeling was so strong, she got up and slipped out of the office to make sure.

Signing for the file, Frankie left the exhibits officer and moved away. At the back of the dingy room, she sat down, turning on a desk lamp, opening up the box that David had initialled. Breaking the seal, she took the stones out, studying them, rolling them between her fingers. They had already been examined forensically and had been found to be free of DNA. They were extremely tactile: different shapes, sizes and textures. Some were smooth, others pitted, giving them a spongey appearance. Some were both. They were all beautiful and individual, multifaceted, multicoloured. One had a rainbow effect, as if two stones had fused together over time. She imagined David's nan threading one with string to hang beside his bed when he was a little boy, an image that made her smile. Whatever power the old lady believed the stones contained, it was she who'd sheltered him, keeping him and Luke safe, the family together.

A noise made her jump.

'Where's Frankie?' Stone was standing on the threshold of the incident room, hanging on to the handle of his office door. Detectives looked up, nonplussed. David's eyes flew to an empty seat. Frankie's body armour. Her mobile phone. Feeling his stomach somersault was like déjà vu. She'd done it again – another disappearing act. He moved into the room, a face-off with Abbott who'd been instructed to keep eyes on her. His answer was out of his mouth before the SIO had time to ask.

'I don't know, guv.'

David swore. 'Anyone?'

Blank faces stared back at him.

'Mitch, locker room. Indira, female restroom. Now!'

The two rushed out and were back within seconds shaking their heads. Frankie had told no one where she was going and, with their attention on a mountain of paperwork, no one had noticed her leave. David walked to the window and looked out, then realised that he wasn't thinking straight. Her car wouldn't be there. She wasn't using her own transport.

He turned to face the room.

'Find her!'

Odin stones had a magical quality. Living in a coastal town as she did, Frankie had spent a lot of time wandering the beach, collecting and examining the jewels of the sea to take home:

stones, shells, driftwood. Mineral specimens had always fascinated her. For centuries they had been turned into artisan jewellery, unique and collectable.

She felt cold. Unusual. The windowless room was always stifling, particularly so at this time of year. But the draught was real, not imagined. Thinking that someone had opened the door and come in, she replaced the stones in the box and closed the lid. She looked around expecting to see a colleague standing there. Nothing. The exhibits officer was nowhere to be seen. Her mind was playing tricks.

'Where have you been?' David barked as she walked back into the incident room. He was angry, hands on hips, face like thunder. He had the look of Bright, of her dad, the mantle of a true SIO. 'The whole team has been searching for you.' He was more het up than she thought reasonable, but a glance at the clock made her realise that she'd been gone longer than intended. Over an hour. Impossible. For a moment, she wondered if she'd fallen asleep away from the constant din in the office, the unremitting phone calls, the chat. Either way, her prolonged absence from the office had sent her guv'nor into a blind panic.

She apologised.

Like his nan had watched over him, he'd been watching over Frankie since the horrific incident on Gateshead quayside that could have been so much worse for Andrea. Frankie hoped he didn't ask any awkward questions. Another glance at the clock, a check of her watch. She simply couldn't explain the time slip.

But there was more to it than that. Detectives had downed tools, all eyes turned in her direction. Frankie's heart nearly stopped.

'Don't tell me there's been another.'

'No, it's not that.'

Relieved, she blew out a breath.

'Can we take this into my office?' David said. 'Dick, you too.'

'We're on!' David said as Frankie shut the door behind her. 'Three hits on the confidential cover file: Dunne at 15.34, Mouth of the Tyne at 16.06 and CSI Nathan Cartwright at 16.55.' He paused, giving her time to process the new information, telling her that while she was out – he stressed the word out – Abbott had come up trumps. 'He checked the exhibits log and made notes before informing me – the reason I came looking for you.'

He was still pissed off.

Frankie repeated her apology.

As always, Dick had her back. 'We can ignore Dunne,' he said, trying to avoid a post-mortem on where she'd been. 'He's already been eliminated from our investigation. I did a job on him when we suspected him of passing information to the press. For one of the murders, he was tied up in court. For another, he was interviewing witnesses in this very building for Sharpe. It's all on record, which puts him in the clear.'

Frankie couldn't get it out of her mind that the stones she'd been examining a moment ago had somehow helped. It was rubbish, of course, and she didn't share the thought. 'Well, Mouth of the Tyne doesn't fit the description of our suspect in any way . . .' Her focus drifted from Abbott to her boss. 'You saw him at the pub, guv. He's a man mountain, sixteen stone and five eleven.'

'I agree,' Dick said. 'But just to be on the safe side, I made a few calls. He was on duty at the time Alison Brody was killed. Ditto for the estimated time of Catherine Bennett's death. I can tell from the log of the jobs he was given that he was engaged elsewhere.'

'You can prove that?' David asked.

Dick grimaced. 'Not conclusively—'

'On duty doesn't mean he couldn't have committed an offence.'

'Point taken, but he responded to jobs at various locations, none of which were near our crime scenes. He was also double-crewed, guv. I just spoke to the witnesses he interviewed. On both occasions, he was there with a female officer who'll be able to confirm that. I didn't speak to her for obvious reasons.'

'That's a good move,' Frankie said. 'We need to eliminate him without actually talking to him, but my guts are ruling him out. He didn't get his nickname by accident. He's nosey. Always has been.'

'He's also been bending Indi's ear,' Dick said. 'Digging for information since her undercover op on Wednesday night, trying to get her to open up and find out what's going on.'

'Isn't that exactly what you'd expect if he's dodgy?' David said. 'Is he on duty now?'

'No,' Abbot said. 'But shouldn't we leave him be?'

'Dick's right,' Frankie said. 'If we drag him in here, we'll be handing him something he can really blab about. Assuming it's not him, it'll tip off the real offender that we're on to him. We need to give your sting more time to ferment, guv. Time for off-duty officers to come in and join the rumour mill. It'll scare the shit out of our target and could ultimately save a life. He won't act until he knows the score. In the meantime, we focus on Cartwright.'

David was nodding. 'He's now our prime suspect,' he said. 'If we're really lucky, his job sheet will show that he was in attendance at the burglary.' He glanced at Frankie. 'Pull his personnel file.'

'Indi is on her way to HQ to pick it up,' Dick said.

'Good. Keep your mouths shut about this and tell her to do likewise. Dick, you're not required over the weekend. Frankie and I will work on Cartwright independently.'

'Sir.' Abbott left them to it.

'I assume you're free?' Stone didn't ask where Frankie had been.

She'd given him a fright and felt bad about it. 'I am if you take me home . . . I love my old man dearly but I'm sick of him and Mum fussing over me. You can take my spare room and play bodyguard if you like, but we'll get nothing done if we have an audience, let alone a spare SIO.' Frankie was almost begging. 'What do you say? You and I need to do this without outside interference.'

'Good plan. Check in with Rae. I'll call Ben.'

The sun was setting by the time they arrived in the fishing town of Amble where Frankie lived. Her home was in Coble Quay, a relatively new apartment block in an area that was fast becoming the place to live, a cosmopolitan café culture building up around the water's edge. The first time he'd been there was to visit Ben when Frankie wasn't home. Then, as now, he'd fallen in love with the place. The scene beyond the floor-to-ceiling picture window drew his eye, a pink, purple and orange sky reflected on shimmering water.

'May I?' He was desperate to get outside.

'Please do . . .' Frankie walked away, a smile developing as she spoke over her shoulder, taking glasses from a cupboard. 'That's always the first question anyone asks.'

Sliding open the patio doors, David went outside onto the balcony to take in the busy marina and far-reaching views of the Coquet Estuary, historic Warkworth Castle in the distance. Frankie arrived by his side, with a bottle of red and two wine glasses. He took the bottle from her and began to pour, then leaned on the railing facing out to sea. 'You must love living here.' He glanced sideways. 'My place is great – I love the countryside – but this is something else. I can't imagine why Ben wanted to leave it all behind and move in with me.'

'He loves you, that's why, even if he might not always show it. It was clear that he needed you and not me. I'm proud of you, David. You've worked wonders with him. You want to sit out for a while? I do my best thinking here.'

He nodded. 'Thought you'd never ask.'

Frankie lit candles as he sat down, a breath of sea air and the sight of colourful boats in the harbour below lifting their spirits after a traumatic week. The minute she left the incident room, he felt her relax. No wonder. The excitement that they might be on to something big was still there, but her fear of being hunted by a vicious killer vanished the minute they left the city.

The sound of rigging slapping against yacht masts took his attention, adding to the serene atmosphere, interrupted only by the screech of seagulls – a small price to pay for those lucky enough to be living close to nature on the Northumberland coast. David felt a strange affinity to the place, even though Amble was not a town he'd spent much time in. His nan favoured Seahouses, further north, where they could catch a boat to the Farne Islands when he and Luke were kids, a wildlife experience no one visiting the area could afford to miss. The image of his brother was strong: wrapped up against the elements, a cheeky grin – he loved nothing more than being outdoors.

Frankie's voice pulled him from his reverie. 'Shall I get Cartwright's file?'

'Now?' He glanced at his watch: 21.15. If he knew anything at all about her it was that she had no stop switch when it came to work. Despite the convivial surroundings, she'd rather go inside and get cracking. She'd been skimming Cartwright's file as they headed north. 'Wouldn't you rather take the weight off tonight, find something to eat and tackle it in the morning? We've been working flat out since early doors and I'm clamming, even if you're not.'

'Just a quick peek . . .' She was practically begging. 'I'll never sleep otherwise.'

'Food first, then overtime. Unpaid!'

'Can we at least eat in? I don't look good in Kevlar.'

He laughed.

Her disappointment dissolved. There wasn't a hope in hell of her going to bed without checking out the crime scene investigator who'd attempted to access their confidential file. If it hadn't been for her tenacity and intuition, the enquiries she'd carried out following her interview with Trish Conway, they'd be nowhere. How could he knock back a request to keep going?

David left the apartment bound for a takeaway. Frankie had recommended either the Golden Harbour – if he fancied Cantonese and Szechuan food – or Sea and Soil, a local bistro. Before leaving, he'd insisted that she'd lock and bolt the door, ordering her to stay off the balcony until he got back. On the first floor, with a video entry system in place, he figured she was safe.

By ten o'clock they had scoffed their meal and cleared away. Frankie made coffee, divided Cartwright's file, giving half to David, keeping half for herself. They sat down at a small glass table by the window, excited at the prospect of what they might find. They had been reading for half an hour, making notes as they went, when someone rang the intercom startling them both.

David was instantly on alert. 'Expecting anyone?'

Frankie shook her head. 'No one.'

'How the fuck did they get in?'

'Relax. They're outside. No key. No entry. They didn't get in.'

A rap on the door. 'They did now.'

'Could be a neighbour.' Her voice broke as she said it.

'And it might not be . . . I thought you kept yourself to yourself.'

'I do.' She could tell that he was worried.

The hairs on David's neck stood to attention, his body's

reaction to a perceived danger. If their target had changed his MO once, it stood to reason that he could do it twice. With no way of knowing that Frankie had company, he might have decided to take her out before going to ground. 'Go in the bedroom and stay there. If you hear a racket, you know what to do.' He pointed to the mobile in front of her. 'Don't hesitate.'

Scooping it off the table, she stood up and made a move.

For once, she didn't argue.

Frankie's bedroom was directly opposite the front door. Once her door closed, David slid open the spyhole cover. No one there. Tipping his head, he put his ear to the door and listened. Nothing. He checked the video entry screen waiting to see if anyone exited the building. They didn't. And suddenly, he was in London, in Jane's flat, watching her life ebb away.

Another knock.

Turning back to the door, David blew out his cheeks. Her unexpected caller was persistent. Again, he used the spyhole. A man was standing outside, his back to the door, a dark hoody hiding his ID. Tall and well built, he didn't fit the physical profile of the offender they thought they were hunting, but the SIO was taking no chances. He shot down the hallway into Frankie's bedroom, urging her to follow him and ask who was at the door. He didn't want to tip off their visitor that she wasn't alone.

She nodded her understanding.

David took off his jacket, ready for trouble.

Her eyes homed in on the firearm strapped to his chest. 'What the fuck is that?'

'Your defence.' Unclipping his holster, his hand closed around the gun. 'Bright insisted.'

Enough said. There was no time for a debate. David never meant her to see it. It was enough to know that he could and would use it to protect her. As a former specialist armed response officer in the Metropolitan Police, he had the necessary qualifications and paperwork to carry a firearm. With a credible threat to her life, the head of CID had authorised its use until further notice, including lethal force if required. Frankie was about to follow him back to the front door when they heard a click. Someone was trying to enter.

'Change of plan,' David whispered. 'Make the call and keep out of sight.'

'Under the bed with my baseball bat? I don't think so.'

'You're the target. Stay here.'

Frankie grabbed his arm. 'David, be careful.'

She was already on the phone to Control.

55

David crept from the room, closing the bedroom door quietly behind him, the safety catch of his Glock off before he made it to the living room. The door clicked open. He could hear footsteps approaching, closer and closer still. His mouth dried up. Extensive firearms training had equipped him to deal with an armed threat. He'd drawn a weapon many times but, up to now, he'd never had to fire one in a live situation. The thought of having to do so disturbed him. He knew then that he could never have taken revenge on Jane's ex in cold blood. A piece of shit he may have been, but the fantasy and the reality of taking a life were poles apart.

Frankie stood stock still behind her bedroom door, the phone in her left hand, ready to give a running commentary to Control if there was any commotion. Slipping it into her pocket, but leaving the line open, she lifted her weapon, prepared to use it if necessary, knuckles turning white as she gripped it tightly with both hands. If David thought she was joking about the baseball bat beneath her bed, he was sadly mistaken. There was silence for a second or two and then movement. There was definitely someone in the apartment.

Keeping his back to the living room wall, David waited for what felt like an age, heart pumping hard. He counted the seconds, imagination in overdrive. He visualised the intruder doing the same as he proceeded down the hallway: five feet . . . four . . . three – he sucked in a breath – two . . . one.

A giant moving shadow appeared on the floor in front of him.

David raised his right forearm at the first sight of the hooded figure. 'Armed police!'

The man turned his head.

'Whoa!' His hands were up.

'For fuck's sake, I nearly blew your damned head off!' Wiping sweat from his brow, David secured his weapon, returning it to its holster. His nephew's eyes were like saucers, hands still in the air. He was hyperventilating at the sight of the Glock that seconds ago had been pointed at his chest. David raised his voice. 'You're safe, Frank. It's Ben.'

Frankie blew out a breath, heart rate returning to normal. Propping the baseball bat against the wall, she opened the door, arriving in the living room, pale-faced, eyes seizing on David's nephew. 'You bloody idiot! You scared the hell out of me.'

'I still have a key,' Ben said, innocent eyes staring back at her. 'And after what happened to Andrea, I wanted to make sure you were all right.'

'Well, I'm not!' She was almost yelling.

A voice, tinny and far away took her attention: 'Control to Mike 2151. Backup on the way.'

Frankie took her mobile from her pocket, lifting the device to her ear. 'Control, stand down. False alarm.'

'Control: Roger that.'

She hung up, eyes fixed on Ben's. 'You couldn't have called first?'

'I buzzed you on the way in. I'm sorry.' Such an angelic face.

'So you should be!'

It was clear from Ben's expression that he was scared stiff. Frankie burst out laughing and threw her arms around him, catching David's eye over his shoulder.

He smiled at her. Bollocking his nephew was a natural reaction, a pressure release, like sounding off at a pet who'd run into the road and almost got himself killed. As the lad stepped away, he apologised again, the seriousness of the situation dawning on him. Working with Wells had been fun, but this was something else. Lives were at stake. People he cared about. This was serious shit. He'd gone there to comfort Frankie and instead had made the situation ten times worse. David couldn't help but feel sorry for him.

His mobile rang: *Control.*

He took the call. 'Stone.'

'Everything OK your end?'

The call was expected. The controller was checking in, as he was duty bound to do. Frankie could have been under duress when she'd asked him to stand officers down. David confirmed that all was fine and that they no longer required assistance, then hung up, shaking his head at Ben.

56

After last night's drama, not much work had been done. Ben hadn't arrived at Frankie's apartment alone; Wells had driven him there and waited in the car for him to say a quick hello. When he didn't materialise, she came looking. Minutes turned to hours and before they knew it, it was almost one a.m. When Frankie finally got shot of them, it was too late to delve further into Nathan Cartwright's background. Exhausted, she decided to call it a day, a decision David agreed with wholeheartedly.

Five hours later, Frankie woke as dawn light entered her room through the blinds, a natural alarm clock in summer. She got up and made coffee. There was no sign of David, so she carried her mug out onto the balcony and sat down, taking in an ever-changing view as the darkness lifted and Amble came to life.

Daybreak was her favourite time of day, a chance to get her mind straight before heading to a busy incident room, a daily ritual of peace and quiet before the madness began. On the weekends, she'd sit there for hours observing cloud formations, reading books and newspapers, chatting with Andrea or her old man – a direct line to his den – or just enjoying her bird's-eye view of the harbour, watching greedy gulls swoop down from the roof of her apartment block to squabble over whatever was available on the jetties below. Better still, a friendly seal – a big lad – a regular visitor who often lounged around on his back in the harbour, smiling at her.

It was twenty minutes before the patio doors slid open behind her.

'Morning,' David said.

Frankie didn't turn around. 'What kept you?'

'It's the middle of the night.'

His voice was rough, like he'd had a skinful the night before and yet he'd only had a couple of glasses of wine the whole evening. When she finally turned to face him, he looked like death: unshaven, hair ruffled, sleep-filled eyes peering at his watch, mortified by the early hour, by the look of him.

Frankie smirked. 'Did I wake you?'

'Did you even go to bed?'

She laughed.

Back at her apartment, refreshed from a bracing walk, they ate croissants Frankie had remembered to take from her freezer before they went to bed, the only thing on offer at such short notice, then sat down to work. There was a lot they couldn't do without access to the PNC, but Nathan Cartwright's personnel file gave them much of his antecedent history: his references, exam results, schools he'd attended, where he'd studied for his bachelor's degree in forensic science; where he was born, information on parents and siblings, his driving licence details and current posting. Nothing rang alarm bells until Frankie happened on a mention of a previous Blyth address on the back page.

She caught David's eye, letting him in on her find.

He held out the part of the file she'd given him. Frankie noted how enthused he appeared to be, which piqued her interest further. She glanced at the photograph attached to the front of the document, wondering if this was the face of a murderer staring back at her, the man who'd seriously injured Andrea. Stone and Oliver were still unclear exactly who he'd tried to kill with a crossbow.

Such an innocent face.

Contrary to popular belief, where serial killers were concerned there were no outward signs to identify them as dangerous individuals, no obvious giveaways or evil looks

315

that would deter you from making their acquaintance. In reality, most looked the same as everyone else.

'Turn the page,' David said.

'What am I looking for?'

'His physical description.'

Frankie's eyes travelled down the sheet of A4 until she reached the information she was seeking: *five seven, dark hair, grey-blue eyes*. She looked up with a growing feeling that they may have caught a lucky break. So strong was the sense that they were nearing their target, she had to restrain herself from punching the air in celebration. 'He's a dead-ringer height-wise,' she said. 'Studious-looking, isn't he?'

'Yup, and only two years in. He came to us straight off a course at the University of Cumbria. I have to say his appraisal forms are impressive. It would appear that he knows his stuff.'

Frankie tapped the file. 'On a sliding scale of one to ten, he's a nine though, yeah?'

'He's a seven or an eight at best,' he argued. 'I don't want to piss on your chips, but we need conclusive proof before we act.'

She made a crazy face. 'Do you *ever* get excited . . . about *anything*?'

'A good night's sleep.' He lifted a hand to his mouth, suppressed a yawn, throwing a wry smile her way. 'The voice of reason doesn't make you a bad person, Frank. Until we can say with authority that he's a credible suspect—'

'Why else would he try to access the confidential file?'

'Maybe he's just nosey like Mouth of the Tyne. In the Met, I worked on too many investigations where fingers were pointed at dead certs, only to stall when we found out we were wrong. It happened more times than I care to admit.'

'Yeah, yeah.'

'I'm not saying he's not our man. He could well be, but we need more intelligence, something concrete that links him with a victim or a crime scene before we make a move on him. For the time being, we hang back.'

'Then let battle commence.'

Frankie knew that David was right. Cartwright loosely fitted a vague description and had spent time in Blyth, but it wasn't enough. It was the fact that he'd been poking into their business that made him a potential candidate. Still, they couldn't allow their suspicions to blind them to the fact that he may not be the offender they were after. In her eyes, he was a definite maybe. 'I wonder what Rebecca Hill would make of him. I'll give the office a call later and see if she made it in.'

57

David went quiet. He began listing the enquiries he wanted carried out first thing Monday morning and in what order. As he'd alluded to already, he wanted to step back a bit. He looked up. 'I'd like to talk to Cartwright's tutors at Cumbria University before I tackle his supervision to find out who he works with now and which SOCO vehicles he drives. When we have that information to hand, we can check it and his private transport, if he has any, against the ANPR.'

'Five-mile radius of our crime scenes?'

David was nodding. It was the best way to track Cartwright's movements across the force area, beginning with the first deposition site, the last place Catherine Bennet was seen alive.

'How many hours beforehand?' Frankie asked.

'Four.'

Frankie made a note of it. 'And after?'

'Two. He'd piss off quickly.'

At midday, Frankie picked up her mobile, called Middle Earth and asked to be put through to the operator who'd been working with Rebecca Hill on the e-fit, wanting to know if she'd made it in and whether there had been any progress.

'I was about to call you, Sarge.'

'You've finished . . . already?'

'For today.' He paused. 'Put it this way, Ms Hill has been and gone.'

'You don't sound happy about it.'

'We're getting closer, but I think we need another pass at it.'

'Dammit!' Frankie's rolled her eyes at David as the operator continued to fill her in. 'Hang on a sec.' She muted the call. 'When we spoke to Hill she gave the impression that she could describe her weirdo to a T. It seems that's not the case. The operator hasn't lucked out altogether, but the woman we'd hoped was our star witness was too drained to stay long apparently. She hasn't eaten for days and was obviously dehydrated. He said her concentration was woeful . . .'

She put the phone on speaker.

'Anything else?' she asked. 'The SIO has joined the call.'

'She kept saying that the eyes of the suspect weren't right. Whilst the composite image looked, quote "a bit like the man she'd seen on the train" unquote, her reaction didn't fill me with confidence. I know you were banking on a good e-fit but we haven't got one yet. Ms Hill needs more time.'

'Wing it over,' David said. 'May as well take a look at what we have got.'

'Will do, guv.' The operator hung up.

Seconds later, an email pinged into David's inbox. He'd seen e-fits tested while working down south. Under the direction of a witness, using composite imaging of facial features, an operator had created a good reconstruction of one of his Met detective colleagues. It was fascinating to watch it evolve, but the process had its limitations. Though quicker to put together than the old-fashioned sketch artist method of providing a physical likeness of a suspect, they were only as good as the eyewitness, often producing comical results no one took seriously. Without atypical facial features, they often looked samey . . . and so it proved.

Frankie laughed when she saw the image. It was pathetic, nothing more than a caricature. David swore under his breath. The image looked nothing like Cartwright who, it had to be said, had few distinguishing features that made him stand out. In the photograph on his personnel file, his face was oval, whereas in the e-fit it was more rounded. The only way it could be the same man was if he'd put on a lot of weight since his employment with Northumbria Police began.

You could say he was Mr Average.

They ploughed on, making calls, lining up appointments for the following week. During a much-needed break, a chance to stretch her legs and make a cup of tea, Frankie rang Rae from her kitchen. As she hung up, David's voice reached her from across the open-plan room.

'How is she?'

'Sitting up in bed, complaining that she wants to go home.'

'A good sign.'

'Very.'

Frankie carried the tea out onto the balcony. The weather had improved, not that either of them had noticed, so intense had their concentration been. Her small but perfectly formed outside space was bathed in sunshine. Slipping her sunglasses on, she sat back focusing on the horizon, her mind returning to her suspect. 'Cartwright hasn't put a foot wrong,' she said.

'On his killing spree?'

'In life,' she moaned. 'His file sucks. No one has a bad word to say about him.'

'No one is that squeaky clean,' David said. 'Even you.'

'Especially me.' She fell silent.

David could see the wheels turning. 'Where are you?'

'What?'

'I asked you where you'd gone. I seem to be sitting here on my own.'

'I'm lost, if you want the truth.' She let out a big sigh, took off her sunglasses and scraped her hair back off her face. 'Aren't you? If you really want to know, I was thinking about the Odin stones. For the life of me, I cannot fathom their relevance. Help me out, David, I'm clueless.'

'Join the club.'

'I can't even take a punt.'

'We might not understand their significance but they sure as hell mean something to the killer. He could be just dicking us around . . . Or absolving himself in some way. I reckon he has a screw loose.'

'I'm not so sure—'

'About him or the stones?

Frankie dropped her gaze.

'Don't tell me they got to you—'

'Let's just say, I'm prepared to be open-minded—'

'Since when?' He laughed. 'Ha! My nan would be stoked.'

'Don't take the piss.' She went quiet, eyes on the horizon, deep in thought. 'And why leave the stones and then take a risk by returning to the scene of his crimes to scrawl graffiti?'

'That's a good question.' He stopped teasing her. 'Maybe he thought we'd missed them. Sharpe did. And if it bothers him, they mean even more to him than we thought.'

Her phone rang.

She checked the screen. 'It's Dick.'

David frowned. 'If he's ringing you at home on a rest day it must be important. Put the phone on speaker.' She did as he asked and let him speak to Abbott directly. 'Dick? What's up?'

'I just got a call from Carlisle CID, guv. They found the guy the conductor saw on Joanna's train, the one you asked me to trace. His name is Mark Richards. He's a season ticket holder and lives in Carlisle. Has done for years. The bad news is, he remembers nowt. I'm sorry not to have something more positive.' Abbott gave the man's address and hung up.

Frankie raised an eyebrow. 'What did I tell you about men on public transport.'

'It was always a long shot, Frank.'

'My life story . . . I think we should interview him ourselves though, don't you?'

'For what purpose?'

'He lives in the same Cumbrian town where Cartwright studied forensic science.' Frankie let the implication hang.

'You're suggesting he knows Cartwright and is covering for him?'

'We won't know until we ask him.'

321

58

Their in-depth research on Cartwright continued throughout Sunday. By the end of the day, David could see that Frankie was flagging and with exhaustion came an emotional response to their case. He didn't know what had triggered her downward spiral, only that it had torn the dressing from a festering wound and she needed help fixing it. He'd gone out for some air. When he returned, she was out on the balcony, a lit candle on the table, a glass of wine, and something else: a photograph of a young woman held so tightly in her hand, her knuckles had turned white. David couldn't take his eyes off it.

'Show me,' he said.

Reluctantly she handed it over, pouring him a drink as he sat down. She couldn't look at him. David studied the image for a moment. It was no surprise that the happy snap was of her late sister, though he had no way of knowing how significant it was, the last one taken on her fifteenth birthday, three months before she died, the same photograph Frankie had been staring at in her father's den ten days ago.

He handed it back. 'She's a lot like you.'

'Only better looking.' With monumental effort, she tried to return his smile but didn't quite make it. There was torment in her eyes but he could see that she wanted to talk. 'Even dead, she manages to outshine me,' she said.

The comment shocked him.

His reaction prompted further explanation. 'My old man can't let her go, David. Her death destroyed him, as a husband, a father, even as a copper, if the truth be known. Ironic, isn't it?' She filled up. 'The best detective of his generation and yet he couldn't catch his daughter's killer. Naturally, he was prevented from taking part in the official investigation. I wish he had. With the case undetected, he'll never stop searching for the man who took her from us. That's why he has a special den. It's not to get away from Mum, Rae and I, as he'd have you believe. Or to spend time with Joanna, though she has a special place in there. It's not a shrine, David. It's a makeshift incident room. Behind the wood panelling, there's a fuck-off murder wall bigger than ours at Middle Earth. I was eighteen when I found it.'

David had never seen her so traumatised, even after Andrea's injury. The night he was promoted to his present rank – reinstated to the position he'd held in the Met – he'd been invited into her father's den. The two men had shared a drink together, man-to-man, behind closed doors, and yet he'd never had an inkling that the room held unspeakable horrors for Frank Oliver II.

'Joanna was murdered pre-HOLMES,' Frankie added. 'There was no computerised system of recording then. Before Dad retired, he copied the murder file in its entirety: every shred of evidence, witness statements, the whole shebang. Against regulations, I know, but he couldn't help himself. You could say he's been carrying out an unofficial review of the case for a quarter of a century . . .'

It was good that she'd finally opened up but David was struggling to find words of comfort, so he kept silent and let her speak.

She was avoiding eye contact. 'He won't let me touch it. He doesn't want me to see what he saw. There are literally boxes and boxes of evidence in his cupboard behind lock and key. I've seen it all. Every time Mum leaves the house, he's in there. Every time they both do, I am. I know where he hides his key.' She necked half a glass of wine in one go. 'There's even a statement from the uniform he met at the crime scene. It's bleak, David. He described Dad's reaction when he arrived and realised it was Joanna lying there. He lost it. He didn't have to be restrained or anything – he's too much of a pro to have contaminated the scene – but you can imagine what he went through.' Now she looked at him, her voice wavering as she continued to unpick the past. 'It was hard enough when he told me that Joanna was never coming home.'

'Were there clues, initially?'

'A white van . . .'

This made sense. David remembered her reaction to a white van during their last case in general CID, before they moved to the MIT. The sight of it made her shudder. She was too slow to turn away, though she tried to hide it. In the middle of an investigation, he didn't question her. It hadn't seemed appropriate at the time. And now, with the benefit of hindsight, that was proving to be a good move. Raking up the past was torturing her.

'They never found it?'

She shook her head. 'Despite a public appeal, no one came forward. Dad couldn't cope with that. Joanna was his angel, more like him than he cared to admit, despite her problems. Rae and I were important to him, but not like her. Her death consumed him. I used to think that the fact that we were still breathing meant nothing to him.' Her voice broke as she said it. 'Whoever was responsible didn't just rob us of Joanna . . . he robbed us of a father too.'

'Frankie, your old man adores you.'

'I know, and the feeling is reciprocated, but don't be fooled. The Frank Oliver you see, the one everyone sees, is a front. Behind his jokey routine, he's a dead man walking.' She swallowed hard, on the edge of something that was breaking her heart. 'Evidence went missing: Joanna's Levi Jacket. There's a picture of it on his murder wall. When DNA testing was developing, it was one of the first pieces of evidence to be sent to the lab for retesting. HQ was at The Kylins back then and the jacket wasn't there when it was sent for. Dad suspected a deliberate cover-up.'

'Jesus! I'm so sorry.'

'Yeah, me too.'

He put a hand on hers. 'Frank, you should have told me.'

'I'm telling you now,' she said. 'That's why I went missing from the incident room. I was checking on the Odin stones, making sure we still had them in our possession. Why I didn't want to believe that we were looking for an insider.'

She looked out to sea as if she'd find answers there.

In David's head, and hers two, there was no difference between a bent cop or dodgy CSI. Either one was a disgrace to their office. It was a serious – in their present case, murderous – breach of trust. If only he'd known that Frankie had additional, very personal, reasons to hate them. Dealing as they were with a loathsome individual at the very heart of the force must be like holding up a mirror to her past. No wonder it was driving her mad.

And still she wasn't finished . . .

She turned to face him. 'My old man has photocopies of station records documenting every officer on or off duty around the time of Joanna's death: on holiday or sick; attending court; even those who'd taken a couple of hours off are marked on that sheet, civilians included. It's a walking-talking record of life in every nick for the time period. Again, this was pre-computerisation, an A2 sheet kept up-to-date by station sergeants. God only knows how he got hold of them.'

David tipped his head on one side. 'He has a lot of friends.'

'And one of them is Abbott. The word theft springs to mind but I'll never hold that against him.'

David guessed what was coming.

She knew.

'It was Dick who told you about Joanna, wasn't it?'

His silence spoke volumes.

Now he understood. Everything she'd told him made perfect sense: her sadness at the crime scene; her public slanging match with Dunne; her over-the-top reaction to his own suggestion of working beneath the radar in case they did something that would render evidence inadmissible further down the line; her loyalty to her father and decision never to speak of her trauma.

She bent down and picked up her bag. Unzipping the side pocket, she pulled out a folded newspaper cutting, browned with age, so flimsy with having been read and reread over the years, she had to unfold it very carefully in case it fell apart. He took it from her. In the article, there was a reference to friends Joanna had spent time with on the evening she was murdered.

He looked up. 'She'd split up from her mates?'

Frankie nodded. 'One of them was Jack. Sixteen at the time. He was a bit of a wrong 'un, keen on Joanna, though she couldn't stand the sight of him. Mum and Dad used to laugh about it. It didn't stop her hanging out with him. Peers were important to them both. Jack had cool friends, and she was going through a rebellious stage, accusing Dad of being hard on her because of what he did for a living. Jack identified.'

'His father is a copper?'

'His father is Windy.' AKA their former boss, Superintendent Gale.

'Jesus!' David squeezed the hand he was still holding.

'When the Levi jacket mysteriously went missing, my dad made allegations he couldn't prove, accused Windy of losing evidence to protect his son. Dad retracted them later and made an apology, but by then the damage was done. That's why Windy can't stand the sight of him or me.'

'This cutting says a witness saw her with a boy earlier in the evening.'

'That was Jack. He left her and went home alone . . . allegedly. My old man has never managed to disprove that. David, he'll stare at his murder wall forever and he won't see shit. He's too close to it. He needs to drop it before it kills him too.'

There were tears in her eyes as she shared the part that hurt the most. 'It's guilt that's driving him.'

She stalled.

David gave her a nudge. 'However bad it is, you can tell me, Frank.'

She wiped a tear from her cheek with the back of her hand. 'There was a row before Joanna went out that night. Dad had a real go at her. She'd been yelling at Mum and he wouldn't stand for it. Joanna tried contacting him from a coin box an hour before she died. He was on duty and ignored the call. He'll never be able to forgive himself.'

'Does your mum know? Rae, Andrea?'

Frankie shook her head. 'He only told me because I forced it out of him. He'll spend the rest of his life trying to absolve himself. What scares me the most, what I really can't bear, is the thought of him dying without knowing the truth.'

'Can I do anything to help?'

'Don't help me. Help him. Not now, we have enough to do, but when this case is over, will you at least try to make him understand that he's not alone?'

'How?' David didn't try to hide his scepticism. 'If he won't confide in you, he sure as hell won't talk to me.'

'No . . . you're wrong.'

'Frank, he hardly knows me.'

'He knows enough!' She held his gaze, a guilty expression creeping across her face. 'I told him about you and Jane. I'm sorry, I shouldn't have broken your confidence, but I was worried about you. You two have a connection that he and I will never have. He won't let me in, but he might – just might – listen to you.'

David found himself agreeing to her request.

One day soon, he'd talk to her father.

59

They didn't speak of the previous night's conversation on the way to Middle Earth on Monday morning. Briefing notes prepared by Frankie over the weekend were handed out, the Murder Investigation Team given instructions to read and digest every word before the meeting began. Afterwards, background checks began in earnest with Abbott in the driving seat, freeing Stone and Oliver to leave Wallsend bound for Cumbria University's Fusehill campus, an hour and a half away.

The miles flashed by as they drove westward across the A69 trunk road, bypassing the Tyne Valley village of Corbridge, the market town of Hexham, and on through Haydon Bridge and Haltwhistle, a journey through stunning countryside, much like that surrounding David's home.

Cartwright's former Forensic and Investigative Science tutor, Professor Helen Davidson, was waiting for them when they arrived. David could have called rather than make a personal visit, but he wanted to talk to the woman who, for three years, had taught his suspect to apply chemistry, biology and physics at crime scenes, in laboratories and courtrooms, the very woman who'd given him the scientific know-how to boost his job prospects.

Davidson took them to her office for some privacy. She was tall and lean, a woman in her mid-late forties with sharp green eyes and red hair, years of academia lining her face. When Frankie called her, she was understandably concerned to learn that the man in charge of a murder investigation team in a neighbouring authority wanted to talk to her urgently. David kicked off the interview . . .

'Thank you for seeing us, Ms Davidson.'

'Helen,' she said.

'I'm DCI Stone. I believe you've already spoken to DS Oliver on the phone.'

'Briefly.' The professor smiled at Frankie, then shifted her gaze to the SIO. 'How can I help?'

'We're investigating a series of murders across the county border,' he said. 'No doubt you're aware of them?'

'There's been so much press coverage, it would be hard not to be . . . Awful business.' The intrigue slid off her face, replaced by a much darker emotion. 'I hope none of my former students has cocked up the evidence.' The comment was not said in jest. The woman was obviously as concerned about negative publicity as the detectives were, keen to protect the reputation of an academic institution with a history of excellence for more than a hundred and fifty years.

Ignoring the fishing expedition, David cut her off. 'It goes without saying that this conversation must remain in the strictest confidence. Until we're in a position to make an arrest, it's imperative that we conduct our investigations in absolute secrecy. We have not, neither do we intend, to go public with this or even share it within our own force, not for the foreseeable future anyway. There's an embargo on the information beyond the Murder Investigation Team, which is why we're talking to you first. You can imagine the fallout should we be proved right. It will reflect badly on us, on so many levels, as I'm sure you will appreciate but, more importantly, it might help the offender and ultimately could lead to another tragedy.'

'You have my word,' she said.

Stone gave Frankie the nod to continue.

'We have reason to believe that we have a credible suspect,' she said. 'An ex-student you used to teach here at the university. He began his studies in 2011 and is now working for us as a Crime Scene Investigator. Before we speak to him, or his supervision, we'd like the heads up on what you thought of him. I'm told that many of your graduates apply successfully to Northumbria.'

'Yes, they do.' Davidson was racking her brains for a name.

The SIO gave her one. 'The suspect is Nathan Cartwright.'

'Nathan?' Her eyes travelled back and forth between the detectives, her reaction instantaneous and heartfelt. She was shocked and horrified by the suggestion. 'There must be some mistake.'

'You rate him?' Frankie didn't wait for an answer. 'I'm surprised you remember him. You must have hundreds of students passing through.'

'Not like Nathan . . . What can I say? He was academically brilliant, top in his year. His critical thinking was as good as anyone's. He was an accomplished student, his attention to detail second to none, as was his written work. His assignments will all be on record if you want to see them. I'm sorry to repeat myself, but he really was a cut above. No one could touch him. In fact, he was so good, I was rather hoping he would stay on here, or spend some time in the field, then come back to us and pass on his expertise to others.'

'He turned you down?'

The professor nodded. 'Sadly, yes, despite my backing. Others would have jumped at the opportunity, for no other reason than the fact that a career in academia would have been more lucrative financially. Nathan wasn't having it. He had his heart set on doing the job, rather than teaching it. I was very sad to see him go.'

David was keen to move on, return to the office and find out what progress Abbott had made. 'Leaving aside his academic achievements for a moment, what was he like personality-wise?'

'He was a very nice young man, helpful and polite which, I have to say, is not always the case. Rarely have I come across a character quite like him. His behaviour was exemplary the whole time he was here. You can ask any member of staff.

Classroom or laboratory, they'll give you the same answer.'

From what the detectives had read in Cartwright's personnel file, Professor Davidson's judgment was echoed by Northumbria Police's own HR department. The CSI had aced his assessment and his supervisor couldn't fault him, which is why they wanted the tutor's opinion before speaking to her. David glanced at Frankie. All supervision had their favourites, him included.

'Did he have friends, girlfriends?' he asked.

'No specific girlfriends as I recall, but he was very popular and outgoing, well liked by fellow students.'

The detectives spent a further half hour with Helen Davidson. She stuck resolutely to her opinion of Cartwright. Nothing negative had come to light regarding his temperament. He was, to all intents and purposes, a model student throughout his time there.

They left the university for the address Abbott had given them for Mark Richards, the season ticket holder who'd shared the fateful journey with Joanna Cosgrove on the night she died. He'd not noticed her get off in Stocksfield, nor the man who'd followed and murdered her. Disembarking at the Carlisle terminus, Richards was unaware of the unfolding drama in Northumberland until the next day when news of Joanna's death was reported in the press.

Crucially, he denied ever having met Cartwright.

Just as they were setting off back to base, Frankie's phone rang. 'How's it going, Dick?' To save him repeating himself to the SIO, she switched to speaker mode. 'We lucked out in Cumbria. Please tell us you have better news.'

'The team's hard work is paying off,' Abbott said. 'I have lots to tell. Firstly though, Hill rang in to speak to you. When I told her you were out, she gave her apologies for her abysmal attempt at an e-fit. She's fully recovered now and is coming in tomorrow to finish it off.'

'About time. What else? You said lots.'

'You're a chip off the old block, Frank. Patience was never your old man's strong suit either.' Abbott laughed, unaware of the awkward exchange taking place in the car sixty miles away as he carried on talking. 'Since you left, Mitch has been through Cartwright's school records. He was in trouble for spraying graffiti as a fifteen-year-old. The ANPR also threw up some interesting intelligence. Cartwright has private transport and I have a list of sightings as long as your arm for that and his SOCO vehicles. He's been all over the knot end, at locations across the force area, one or two you need to know about.'

'Like what?' Frankie said.

The atmosphere in the car was electric. Mentally and physically crossing her fingers, Frankie glanced in David's direction. He kept his eyes on the road, flooring the accelerator as they drove east. There was no doubt in either of their minds that Dick had found something monumentally significant.

'We plotted his movements and found that he was called out to a dwelling house burglary in Dipe Lane, Boldon,' Abbott continued. 'One of the flash houses along the road from the Golf Club, days before Alison Brody's body was discovered at the cemetery, which puts four, not two, CSI's in the vicinity within a few days, any one of whom could've seen her in the area. She practically lived on the doorstep, so we have more work to do.'

'That's all we need.' There was a bitter edge to David's voice. The excitement from a moment ago evaporated as quickly as it had arrived. 'So which crew went to the golf club?'

'CSIs Percival and Grant, guv.'

'Then it's not as bad as it sounds,' Frankie said. 'I know Percival. He's an old soldier, nearing retirement. I see him occasionally and happen to know he's paired with a female investigator at the moment. That'll be Grant.' When Abbott confirmed it, Frankie added: 'Given that he's old and she's female, it kind of rules them out if we're looking for a young-ish male. I'll have a quiet word with him.'

David looked at her. 'Can you trust him to keep shtum?'

'Yes.'

'OK, do it. And tell him he'll lose his pension if he breathes a word of it to anyone.'

'Something else you should know,' Abbott cut in. 'Cart-wright's supervision changed a year ago.'

'Is that relevant?' Frankie asked.

'It is if it's Scissor Mouth.'

'You're kidding me!'

David had no idea who they were talking about or why the nickname had raised the spirits of detective sergeants on either end of the phone, only that it had. Pulling hard on the steering wheel, he turned into a layby, braking hard, throwing Frankie forward in her seat. He turned to face her. 'Scissor Mouth?'

'Work it out,' she said.

'Sharp tongue?'

'Razor sharp. If anyone fits the victim profile it's Stephanie Craven. She's a pro, highly ambitious and good at her job, but she doesn't suffer fools. She's a bit of a motor-mouth, an obvi-ous target for our suspect. If Saint Cartwright is on her team, we're heading in the right direction. If we're serious about lifting him, Craven needs protection until we pick him up.'

'She's got a few days off.' Abbott had already checked.

Frankie had almost forgotten he was still there. 'Find her. She needs to be in a safe house.'

'Want me to fix that up too?'

'No,' David said. 'Frankie can do that from the car and let you know which one. Get over there now. I want her out of that house, no arguments. When you've sorted that, find out what shift Cartwright is on and bring him in.'

'I'll do what I can, but I'm reliably informed that he's on leave, a sudden request on Friday afternoon, hours before he tried to access the confidential file. Call me an old cynic but I'd say that's quite a coincidence, wouldn't you? More mud to sling at him when he's interviewed.'

'Find him!' David said. 'No arrest. Let's see if he'll cooperate voluntarily.'

'And if he won't?'

'Lock him up.'

Three bleeps came through the speakers.

Abbott was already gone.

60

The window was open, the radio on, a Leona Lewis track he recognised: 'Run'. How apt. He was eyeing his target through binoculars, thoughts of what he was about to do to her exciting him. He'd dreamed of this day for so long, fantasised about it, every action, every word he'd say to her. It wouldn't take her long to work out what was going down. And, on this occasion, he'd make damned sure that she'd shut her mouth and listen. She was bright. She'd take in the what, why and when immediately. The 'how' might present her with a conundrum, but he had that covered.

A grin was developing at the edges of his mouth.

Perfect your craft.

Her words, not his – and that's exactly what he'd set out to do.

It was her hostility that got under his skin, time and again, day in, day out. He wanted in on the action and she was standing in his way, failing to spot his potential. Some people needed a leg up, that's all. No shame in that. He just couldn't cope with the mundane work she threw at him, stuff below his pay grade. He wanted a decent gig and was done with being passed over.

He relaxed.

It wasn't all bad news. His was an improving situation. Outside of his normal line of work, he was flying. He'd come to enjoy the experience of operating alone. Doing her required no second skin. She glanced out the kitchen window, as if she'd heard him, looking straight at him and yet not seeing him. He was well hidden, lying in the undergrowth at the bottom of her garden, camouflaged. He zoomed in as she dropped her gaze, picked up a knife, busying herself on the kitchen bench. Who knew that someone so unpleasant at work would come across as the epitome of domestic bliss at home.

It didn't last.

A flash of irritation crossed her face. He wondered what had flicked her switch this time. Her eyes were on him again. He liked to think that she felt his presence as she peered out from within, though she showed no sign of it. She was alone in the house. He'd made sure of that. She had no dog either. Hated them, she said. Her mouth was moving now. He was too far away to hear what was being said. Talking to herself, most probably. Swearing under her breath, her default position; that twisty mouth making her appear ugly, more so than she was in reality.

Unless she was singing . . .

Did hags like her sing?

Putting the knife down, she washed and dried her hands quickly and killed Leona's angelic voice with one jab at the radio. Scooping her mobile off the kitchen bench, she barked at the caller. 'Craven!'

Frankie was relieved to hear her voice. Whatever the Crime Scene Manager's faults, the detective sergeant couldn't bear the thought that she'd come to a sticky end like Catherine Bennett, Alison Brody, Margaret Robson and Joanna Cosgrove. If Craven was on the target list of a depraved killer, she was in grave danger and Frankie would do anything and everything in her power to keep her safe. Cartwright may not fit the profile of a serial killer, but then neither did Fred West.

And he was clever too.

Professor Davidson's words broke loose from Frankie's memory, floating into her consciousness, a comment that sent a shiver right through her: *No one could touch him.* She chose her words carefully to avoid spooking the woman on the other end of the line. 'This is DS Frankie Oliver, Stephanie. We have a situation. It concerns our ongoing murder case. I need your help.'

'Then call my office.'

'I did. You're not there.'

'That's because I'm on rest days.' *Not even a chuckle.*

'I'm aware of that, but this is urgent.'

'Well, be aware of this . . . I'm busy.'

True to form, she was bad-mouthing the person who'd interrupted her day off. Someone had to put a stop to it – and he was that someone. A beetle scuttled across the ground in front of him, zigzagging across warm earth, just as she would crawl, on her hands and knees, begging for her life before he snuffed it out. The mere thought of it made his heart race. She'd made him feel small and insignificant, like the bug on the ground before him; now it was time to turn the tide of abuse he'd suffered for the best part of two years. He'd make her pay for belittling him, sadly without the benefit of an audience, as she so often had – but hey, as powerful as he was, he couldn't have everything.

'Not too busy for this, I can assure you.' Frankie rolled her eyes at David and made scissors with her fingers, a cutting gesture: *I told you so.* She couldn't get a word in edgeways. Craven was in a panic, baking a cake for her mother's seventieth birthday party. She was behind schedule and didn't have time to chat, in person or on the phone . . .

David's mobile bleeped an incoming text.

'Dick,' he whispered.

Pressing the message icon, he read the text, turning the phone to face her:

Mitch lucked out with Cartwright. Not at his home address. Officers deployed to find him. I'm en route to Craven.

*

The Crime Scene Manager was still giving Frankie earache.

'Steph, button it. I haven't got time to piss about. We believe you may be in serious danger. Stay where you are, no ifs or buts. You know DS Abbott, right?' Craven confirmed it. 'He's on his way to you. Don't answer the phone or the door to anyone until he arrives. He'll be with you in ten to explain.' Frankie hung up.

As Craven picked up the knife, he was on the move, backing out of his hidey-hole, doubling back and around the side of the house, out of her line of sight. The patio door at the rear was ajar, curtains billowing through the narrow opening. He stood up, took in a deep breath, his weapon of choice held tightly in his hand. He stepped over the threshold, a silent entry. He was ready.

61

'The date is Monday, 25 July 2016. The time is 8.05 p.m. I'm DS Richard Abbott. Also present is DC Paul Mitchell. This is a voluntary interview with Crime Scene Investigator Nathan Cartwright. Thanks for coming in, Nathan. For the tape, you are here voluntarily. You do not have to say anything and can leave at any time. You are not under arrest but may have representation if you so wish.'

'No, I'm good, Sarge.'

He looked it.

It was important to identify the purpose of the interview and give him enough of an explanation to enable him to make an informed choice on whether or not to cooperate, with or without a brief or union rep to hold his hand. The interview Abbott was about to conduct had been planned and rehearsed while they tried to locate him. Dick had been warned to stick with the script as outlined by the SIO.

David was in the viewing room next door with a direct line to Abbott's earpiece should he feel the need to prompt him. He would only make an arrest if Cartwright incriminated himself. Like her father twenty-five years ago, Frankie had been ruled out of taking any active part in the interview for two reasons: because she may have been the intended target of the crossbow; and due to a personal connection to Andrea McGovern, the injured party of that attempt to kill. Although David had agreed that Frankie could sit in with him, she was having none of it. An image of her arrived in his head.

'No, I'm out, David. You're on your own.'

'Technically, you'd be an observer.'

'"Technically" is an idiotic word that lets scumbags off. This has to be done right. More importantly, it has to be seen to be done right. A savvy defence barrister will be all over it otherwise.' And that's how they'd left it.

Abbott was ready to begin. 'As you may know, we are investigating a series of major incidents in this force area,' he said. 'And we're hoping that you can assist us with that.'

'The Sleeper, right?'

Abbott gave him hard eyes. 'The use of a pseudonym isn't helpful, Nathan. We don't take our information from the press and neither should you.'

'Sorry.' Cartwright looked genuinely shamefaced. 'I can't see how I can help, but fire away.'

'As part of our ongoing investigation, we've done a check on the ANPR for vehicles in close proximity to our crime scenes. Some driven by you were caught on camera. I'd like to know what enquiries you were making at the time your vehicle was spotted.' He pushed an A4 sheet across the table. 'This document is a copy of your works vehicle and the locations we're interested in. Does everything look in order to you?'

Cartwright glanced at the sheet. 'Yes.'

'You have kindly supplied us with your works schedule and we'll use that information to conduct this interview. On this date' – Abbott used his finger to point at the relevant place on the page – 'you used this vehicle . . .' Just so that Cartwright couldn't dispute this later and for the benefit of the tape, he read out the registration number. 'Is that correct?'

'If you say so, yes.'

'What were you doing in the area?'

'I was at a crime scene in Boldon. It's on the schedule.'

'Were you alone at the time?'

'No, I was double-crewed.'

'With whom?

*

340

David sat forward, waiting for a response, his eyes fixed on the suspect. Cartwright was just as Professor Davidson had described him: unflappable, polite, measured in his response. Abbott's interview technique was exactly the same. There was no one in the Murder Investigation Team the SIO trusted more to take this one on, apart from Frankie.

'I usually work with Brian Priestley,' Cartwright said.

Mitch was scribbling on a notepad.

'And how is that working out?'

'Fine.'

Abbott changed tactics, reassured by the knowledge that the woman he was about to refer to was in a safe house out of harm's way. 'How's your relationship with your manager, Stephanie Craven?'

'I have no problem with her. She's firm but fair.'

'You seem very calm, if you don't mind me saying.'

'I'm shitting myself.' And he was.

David almost smiled. So far, so good. Dick hadn't got to the good bits yet.

'I'd like you to take a look at this document,' Abbott said, another sheet of A4 crossing the table. 'In case you're unfamiliar with it, it's an audit trail of a computer file.'

'I see that. Am I allowed to ask what it has to do with me?'

'I'm coming to that.' Abbott paused. 'At 16.55 on Friday, 22 July, your access card was used in an attempt to view a confidential item on the force exhibits log. As you can see, it matches the file on the sheet I've just given you, this item here.' Abbott pointed it out. 'Why did you attempt to access that file?'

'I didn't.'

'The file in question is confidential. Did you notice that?'

Cartwright glanced at the audit trail and nodded.

'For the tape, please,' Abbott said.

'Yes, I can see it's marked as confidential.'

'You are not authorised to view that file.'

'I told you, I didn't.'

'It's quite clear that someone did, using your card. It would be hard to forget, Nathan. You'd have received a computerised message to say that access was denied.'

'I swear to you, it wasn't me.'

'Have you ever tried to access information you're not authorised to view?'

'No, I have not.'

David was impressed with the way the interview was progressing next door. Abbott was asking all the right questions, urging Cartwright to take another look at the list. The suspect held his gaze for a moment or two. There was no defiance there, just steely determination, an honest face, an open stance, but a hint of guilt nevertheless. It was the first time he'd looked flustered since the interview began.

Abbott had noticed it too. 'Is there something you want to tell me, Nathan?'

'No, yes . . .' Cartwright hesitated. 'Look, if I'm guilty of anything, it's stupidity. If I go for a slash, I leave my card in my computer. Most of us in the office do.'

'You're suggesting that someone else used it?'

'That's exactly what I'm suggesting.'

Abbott hit him again. 'Your private vehicle was seen leaving your base within half an hour of that attempt.'

'That's understandable. Unless there's a job on, I knock off at half past five.'

'That may be the case, but this was the very same day you asked for a week's leave at short notice, a request that was subsequently granted. There is a note on your personnel file to that effect. Would you be willing to tell me why you put in that late request?'

'It's personal.'

Abbott made him sweat a while.

Cartwright seemed unwilling to answer.

'Nathan?'

'If you must know, I have a medical problem, a weak bladder. It's not something I like to talk about. The details of my urologist and hospital appointments are on my phone. I had an in-patient admission. It was brought forward due to a cancellation.'

Abbott continued. 'I'd like you to account for your movements for the dates and times outlined in this document.' He passed yet another sheet of paper for the suspect to look at. Cartwright had already worked out that the times and dates coincided with four murders and the attempted murder of a female Traffic cop.

When Cartwright stood up, David was half-expecting him to end the interview and walk, and was impressed when he didn't. Instead, the CSI pulled out his phone and handed it over. Abbott thanked him, then hit him broadside, asking for permission to search his house. Cartwright handed over a set of keys. Just like that. These were hardly the actions of a guilty man.

He sat down.

'You used to live in Blyth,' Abbott said. 'Is that correct?'

'A long time ago, yes.'

'Do you know Catherine Bennett?'

Cartwright began to sweat. 'She's a local celebrity.'

'Answer the question, please.'

'Of course I know of her, everyone does, though we've never met. She's a talk-show host. Her parents and my grandmother live around the corner from one another.'

'Have you ever seen or spoken to her, in person?'

'Seen, yes. Spoken to, no.'

'OK, is there anything else you'd like to say?'

'For the record, I never killed anyone.' Cartwright pointed at the mobile lying on the table between them. 'That phone never leaves my possession. You should be able to track my movements from it. I keep a very detailed digital calendar. Feel free to keep the phone for as long as you like. And before you ask, I was off duty for every one of those offences, barring the attempt on Inspector McGovern's life.' Another flash of guilt. 'You're going to think this is awful, but I was gutted when I didn't get called out for one of them.'

'You have a fascination for dead bodies?'

'No . . .' He let out a sigh of frustration. 'My supervision told me that I'd earned the right to be involved in the next major incident.'

'Maybe you were,' Abbott never took his eyes off Cartwright.

'No. I was excited at the prospect, that's all.'

'Haven't we all been?' David's voice arrived in Abbott's ear. 'Ask him about his penchant for graffiti.'

Abbott glanced briefly at the CCTV camera located in the corner of the room, a sign that he'd got the message. He checked his notes, making the CSI wait. 'I have it on good authority that you were in trouble at school for spray-painting graffiti on a wall. Is that correct?'

'I'm not proud of it.'

'Do you have a tag?'

'I've not done it for years.'

'That's not what I asked.'

'Then yes . . . but I only do legal stuff now. Believe it or not, you can earn a lot of money from a commission. I can show you if you like. There are images on my home computer and, for the record, I never painted RIP at the crime scenes either.'

'How do you know about those?'

'Twitter.'

Abbott's voice was harder than before. 'The tag, Nathan.'

'Odin, my tag is Odin.'

*

344

'Jesus!' David was off his seat, congratulating Abbott through his earpiece for leaving the best till last.

Next door, Mitch could hardly contain himself and Abbott wasn't quite finished . . .

'Odin is the god of war and death in Norse mythology, isn't he?'

Cartwright's head went down.

The detectives gathered up their papers, readying themselves to end the interview.

Relief was too short a word for the emotion David was feeling. He was about to leave too when Frankie burst through the door behind him. He swung round to face her. Given the vociferous tone with which she'd voiced her objections to joining him, or even observing the interview taking place, he hadn't expected to see her until the proceedings were complete. He was about to give her the good news when she lifted her finger to her mouth silencing him. She leaned across him, turning off his equipment and with it the means of further communication with Abbott. Taking no chances, she handed David a note:

It's not him! We got the wrong CSI.

62

No SIO's job was ever easy. Most days it was an emotional seesaw, up one minute, down the next, or vice versa, a stress-inducing head batter he could do without. What he could do with right now was a stiff drink – two, if he could manage it. He'd held the MIT back in case there were urgent enquiries to be made following Cartwright's interview and possible arrest. Knowing that Abbott and Mitch would be bitterly disappointed with the unexpected turn of events, David allowed them their moment of glory, then asked them to sit down and gave Frankie the nod to take the floor. She had a tale to tell and everyone present had to hear it.

She focused on Abbott. 'I'm sorry, Dick. The boss told me the interview was spot on, but we need to take a step back a moment. I know the evidence is pointing at Cartwright but it's circumstantial. It's not him, at least I don't think it is, so we're not breaking out the beers just yet.'

Abbott didn't look happy. 'Tell me,' he said.

'You were the one that put four CSIs in the Boldon area, right? Two double crews.'

'Yeah, but you said Percival's too old and Grant's female—'

'Correct, but while you and Mitch were busy interviewing, I had an illuminating discussion with Percival. While he and Grant were at Boldon Golf Club, guess who turns up out of the blue?' She didn't wait for an answer, but it was clear that Dick had made the jump. 'Cartwright was there,' she said. 'Along with his opposite number, Priestley.'

'That's good, isn't it?'

'Frankie scanned every face in the room.

David studied her.

She was animated, her eyes sparkling, a detective with

important information to share. 'I'm paraphrasing here, but bear with me. Just as Percival and Grant arrive at the golf club, they see a second CSI vehicle arriving. They get out of their car. The four of them greet each other, as you do. Priestley's ribbing Cartwright, calling him names. Cartwright slopes off in a mood, heads into the clubhouse to take a piss. Hold that thought . . .' Frankie paused. 'At this point, Alison Brody arrives and lets fly at the other three about the lack of progress, the fact that she's got an event to run, accusing them of standing around with their thumbs up their arses preventing her from doing her job. Percival didn't have a clue who this angry woman was. She demanded to know who was in charge, had a go at him and left, so when a body was found in the graveyard next door it never occurred to him that it might be her.'

'C'mon!' Abbott said. 'He didn't recognise her?'

'Have you seen me when I'm angry, Dick?'

Everyone laughed.

'The photograph issued to the press after Alison's death was the usual sickly, smiley one families usually put forward,' Frankie explained. 'The best they could come up with. The one that showed their dead loved one in a good light.' The team understood. Most families did it. 'Sharpe may have made mistakes as SIO, but he was careful not to release Alison's company details to the press, nor her profession, I checked.'

'So how does that change anything?' Abbott asked. 'You've linked Cartwright to a murder victim. I'm not saying he's guilty. On the surface, he appears to be a good bloke. He cooperated fully in interview, but there's evidence to tie him to these offences.' He threw it out there. 'His works vehicle was picked up on the ANPR close to two crime scenes; his computer access card was used in an attempt to view confidential data; he was off duty on the dates of all four murders—'

'Which most likely means that Priestley was too, if they're paired up,' Frankie argued.

'Agreed, but Cartwright is also the right age and physical build.'

'And so is Priestley, according to Steph Craven. I just spoke to her.' Frankie was on a roll and asked Abbott to hear her out. She wanted everyone on the same page. 'The crucial thing here is that Cartwright wasn't present during Alison Brody's angry outburst. He did not see her—'

Dick cut her off. 'Or he did but knows he has three colleagues who'll swear under oath that he wasn't there. Sounds like the perfect alibi to me. Who's to say he didn't clock her from inside the clubhouse? Cartwright's graffiti tag is Odin, for Christ's sake. What more do you want?'

David loved it when detectives challenged each other's theories and provided information to back up their point of view. He focused on Abbott. 'Dick, all you've said is true, but I'm inclined to go with Frankie on this. The evidence is all circumstantial. I just had a word with Cartwright off the record. He's known Priestley since they were kids. It stands to reason that there's very little they don't know about each other.'

'Priestley's not Craven's cup of tea, I can tell you that much,' Frankie said. 'If it looks like a set-up and it smells like a set-up . . .' She let the sentence hang.

'Dick's right though,' Mitch said. 'There's too much on him to let him go.'

'We are not letting him go . . .' David made that clear. 'At least not yet, but neither is he under arrest. He's agreed to stick with me this evening on a voluntary basis. He's happy for us to keep his car, his phone, and I need to search his house. When I leave here, that's where I'm heading.'

Someone had their hand up, her focus on Frankie. 'You're sure Cartwright wasn't present when Alison was shouting her mouth off?'

'Not according to Percival. I haven't yet corroborated that with Grant, but I will.'

'It must have been a long piss,' someone else said.

'That's the only bit that doesn't fit,' Frankie had to concede.

'Yes, it does,' David came to her rescue. 'In interview, he said that he has a urinary problem requiring surgery. He's booked into the Nuffield Hospital. That's the reason he took leave at short notice. He claims his admission letter is in the house. Lately, his medical condition has become a problem for him, the reason he gave for leaving his access card in his computer. He claims he's up and down like a yo-yo and it takes time to log in and out.'

'Unless he's covering himself,' Indira said.

'That's a possibility, but why would he lie about something that can so easily be verified?' David focused on Abbott. 'Dick, I want you to tag along with me tonight. There are supplementary questions to put to Cartwright. Namely, why he turned up at someone else's crime scene, though I suspect we already know the answer if he used the gents. I want to know what Priestley talked about when they left. Did he say anything odd? What was his demeanour?' David scanned the room. 'Are we done?'

Heads were nodding.

David thanked Frankie for her input. 'I'll have someone take you home.'

'I'm not going home.'

'Yes, you are.'

'Relax, guv. I'm staying with my old man. He's on his way in with Kevlar jimjams.' She scanned the team. 'Watch yourselves on the way out. The stupid sod probably hired an armoured car.'

The door to the incident room crashed open. Her father strode in, like he'd never been away, the eyes of every detective turned in his direction, a spontaneous round of applause taking him by surprise. Frankie wondered if he'd been buzzed in at the front desk or let himself in at the back as Sharpe had done. She felt guilty for ever having doubted him.

'What did I miss?' her father was asking.

He didn't get an answer.

David shook hands with him, meeting Frankie's eyes over her father's shoulder. Apart from the SIO, only Abbott knew how serious Frank Oliver Snr was about protecting her. He'd do anything to preserve the life of his child. Frankie smiled back at David, a very different person to the one he'd spent the weekend with, more relaxed now he knew the truth about her sister. The ghost of Joanna Oliver would remain with her for the rest of her life – as Jane's would remain with Stone – but for now they were resting.

'We'll come back to this tomorrow,' David said. 'Dick, you're with me in case Cartwright is our man and tries to make a run for it. Pam, I want an ANPR check on Priestley's private vehicle. Mitch, Indira, I want eyes on him. Any sightings, let me know. If you find him, I want him under surveillance at all times. Until we know the extent of their involvement, we cannot afford to lose sight of these two. Frankie, can I have a quick word? The rest of you, go home. Get some kip. I want everyone in bright and early. Let's wrap it up.'

63

David asked Frankie to call in a team of crime scene investigators before she left Middle Earth, delaying her departure and his, then he left the incident room with Abbott, collecting Cartwright from the interview room on the way out, taking him with them as planned. He said nothing as he left the building and neither did the SIO. He had no intention of sharing the fact that he now had another credible suspect in his sights.

Following Frankie's unscheduled input, murder detectives were divided over Cartwright's guilt but willing to accept the need to investigate thoroughly and get it right, rather than rush into something they would regret if they got it wrong. The CSI had cooperated fully and was still doing so voluntarily, though he wasn't out of the woods yet. He was under suspicion, though not under arrest; that decision would come later.

Frankie was deep in thought as she watched the three men leave. As she got into her father's car, her mind replayed the briefing she'd just come from: the team's conviction that they were closing in on their target taking a dive; the defeated look on Abbott's face, even though he accepted that there was a valid reason to take another look at the evidence; David's willingness to listen to her point of view . . .

He didn't even think twice.

Holding on to that thought was Frankie's only saving grace. She was gutted not to be out and about with him, or leading the charge in the search for Priestley, a role a couple of young DCs had taken on. Mitch and Indira would be thrilled at the prospect of chasing him down, working late into the night for no financial reward. They would do so because they were professional, because they cared deeply about public safety, but most of all they would do it on behalf of victims who couldn't speak for themselves.

In a way, Frankie had been foiled by her own diligence, turning the enquiry on its head when the MIT thought a lock-up was a dead cert. In almost every major investigation, there was a turning point when intuition took over and the focus switched unexpectedly. Those moments were pivotal. Instinctively, she felt that her conversation with CSI Percival was a prime example. Understanding the wisdom of why she'd been sidelined didn't make it any easier to take.

She glanced at her father. He'd hardly said a word since they'd left the car park. And as they joined the open road, it hadn't passed her by that he was being vigilant, checking his rear-view mirror more often than usual on the lookout for a tail, taking the perceived threat to her wellbeing seriously. The atmosphere in the car was grim.

'You OK, Dad?'

'Living the dream. You?'

His joke fell flat. She may be the one wearing a bulletproof vest, but humour was his body armour, a way of coping when his head was down. Always had been. Occasionally, not often, he allowed the cloak of survival to slip, though never in front of her mother, Rae, Andrea – or anyone outside of his immediate family. Only Frankie knew that, beneath the veneer of coping, he was suffering in the worst way possible, pushing himself to the limit, enduring a private hell she desperately wanted to end. David was the key, she was sure of that, the one person she believed might make it happen.

Cartwright's place was exactly as Stone and Abbott expected: small but tidy; a traditional Tyneside two-up two-down in the city's east end. He was doing his best to keep cool, but even the innocent gave off signs of embarrassment and apprehension when they were in a corner and under suspicion.

Crime scene investigators were there when they arrived, a team Frankie had drafted in from Durham Constabulary, telling them it was an urgent job that couldn't wait till morning. Cartwright sat down, watchful as they went about their business. His connection with Northumbria's own scientific aids team ruled them out of taking his life apart. Though he had never voiced an opinion, it occurred to the SIO that he was as bright as Professor Helen Davidson had said he was.

Cartwright was deep in thought, his focus on Abbott. He'd already worked out that not one, but two CSIs from his own force were under scrutiny. And though Dick had been careful not to flag any particular interest in Priestley, Cartwright had a name in his head. No one was better placed to use his access card to view a confidential file.

David almost felt sorry for him.

Mindful of the possibility that one CSI might be planting evidence to frame the other, using an outside force to search Cartwright's home was not only the right thing to do – it was the only thing to do. Frankie was right. The MIT had to be seen to be doing things by the book. They would leave themselves open to criticism if they didn't handle sensitive enquiries with professionalism and fairness. Many a badly handled case had been overturned.

Frankie sat quietly in the passenger seat of her father's car, a lead weight in and on her chest. Suppressing a full-on yawn, rubbing at tired eyes that weren't coping well with the glare of headlights coming the other way, she glanced at her father. 'I'm exhausted. How's Andy doing?'

He didn't utter a word, just looked at her as if to say: *Thought you'd never ask.*

His grumpy reaction irritated her. 'I've been busy, Dad.'

'You shouldn't be at work.'

'Was I hearing things when you told David that, given the

same set of circumstances, you wouldn't want to back off either, or words to that effect? For the record, Andrea's a mate as well as an in-law. I've been checking on her, calling Rae for updates every couple of hours and Ben's been calling in person too.'

'Then why ask?'

Frankie kept her thoughts to herself. It was unlike him to be spiteful. Then again, he hadn't been himself lately. Outwardly, he was the life and soul, but the tension was there for those who were observant: the worry lines, the hair loss, the tortured eyes she could hardly bear to look at.

Craven's counterpart in Durham Constabulary had muscled in, arriving to check on progress. If there was any publicity to be gained from locking up a quadruple killer, he wasn't going to be left out. He'd described his team – one male, one female – as the best in the business. They would turn the job around in double quick time – and they did.

'How long do you anticipate being here?' It was the first time Cartwright had spoken since they had left Northern Command HQ.

Abbott shrugged. 'You know the score, Nathan. It'll take as long as it takes.'

'What are you expecting to find, if I'm allowed to ask?'

'You're not.' Abbott was too experienced to give away that information. 'You need to be somewhere?'

'I need a piss. Feel free to search me before I go.'

'That won't be necessary,' David said, a nod to Abbott.

The DS left the room, mounting the stairs to check the bathroom. The female CSI was on the landing. He pointed at the bathroom door.

'All done,' she said. 'There are some prescribed drugs in the cabinet.'

'Thanks for the heads-up.'

Dick pushed the door open. There was a small window

in there, large enough for Cartwright to crawl through and make good an escape if that was what he had in mind to do. Though he'd not given off any signals that he'd take flight, he knew the seriousness of the charges he was potentially facing and was undoubtedly concerned. People who were frightened often panicked. Facing a life sentence, the guilty ones might even attempt suicide. Abbott couldn't afford to let Cartwright out of his sight for a second or turn his back on him. Many a rookie had come a cropper doing that. Abbott returned to the living room. 'C'mon. And leave the door open.' He was taking no chances.

Frankie's father put his left hand out and squeezed hers, voicing an apology.

'Don't be daft,' she said. 'I know you worry. So do I, but Andy's a fighter. Her recuperation will take a while but she's going to be fine, Dad.' Her eyes were back on the road, her mind on the job. 'Can you turn right here?' She pointed to a junction up ahead.

'Are we off clubbing?'

'No.' Her laughter was short-lived as he overshot the turning. 'Dad, you missed it. I meant the last street, the one you just ignored. It's OK, you can take the next one.'

'David said straight home, no detours.'

'Did he?' When her father carried on without deviating, it angered her. 'I have one more thing to do before I knock off, possibly two.' She held up her mobile. 'Either you can take me where I want to go, or I'll call a squad car and tell them I've been kidnapped. Under the circumstances, I don't have to draw you a picture of what'll happen next.'

'Where are we going?'

'Gosforth.'

'Nice try.' Another missed turning.

Frankie swore under her breath. 'Dad, it's important.'

'So is getting you home.'

'There are some retirement apartments just off the High Street I need to visit.'

'For what?'

She tried to humour him. 'Thought I might get you in there if they have room.'

'Cheeky bugger.' Another check in the rear-view. The road behind was empty. Her father wasn't the only one on the look. He glanced at her. 'I'll have you know I'm in my prime, young lady. And how many times have I told you that you need a good excuse to be out late on a school night?'

'Dad, I'm not a five-year-old.'

'So, tell me where we're going or make that call.'

'That information is restricted—'

'So is my ability to turn right.'

Frankie punched his arm. 'OK, not a word of this to anyone.' If there was one person in the world she could confide in, it was her father. She knew she could trust him, even with information that was top secret. 'It's an unofficial safe house. Remember Stephanie Craven?'

'Yeah, I know Steph. I have a lot of respect for her. Like you, she speaks her mind. And, just like you, she has her faults. She's another one who can't take no for an answer.'

Frankie's tone was flat. 'We think she's in danger.'

'She is,' her father joked. 'It's hard to talk with a mouth full of razors.'

'Under the circumstances, that's not remotely funny, Dad. As crazy as it sounds, we figure she's the reason our scumbag flipped out and started reducing the female population. She's completely devastated. I want to check on her, make sure she's safe, but first I have a call to make.'

No modern-day SIO wanted to lock up a professional colleague and have to release him later. Throughout the search of his home, Cartwright was the most agreeable suspect David had ever come across in fifteen years of policing. He'd answered every question put to him. So far, the Durham team's efforts had recovered nothing over and above what David had been led to believe they would find and, very soon, he had a decision to make: arrest or release. The burden of proof was his.

Responding to the SIO's solemn expression, Cartwright got up and started pacing the living room as the Durham team worked their way through his home room-by-room. Being in the job himself, he didn't need to imagine what was going on. He'd know exactly what they were doing and how meticulously they'd be doing it. The female CSI arrived in the doorway in protective clothing: a white forensic suit, gloves and mask, paper shoes.

'Sir?'

The SIO turned and followed her out. She'd obviously found something of interest, some physical evidence she thought might be of value to the investigation and wanted to run it past the lead investigator. Abbott could see that Cartwright was rattled. Their eyes met, a brief exchange, the two men checking each other out as a muffled conversation took place on the other side of the living room door.

'So what happens now?'

It was a throwaway remark from Cartwright. A daft thing to say, given his knowledge of procedure and evidence collection. A flash went off in the hallway as photographs were taken, a permanent visual account of what was going on, out of sight of the man whose house was being searched. Extensive notes of what and where each item had been found would be noted in a log.

'Not up to me,' Abbott said. 'The search is far from over. When it is, my guv'nor will let you know.'

The SIO emerged from the hallway, a split-second glance at Abbott from behind Cartwright's back: something had been found.

Cartwright looked over his shoulder, approached the SIO. 'Sir, may I have a word?'

David nodded, his eyes giving nothing away.

'If it makes it easier for you, you can keep me overnight in a cell or in the medical room,' Cartwright said. 'You can lock me in if it'll make you feel any better, just don't lock me up.' His eyes were misting slightly. 'I'm going places, guv. And so are you. I can see where you're coming from, but it won't look good on my CV or yours if you arrest me. I know how important this case is for everyone concerned. I have a sister, a mother, terrified to leave their homes. Believe me, I want the offender caught as much as you do.'

And still David didn't speak.

Cartwright tried again. 'Look, I can see you're nervous of letting me go. So would I be, in your shoes. Guv, I'd rather be in the station in case anything else happens. I want you to prove that I wasn't involved.'

David said nothing in return, just looked on as Cartwright retook his seat. It was quite a speech. He was either a capable and honest Northumbria Police specialist, caught up in a murder investigation through no fault of his own and being set up by his professional partner; or he was culpable, impersonating an innocent man with the artistry of a character actor, a sophisticated subterfuge if he could pull it off.

David just couldn't be sure which one.

64

Frankie cleared her throat and tried to sound breezy. 'Rebecca, I'm sorry to call so late in the day but I'd like to switch the venue of your meeting with our e-fit operator. I've given him instructions to meet you at Central Area Command at Etal Lane instead. It's around the same distance for you but easier to get to. I'll text you the postcode when I get off the phone.'

'Have you made an arrest?'

'Not yet—'

'But you're going to?' Hill wasn't stupid.

Frankie didn't admit or deny it. She'd moved the venue to another nick for obvious reasons: detectives couldn't risk her bumping into a suspect at Middle Earth. There was no doubt in her mind that the chemical engineer had already worked that out. 'There are multiple investigations ongoing,' Frankie said. 'The MIT is just one cog in a very large wheel. We're pushed for space, that's all.'

She left it there and hung up.

'Nicely done,' her father said, indicating to leave the A1.

Ending the call with a half-truth was the only way to quell Hill's suspicions and put an end to her questions. Frankie was too busy texting to respond. One of the texts she sent was to Hill, the other to Craven's private mobile number, giving advanced warning that she was almost there, having tipped her off before she left the office of her intention to visit.

The car came to a halt directly outside the entrance to a block of retirement apartments. Frankie's father ignored a No Parking sign, getting her as close to the front door as possible. The building was smart, purpose-built, architecturally designed.

This was comfortable living for the over-fifties in a leafy, up-market suburb north of Newcastle. The Crime Scene Manager looked drawn as she let them into a room furnished to a high standard, designed to impress visitors. She seemed pleased for some company, but mortified to see Frankie wearing Kevlar, her retired father acting as escort having refused to wait in the car. If Craven was in any doubt of the seriousness with which the police were taking the threat to her life, it was dispelled at that moment.

They sat down in the guest suite.

Frankie's eyes travelled around the room before landing on the woman whose life she was trying to protect. 'How are you doing?' She held up a hand. 'Sorry, that was a ridiculous thing to say given your situation—'

'And yours.' Craven's eyes were on Frankie's body armour. 'How's Andrea?'

'She's fine.' Frankie glossed over that one. She didn't want to talk about it in front of her old man and tried to lighten the conversation. 'Abbott told me that when he offered you a safe house, you thought it was a wind-up.'

'I did. You lot are so convincing. I've had my leg pulled before, no names, no pack drill.' A quick glance at Frankie's father produced an unexpectedly warm smile from both of them. They had more history than Frankie had been aware of. 'Abbott soon put me right,' Craven added. 'He can be quite persuasive when he wants to be. He let me grab a few things and practically frogmarched me from my house. The problem is, my mother has been in here less than a fortnight. She now thinks I'm moving in.'

'How was the party?' Frankie asked.

'Minus a cake,' Craven said bluntly. 'It's still on the kitchen bench. I told her I dropped it and she laughed like a drain. She said it was divine intervention. She never wanted any fuss.' She paused, a moment of humour but also unrivalled sadness. 'Is it true what Abbott said, that I might be the reason for the deaths of four women and the attempted murder of your sister-in-law?'

Frankie raised a sceptical eyebrow. 'I'm sure that's not what he said—'

'It's what he implied.' Craven was more upset than angry.

Frankie was about to speak when her father cut her off. She'd asked him to keep quiet, but he couldn't help himself. 'None of this is your fault, Steph. You're not responsible for the twisted logic of a madman. That's down to him and him alone.'

'He's right,' Frankie said. 'You can't blame yourself for any of this.'

Craven had something on her mind . . .

It took a while to surface.

'Am I allowed to offer an observation?' She took in Frankie's nod but would have voiced it anyway. 'I'm not buying your choice of suspect. On a sliding scale, Nathan Cartwright is a genius, not a maniac. There may be a fine line between the two, but he'd never harm anyone. Just so you know, you've got the wrong man.'

Frankie thought so too.

'There's been no arrest. Nathan is a voluntary attender at this stage.' Frankie might be on the subs' bench, but she was still a murder detective. Her visit wasn't purely benevolent. She had an ulterior motive: she wanted information. 'You can't breathe a word of this Steph, but I'd like your opinion on Brian Priestley.'

'Now that I could believe.'

Craven's eyes grew dark, a look that hadn't been there a moment ago. It was as if someone had flicked a switch. She tried very hard to hide it but Frankie was already poised to ask a question . . .

'Steph, what is it?'

'Nothing, I'm just being paranoid.' She looked away.

Frankie glanced at her father.

He shrugged.

As the Crime Scene Manager looked up, a tear escaped her right eye, dribbling down her cheek. She wiped it away with the back of her hand. Underneath the bravado, the attempt at humour since her visitors arrived, it was clear as day to both of them that this formidable woman was in bits.

Frankie recognised terror when she saw it.

She gave her a gentle nudge. 'Steph, tell me . . . I'm here to help.'

Craven took a deep breath. 'Before I left home with Abbott, I went to secure the back door,' she said. 'I was sure it was open more than I'd left it. Given Dick's urgency to get me out of the house, it sent a chill right through me. I didn't say anything because, frankly, I didn't want to believe it, or even acknowledge the thoughts running through my head. Between you and me, I couldn't wait to get out of there.'

Frankie's stomach turned over.

Craven's failure to tell Abbott was a mistake, one a woman in her position ought not to have made, and probably wouldn't have had she been thinking straight. They might've found evidence. Still might, if Frankie had anything to do with it. If Cartwright or Priestley were in or near the house, they'd backed off when Abbott drove up. A lucky escape that had occurred to Craven now she'd had time to think about it.

No wonder she was trembling.

Her father's voice interrupted Frankie's train of thought. His question was unambiguous. 'Does anyone at work know where your mother lives?'

Craven shook her head. 'I never discuss her or anything personal at work, as well you know. I'm as safe here as anywhere, Frank.'

'You sure?' Frankie asked. 'Just say the word and I'll move you.'

'I'm fine. Don't fuss.'

'OK. The offer stands if you change your mind.' Frankie

backed off. 'You wouldn't happen to have a photograph of Priestley to hand?'

'There'll be one on his personnel file.' Realising she was stating the obvious, Craven reached for her bag, took out her phone and began scrolling through the images contained there. Once she'd found what she was after, she handed over the device. 'That's him, third from the left, at last year's Christmas party.'

Priestley was a geeky-looking twenty-eight-year-old, a loner with an unhealthy fascination for death, according to Craven. Now she'd started down that road, Frankie couldn't shut her up. In the photograph, he was standing shoulder to shoulder with Cartwright. They were of a similar stamp, so close in appearance they could easily have been related. Percival was there too. At six three, he towered over the other two, creating a good height comparison. Frankie felt sure that Priestley was the perpetrator, but she still had to prove it.

'Is this a good likeness of Priestley now?' she asked.

'Absolutely.'

'He hasn't changed his appearance in any way, dyed his hair, grown a beard, moustache or sideburns?'

'No.'

'Can you send the image to me until I can get my hands on his personnel record?' She didn't need to ask twice. Craven did it right away. Frankie flagged the email for ease of access later, then looked up. 'How is he with authority figures?'

'Resentful,' was Craven's one-word answer.

'And otherwise?'

'Doesn't say much. Never has. He can be fun occasionally, but he's a moody bugger, hard to read and work shy, the kind who thinks the world owes him a living. Confidentially, I've marked him down. He'll be on his way soon, if I have any say in it . . .' She stalled. 'Unless he gets me first.'

65

Frankie couldn't settle. There was much going on that she wasn't part of and still no update from David. With the strong urge to do something, she stopped pacing and sat down in her father's den to text Mitchell, asking if he was still out and about. He was, though the text that came back was from Indira. Relieved to hear that they were still at it, Frankie called her on her own number, but the phone was switched off. Swearing under her breath, she tried Mitch and could hear road noise when he picked up.

He was mobile.

'What's the score?' she asked. 'Any news on Priestley?'

'None. No lights on at his place. We waited until midnight and he didn't show. His vehicle wasn't there and there's no update on the ANPR. We gave his neighbours either side a knock. One lot had no clue. They didn't seem to know him. He keeps himself to himself, though they describe him as quiet and polite. A couple of weeks ago, the guy on the other side saw him lifting stuff into a van. He's not seen him since and seemed to think that he'd moved out—'

'Fuck! He could be anywhere. Is he a tenant or homeowner?'

'Tenant. They all share the same landlady, a Mrs Flynn.'

'Did you get her number? I'll get her out of bed.'

'Indi did that already, Frank.'

'And?'

'Flynn's not aware of him leaving, though her properties change hands on a regular basis. Not all leaseholders give advanced warning when they leave. The ones that owe her money often do a bunk, but she seemed surprised by the suggestion that Priestley might have been one of them. She's had no problem with him. Quite the opposite. He pays up on time. Keeps a tidy house. The woman has never heard a squeak out of him. Maybe the neighbour is wrong.'

'Yeah, and maybe he's not.' Frankie's tone was vitriolic. 'And he'd hardly leave a forwarding address if he's who we think he is. Hold on . . .' Frankie's father had come in to say goodnight. Seeing that she was on the phone, he blew her a kiss, pointing at his watch, her cue to go to bed. Nodding a promise not to stay up too late, she went back to her call as he left the room. 'Sorry, Mitch. Have you informed the boss?'

'Indi was about to when your text came in. She ran out of battery.'

'I gathered as much. Tell her not to bother. I'll do it myself. Anything else?'

'We lifted a black bin liner from Priestley's dustbin. There's a fortnightly collection and they're due tomorrow. I thought it best to grab it while it was still there. I had a quick look at what was on top, but I knew you'd want to preserve what was underneath. It looked like common or garden domestic rubbish to me. I'm on my way to Middle Earth with it now.'

'Good job! I'm proud of you both.'

'Be sure to tell the boss. We'd like a permanent posting.'

'Done,' she said. 'Oh, and Mitch? Craven thinks someone was in the house and backed off when he saw Dick drive up. If that's the case, she had a lucky escape. I want her house and garden processed ASAP. Pass the message on when you get back to the office.'

'Will do.'

Wishing him good night, or what was left of it, Frankie hung up.

She put her feet up on her father's desk and leaned back, staring at the ceiling, her mind unable to shut down. Even though the evidence was stacked against Cartwright, the more she thought about it, the more convinced she became that Priestley was their man. She accessed the photos app on her iPhone and clicked on the image Craven had supplied of the Christmas party. Frankie had only given Cartwright and Priestley a cursory glance when she was at the safe house – and then it hit her . . .

She'd seen these two before.

They were leaving Middle Earth on the night she'd seen Sharpe in the corridor outside the major incident room. She knew now that if the retired officer had been in the MIR, it was for no other reason than to shake David's hand and wish him all the best with an investigation he'd failed to resolve before his sudden departure – a decision that had probably left him with a sense of dissatisfaction, if not full-blown guilt. Conceivably, one or both CSIs she'd passed on the way in might have had access to the incident room and/or given her that weird sensation that she was under surveillance.

She shivered.

Could the two be in cahoots?

The idea was discounted as quickly as it arrived. With the Odin stones and graffiti pointing at one of them, it made no sense. It made Frankie's blood boil to think that she'd come within feet of them without knowing it at the time. It was too late to call Steph Craven, so she sent a text:

Did Priestley move house recently?

No change of address notified.

OK, thanks – get some rest.

Is there anything I can do to draw him out?

No. It's too risky.

I'd like nothing better.

We might be too late.

What do you mean?

We suspect he's on the fly. Stay put.

Frankie had only been mildly surprised when she got an immediate answer to her text. Like her, Craven probably couldn't sleep and was unlikely to do so now she'd been told that Priestley might have fled. She'd hesitated before telling her, then Andrea popped into her head and the decision

366

was made: she owed Craven the benefit of advance warning. Frankie got to her feet to stretch her legs and made another call. David picked up immediately. He was back in the office and she wished she was too. She fed back what Mitch had just told her, asking if he'd fared any better. The news was equally depressing.

Durham Crime Scene Investigators hadn't found much evidence in Cartwright's house, he told her. 'No wax jacket, Odin stones, blue rope or crossbow. No illicit material or literature of the kind we might expect to find if he'd been guilty of extreme violence. There were cans and cans of spray paint in an outhouse in the rear yard, but then he hadn't denied his interest in graffiti. When it was found, he showed us the images he'd referred to in interview, legitimate commissions he described as street art.'

'What about his hospital admissions letter?'

'Yup, that was there too. His surgery is scheduled to take place tomorrow, in case, like me, you've forgotten what day it is. It's all here, Frank. Confirming everything he told Abbott. I've retained his computer. I'll get the techies on to it first thing in the morning.'

Frankie ran a hand through her hair.

Her eyes travelled around her father's den and came to rest on Joanna. A lump formed in her throat and made her want to bawl. 'And what are you going to do with Cartwright?' She didn't wait for an answer. 'You can't let him go. You'd never forgive yourself if it's him and he kills again—'

'Frank, stop!' David's tone went from harsh to reassuring. 'Cartwright's going nowhere until I say so. He practically begged me to hang on to him. He's in the medical room as a voluntary attender. He can't get out of the cell block. The custody sergeant will keep an eye on him. Now hang up and go to bed.'

66

When David let himself into his house at almost two a.m. Ben came in to greet him, eyes filled with sleep, hair ruffled and damp with sweat. Apologising for waking him, David poured himself a whisky and sat down heavily on the sofa in the living room to drink it. He'd hit a brick wall. When Ben made no move from the room, David knew he had something on his mind.

That made two of them.

'Have you looked in a mirror lately?' Ben said. 'You look like Desperate Dan.'

'And that's exactly how I feel.' David was almost too tired to laugh, but he did as he stroked rough stubble on his chin. 'That's what happens if you're chasing down a villain with a bit of nous. With the shift I just put in, four deaths and one attempted murder to solve, I reckon I've got an excuse to look shabby.'

'Word is, you've got someone in custody.'

David met Ben's eyes over the top of his glass. 'Word is not always what it's cracked up to be. Remember that.'

'Belinda said—'

'I don't give a shit what she said, to be honest, so unless you can tell me where you're getting your dodgy information, fuck the hell off and make us a cheese sarnie. I'm famished and I'm all out of cow pie.'

Ben grinned. 'It's not true?'

'It's not true.'

Before Ben made it back to the living room, David had fallen asleep. He woke up in a crumpled suit four hours later, to find a curled-up sandwich on the table beside him. He ate it for breakfast, washing it down with a cup of strong coffee, then had a shave while he waited for Ben to get out of the shower. Within twenty minutes, they were dressed and on their way to the car.

The lad waited until they had climbed in, then swivelled in his seat to face his uncle, asking him to hold on a second before pulling away, that same expression he had the night before, like he had important information he couldn't wait to share. David thought he was going to mention Wells' theory that he had someone under arrest:

'Ben, I haven't got time for a Q&A. Drop it, eh? Take my word for it. We have no one in custody.' It wasn't a lie.

'That's not what I wanted to talk to you about.'

'Well, make it quick. I have a briefing to conduct.' David put his key in the ignition and turned the engine over.

'Belinda dropped me off early yesterday. She was going to the theatre—'

'I said quick, Ben.'

His nephew apologised. 'When you didn't turn up for dinner, I was bored, so I had a look around the Internet. I found something you need to see. The Twitter stream on the #BalticShooting hashtag had almost dried up,' he explained. 'But a new user posted this photograph at around eight forty-five last night. I grabbed a screenshot in case the user deleted it.'

David took his phone from him.

The image was of Frankie, taken on the Gateshead side of the River Tyne. She looked unconcerned and appeared to be waiting for someone: Andrea. What was even more interesting was that the Millennium Bridge in the background was down. It had been raised just as the Traffic officer was shot with a crossbow and had been kept open for a couple of hours afterwards on Frankie's instruction. David noticed that the username on the screenshot was made up of a series of letters and numbers that meant nothing to him.

'This here . . .' He pointed to the right side of the screen where *54m* was displayed. 'I assume that means fifty-four minutes before you captured the image. Tell me you wrote down the exact time you did that.'

'Do I look stupid? Anyway, I didn't need to.' Trying hard not to take the piss, Ben pointed at the top of the screen which timed and dated the screenshot. Underneath yesterday's date, the time 20.28 appeared. Unwittingly, he'd just handed Cartwright a cast-iron alibi. He was in voluntary attendance at Middle Earth, being interviewed by Abbott at the time, his mobile phone in the possession of the police, all of it witnessed by the SIO from the adjacent viewing room.

A feeling of pride swelled in David's chest.

He locked eyes with his nephew.

'Ben, this is gold.' He grinned. 'You just ruled out the person we didn't have in custody.'

'How?' asked Ben.

David explained.

They didn't speak much after that. On the journey into town David's mind was fully occupied. He didn't do Twitter but knew enough to know that anyone who did had to possess an email address to create an account. He dropped Ben off at the newspaper office before heading for the mother of all briefings, but first he had something important to do, a task that would give him a great deal of pleasure.

As he entered the medical room, Cartwright stood up, his face pale, wide-eyed as if he feared the worst. It was the obvious conclusion to jump to. It wasn't every day you get a visit from a busy SIO. 'Relax, Nathan . . .' David's phone rang, preventing him from delivering the good news that he was free to go. Ben's name appeared on screen. Irritated by the interruption, David was about to mute the call and let voicemail take a message when Cartwright's expression stopped him.

He held up the phone. 'I'll have to take this.'

'Sir.' Cartwright sat back down.

David walked out into the corridor, closing the door behind him. 'This had better be good, son.'

'You do know about scheduled tweets, right?'

David listened as Ben explained that it was possible to write a message on the social media site and post it at a given time. The SIO blew out a breath. 'Thanks,' he said. 'You just saved me making a complete tit of myself.'

Cartwright was back in the mix.

67

MIT detectives were given instructions to examine Priestley's worksheets during the briefing, a job they had already done on Cartwright – two CSIs still in the frame. When Frankie joined David in his office afterwards, she didn't look happy and he knew the reason why. He owed her an explanation for his about-turn on Cartwright and shared Ben's find on social media, disclosing his own – potentially fatal – mistake of thinking it was safe to let him leave until Ben tipped him off.

The screenshot shook Frankie to the core . . .

She'd come closer to a killer than she knew.

'Ben changed your mind?'

'Yes and no,' David said. 'I almost didn't take his call. But when I told Cartwright to relax, it was his egotistical expression that made me reconsider, a flash of relief, but also smugness. I could be wrong, Frank. On four hours' sleep, maybe I saw something that wasn't there, but equally he could be playing us.'

'That doesn't make sense. Why would he point the finger at himself?'

'Because he thinks he's untouchable. Steph Craven called him a genius. Professor Helen Davidson seemed to agree with her. Maybe he's starting to believe the hype.' David took a moment to gather his thoughts. 'Clever doesn't stop him also being devious – and there's nothing more so than organising your own alibi, is there? Besides, it makes as much sense as Priestley making a run for it after spending so much time and energy trying to implicate his professional partner so he could get away with murder.'

'I suppose.'

Frankie's head went down as David's had when he'd

walked away from the cell block. The seesaw effect of not knowing which way to jump was frustrating and emotionally draining. There was no getting away from it: the enquiry was again coasting to a crawl, like a car heading into snarled-up traffic, except for them the journey was far from over. They had nothing concrete. What they needed was a smoking gun.

'What did you say to Cartwright?' Frankie asked.

'I didn't. I left him to sweat.'

'And if he starts to crow about the time he's spending in the cell block?'

'Then I'll arrest him. You said yourself, there's too much at stake. We can't afford to stand off and keep our suspects under surveillance, assuming we ever find Priestley. There's still no news of him. If we were to let Cartwright go and lose sight of him, and another woman is attacked, it would be fatal for her and curtains for us. We'd be crucified in the press. I'm not about to let either of those things happen. Cartwright stays put until we know which one is responsible. I don't want to lock him up yet because then we're on the clock. For now, we keep investigating. We'll get there, Frank.'

She was nodding, a glance at her watch: 08.50. 'Priestley's due in at nine. Dick is at his office, waiting to see if he turns up. Maybe then we'll have a clear indication of who we're after.'

Frankie watched as the big hand on the clock clicked forward a notch, reaching the hour mark. A few seconds later, Mitch knocked on David's office door and poked his head in, his focus on Stone. 'Excuse the interruption, guv. I know you said to hold all calls until further notice, but Dick is on the phone. It's important. OK to put him through?' A nod from David. Mitchell switched his attention to Oliver. 'CSI Grant is here to see you, Frank.'

'OK, tell her to wait.'

The young DC disappeared. Seconds later, the internal

phone rang. Picking up, David put the phone on speaker and waited for an update from Abbott. He sounded like he was running.

'Frankie and I could do with some positive news,' David said. 'Tell us you're out of breath because you slapped the cuffs on Priestley.'

'If only that were the case, guv. He rang in before I got there, asking for compassionate leave for a couple of days. Craven wasn't in work to ask her, but we knew that already and so did he. Percival is covering for her but was otherwise engaged when the call came in. The idiot who answered told Priestley that they weren't that busy and said it would proba- bly be OK. He asked no personal questions, quote "in case it upset him" unquote. Can you believe that? Priestley was in a hurry to get off the phone.'

'I bet he was,' Frankie said.

'He said he was heading north and asked the call-taker to leave a note on his behalf. Percival went ballistic when he saw it and so did I. I reckon that's the last we'll see of Priest- ley for a while. Sounds to me like he's giving himself a head start—'

'Pound to a penny he's heading south,' Frankie said sourly.

'Is there any update from Technical Support on Cartwright's computer?' David asked.

'No, but that Twitter account you talked about at the brief- ing has been nailed down. We have an email address—'

'Great!' David was off his chair, hand poised in mid-air to give Frankie a high-five.

'Not so great,' Abbott said. 'It belonged to PC Duncan Carr, the same Duncan Carr who was buried on Tuesday. If Sharpe knew he'd died, pound to a penny the account holder did too, or he read Jack's obituary in the *Journal* and, realising the address would still be active, thought he'd have some fun at our expense. I'm sorry, guv. We're not going anywhere with it.'

'Damn it!' David slammed his fist on the desk, his eyes on his 2ic. 'What did I say about devious?'

Bitterly disappointed, Frankie got up and left the room.

Grant stood up as Frankie left David's office. Frankie took her to the staff canteen, bought her a cup of coffee, then sat down beside her, asking the CSI to describe, in minute detail, everything she could remember of her encounter with Priestley and Cartwright at Boldon Golf Club. Her story confirmed Percival's to a T: Cartwright never laid eyes on Alison Brody in their company.

Thanking her for her time, Frankie got to her feet. She was almost at the door when more questions bubbled to the surface. She retraced her steps. May as well get Grant's personal take on the two men while she was there – a female perspective in a case of this nature was crucial.

'What do you think of Cartwright?' she asked.

'He's a nice lad. Very professional. We've worked together once or twice.'

'And Priestley?'

'He's an arrogant dickhead. I don't rate him and neither does the boss. Put it this way, Craven gives him the routine stuff, the jobs no one else wants, not those where lives are at stake like the one you're dealing with. She paired him with Cartwright hoping that he'd learn something, but guys like him rarely do, in my experience. By the way, I've just finished searching the contents of his bin. It may not be what you want to hear but I found nothing but domestic rubbish.'

'I want to see it,' Frankie said.

'It's a bit smelly.'

'Let's go.'

Grant's description of Priestley stuck with Frankie as they made their way along the corridor. The stuff Mitch had collected from his bin was laid out on a trestle table on a brown-paper lining. Frankie put on a pair of nitrile gloves and a mask to examine what was there and took a good look through it, moving along the table inch-by-inch: empty beer cans, squashed cartons, torn paper smeared with food, scrunched up tin foil and general household waste. About three-quarters of the way along, a small plastic bottle caught her eye. The sight of it made her heart leap. A half-empty bottle of contact lens solution . . . Or was it half-full?

68

Frankie placed the bottle in an evidence bag and made an urgent request to have it analysed and examined for finger-prints. She asked the custody officer to pay a brief visit to the medical room for an information-gathering exercise. Then she went in search of David to inform him of her find. 'Today was bin collection day,' she said. 'Priestley knew, or thought he knew, that with Cartwright helping us with our enquiries we weren't looking at him. Only, thanks to Percival and Grant, he was wrong about that.'

She paused, allowing him to catch up.

'David, Cartwright just told me that Priestley doesn't wear glasses or contact lenses and, even if he did, who throws this stuff away? It's expensive. Hill's description of the man she saw on the Durham train led us to believe that he was changing his appearance in order to hide his identity. From that point on, we've been of the opinion that he was disguis-ing himself. Well, now we have something that might help prove it.'

'Might being the operative word,' David said. 'At best it's more circumstantial evidence.'

'But it gives us reasonable grounds to suspect him, yes? Enough to convince a magistrate to give us a search warrant for his home. The neighbour was wrong. His landlady has just confirmed that his kit is still there.'

'Do it!' He smiled at her. 'Put on your sincerity specs and tell them we suspect he's gone to ground. I'll head over to Central Area Command and check on the e-fit.'

It was all the impetus Frankie required to get going.

She obtained an immediate warrant to search Priestley's home.

What she found there was zilch; on the face of it nothing that tied him to any victim or crime scene. Anticipating his arrest, he'd got rid of all incriminating evidence, apart from the bottle of the lens solution she suspected he'd dumped at the last minute, unaware that Mitch would get to it before the bin men did. A team of CSIs were still at the house. Hopefully they might find something Frankie couldn't see with the naked eye.

The hunt was on to find and arrest Priestley.

With the SIO otherwise engaged, Frankie was directing operations in the incident room, waiting for news on the suspect's whereabouts – and finally it came in an excited call from Abbott.

'You were right,' he said. 'Priestley was travelling south, not north. The ANPR had picked up his private vehicle on the M6 near Manchester. Four police vehicles carried out a hard stop on the motorway following a lengthy chase.'

She listened carefully as Abbott gave her the details. Traffic officers involved didn't know Andrea, only her current predicament – Frankie had made sure of that – and there was no greater motivation to take Brian Priestley into custody than knowing that an officer he'd attempted to kill was one of theirs.

No longer confined to barracks, and with the suspect under arrest and on his way back to the north-east, Frankie was free to come and go as she pleased, but she wasn't leaving the major incident room. Not now. There was too much to do in the office, not least of which was planning an interview that might draw the offender out. She was halfway through doing that when she stopped writing. Scooping up the phone, she called Craven, updating her on progress, asking her to come in. Fifteen minutes later, she arrived and the two went into David's empty officer for a chat.

*

By the time the suspect arrived back at Middle Earth in the late afternoon to face his accusers, the SIO was in possession of the e-fit Rebecca Hill had helped produce, a good likeness to the blown-up image on the murder wall, the snapshot Stephanie Craven had supplied and the official profile photograph attached to his personnel record. The e-fit convinced the doubters that he was the man they had been hunting for a little over two weeks. He may have been guilty of intimidation – Rebecca Hill was terrified on that train when he got on at Durham – but he'd been careful not to speak to her. As such, there was not a lot they could charge him with in that respect. As despicable as his behaviour was, they wanted him for more serious offences than that. So far, he'd said nothing in interview that would link him to a murder case.

At Frankie's insistence, the Murder Investigation Team did everything by the book, gathering intelligence, identifying gaps in Priestley's story as messages were passed back from those who were observing David's interview with him. None were gaping holes, if the truth were known. Priestley had been and was being careful. His responses were scripted and well rehearsed, designed to deflect blame on to Cartwright, though he claimed that they were friends.

As a graduate of Cumbria University, he too was known to Professor Davidson. She claimed that he was clever, though not in the same league as Cartwright, echoing Craven's professional opinion that he'd failed to apply himself.

Frankie turned to Abbott. 'Get on to PolSA. See how they're coming along with the search of Steph Craven's house and garden. There may be something more we can throw at him.'

'I'm on it,' he said. 'Is there any news from the boss?'

'Priestley hasn't coughed.'

Abbott gave her a pointed look. 'Would you?'

69

Frankie turned the case over in her mind. As with the missing physical evidence, there was nothing on Priestley's phone or SIM card that could be classed as hard evidence: no contacts that stood out, no dodgy internet searches or covert recordings. A second computer, a laptop, found in his car was being examined as a matter of urgency. Cell site analysis had helped place him at various locations, producing a detailed record of where his mobile was as it passed between phone masts around the region, though none close enough to the scene of any crime to implicate him. The most illuminating thing they discovered from the mobile device were periods when it had been switched off, adding some weight to the case against him.

'It's not enough,' Frankie whispered under her breath.

'Sarge?'

She looked up to find Mitch standing by her desk. Frankie's discussion with Craven had borne fruit. The Crime Scene Manager had told her that on the day Andrea was shot, Priestley had been very close to the crime scene and, with her insight, Frankie thought she might be able to prove it. She'd sent Mitch off to investigate.

'Have you got something for me?'

'As it happens, I do. Priestley walked into Gateshead nick within minutes of the incident on the quayside, just as you were raising the alarm. He made a song and dance about being out of battery to a female member of the admin staff. I just spoke to her. She gave a statement to that effect, describing him as unperturbed.'

'Did he mention the mayhem going on down there?'

'Briefly.'

'So why didn't he respond to the call-out for all units?'

'He's not a copper—'

'He's not a human either,' she said. 'What self-respecting member of staff – detective, uniform or civilian – would ignore a call-out like that?'

'No one I know,' Mitch said.

'Other CSIs came to my aid. He was aware and did nothing? Fucking moron.'

'There's more . . . Priestley used the office phone to check in with his unit.'

'Yeah, Steph told me. It was her he spoke to.'

'He was probably covering his back, but it's backfired on him. It places him close to the scene and alone when Andrea was shot.'

Mitchell didn't mention the crossbow for fear that it would upset her. He was sensitive like that and Frankie appreciated the gesture.

'Where was Cartwright?' she said.

'At the Jesmond Nuffield, an appointment with his urologist, just as he said he was. Priestley dropped him off there.'

'You're absolutely sure?'

'Certain. I confirmed it with the receptionist.'

The team needed more to make a charge stick. Frankie's eyes strayed to her computer, to Priestley's work schedule, her father's words arriving in her head, pressing on the inside of her brain, crushing her, urging her to make a connection that she could use to her advantage or that of the SIO.

Everything you see is a signpost.

Minutes later, a CSI she'd seen at Priestley's house approached her desk. He updated her, then turned to go. He had another job on and needed to hand in his forensic suit to the exhibits officer.

'Fuck!' It came out like an explosion.

'Sarge?'

Ignoring Mitch, Frankie logged on to her computer, pulling

up Priestley's work schedule to compare with the estimated times of death for all four victims, then grabbed her bag and raced for the door, leaving her young colleague standing with his mouth open.

'Frankie?' he called after her. 'Where are you going?'

'To catch a killer,' she said. 'Tell the boss.'

She was gone.

70

When the SIO returned to the incident room, giving the prisoner a break from questioning as he was required to do – even scumbags like him had rights when it came to periods of detention – no one knew where Frankie was. An hour passed. Frustrated, unable to reach her or understand the cryptic message that Mitchell had passed on, David recalled Priestley's brief to the interview room, heading back to do battle with his client, with renewed determination and, it had to be said, enthusiasm with Abbott as second chair.

Frankie tapped her fingers on the counter while white-coated lab technicians went about their business. She had eyes only for one, a young woman of Chinese descent who had agreed to do a rush job. The result Frankie was hoping for was the only way she could take a crack at the man who had the audacity to believe that he was untouchable. After three long hours, the Chinese scientist looked out through the window of her laboratory, locking eyes with Frankie through the glass, a silent message contained in her expression. She may just as well have raised a thumb.

Reminding Priestley that he was still under caution, the SIO sat back in his chair thinking about what Frankie just told him, a relaxed pose before he began. 'I'd like to refer to your first interview, if I may.'

Priestley said nothing.

'I've asked you this before, but you've had some time to think it over, so can you please confirm whether or not you've been involved in any capacity' – David stressed the last three words – 'at any of the crime scenes I referred to earlier. Just to refresh your memory, the locations are listed here, along with the names of five victims. Your solicitor might like to see it too.' Pushing the list across the table, David glanced at the brief. 'Actually, you can keep that one, sir. I have another copy.'

Blyth promenade: CATHERINE BENNETT (28)
Boldon Cemetery: ALISON BRODY (34)
Telford Bridge: MARGARET ROBSON (59)
Stocksfield station: JOANNA COSGROVE (37)
Gateshead Quayside: INSPECTOR ANDREA McGOVERN

The SIO waited.

Not a flicker from his suspect.

A face-off.

Priestley had a degree in smug. During the previous interview he'd said very little. Facing such serious allegations, this was only to be expected. He'd have been fully briefed to say nothing at all. Often in situations like these, offenders – even the most narcissistic among them – incriminated themselves while being questioned by detectives trained to trap them into making a mistake.

'Mr Priestley?' Stone applied gentle pressure, keeping his voice level. 'Do you need more time to consider your response or consult with your solicitor?'

'No.' Priestley slid the list across the table to his brief and crossed his arms, a bored expression on his face. 'I was not present at any of those crime scenes.'

'Are you absolutely sure?'

'Yes, how many more times do I have to say it?'

It was the first show of contempt.

David put on his best worried face, acting as if he had little to throw at him. It was clear from Priestley's supercilious expression that he'd expected a more aggressive stance from the SIO investigating four murders and the attempted murder of a police officer. So far, the interviews had fallen woefully short of the interrogation he'd expected. That was about to change.

'I believe you,' David said.

This threw the suspect.

It threw his brief.

The SIO's strategy was working: let his adversary think that he was holding the better hand and then trump him by turning up the heat. 'That is to say, I believe that you were not there in any official capacity. I'd like to share with you the reason for that belief. My officers have been working hard on this case, particularly DS Oliver.' Convinced that Frankie was the target of the crossbow shooting, David threw it out there to see what reaction he might get, his eyes never leaving the suspect.

Mention of Frankie Oliver almost made Priestley laugh. If Stone thought he was going to cough to any of these offences, he was sadly mistaken. The MIT had nothing on him. They both knew that. No matter which way they looked at it, the evidence was pointing at Incontinence Man. No judge worth his salt would convict anyone else.

No sweat.

As he'd told his solicitor, his trip south was genuine. His brother was in a Manchester hospital with sepsis caused by a rusty nail puncturing his work gloves on a building site. A stroke of luck, it had to be said, providing him with a genuine excuse to leave the area, as detectives would discover soon enough. Stopping him on the M6 would make them look stupid – not to mention callous, given the fact that his brother was fighting for his life and would probably croak. Detectives didn't need to know that they hated one another, did they? And if his brother happened to survive, so what? It wouldn't be the first time that estranged siblings had decided to support one another on their death bed, whatever their history.

Bring on the role of Good Samaritan.

Across the table, the SIO's hard eyes stared back at him. Like he could give a shit. The great Met detective wasn't a patch on Craven and he was making mistakes. Oliver was a case in point. It was true that she'd been on his hit list, but then he'd reconsidered. Her family were tight and well respected, revered throughout the force. Killing an in-law made perfect sense, handed him the opportunity to see them all grieve.

Priestley's eyes reflected an emotion that mystified David, as if he'd got this wrong and Andrea was the intended target all along. With no time to dwell on it, he moved quickly on. Now he had the upper hand, he didn't want to let it go. Eyeballing his suspect, David upped the ante, trying to get a rise out of the man facing him. 'DS Oliver's enquiries with your supervision were illuminating,' he said. 'Your line manager revealed that you're "not ready to investigate the ultimate crime". She's right, isn't she? You're not up to the job, are you? The truth is, you never have been.'

The suspect's expression changed instantly.

'You disagree?'

Priestley had no answer to give.

If he did, he didn't voice it.

'Did no one ever tell you that devious doesn't equal clever? You didn't agree with her assessment, did you? So you hatched a plan to make her sit up and take notice. Yours must be quite a persecution complex.'

'I have no idea what you're on about.' Priestley was rattled.

'Oh, I think you do.' David hadn't yet referred to Stephanie Craven by name. He would, though he had no need. He'd already scored a bullseye and, thanks to Frankie's diligence, was about to go in for the kill. 'So far, in your work as a CSI you've dealt with minor offences, the grunt work, isn't that so? I can see from your expression that it's a crushing disappointment to you, given that others who graduated in your year have moved on to more serious investigations, sexual assaults, rapes and robberies . . . and will soon move up to murder cases, CSI Nathan Cartwright among them. How does that make you feel?'

Priestley's counsel stopped scribbling and raised his head. 'Relevance, Detective Chief Inspector?' It was the first show of real concern from the solicitor who, up to that point, had sat quietly making notes, satisfied with the way things were going, confident that his client had taken his advice and given away nothing that would send him down for life. Like Priestley, the brief was on the back foot now, sweating on this line of questioning, concerned where it might ultimately lead.

'My apologies,' David said, then hit the suspect again. 'You wasted your time leaving a trail of evidence to implicate Cartwright – a betrayal of the worst kind, in my opinion. The Odin stones and graffiti was your insurance, wasn't it? All of it designed to throw us off the scent and shift the blame elsewhere in case we got too close. And when we did, you bottled it and ran away.'

A look of irritation passed from prisoner to SIO.

Or was it hatred?

Priestley panicked, unaware that his body language was giving him away. Beads of sweat had formed on his upper lip and his chest rose and fell more deeply than it had before, proof that he was under some pressure, unable to control his emotional response to the SIO poking fun at him. Hands that had previously been relaxed in his lap were now firmly clenched, turning his knuckles white.

Priestley followed Stone's gaze. It took monumental effort to unfurl fingers that were digging into the palms of his hands. When he looked up, he felt his stomach heave. The look in the SIO's eyes was a dead giveaway.

He'd found something . . .

But what?

Priestley dropped his head, avoiding eye contact. Thinking time. He'd been so careful to cover his tracks and lay the blame at Cartwright's door, evidence that could be attributed to him and him alone. He'd got rid of every scrap of clothing he'd worn and, as far as he was aware, there was nothing concrete to tie him to these offences. A good barrister would laugh if the Crown Prosecution Service presented only circumstantial evidence in a case like this, casting doubt on his culpability, enough to convince a jury that there was insufficient evidence to convict him.

He raised his head – no need to panic.

The suspect was not a man who liked to be told that he was substandard or lacking in any way, much less a coward who'd run at the first sign of trouble. A blind man on a galloping horse could see that he was under pressure – and that's just where Stone wanted him. He, on the other hand, was serenely calm, as was Dick Abbott, the detective by his side. No hint of agitation from him, just the quiet confidence of an officer with years of experience of interviewing scumbags like Priestley.

An unspoken message passed between them: *Shall we tell him now?*

Aware of what this would do to Priestley, slowly and deliberately Stone turned to face him, leaning forward, a not-so-subtle attempt to antagonise him further. Resting his elbows on the table, a benign expression on his face, all de-signed to take the rise out of his prisoner.

'Did you seriously think that you'd get away with it?'

David felt nothing but contempt for the man.

Time to wind up a gear.

'You look upset, Mr Priestley. You have my apologies . . . Both of you . . . That was never my intention. I was merely trying to establish that there would be no cross-contamination issues with my current investigation.'

Priestley drew in a breath, wiping his face with his hand, an agitated glance at his brief: Say something!

The solicitor leaned in, whispering in his client's ear

– probably advising him to keep his mouth shut and let him do the talking, before turning to face Stone. 'My client has already stated several times that he was not deployed to any of the incidents referred to here.' The brief waved the list at David, a hard edge to his voice. 'Neither has he been near the deposition sites since. As a crime scene investigator, he's as upset by these murders as the rest of us. Now, can we move on?'

'Thanks for clarifying that, sir.' David's eyes shifted to his prisoner. 'Only, that's not true, is it, Mr Priestley?'

'I've answered your question.'

The SIO crossed his arms, his turn to appear smug. 'You've shot yourself in the foot, Brian. You should have taken more notice of your university tutors. You know as well as I do that after every crime scene investigation, forensic suits are retained in evidence as exhibits, sealed and signed.'

'I told you, I wasn't there.'

'You murdered these women, didn't you?'

'No.'

'I have proof that you did.'

The brief looked up. 'Then perhaps we could hear it.'

'As you wish.' David focused on his suspect and only him. 'You should have paid more attention to your training. I'm sure your tutor Helen Davidson taught you well. I know for a fact that Stephanie Craven repeated the basic principle of your role. You really shouldn't wind up my 2ic. It makes her try harder. Unlike you, she knows that every contact leaves a trace and that you just have to find it.'

'DCI Stone—'

David cut off the solicitor's objections before he could finish. 'After you murdered Margaret Robson, you were called upon to attend a burglary in Annitsford eleven miles away. For the tape, I'm now showing the suspect exhibit AJ25. This forensics report should be very familiar to you. Perhaps you'd like to explain – given your absence from any of the murder scenes contained on that list, as you've stressed, time and time again – how a strand of Margaret's hair and fibres from the faux fur hood of the jacket she was wearing on the night she died were found on the inside of a forensic suit worn by you and handed to an exhibits officer fifty minutes later. Who, by the way, has genuinely not been involved in the multiple-murder incidents I'm currently investigating.'

Priestley knew he was done for.

71

A week later, David found Frankie sitting alone on the Amble dock, a half-eaten carton of fish and chips lying on the ground beside her. She seemed to have lost her appetite. Unaware of his presence, he watched her for a while, observing her stillness, her ashen face, wondering why she looked so overwrought. It was her intuition and exceptional detective work that had finally broken through the logjam and solved the case. A long shot, but one that managed to pan out and close the investigation. From Priestley's work schedules, she'd calculated that to have killed Margaret Robson, he must have gone straight to work afterwards, having been ordered to attend an urgent job by Craven, a woman he hated with a passion.

The irony.

There was no doubt that she'd been on his hit list and would now be dead had Abbott not arrived in the nick of time. Priestley had been charged with four counts of murder and one of attempted murder. Andrea had been discharged from hospital, was back home and on the mend, expected to make a full recovery, milking it for all it was worth according to her wife, Rae. Cartwright had returned to Craven's team, absolved of any wrongdoing, accepting an apology from the SIO, unable to believe that his co-worker and former friend had left a trail of clues, like breadcrumbs, leading to his door.

Envy as well as hate did things to people who were unhinged.

The evidence-gathering would go on. David had yet to submit the murder file to the Crown Prosecution Service, but it was shaping up. Detective Chief Superintendent Philip Bright, head of CID, had commended the MIT on what had proved to be a harrowing case for all concerned. He was thrilled that a dangerous man would spend the rest of his life in prison and that Catherine Bennett, Alison Brody, Margaret Robson and Joanna Cosgrove could finally be laid to rest.

'Why the long face?' David said.

It was a daft question, one he knew the answer to: there was no such thing as justice for bereaved families whose loved ones had been brutally murdered – only closure. They would endure a lifetime of grief. David understood that more than most. Jane's death had broken his heart. He'd never get over it. The same could be said of Joanna and Frankie Oliver.

Not counting Andrea, the current investigation had taken its toll on many detectives, three in particular: two serving, one retired. Two of the three were no longer hiding dark secrets. The case had forced them to delve into their past, revealing and examining their innermost horrors, cementing relationships, personal and professional, that the SIO knew would go on forever. There would be no celebration, of this or any other case, while Joanna Oliver's killer was at large. As for Frankie's father? David had it covered.

'I've spoken to your old man,' he said.

Frankie almost lost it as she turned to face him, swallowing down the lump in her throat, as close to tears as he'd ever seen her. She didn't ask how it went. Maybe she didn't want to know. Maybe it was too painful to revisit now. Maybe it was enough to learn that a conversation had taken place and that the healing could begin.

David sat down beside her, legs dangling over the edge of the marina, a calm North Sea directly in front of them, the sun reflecting on a shimmering body of water. Slipping his hand in hers, he gave it a squeeze and, with the other, took a newspaper from his back pocket. As he handed it over, Frankie glanced at the headline, her eyes travelling down the page. Wells had written her exclusive. There was no mention of Ben in the article – not surprising, given that he shared a surname with Stone. It didn't bother the lad. He was maturing, turning the corner, making a go of it. David was immensely proud of him and the part he'd played in apprehending a killer.

'Where are they?' Frankie asked.

'Celebrating, I should imagine,' David said. 'Which is what we should be doing. By the way, Ben now has a penchant for strawberry daiquiri.'

She smiled. 'You're an amazing dad.'

'Those were my exact words to yours when I saw him earlier.'

'He is . . .' The smile melted away. Another squeeze.

'We'll get him one day, Frank.'

Frankie gripped his hand tightly. That's all she wanted to hear.

Acknowledgements

The Insider marks a milestone for me as it's my tenth book. All I ever wanted was to write one . . . but I got the bug and couldn't stop.

This is the second outing for newly promoted Detective Chief Inspector David Stone and Detective Sergeant Frankie Oliver, a complicated four-hander investigation that tests them to the limit, as it did me on occasions.

I'd like to acknowledge everyone at Orion publishing house. Working with you this past year has been a dream. Special thanks to my fabulous editor, Francesca Pathak; assistant editor, Bethan Jones; publicist, Lauren Woosey; marketing guru, Lynsey Sutherland; designer, Tomás Almeida; and freelance copy-editor Anne O'Brien, who has been with me from the very start of my writing journey.

Thanks also to Oli Munson – the best agent any writer could wish for – and everyone at A.M. Heath Literary Agency who work so hard on my behalf. To readers, bloggers, booksellers and librarians who've recommended my work to others, I appreciate everything you do for me.

Many thanks to Captain Kim for help with long-haul flight information. Also, Debbie and Ange whose apartment now belongs to Frankie Oliver. I hope I did it justice.

To my wonderful family: Paul and Kate, Chris and Jodie, Max and Frances, Daisy, Finn and Mo. Without your patience, sacrifice and support I'd have given up scribbling years ago. I love you all.

Stone & Oliver will return in
Mari Hannah's next gripping novel

The
Scandal

Keep reading for a special early extract now.

Prologue

Nancy fled the building, a mixture of relief and fear flowing through her body, an adrenaline rush the like of which she'd never known. The feeling that she was under surveillance even as she drove through the staff car park was like a knife plunged deep into her back. She'd left her resignation on her desk with little explanation. Circumstances beyond her control wouldn't cut it . . . Not a hope in hell. She'd been too vocal for her own good. Too vociferous in her defence of the defenceless. Hers was a just cause. It had put her in danger more than once, but this had never been about her welfare. In one way, the assault had clarified matters, a backhander so violent it had thrown her clear across the room. No witnesses; they were too clever for that. That slap, delivered with such venom, was counterproductive. A signal – if one were needed – that she couldn't change things from the inside. There was no other way . . .

She had go.

It had taken months to make the decision. Using what she knew had ramifications. It would blow the lid off a situation that was out of control. To do it right meant meticulous planning, evidence collection and recording: photographic as well as the notes she'd kept in her journal: names, dates and times. In the meantime, without telling a soul she'd sold up, moving to a place where no one knew her in order to distance herself from those seeking to silence her. Handing in her notice with immediate effect was only the beginning.

She'd have to be careful now.

As she drove teary-eyed from the estate, the faces of those she cared for scrolled before her eyes like movie credits: Bill, Edna, Molly, George and countless others who'd gone before.

Unloved in a lot of cases. The forgotten ones she called them: isolated, indecisive, just plain weak. When they found out she was gone without saying goodbye they'd feel abandoned – but telling them was out of the question. Taking them into her confidence was never an option. A slip of the tongue overheard would tip off the very people Nancy was anxious to expose, leaving those under her care and protection vulnerable – or worse, taking away her ability to blow the whistle.

Nancy sighed.

Her colleagues didn't want to know. One by one, they had turned away, preserving their jobs, keeping the status quo. Who could blame them? For years, they had been operating in a culture of fear. She wondered if they had been paid for their silence. Blood money.

How could they?

A single drop of warm liquid fell from her eyelid, dribbled down her cheek, hot and salty as it crept into her mouth. There would be no tears from those she'd left behind. In many cases they had passed away already. The dead don't cry or complain. A majority would forget her by morning. And yet she could hear them weeping, baffled by a sudden and inexplicable change in circumstances, waiting, wondering if she was ever coming back. That gut-wrenching thought was more than Nancy could bear.

If only it were possible to consign her own observations to oblivion. It wasn't. She felt guilty then. There was nothing worse than memory loss. And yet, if she were honest, she'd wipe her own hard-drive if she could. The thought alone was despicable. Cowardly. It lingered in the back of her mind as she passed through the iron gates and out onto the open road, her decision to go gnawing at her conscience. She worried that her actions would leave those she might never see again caught in a trap with no way out. At least not in the short-term . . .

The word stuck in her throat, tears stinging her eyes.

The short-term was all they had left.

What Nancy did next would determine the rest of their lives and that of countless others, a responsibility that she alone could shoulder. Worse than that, these were no isolated cases. There had been many prosecutions over the years, the accused lifted by police and put before a court of law, some sent to jail. And still it went on. Her actions weren't an exercise in conscience clearing. At every turn, she'd spoken up. On each occasion, she'd been told to shut the fuck up or face the consequences . . . And the consequence had just rounded the bend in her rear-view mirror.

Oh God!

He'd found the letter sooner than she'd hoped. She imagined him sniffing around her office, opening drawers, his dirty fingers all over her stuff. Curious to know what was inside a letter addressed to her boss, he'd have broken his neck to get over there, a sneer developing as he was sent after her . . . Nancy didn't want to know what his instructions had been.

'Deal with it!' most probably.

And deal with it he would.

Nancy's stomach took a dive, the stress of what he had in mind bringing on arrhythmia, a condition she'd endured since her early twenties, a skipped heartbeat that seemed to last forever, followed by a thunderous shake of the vital organ struggling to right itself beneath her ribs, like a car battery spurred into life by jump leads. She'd never outrun the Land Rover on this remote stretch of road, though she'd do her damnedest to escape the man in the car behind . . .

Or die trying.

Up ahead, a beam of light across the road. A lucky break . . . An articulated lorry on its way out of a stone quarry, slow-moving with a heavy load. Braking, she flashed him out. The vehicle moved forward, a lumbering beast, its cab moving one way, the trailer seeming to disconnect as the driver turned the wheel. Nancy waited . . . the Land Rover gaining ground.

She had one shot.

Just one.

Flooring the accelerator, she took her chance, pulling out, squeezing her Fiat through the narrow gap between the lorry cab and trees lining the opposite carriageway. Blinded by headlights, Nancy pulled hard on the wheel, swerving to avoid oncoming traffic, missing the lead car by a whisper, a long line of cars preventing the four-by-four from overtaking. An angry, elongated blast of a horn from behind.

Nancy stared wide-eyed into the rear-view mirror.

The lorry slowed in response to the maniac behind, frustrating the tailing vehicle. The four-by-four countered, poked it's nose out from behind, disappearing just as quickly, repeating the process over and over again in an attempt to get by. Nancy drew her eyes away, trying to concentrate. More horns. Flashing headlights. Road rage just might save her skin.

A clear image of the man chasing her arrived in her head: evil eyes, dark pools of hostility burned into her memory, callous hands gripping the wheel, foul-mouth screaming abuse. He was not a man you messed with. Nancy glanced at the speedo; it was climbing – seventy, seventy-five, eighty – increasing the distance behind. She prayed that there would be no break in the oncoming traffic. If she could make it to Devil's bend, she could take the back woods, switch off her headlights and call for help. It wouldn't be swift to arrive. This was rural Northumberland. No cops. Only robbers. She had more chance of dating Idris Elba than seeing a squad car at this time of night.

The man in hot pursuit would show no pity. Nancy knew that. Inflicting pain was his thing, acting like an aphrodisiac. Doing someone's dirty work handed him the power and kept his employer's hands clean; the meaner he could be, the better he liked it. Distracted by that scary reality, Nancy miscalculated the angle of the bend. She took the corner too fast, tipping her vehicle on to two wheels momentarily.

She opened her mouth to scream but no sound came out.

The Fiat hung in the air, seemingly in slow motion, before righting itself, crashing to earth with a thud, shaking the chassis like a toy. She almost lost control of the steering wheel as the car bumped over uneven ground, rattling the interior and her along with it. Taking her foot off the brake, she killed the lights, her eyes stuck fast to the darkness where her wing mirror belonged, hoping that the lorry – and, crucially, the four-by-four – would coast by without seeing her. As it did, she blew out a breath, turned her lights back on and drove further into the wood.

Cutting the engine, she wept, white noise filling her head, fists clenched so tightly her nails dug into the palms of her hands. She was struggling to get breath into her lungs as she squinted into the forest, the trees like malevolent figures standing guard. An owl hooted, irritated by the disturbance. Shivering in the dark, Nancy fumbled her phone from her pocket, losing it in the footwell as it slipped from a shaky hand. A fingertip search failed to locate it.

She tried again.

Nothing.

'Come on!'

Another car flew by on the road behind, a streak of light, like a comet in the Northumberland sky. Turning the light on to find the phone wasn't an option. It would act like a beacon in the pitch-dark forest, pinpointing her exact location if he doubled back. Stay calm. It has to be here somewhere. She tried again with her left hand, then her right, walking her fingers across rubber matting caked in dried mud. Her little finger nudged a solid object. The device had bounced and lodged itself on its edge under the door sill. Finally! Using her thumb to activate the screen illuminated the car. A waste of time. What the fuck? No signal.

Nancy panicked.

If she had to wait till morning with the engine off, she'd freeze to death. Tonight, minus five was forecast. A light appeared on the road behind her: headlights that sent a shiver down her spine. The beams didn't flicker or change as she stared at them. They were stationary . . .

Weren't they?

Nancy held her breath . . . one, two, three seconds . . . four. Switching off her phone, she scanned the surrounding vegetation, imagination in overdrive. Had he left his vehicle on the road? Was he heading out on foot, stalking her with intent to do her harm? No . . . The lights were on the move, inching closer and closer to the junction where she'd left the road. Out of the car now, she legged it. Fifty yards, no more. Ducking down, she waited, praying that the open door of the Fiat would give the impression that she was long gone.

From her position, she had a good view of the road. The approaching vehicle slowed, turning in, illuminating the dense and eerie forest, her car along with it, the interior light still on. Momentarily, Nancy froze, her face pressed against the rough bark of the tree she was clinging to, senses on high alert. She shut her eyes, the better to concentrate on sound. James always did that when she read to him.

Blinded by headlights, she couldn't see the shape of the car clearly and prayed that this was not the one she was hiding from, that it was someone else, a couple of lovers perhaps, a clandestine rendezvous. In seconds, she realised she was wrong. There was no disputing the clunk of the door of a high-end motor.

The Land Rover.

Opening her eyes, Nancy shuffling sideways. A dark, menacing shadow passed across the headlights of the four-by-four. A twig snapped behind her. She dry-heaved. There were two of them? Had they set a trap, a pincer movement to flush her out? She swung round to find the eyes of a stag staring back at her, ears pricked up, aware of the danger.

That made two of them.

As it bounded off into the forest, Nancy turned back. The figure was on the move, a torch in his hand, its beam sweeping left and right, left and right, like a searchlight looking for survivors in a deep and dangerous sea, except for Nancy there was no lifeboat or crew to pull her to safety. The flashlight was now trained on her empty Fiat, then suddenly it changed direction.

Move, MOVE!

Nancy prayed that nature would provide enough cover. She crouched low, scrambling across rough terrain on her hands and knees, over the stumps of felled trees, snagging clothing, brambles lacerating her skin as she moved through the brush. In her rush to stand upright, her wedding ring caught on a branch as she propelled herself forward, dislocating her finger. The pain was excruciating, stopping her dead in her tracks.

The thought of James – gone six years – gave her strength. In spite of the crushing grief of losing him, she'd kept her side of the bargain to carry on. He was a good man, a kind man. Irreplaceable. A voice, weak and croaky, arrived in her head. 'Without me around to hold you back, you can do anything you want.' He'd winked at her. 'You could go back to law school or take up the voluntary work you're always banging on about. Fight the good fight, Nan. It's what you've always dreamed of. Whatever you choose, you'll be brilliant at it. Give it your all . . . Not for me or the kids . . . Do it for yourself.'

Nancy could feel his bony hand attempting to squeeze hers, but there was no strength in it. He was tired. Ready to say goodbye. She wasn't. Somehow, she'd managed a smile, a lump forming in her throat, their plans in ruins, the idea of losing him breaking her heart.

'Promise me you won't dwell on what you can't have,' he said.

'I promise.'

'We've had a ball, haven't we?'

'You bet.'

'No tears?'

God, how she wanted to roar. A little shake of the head was all she managed in reply.

James winked at her. 'I'll be with you every step of the way, Nan.'

'I know.'

Two days later, he was gone.

James had known that. even as a kid, if she'd seen injustice, she felt compelled to confront it. Right now, she could be forgiven for thinking she'd picked a fight she couldn't win. A sob left her throat as she stared ahead through pools of water. As she propelled herself further into the forest, inch by painful inch, Nancy was aware with every step forward that the only exit was behind her. She'd have to find a place to hide, a crawl space in the undergrowth. Later, when the coast was clear, she'd double back to the main road, flag down a car and get a ride. The only alternative was to make for high ground where she might find a signal.

Might.

With superhuman effort and James's encouragement urging her on, she hauled herself upright, prepared to do whatever was necessary to get out of there and finish what she'd started. Each time the flashlight reached her, she took cover, turning her body sideways to make herself invisible, setting off only when it moved away. She sprinted, arms like pistons, darting left and right. Better a moving target than a stationary one. The gunshot was a warning to stand still. In this part of 'the Shire' no one would hear, let alone question it: a poacher, gamekeeper, deerstalker – someone in for the kill on a lonely woodland track. Given her present predicament, the description was apt. The man with the firearm was a hunter, Nancy his prey.

**Don't miss out on the rest
of this brilliant novel
– order now.**